THOMAS PAINE

COMMON SENSE FOR THE MODERN ERA

THOMAS PAINE

COMMON SENSE FOR THE MODERN ERA

Edited by

Ronald F. King
& Elsie Begler

San Diego State University Press
San Diego, California

Copyright © 2007 San Diego State University Press.

All rights reserved. No part of this book may be used or reproduced in any manner whatsoever without written permission except in the case of brief quotations embodied in critical articles and reviews.

Thomas Paine: Common Sense for the Modern Era is published by San Diego State University Press, San Diego, CA 92182.

Digital cover image based on "Thomas Paine", an oil painting by Auguste Milière (1880), after an engraving by William Sharp, after a portrait by George Romney (1792).

Book design by Guillermo Nericcio García and Lorenzo Antonio Nericcio for memogr@phics designcasa.

Thomas Paine: Common Sense for the Modern Era is first in a series of publications made possible through the James Hervey Johnson Charitable Trust.

ISBN: 1-879691-87-6

FIRST EDITION

PRINTED IN THE UNITED STATES OF AMERICA

ACKNOWLEDGEMENTS

The editors would like to thank the James Hervey Johnson Charitable Trust and San Diego State University for making this conference possible. Kevin Munnelly, Trustee of the James Hervey Johnson Trust, and Paul Wong, Dean of the College of Arts and Letters, provided the inspiration and gave continued encouragement. Dawn Marsh Riggs did much of the initial work in putting the conference program together. Michael Kriezenbeck helped coordinate practical arrangements. The International Studies Education Project (ISTEP) did a wonderful job of including high school teachers from the San Diego region and publicizing the event to the wider community. The editors express special thanks to Howard Dratch and the Summerset Foundation for the high quality videotape of the proceedings and for its transcription. Harry Polkinhorn, Director of San Diego University Press, served as always as wise shepherd, guiding the manuscript from rough text to finished volume.

Finally, the editors would like to dedicate the volume to Thomas Paine and his enduring legacy. In these trying times, he restores to Americans the essence of our democratic, revolutionary soul.

CONTENTS

Preface, by Ronald F. King / 10

Part I: Keynote Addresses

    INTRODUCTION: ELIZABETH COBBS-HOFFMAN / 14
Joyce Appleby / 15
"Thomas Paine and the Intellectual Underpinnings of American Democracy"

    INTRODUCTION: EVE KORNFELD / 37
Eric Foner / 38
"Thomas Paine and the American Radical Tradition"

    INTRODUCTION: MICHAEL KREIZENBECK / 60
Brian McCartin / 60
"Thomas Paine: Giving Cause for America and Freedom to Mankind"

    INTRODUCTION: WILLIAM WEEKS / 77
Susan Jacoby / 77
"The Religious Radicalism of Thomas Paine: Why the Age of Reason Still Threatens Unreason"

    INTRODUCTION: RONALD F. KING / 97
Harvey Kaye / 98
"Paine and America's Unfinished Revolution"

Part II: Panel Papers and Discussions

Panel 1: The Tricks of Tom's Trade: Language Use and Rhetorical Devices
    INTRODUCTION: ELSIE BEGLER / 119
Moderator: Tony Freyer / 119

Seth Cotlar / 121
"Tom Paine's Readers and the Making of Democratic Citizens in the Age of Revolutions"

Timothy Killikelly / 138
"Examining Common Sense: A Gramscian Analysis of Thomas Paine"

Hazel Burgess / 151
"Thomas Paine: The Great Philosopher Unveiled"

Panel 2: Paine, Political Ideology, and Democratic Reform Movements
Moderator: Dawn Marsh Riggs / 173

Kenneth W. Burchell / 174
"Birthday Party Politics: The Thomas Paine Birthday Celebrations and the Origins of American Democratic Reform"

Bryson Clevenger, Jr. / 190
"Paine, The British Labor Movement, and Irish Politics"

David M. Robinson / 207
"Agrarian Justice: Paine, Jefferson, Crèvecoeur, and Economic Egalitarianism in the New Republic"

Panel 3: Paine, Religion, and Politics
Moderator: Vikki Vickers / 226

Eric R. Schlereth / 227
"Remembering Thomas Paine and Reckoning with Religion in Antebellum American Politics"

Nathalie Caron / 245
"The Relevance of Thomas Paine's Religious Thought Today"

Kirsten Fischer / 260
"'As Near to Atheism as Twilight is to Darkness': Tom Paine's Deism in a Religious Republic"

Panel 4: The Right of Revolution and the Legitimacy of Governments
Moderator: Ronald F. King / 274

Jason S. Maloy / 275
"The Paine-Adams Debate and Its Seventeenth Century Antecedents"

Drew Maciag / 289

"Revenge of the Anti-Paine: The Uncommon Wisdom of Edmund Burke (and Why It Still Tries Our Souls)"

Aaron Keck / 301
"Thomas Paine and the Right of Revolution"

Contributors / 315

PREFACE

Ronald F. King

There is a delightful story told in Jack Keane's biography of Thomas Paine. Upon his return to America, Paine encountered on the streets of New York the young author of a disparaging and fallacious account of the great firebrand's religious views. Paine asked the author whether he had profited financially from the work and was answered in the affirmative. "I am glad you found the expedient a successful shift for your needy family," he continued, "but write no more concerning Thomas Paine; ... try something more worthy of a man" (Grove Press: 1995, p. 496). Commentators have, of course, long disregarded this advice. They have written extensively about the life, works, and impact of Thomas Paine, and found it a most worthy undertaking. Yet the lessons that Paine has to teach have not always been well received. Only gradually has the tide turned and opinion become more favorable toward one of the most significant of our founding fathers. Even today, Americans are often reluctant to acknowledge our debt to Paine, and to engage in frank conversation with him about individual liberty, social-economic justice, the capacity of ordinary citizens, and the political conditions that can fetter or further such ends.

This volume is the consequence of a conference held at San Diego State University on October 21-22, 2005. It is intended as the first in a series of conference-based volumes focusing on historical individuals whose independent spirit, freethinking, and controversial views have become essential to the definition of the American experience. It is fitting that Paine takes first place within this series. As a revolutionist in three countries— America, Britain, and France—his pen helped shape the emerging liberal democratic world of the late eighteenth century. In America, he gave voice to the *Common Sense* of colonial discontent and provided needed encouragement at times of *Crisis* when the democratic *Prospect* seemed most bleak. In Britain, he challenged hierarchical monarchy and articulated a vision of the basic *Rights of Man* that resulted in his trial and conviction for seditious libel. In France, he envisioned a dawning of *The Age of Reason*, was elected as a delegate to National Convention, but spent ten months in the Luxembourg prison at the height of the Terror.

Paine was far more than the most visible and eloquent propagandist for the birth era of liberal revolution. He merits our attention, intellectually, by the content of his prose and the depth of his vision. Politically, Paine advanced and defended the institutions of democratic self-government and the ability of ordinary individuals to direct their own affairs. Philosophically, he gave quintessential expression to an Enlightenment perspective based on the unity of nature, science, reason, and free inquiry. Economically, he represented the class of emerging small entrepreneurs seeking increased opportunity, and he promoted the idea of a welfare state on the assumption that everyone was not fully responsible for their situation, and of course religiously, he articulated a personal deism, a simple faith in the creator of our beautiful and potentially bountiful world, in contrast to the alleged dogmatism and artificial complexity of belief propagated by institutionalized churches.

A conference devoted to Thomas Paine certainly has plenty to discuss. Moreover, it involves more than an exercise in the history of ideas. Paine's writings remain controversial, and his principles continue to confront those who would prefer to rest quiescent in the face of social exploitation, political domination, and the unquestioned authority of received wisdom. The theme for the conference, and also for this volume is, therefore, "Thomas Paine: Common Sense for the Modern Era."

Not surprisingly, there were both common points of emphasis and some degree of disagreement among the scholars participating in the conference. There was considerable discussion about Paine's education and how conscious he was of the intellectual influences upon him, his principles, and his times. There was discussion regarding Paine's understanding of developing capitalist society and the diagnosis of economic as well as political injustice in his thought. There was discussion about the depth of Paine's religious beliefs, and the relationship between the deism that he proclaimed and the atheism of which he was accused. There was discussion of Paine's position within the Enlightenment project and of the potential limitations inherent to that project. There was discussion regarding just how revolutionary Paine was in the originality of his ideas and in his commitment to an ever-changing society. There was discussion about the extent to which Paine was neglected historically. There was discussion about the extent of

Paine's relevance for contemporary politics, addressing both his particular social analysis and policy prescriptions and his role as a symbol for those dedicated to the movement for progressive reform.

For the most part, the conversation recorded in this volume should be interpreted as internal to a community of scholars all of whom concur regarding the merits of Thomas Paine and the importance of Paine studies for our understanding of the American condition, with one notable exception. Dr. Hazel Burgess, whose husband claims to be descended from an illegitimate child born to Paine and Marguerite de Bonneville (itself a contested fact), argues that Paine was little more than a scribe, who worked merely as a hired pen at the service of activists more knowledgeable and capable than he, yet who feared the consequences of visible authorship. It is a contentious position, based on an inventive combination of evidence and inference, which prompted considerable debate but no endorsement from the experts in attendance.

This volume mirrors the organization of the conference, consisting of both keynote lectures and expert panels on identified topics. The keynote texts have been edited and revised by their authors, but are based on the transcripts of their oral presentations. As such, they sometimes lack full bibliographic references. The panel presentations came from formal papers, which have been collected and are exhibited thematically. The volume has kept the informal tone of the conference, and includes excerpts from the "Question and Answer" sessions that made the conference especially lively and engaging for all in attendance. In structure, therefore, this volume sits somewhat between a proceedings and an anthology.

The book begins with the keynote lectures from two of the most prominent historians of the early American republic, Joyce Appleby and Eric Foner, both former presidents of the American Historical Association and of the Organization of American Historians. Professor Appleby addressed the intellectual influences that came together in the work of Thomas Paine. Professor Foner addressed the importance of Paine for his time and as an enduring influence on American progressives. The two lectures thus provide an appropriate frame for the subsequent discussion.

The other keynote speakers included: Brian McCartin, President of the Thomas Paine National Historical Association, who highlighted the role of Paine as revolutionary catalyst and who also brought to San Diego an exhibit of Paine memorabilia; Susan Jacoby, noted author and journalist, who discussed Paine's religious radicalism and its contemporary meaning; and Harvey Kaye, Ben and Joyce Rosenberg Professor of Social Change and Development at the University of Wisconsin, Green Bay, who detailed the relevance of Paine for generations of American political, social, and economic dissenters.

The four organized panel discussions concerned: Paine the rhetorician, whose voice moved nations; Paine the political ideologist, who inspired democratic reform movements in many contexts; Paine the religious critic, whose emphatic freethinking has liberated and enraged across generations; and Paine the revolutionary proponent, whose thought helped shape the legitimacy and constitution of governments.

The consensus among both scheduled conference participants and audience alike was that the words and actions of Thomas Paine persist as relevant, not just for his own time, but for the modern era as well. Paine's American homeland has been transformed in ways he would not find recognizable and most likely would not have endorsed. Yet his voice remains most resonant, as a reminder of what this country might have been and always has the potential to become.

THOMAS PAINE AND THE INTELLECTUAL UNDERPINNING OF AMERICAN DEMOCRACY

Joyce Appleby

Elizabeth Cobbs-Hoffman

I am Elizabeth Cobbs-Hoffman, chair of the history department, and I hold the Dwight Stanford Chair of American Foreign Relations here at San Diego State University. It is my pleasure to introduce Joyce Appleby, professor emerita at UCLA. She is past president of the Organization of American Historians; also of the American Historical Association; also of the Society for the History of the Early Republic—all the outstanding historical associations to which anyone of her qualifications could possibly aspire. Before becoming a professional historian, incidentally, and I think this might be the most charming and amusing factoid about Joyce, she worked for *Mademoiselle* magazine and the *Pasadena Star News*. Professor Appleby has long taken an interest in bringing history to a larger public, which is in the spirit of Thomas Paine. As co-director of the History News Service, she facilitates historians writing op-ed pieces for newspapers in which contemporary issues are embedded in their historical context. For all of these reasons, it is my honor to welcome Joyce Appleby.

But there are two other reasons that I would like to take just a moment to comment upon. First, Joyce Appleby has been a source of inspiration to a generation of historians, not just for her prodigious research, but for her defense of what Thomas Paine would have called plain truth, or common sense. Democracy and history, she has argued, always live in a kind of tension with each other. Nations use history to build a sense of national identity, pitting the demands for stories that build solidarity against open-ended scholarly inquiry that can trample cherished illusions. The response should be not nihilism but a pragmatic skepticism that refuses to descend into relativism. It must be based on criticism and debate, dissent and irreverence, without eliminating the possibility of some truths prevailing for centuries. One of the responsibilities of the historian is to record both the survival and the reformulation of old truths. I would like to praise Joyce Appleby as a person willing to debunk false heroes but not to disparage heroism, willing to be critical but unwilling to be cynical, a person who urges us to investigate the truth, not to deny it, but in order to honor the existence of truth. This reminds me of the beautiful little Paine quote, which is printed on the free bookmark distributed today by the Paine Historical Association: "To argue with a man who has renounced the use of reason, and whose philosophy consists in holding humanity in contempt, is like administering medicine to the dead." I believe that Joyce Appleby is a person who does not hold humanity in contempt, despite her understanding of its foibles. Instead, she administers medicine to the living.

There is a second reason that it is my honor to introduce Joyce Appleby, which is that we at San Diego State can say, "We knew her when." That is, she was a professor of history at San Diego State for 14 years before she went on to UCLA. While we can take no credit whatsoever for her ensuing successes, we are nonetheless very proud. I hope you will join me in welcoming Joyce Appleby as she gives a talk on "Thomas Paine and the Intellectual Underpinnings of Democracy."

Joyce Appleby

Thank you for that very thoughtful introduction. This conference represents a convergence of two things that I hold in great esteem. One of them is the scholarship on Thomas Paine and the other is San Diego State University where, as Elizabeth said, I began my teaching career in 1967.

The subtitle to my lecture tonight is "and the intellectual underpinnings of democracy." I gave a lot of thought to picking the word "underpinnings" — *intellectual underpinnings*. I could have said *intellectual roots*, but I don't really like that organic metaphor. It is too deterministic. An acorn doesn't have any choice but to become an oak, and that isn't the way things are in human existence. The same thing is true of *intellectual origins* of democracy, for it, too, has that organic sense. I could have used *intellectual arguments* for democracy, but that would have suggested that I was going to talk about debates for and against democracy.

Underpinnings has the virtue of being exactly what I wanted to talk about. The metaphor is architectural. *The building of democracy* would indicate the sentiments in favor of democracy that were developed in the eighteenth century, but *underpinnings* goes down a little bit further to the supported assertions that under-gird democracy, and that's exactly what I want to do: go into these deeper assertions.

I do this because the unexamined assumptions of the traditional worldview were hostile to democracy. In fact, they were the greatest obstacles towards the emergence of democracy in the modern era. Before reason-able men and women could think about democracy as a practice, these traditional assumptions had to be addressed and challenged. This process took place in the seventeenth and eighteenth centuries, with the confrontation of old ideas about power and governments by some new propositions, and Paine figures, in my talk, as the master synthesizer of these new political affirmations coursing through Western Europe and America. In other words, before there could be democratic regimes in the world, there had to be an intellectual revolution, and Paine was the catalyst of that revolution.

In arguing this position to you, I am putting myself at odds with the great expert on democracy in America, Alexis de Tocqueville, that redoubtable Frenchman who came to the United States in the 1830s to examine this new phenomenon of democracy. Tocqueville continues to be read today, largely because of his stunning insights into the culture of democracy that he discovered in the United States. In no way do I wish to take exception to these wonderful observations of Tocqueville. But I do disagree with the way in which he treated the emergence of democracy in the United States as a natural force, occurring without the prompting from any ideas or as the consequence of any clash of ideas among men and women who were obsessed with ideas.

Tocqueville construes the origins of American democracy as the unfolding of inexorable tendencies rather than as a succession of political choices that leaders and voters had to take over a two-decade period. For Tocqueville, the "equality of condition" (a phrase he uses over and over) in the United States serves as the main motive force in his book, *Democracy In America*. It's like a *deux ex machina* that is summoned to explain a variety of natural preferences. Tocqueville thinks that democracy in America was a natural force, and his book is filled with naturalistic phrases. He depicts democracy as washing away old habits of thought. He sees that the equality condition flowers in the society. Sometimes he mentions factors that might have led America to become democratic, like New England town meetings in the seventeenth century, but they are very tenuous connections.

Arriving 56 years after Americans had announced their independence, Tocqueville marveled at the pervasive purchase of democratic mores, and he read their vigor back into the past. He contributed to the American penchant for thinking of political phenomena as natural, as inevitable, as a force independent of ideas. Astute as Tocqueville was, he failed to investigate the political views of the founders of the American republic, and hence he missed the roiling conflicts of the 1790s and their critical importance. Perhaps this was because he hung out, while he was in the United States, with the Federalist elite, the ones who had been defeated by the democratic forces, who preferred to think that they had been pushed aside by the hand of God rather than the arm of Thomas Jefferson.

In discussing the intellectual underpinnings of democracy, I want to start by listing the propositions that had to be rethought before people would take seriously democracy as an alternative to monarchy, or as an alternative to the British mixed constitution, or as an alternative to some eighteenth century variant of classical republicanism. Here they are.

One is the exaltation, even mystification, of authority as essential to maintaining order, as one of the principle assumptions of a traditional worldview. The second is a reverence for the past. Within the tradition of Christians, that reverence was traced back to the virtue in the Garden of Eden. For those people of a more philosophical bent, it was traced back to classical Greece. In any case, it was the past that had shown the pinnacles of human achievement. The implication, of course, is that there was kind of a falling off from those pinnacles in the present.

The third is a deep fear of change, that change can only bring destruction or a deterioration of values, that change is evidence of degeneration. Change, in Pocock's words, would throw men and women back into the terrors of history. There was also, in the traditional worldview, a submergence of the individual into the group, a view that stressed the attachment to community and emphasized the importance of membership, of belonging. One saw the whole as greater than the sum of the parts.

But perhaps the most entrenched obstacle to a new conception of a political association was the belief in a natural inequality. The world was composed of the few and the many—the few talented, ardent, wise, brave people, and the many ordinary people whose work was going to sustain these few. It was deeply embedded in the traditional worldview.

I once had a few extra days to spend in London, and I spent the days reading the critics of Thomas Hobbes's *Leviathan* at the Goldsmith's Library. I assumed that the critics would, like most contemporaries, be appalled by Hobbes's description of life in the state of nature as being "solitary, poor, nasty, brutish and short." Not a bit of it. Not one of these critics ever mentioned that. What horrified them was Hobbes's assertion of natural equality. Hobbes begins with that premise. This was just unthinkable to them. It was a feature of hierarchal society that ordinary people were base, if not actually vile, that they were stupid and ignorant. This conviction about ordinary people provided the social glue for upper-class rule. It was horrifying when someone would come along and say that no, they were really equal. Hobbes's critics denied the capacity for independent judgment that Hobbes bestowed upon individuals. One writer said of Hobbes, "He discourses of men as if they were Terrigene, born out of the earth, come up like Seeds, without any relation one to the other," when we all know that "by nature, man was made a poor, helpless Child" who confides and submits to his parents.[1]

Once placed in doubt, these older beliefs could be replaced by a cluster of new discourses, converging on a novel understanding of the human situation. It's adumbrated first in Thomas Paine's *Common Sense*, and then the new ideas become politically institutionalized in the new United States with the election of Thomas Jefferson as president in 1800. That campaign featured a genuine contest of visions, even if it was also unmatched in American history for vilification and vituperation. Nonetheless, there were ideas at the center of it.

The new core beliefs highlighted the voluntary cooperation of human beings, demonstrating that they could take care of themselves without the firm direction of authority figures like the magistrate, the minister, or the father. They also said that this capacity to take care of oneself was a part of the human endowment, and hence it was universal and equal, making social change an evolutionary process that over time would enhance the human prospect. These ideas represented a stunning re-evaluation of human beings as reasonable, self-governing creatures whose free interactions would end in development, rather than in mere change.

Here we have the opposing paradigms of social orders. What has absorbed my curiosity — and I hope will engage your curiosity — is the question where these new ideas came from. It took a lot of strands to weave together an alternative picture of what human beings were capable of, what the world was composed of.

Both Thomas Hobbes and John Locke relied on the premise of equality for their theories about the origins of political obligation. They were interested in the basis for human beings obliging themselves to accept government. But in neither writer does equality last long. It exists as a premise in the state of nature, yet once human beings reason themselves out of that state of nature, they enter into a society in which there is a lot of inequality — different in both writers but still there. The assertion of equality is important because Hobbes and Locke are major figures. But I think we have to recognize that it really plays almost a technical role in their political philosophy.

However, while these two men were writing, there were other English thinkers who were examining a new source of empirical data, and that was how people behaved when they bought and sold in the market. For over a century, those watching the phenomenon of an expanding world trade put into circulation commentary that depicted men and women as steady self-improvers, drawn naturally to the producing, selling, and buying that drove the market, by the desire that they had for bettering themselves. These observations were scattered all over the seventeenth century in English publishing. They were in pamphlets, they were on broadsides, they were in how-to books, and they were in learned tomes. There were learned tomes by men like John Locke, Isaac Newton, Daniel Defoe — they all wrote about the economy as a kind of a sideline.

They all converged on the same conclusion, that reasonableness characterized human behavior in commercial dealings instead of human impulsiveness— the wicked, stupid, capricious conduct that is depicted Sunday after Sunday in Puritan sermons or in all Elizabethan drama. These observers were seeing that market participants calculated costs and benefits. Finally, they were led to believe that there was a uniform response from market bargainers. People could be counted on because they counted their interest. By mid-eighteenth century, Samuel Johnson could comment, "there are few ways in which a man can be more innocently employed than in getting money."[2]

Another fact about these market analyzers was their tendency—from the very beginning of this discourse, in the 1620s—to consider the round of producing and selling and paying for goods as somehow natural, because it was as consistent as water running downhill. With trade generating new levels of wealth, economic writers continued speculation about the dynamics behind this evolving system of enterprise and exchanges. Gradually they recast the economy as a natural system, working invisibly to produce harmony among buyers and sellers, instead of being a disordered hodgepodge of activities that required careful political control.

From this assumption came the even more powerful idea of change over time as development, a steady process of improvement, rather than convulsive episodes of feast or famine, escape or disaster. I'm going to offer evidence of this intellectual development with two quotations. One comes from Thomas Mun, who wrote in 1623, and the other from a very astute critic of John Locke.

Mun was the first to analyze the trading universe as a coherent and mutually supporting community. He also insisted upon the autonomy of trade. (This perhaps doesn't strike us as strange, but in that era, the economy was definitely under the political control. People did what they were allowed by ornate regulations in the economic realm, and so this is a sort of smashing idea.) Mun wrote, "Let the mere Exchanger do his worst; Let Princes oppress, Lawyers extort, Users bite, Prodigals waste . . . so much Treasure only will be brought in or carried out of a Commonwealth as the Foreign Trade doth over or under balance in values." Then this kicker: "And this must come to pass by a Necessity beyond all resistance."[3] These trading relations are going to go on; it doesn't matter what you do. They have an autonomy.

My other citation, about finally seeing the economy as an autonomous system, comes from a critic of John Locke. He writes—it's sort of like he's scratching his head—"John Locke pretends that Government had no more power in Politicals then they have in Naturals."[4] In other words, he's acting as though government doesn't have any power over the economy.

Adam Smith drew together a century of theorizing about the commercial system in his mighty synthesis, *An Inquiry Into The Nature And Causes Of The Wealth Of Nations.* Smith wrote, in part, to free the economy from government, you might say, taking economics from Politicals and placing it under Naturals. He describes in great and convincing detail a self-sustaining system drawing on the previous century's speculations and assertions. One of the remarkable features of *The Wealth Of Nations* is that Adam Smith never argues for the concept of human nature that runs through the book, a clue to me that these had already become commonplaces. They had started in observations of economic workings all through the seventeenth century, but by the time Smith takes up his pen, people accept that, so he can toss off lines like, "The principle which prompts to save is the desire for bettering our condition, a desire which, tho generally calm and dispassionate, comes with us from the womb, and never leaves us till we go into the grave,"[5] or it is "not from the benevolence of the butcher, the brewer, or the baker that we expect our dinner, but from their regards to their own interest."[6] Another Smith quote: "The uniform, constant, and uninterrupted effort of every man to better his condition, the principle from which public and national, as well as private opulence is originally derived, is frequently powerful enough to maintain and sustain the natural progress of things towards improvement, in spite of the extravagance of government and of the greatest errors of administration."[7]

Smith is assuming all these things that, as I said, earlier writers speculated about—autonomy, naturalness, consistency, reasonableness. Just as Newton saw uniformity behind the dazzling diversity of planets, meteors, and comets, so Smith found consistency in the multifarious transactions of commerce. He described a system that was not subject to the laws of the state but, on the contrary, subjected the state to its laws. Integral to his theorizing was "The Law Of Unintended Consequences," an arresting insight that put forward the idea that people could be acting in their self-interest, they could be directed at one thing, but the unexpected consequences of it could be the betterment of the whole group. Of course, this was the invisible hand of the market, the concept that Smith popularized. It had all sorts of people competing out of their self-interest, but that competition led them to produce a better product at a lower price, from which the public benefited.

Smith and his fellow Scots also proposed a conjectural history, with change that was obviously irreversible and cumulative. This led to an interest in what might have been the previous stages of history. In their conjectural history, they had the hunters and gatherers. These were followed by the herders, then the farmers, and finally the commercial stage that Smith was celebrating. The discovery of indigenous people to North and South America—which there was much writing about and had been for several centuries—gave a kind of facts on the ground to the idea that there had been this evolution from hunters and gatherers. You could still see hunters and gatherers, as well as herders and shepherds and the like.

These stages supported a perspective that made cumulative change the force in history, rather than what powerful people did. There were these impersonal forces operating, and they were propelling history forward through a slow process of progressive change.

Here was a really astounding reconceptualization of time as development. But there was an even more important and subtle implication to all this speculation: that the economy, rather than the polity, served as a better model for human organization. The polity was exclusive. There were citizens, and then there were many others, including all women, who were disenfranchised. But the economy was embracing. It embraced everyone in its workings, and so it became a model for society. It celebrated everybody who was productive and, perversely, linked beggars with aristocrats among the unproductive forces of the society.

One of the most fascinating documents I ever found was in the Lovelace Collection of John Locke's papers at Cambridge University. I was looking through these papers when I found a piece of foolscap, just like the lined yellow pads we have, and on it Locke had written, "If everyone in the world worked, the world's work could be done in half a day." It was just astounding coming from a man of the seventeenth century, when work was still looked down upon, in a world which distinguished laborers from those elegant members of society, the few, who were so special. I thought, "Ah, here it is. John Calvin has finally found his political theorist."

Much was attributed to trade in the first flush of observation. Commerce, Paine saw, was an alternative to war, in getting people what they wanted. They didn't have to go to war to seize diamonds or rubber, whatever they might want. They could exchange; they could enter into trade. He described the economy as a "pacific system" that works "to cordialise mankind, by rendering nations, as well as individuals useful to each other."

The new market economy had lured people into more consistent work habits. Moralists honored the enhancement of working habits and new mores. One pamphleteer noted that "tradesmen live upon credit, buy much upon trust," and continued, "as they buy upon credit, so they must sell upon trust."[8] It's a new idea, that people were going to trust each other, send goods at long distances and trust that the payment would be returned.

In succession, investigators of the commercial economy had come up with three radical propositions: that human beings were consistent and disciplined and dependable market participants; that there existed natural laws governing the realm of voluntary and cooperative activities; and finally that human history didn't move cyclically but developed through steady improvement.

The infiltration into the popular mind at that time was a development that had profound consequences. It changed the stance of the present towards the past and the future. The expectation of positive improvement in the future denigrated both past and present. Whereas previously the golden age of the Greeks or the Garden of Eden had reminded Europeans and Americans that they lived in a fallen state, now the future could be imagined as golden. The classical notion of cyclical change, that linked human life to the observable cycle of conception and birth, vigorous growth to maturity, inevitable decay and death had been replaced with a new script of development. This took over the imaginative space, once devoted to the poignant story of inevitable degeneration. Fear moved aside to make room for hope.

Downgrading the glories of the past also undermined reverence for authority. As Paine said of the English constitution, it was "noble for the dark and slavish times in which it was erected." With this pithy comment, he dispatched kings and nobles to the dustbins of history. Similarly, Jefferson wrote, one almost suspects with tongue in cheek, that since in his day people had discovered the principle of representation—so that you could have democracy without everybody fitting into one assembly room in Athens—this meant that if we have lost any of Aristotle's writings, it's really not too worrisome. In other words, experience had taught moderns the things that were far more significant than they could get out of Greek philosophy.

With time now parceled out in cumulative effects, incessant processes, sequential patterns, and irreversible transformations, all the rivulets of human activity could be seen flowing into the great river named progress (although that term isn't used until the nineteenth century, but certainly the idea of cumulative development is there). To a large extent, the past lost its attraction, and the present became a mere springboard to the future.

The new description of human behavior in the market as orderly, reasonable, and consistent might have remained confined to the specialized field of economic writings. This would have happened had it not been that its appearance coincided with a new discourse about human equality. Hobbes and Locke, as I just mentioned, had both asserted that men were equal (the distaff side of human nature being ignored), but theirs were not arguments for equality, but rather premises needed for their case about the nature of political obligation.

How equality acquired an emotional and moral resonance in the eighteenth century is obscure. At least it's obscure to me. It emerges in the 1780s and 1790s. The Count de Roederer, who was one of the reforming noblemen in France, talked about the fact that equality had become "the word," the concept of the decade. It's all anyone could talk about, he said. You really want to smile when you think of these bejeweled, ornamented noblemen with their fancy buckles and laces and frills talking about equality in the midst of a destitute populace. But you cannot ignore the fact that this had a moral and emotional quality that the concept of equality had not had before.

As I said, I don't know why or how that change took place. I don't know what led to it. I think some of it must have come from popular literature. The novel was one of the first forms of literature to talk about ordinary people and to invest their emotions with some significance. I think probably some role was played by the religious movements of the time. Thomas Huxley, the nineteenth-century friend of Darwin, is alleged to have thanked God that there was no talk about rights in the Bible. Well, there might be no talk about rights in the Bible, but there's plenty of talk about justice and love and charity, and I think this must have had something to do with the romanticizing of equality.

The problem of assigning a causal role to religion in this new phenomenon is that these ideas about spiritual equality had always been there, and they had not led to upsetting the existing hierarchies before. Still, the outpouring of evangelical fervor—the pietists in Germany, the Wesley brothers in England, the Great Awakening in the American colonies—must have played a part in moving equality from a rather arid, philosophical premise to an ardent affirmation. Its convergence with secular discourses about human behavior made spiritual equality a handmaiden to social equality, and both to a new interest in the latent potentialities of ordinary men and women.

Human nature, another inventive phrase of the eighteenth century, came to be seen as an endowment, a bundle of potentialities rather than a cast of problematic tendencies like the impulse to sin. When John Locke described the infant child as having a blank mind, the *tabula rasa*, this opened up the possibility of imagining a supportive environment, offering yet another challenge to the reigning assumptions about human corruption and utter dependency and invariant wickedness that were collected under the term of original sin. As with the economic discourse, the radical implications of Locke's sensational psychology, which is to say that we learn through the sensations that we experience in our lives, might have remained locked up in a philosophical treatise, like the one that Locke in fact wrote, had there not been, again, fruitful connections to make—the hypothesis about the infants' openness to first impressions suggested that better experiences might lead to an alternative storyline for the human race.

This combination of a new definition of human nature as orderly, with the workings of an economy as natural, the affirmation of human equality, and the reconception of time as a process of development—all these tumbled together became combustible ideas. Perhaps no one articulated an enthusiasm for these beliefs better than Thomas Paine, when he described somewhat wondrously that "there is existing in man, a mass of sense lying in a dormant state, and which, unless something excites it to action will descend with him, in that condition, to the grave...The construction of government ought to be such as to bring forward, by a quiet and regular operation, all that extent of capacity...."

This investment of moral qualities in human beings, just as human beings, further strengthens the idea of natural rights. Natural rights philosophy did not represent for Paine, as it did to most contemporary scholars, a learned discourse going back to the stoics. Rather, it delivered to him a warrant to dismantle hierarchal society so that men and even women, long alienated from their true natures, might recover them.

By the time Paine began writing his incendiary volumes, what I have called the intellectual underpinnings of democracy were in place. They figured in his mind as simple truths. Paine took in a century of theorizing about government and produced not just a justification for Americans' rebellion, but an invitation to all people to consider what they were capable of, and why they had been hoodwinked into thinking otherwise. All these things about human capacity, equality, and rights found their place in Paine's attack on the British monarchy in *Common Sense*. Its resounding success, something comparable to selling three million copies today, tells us something. His pamphlet didn't convince people, as much as his words crystallized opinions they already held.

Echoes of all the speculation about a natural social harmony that I've been discussing find expression in the opening lines of *Common Sense*. Paine writes, "Some writers have so confounded society with government, as to leave little or no distinction between them; whereas they are not only different, but have different origins." He goes on to explain, "Society is produced by our wants, and government by our wickedness; the former promotes our happiness positively by uniting our affections, the later negatively by restraining our vices."

When Hobbes and Locke wrote their great tracts, there were only two states, those of nature and civil society. By the end of the eighteenth century, there was this new concept, society. Society was the realm of voluntary interaction, of freedom where people engaged in activities, made bargains, and entered contracts without being in a state of nature or being under the control of government, and society entered the lexicon as a very powerful concept.

The source of discord in society, according to Paine,

was not human nature but the oppression from those given social privileges. "Male and female are the distinctions of nature, good and bad the distinctions of Heaven." Any other distinctions Paine saw as worse than arbitrary; they were vicious. The differences among men are politically irrelevant. That's a point that Hobbes and Locke made, in explaining why people left the state of nature. But they were now being asserted to ridicule hierarchies that stood in the way of social equality.

The eighteenth-century concept of nature does heavy duty in Paine's frontal attack on the English monarchy. He announced that he had drawn his "idea of the form of government from a principle of nature which no art can overturn, vis: that the more simple anything is, the less liable it is to be disordered." Nature comes in to support most of his assertions. Of independence, Paine wrote, "the simple voice of nature and reason will say, 'tis right," and he offered this shrewd piece of advice, that he "who takes nature for a guide, is not easily beaten out of his argument." Nature was Paine's contrast to the artifices that had given kings and lords their unwarranted power and their intimidating privileges.

For Paine, the implementation of natural rights required radical surgery upon the traditional body of politic. More urgently, the burden of old ways of thinking, of antediluvian concepts, of controlling institutions, had to be shed. Only liberation from our arcane authorities of all kinds would lift the heavy hand of the past from the shoulder of his generation.

These assertions about a naturally ordered mechanism prompted skeptics to ask why, if there had always been this spontaneous order, we have a history that is replete with rebellions and disorders and invasions and brutality of all sorts. The riposte to this challenge was to point out how the over-weaning and overbearing hierarchies of church and state had worked in tandem to suppress the natural human potential. Here Paine was in his element as he castigated kings and nobles in *Common Sense*. "To the evil of monarchy," he wrote, "we have added that of hereditary succession; and as the first is a degradation and lessening of ourselves, so the second, claimed as a matter of right, is an insult and imposition on posterity. For all men being originally equals, no one by birth could have a right to set up his own family in perpetual preference..." Then he goes on to say, it is evident that nature disapproves of these artificial hierarchies, for otherwise why would she so frequently give mankind an "ass for a lion"? I think he's talking about the failure of natural succession to produce lions for kings.

Common Sense proved a godsend for those Colonial leaders promoting independence, because the pamphlet's powerful rhetoric spoke to southerners and northerners alike, to rich and to poor, to farmers and to merchants. Paine considered himself an American, like thousands of immigrants who had come as he had. He took part in both the military and political phases of the Revolution. In the middle of it all, in the darkest days of the Revolution, Paine penned those famous lines: "These are the times that try men's souls. The summer soldier and the sunshine patriot will, in this crisis, shrink from the service of his country; but he that stands it now deserves the love and thanks of man and woman."

Just as the founding fathers were gathering to draft a new constitution, Paine returned to Europe where he threw himself into the French Revolution and wrote a series of books, each one more radical than the former. With the revolution in the United States secure, and a new, more powerful frame of government in place (this would be 1789, after the ratification of the Constitution), most upper-class Americans slipped back easily into the old ways of thinking about the few and the many. To be sure, those who didn't leave with the Loyalists in 1783 did see their nation as proof of the possibility of transformative social change, but it proved easier to persuade ordinary people of human equality than those gentlemen who had benefited so greatly from the conviction that society was divided between the few and the many.

John Stevens was a scion of a distinguished New Jersey patriot family, and he wrote rhapsodically that America should have "the honor of teaching mankind this important, this interesting lesson, that man is actually capable of governing himself."[9] I thought that was interesting because it conflates self-government of a nation with the governing of oneself. Paine made explicit this connection when he announced that "man has achieved mastery over government by participating in it, and thus achieved mastery over himself." We read democracy back into these statements, but I don't think that's what John Stevens was in favor of, or the people in his association. They were for a republic of laws with guaranteed liberties, but they were not for democracy. They continued to feel that it was extremely important to maintain the regime of upper-class office-holding with lower-class political activity confined to voting.

It is difficult to prove, but I feel quite certain that *Common Sense* jump-started a process of radical thinking in Thomas Jefferson, a 33-year-old Thomas Jefferson who read *Common Sense* when he was writing in a very lawyerly way about how Americans might slip the bonds of obligation to Great Britain. While they are very different in their presentation of self, Paine and Jefferson shared sentiments that suggest the existence of a common matrix.

Paine, the deracinated intellectual, was like a seeded cloud, regularly dropping showers of rhetoric. Jefferson, on the other hand, was more like a stealth radical, moving through polite society, not exactly concealing his views but deftly inserting them in quiet words at appropriate moments. He plotted his attack on upper-class rule within the bosom of America's ascendant, revolutionary elite. Jefferson was an anomaly, a tenacious champion of subversive ideas who repeatedly got elected to high office by an electorate of slaveholding, plantation patriarchs. I'll never know how he did it.

Paine stirred people with the pungent prose of a Speaker's Corner incendiary. If indeed I am correct that he radicalized Jefferson, it was among his greatest accomplishments, for Jefferson had the opportunity and the power to change the direction of American political development. He sounded the alarm about Federalist elite sentiments and carried the banner for a new discourse of natural rights and democratic practices until he finally achieved the presidency.

Without the eruption of Jefferson's tumultuous popular movement in the 1790s, the American political order might have mirrored that of England, where an economically progressive propertied class kept radical reform at bay for another century. The Federalists maintained the distinction between the few and the many. They thought a strong central government was essential to public order, and they wanted to maintain as much of a hierarchy as the American mores would permit.

Alexander Hamilton epitomized what Jefferson feared in federal politics. When he had a chance to draft an economic policy for the nation, Hamilton relied on what he called the "durable and permanent" existence of rich and poor and debtor and creditor. The wealthy few would develop new enterprises for the poor, whose lives would be regulated through their economic dependency and if necessary the master-servant law. Convinced of the need for leadership from disinterested and educated gentlemen, Hamilton rejected the notion that ordinary farmers and storekeepers might just as effectively use their own resources to start new ventures for themselves. Illustrative of Hamilton's attitude was his reaction to Adam Smith's idea of a self-regulating trade. Believing that the economy could not flourish without "a common directing power," Hamilton derided Smith's idea as "one of those wild speculative paradoxes, which have grown into credit among us, contrary to the uniform practice and sense of the most enlightened nations."

The key issue became the importance of government to the maintenance of order. Conservatives claimed that men were too unruly to handle new freedoms. After all, if they had been so tractable through the ages, why was history replete with accounts of riots, rebellions, and general mayhem? Democratic reformers replied that people were naturally self-regulating, if given a chance to cultivate their reason and to exercise free choice. It was government with its abusive powers that had created history's record of discord. Federalists focused on the problem of order and feared popular participation and all that it entailed. President George Washington reacted viscerally to the unprecedented phenomenon of ordinary voters forming political clubs to discuss state affairs. He dismissively spoke of them as "certain self-created societies." A member of one of those clubs shot back in a pamphlet, "Whatever the United States might have been previous to the American Revolution, it is pretty evident that since their emancipation from British rapacity, they are a great self-created society."[10]

Tocqueville was not wrong to see strong social forces sustaining democracy in the United States. The nation's mores made possible more radical social experiments than in those countries like Scotland, England, and France that supplied the essential intellectual elements supportive of democracy. The distinguished French economist, Jean-Baptist Saye (from whom we get Saye's Law), lamented to President James Madison in 1814, "In old Europe there are enlightened men who advocate a liberal government, but they are few and *bien timide*. In America they govern the nation."[11]

Failing to examine the origins of the understanding of democracy that Paine propagated and Jefferson institutionalized, Tocqueville described a generic democracy rather than the particular one we actually have — the one resting on certain assumptions about human nature, about the proper ambit of freedom, and the direction of the future.

Now that we have added democracy to our exports, it is urgent — more urgent than ever — for us to excavate the intellectual underpinnings of our democracy and to recognize the roles played by the belief that the economy has solved the problem of order; that freedom liberated the individual from the group; and that time has been programmed for progress. We need to recognize that these are the underpinnings of our democracy.

The essence of these assumptions represented not only a rejection of the past, but of any effort in the name of tradition to curb individual initiative or free choice. We have created a culture; we have built a culture on these underpinnings. It remains to be seen if they can be transported. Thank you.

Question (partly audible): . . . regarding the Constitution and its alleged embodiment of Federalist-like elite assumptions, in contrast to the populism of Paine and Jefferson, of which you spoke.

Joyce Appleby: I don't think the U.S. Constitution has embedded in it ideas of natural inequality or these Federalist social assumptions. One of the reasons is that not everybody who wrote the Constitution became a Federalist. There was a split. Of those 55 delegates, more became Federalists. We have to realize that the two best defenders, Alexander Hamilton and James Madison, end up on opposite sides of this political struggle in the 1790s. Both sides to this debate believe in popular sovereignty. The debate is about how they think that popular sovereignty should be exercised. According to Adams, you can have both popular sovereignty and a nobility, if the people vote to have a nobility. The matter of popular sovereignty at the time of the founding was how to base the government on the will of the people.

The Constitution does seek to avoid rambunctious majorities. It did not establish a democracy in which the voters can do anything they want. The founding fathers gave away power that still cripples us today—for example, the tremendous advantage given to the states. But when Madison writes, in Federalist 51, that ambition must be pitted against ambition, that the ambition of the man must be attached to the privileges of the office, talking about the separation of powers, that's a very un-elite idea of using ambition in this way.

Question (partly audible): . . . regarding the alleged natural alliance of commerce with commercial equality, in contrast to the extensive commercial inequality in the early United States, including slavery.

Joyce Appleby: The alliance of which I spoke appears right in the discourse. I am not saying that it is truly natural; I am saying this is what they observed, and they created a very powerful discourse about the naturalness of it. They were living in a time of great expansion for the ambit of freedom through the economy, so it seemed natural because these were actions that came from individual initiative, rather than being ordered.

About slavery and the persistent discrimination against people of color in the United States, I call that—Ellison has the Invisible Man—I call that the Invisible Contradiction. White Americans continued to celebrate the Declaration of Independence, knowing what they did about the denial of those rights to Black members of the society. It's just a contradiction that people were unwilling to confront, and so they just suppressed it, until it finally erupted and had to be confronted. But I think we'd like to suppress it again, if we could.

Question: Obviously the emergence of market freedom allowed people to be more sociable and created certain commercial virtues. But there are other virtues, more classical virtues, including self-restraint and personal, going inside to an inner light. Both Tocqueville and I believe Paine also warned about too much attention to commercialism. They drive out the very virtues that sustain a democratic character. Could you comment?

Joyce Appleby: I think reformers of all sorts want to make changes, and they don't realize that they're also cutting at the taproots of equality that exist as a part of the changes they're making. In other words, most reformers want the world to stay constant and then to fix what it is they don't like. But you don't do that. You change one thing, and you change other things, and the qualities you talked about are very much at risk in a dynamic commercial society. The whole idea of the group, or sacrificing for the group, for example, is not a commercial idea. American children have to be reared to be individuals, or they're not going to do very well in American society. But that means from a very early age they can't be turned into dependent and interlocking members of a tight family and community. I mean, as we open one door, we close other doors.

Question: I love what you have done exploring political underpinnings and how they came to Jefferson. I am intrigued by the religious aspects that precede all of this. I kept wondering about Erasmus and Luther, as a sort of parallel to what happens here.

Joyce Appleby: As I mentioned, I think there has to be some religious element to the rhapsodic view of equality, very different from these cold, analytic views. I'm sure there is some influence, but of course the problem is that these religious doctrines were there all the time. We do know in Christian history that they do erupt. As they said about Luther, he preached the Old Testament to the poor and the New Testament to the rich. But I think that influence is there.

Question: I wonder if Paine were writing contemporaneously, what issues do you think would attract him? What sorts of positions do you think he might have?

Joyce Appleby: You know, he hasn't lived in our generation, and he doesn't know what we know about the generations between him and us. I find it awfully hard to put Thomas Jefferson or Paine in the 21st century. As the previous speaker said, he might be horrified just how self-interested, how materialistic, how vainglorious, how absorbed we are with getting and spending.

Question (partly audible): . . . expressing curiosity about the *underpinnings* metaphor and the forces that explain it. Now it appears, we're trying to export democracy without taking into account underpinnings.

Joyce Appleby: It's not working. It's like a house without a foundation. This was one of the things that I wanted to show, that U.S. democracy had deep roots, and they were explicit. It wasn't a natural force; there were men and some women thinking these ideas and arguing them through over two centuries, creating a new definition of human nature and human interaction. These are processes of great effort, imagination, and time.

You could have a democracy unlike our demo-cracy. There are other ways to mobilize popular will. We have one that is historically specific. That's what I meant when I said Tocqueville talks about generic democracy. I don't think ours is a generic democracy. I think it's a very particular one.

Question: In the spirit of what you discussed, where people imagined the foundations of democracy and not the generic kind, how can it be exported to other societies where traditionally their history is very unique, very different?

Joyce Appleby: This idea of democracy is now flourishing as it never had. There are more democracies than ever before. The idea is going to be powerful, even in the most traditional societies. But I think it should be a force that is discussed and contended with. I think what seems foolish is to try to impose democracy. That's only my opinion as a citizen; it's not as a historian, because I don't know anything about the contemporary world as a scholar, only as a reader of the *New York Times*.

Question: You expressed some puzzlement about Jefferson's political success in the context where it shouldn't have been, his radical ideas. Can you say more about Jefferson as a political figure and what kind of conclusions you've come to about how he was able to achieve political victory as an elected official, what he was able to do?

Joyce Appleby: I speculated that Jefferson might have been radicalized by Paine, because the things he was writing in 1776 were not particular radical—mostly lawyerly treatises about detaching the American colonies from Great Britain. There were a lot of other things that could have radicalized him. The French Revolution, obviously, might have had the same impact. It made him realize that if one revolution is a revolution, two revolutions are a revolutionary age.

His personal success, I think, had to do with the fact that he was a genius organizer, political organizer. Also, the young ordinary men in America really responded to this idea of flipping the elite and dismantling hierarchies. But Jefferson was essentially a cautious man. Although he said a lot about slavery, the more power he got, the less he did about it. I think he justified this by saying he would lose the support that enabled him to be President, which is probably true, but it's also kind of a weasely excuse. But I think perhaps it holds a clue; even though he had these radical ideas, he did have a sense of what he thought was possible.

How did he become elected? Another element is that he was obviously the shining son of the South, and there weren't any other politicians like him after Washington. Monroe and Madison were kind of quiet people; they were not going to lead a party. By this time, the southerners really feared the New Englanders, and there was a deep antipathy between them. It's hard to speculate about these things.

Notes

Professor Appleby's address was based on her article, "The Intellectual Underpinnings of American Democracy," published in *Daedalus*, 136:3 (Summer, 2007), 14-23,

[1]William Lucy, Bishop of St. David's, *Observations, censures and confutation of notorious Errours in Mr. Hobbes His Leviathan* (London, 1663).

[2]James Boswell's *Life of Johnson*, ed. George Birkbeck Hill (Oxford, 1887), vol. 2, p. 323.

[3]Thomas Mun. *England's treasure by forraign trade*, pp. 218-19; as quoted in Joyce Oldham Appleby, *Economic Thought and*

Ideology in Seventeenth-Century England (Princeton, NJ: Princeton University Pres, 1978), p. 51.

[4] Henry Layton, *Observations*, p. 15; as quoted in *Ibid*, p. 237.

[5] Adam Smith, *An Enquiry into the Nature and Causes of the Wealth of Nations* (New York: Modern Library edition, 1937), p. 306.

[6] Smith, *Wealth of Nations*, p. 13.

[7] Smith, *Wealth of Nations*, p. 306.

[8] *The grand concern of England explained*, (1673), p. 51; as quoted in Appleby, *Economic Thought and Ideology in Seventeenth-Century England*, pp. 188-89

[9] John Stevens, *Observations on Government* (New York, 1787), p. 53.

[10] *Independent Gazetteer*, January 21 and 28, 1795; as quoted in Joyce Appleby, *Capitalism and a New Social Order*, (New York: New York University Press, 1984), pp. 67-68.

[11] Gaillard Hunt, ed., *Writings of James Madison*, vol. 9, pp. 135-36.

THOMAS PAINE AND THE AMERICAN RADICAL TRADITION

Eric Foner

Eve Kornfeld

I am Eve Kornfeld, a professor of history at San Diego State University. My specialty is early American history and Revolutionary America. It is a great pleasure to appear at this symposium, which includes two past presidents of the American Historical Association and the Organization of American Historians. Eric Foner is one of them.

Many of you may know Eric Foner as one of the nation's most important historians of the American reconstruction period, which has been his major concern in recent years. His book, *Reconstruction: America's Unfinished Revolution*, won the Bancroft Prize, the Parkman Prize, and the Los Angeles Times Book Award. You may also have seen or heard of his two prize-winning museum exhibitions on mid-eighteenth century American history, "A House Divided: America in the Age of Lincoln" and "America's Reconstruction: People and Politics After the Civil War," which he co-curated with Olivia Mahoney.

But I always think of Eric Foner as a historian of revolutionary America. When I was an undergraduate at Princeton, I took a large lecture course on the American Revolution, and Eric Foner was my preceptor, a term which probably has no meaning outside of Princeton, but which meant that I talked with him and ten or fifteen other undergraduates about revolutionary America every week. I think it was at 8:00 in the morning, but it was always a treat.

Eric Foner had not long before published a book called *Tom Paine and Revolutionary America*. He was very excited about the concept of republicanism, which soon thereafter became a guiding paradigm in Revolutionary American history. *Tom Paine and Revolutionary America* explored republicanism in its social and political contexts and, as Eric Foner's work always does, connected intellectual, social, and political history. The book was ground-breaking and very exciting in its comparative dimensions, exploring Paine's radical thinking and artisan communities and radicalism on both sides of the Atlantic. It awakened my interest in early American history, which is still very much alive. It is a great pleasure for me to introduce Eric Foner, and it should be a great pleasure for all of us to hear what he has to say about "Thomas Paine and the American Radical Tradition."

Eric Foner

One of the greatest pleasures of being a teacher, especially for as long as I have been, is to see young students of history blossom and become eminent scholars in their own right. It's particularly a pleasure to be introduced by Eve Kornfeld, whom I knew as an undergraduate many, many years ago, it seems. To see her become such an important teacher and writer of history is very gratifying. I want to thank this fine university for putting on this conference about Thomas Paine. Thomas Paine was an international figure. I do think he missed coming to San Diego, although he played a role in the history of many different places during the age of revolution.

Before I begin my talk, I want to tell you how — over a decade ago when I was president of the Organization of American Historians — I learned through Thomas Paine something interesting about how American politics works. I became involved as president of the OAH in the movement to get a statue of Thomas Paine erected in Washington, D.C. There is no such monument. There are in some other places, but not in the nation's capital. There is a statue of Edmund Burke in Washington D.C., because of his support for the American Revolution, but not of his great antagonist, Thomas Paine.

The leader of this battle in Congress was Senator Steven Symms of Idaho. This was somewhat surprising because Symms was far to the political right. It turned out that Symms' dentist, who was also a major contributor to his campaigns, was a fanatical admirer of Thomas Paine. Basically, Symms had told his staff, whatever this dentist wants, you do it. They began sending me letters, one of which said that my book on Paine is the Bbible of this movement. I thought this was an odd way of putting it, given Paine's views of the Bible.

I went and testified before a little commission that decides who gets a statue in Washington, D.C., and where to place it. I testified before this commission why it was worthy to have the statue of Paine in a prominent place within Washington, not just stuck off in some corner. They were mostly concerned about Thomas Paine's religious views. They said to me, "Was Tom Paine an atheist?" I said, "Oh no, no, no, sir. He was a deist." Well, of course that drew total blanks. I had to explain what deism was, as best as I could. Then they said, "Well, if we put up this statue, are religious people going to riot?" I said, "No, I really don't expect that."

The person who testified after me was Professor Thomas Clark, a very eminent historian of another generation, who passed away recently. He was from Kentucky and was introduced to the commission by the senator from Kentucky, who said something like this: "Look, you commissioners, my former teacher, Professor Thomas Clark, one of the most respected men in Kentucky, is coming to testify before you. I don't know what he's going to say, but you'd better do exactly what he tells you. I can't stick around, but I'm just going to remind you of one thing. I am the chair of the subcommittee that handles the budget of your commission. If you don't do what Professor Clark says, you're going to really pay for that." Well, funnily enough, Professor Clark said that there should be a statue, and the commission voted unanimously that there should be a statue. Thus, I got to see how power operates in American politics. Unfortunately, there still is no a statue. In the spirit of our modern era, the authorizing bill said it was to be erected purely by private funds, with no government money, so the statue still not there, but it is authorized, and I hope one of these days there will be such a statue.

Last spring, a conference was held at Columbia University, where I teach, on the subject of the Radical Enlightenment. Jonathan Israel, the author of two large and important books on the subject [*Radical Enlightenment*, Oxford University Press, 2001; *Enlightenment Contested*, Oxford University Press, 2006], spoke and outlined what he saw as the central tenets of this left wing of the broader Enlightenment—they included a strong philosophical belief in the primacy of reason and scientific investigation as opposed to supernatural agency of any kind; hostility to ecclesiastical authority, revelation, prophecy, and belief in religious toleration; insistence that a good society is created by men and not sanctioned by the church; belief in the emancipation of women; hostility to slavery; and the belief that monarchy and aristocracy have no justification and democratic republicanism is the most natural and indeed only legitimate form of state. Key figures included

Spinoza, Toland, Mandeville, Vico, and other thinkers less well known, at least to me.

In the discussion, Israel said that nobody held all of these views at the same time, that he was putting together a series of commitments from a general intellectual community. In reply, I pointed out that Thomas Paine held all of these views (except perhaps the equality of women, although *Rights of Man* did inspire the early feminist writings of Mary Wollstonecraft). In terms of philosophy as well as political action, Paine turned out to be more central than ever to an understanding of the Age of Revolution. My aim tonight is a bit less sweeping—not to give the whole philosophy of Thomas Paine, but to suggest something of Paine's influence in that pivotal, revolutionary era in the United States, and his legacy long after his own lifetime.

Of the men who made the American Revolution, none had a more remarkable career, or suffered a more peculiar fate, than Thomas Paine. Although people recognize his importance in the movement for independence, Paine is not generally included within the most exalted pantheon of founding fathers. While his friends Thomas Jefferson and George Washington, and his ideological antagonist John Adams, came from middle- and upper-class families long established on American soil, Paine's origins lay among the lower orders of eighteenth-century England, and he did not even arrive in America until the very eve of the Revolutionary War. Unlike Alexander Hamilton, another leader of the Revolution born abroad, Paine always remained something of an outsider in America, never developing true local roots here. Paine's profound influence on American events was acknowledged by friends and opponents alike, but after his death he was firmly excluded from the group of revolutionary leaders canonized in American popular culture. His memory was kept alive primarily by succeeding generations of radicals, who rediscovered him again and again as a symbol of revolutionary internationalism, freethinking, and defiance of existing institutions.

Even among radicals, Paine was by no means the most pervasive influence in the development of American radical thought. In England, as E. P. Thompson reminds us, Paine's writing became the foundation text of the working-class movement; in America, however, his aggressive infidelity, his assault upon revealed religion and institutionalized

Christianity in *The Age of Reason* and subsequent writings cut him off from the evangelical fervor that inspired so many reform movements of eighteenth-century America. Many American radicals found they could get their democratic ideals from Jefferson, without having to take on the added burden of Paine's religious beliefs.

It is difficult to find a sustained tradition of "Paineite radicalism" in eighteenth-century America, although Harvey Kaye has recently shown this tradition to be more vibrant than I realized when I wrote on Paine in 1976. However, it would be wrong to underestimate Paine's impact on the evolution of the American radical tradition. I want to argue today that Paine's influence on that tradition was, in fact, profound because more than any individual he defined the terms, created, if you will, the political language of eighteenth-century radicalism. Even those who rejected his religious beliefs could not escape the impact of Paine's radical variant of the republicanism that had come to dominate American political culture as result of the Revolution.

Paineite republicanism provided a vision of the good society, a utopian definition of active citizenship, against which the actual development of eighteenth-century American society often stood in sharp contrast. Paine helped to inspire many of the expressions of radical protest ranging from the labor movement of the 1830s to the Populist uprising of the 1890s. Yet at the same time, the limitation and ambiguities of republicanism as a vision of society, particularly its weaknesses in analyzing the economic, as opposed to the political components of the social order, posed problems that many American radicals found difficult to transcend. Thus, Paineite radicalism both provided inspiration for and set limits to the development of radical thought in eighteenth-century America.

In discussing the complex relationship between Thomas Paine and the American radical tradition, it is necessary first to suggest a definition of American radicalism. I do not propose to be detained by the classic question posed seventy years ago by the German sociologist Werner Sombart: "why is there no socialism in America?" for I am convinced that this is a bad question that has misled many fine scholars into proposing grandiose, abstract theories about American society, all of which have collapsed in the cold light of empirical reality. There have in fact been highly significant expressions of radicalism in American life; the problem for the historian is not to deny their existence, but to explain the unique constraints within which they have had to operate, and their persistence despite a relative lack of success. Instead, I want to focus on what I consider to be the three characteristic expressions of radicalism in American history, and Paine's relationship with each.

The most important radical movements of the late eighteenth and much of the nineteenth centuries derived from the republicanism of the American Revolution, a complex ideology in which the autonomous, property-holding citizen was viewed as the repository of social virtue and the basis of republican government. Alongside this republican radicalism arose a second expression, based on the ideal of the free individual, not, as in classical republicanism, defining his freedom through active citizenship and a commitment to the good of society, but standing rather in opposition to state and society. Generally, this is associated with classical nineteenth-century liberalism. In its most extreme form, this ideology became "native American anarchism" (no, I don't mean anarchism among Native Americans), the homegrown American hostility to all government so prominent in the eighteenth century and with echoes still surviving in American politics today. Finally, by the late eighteenth century, there emerged radical movements based on social class as the fundamental dividing line in American society. In his writings both in America and Europe, Paine helped analyze the new and unique characteristics of the modern industrial order, although he felt fundamentally that the cause of economic problems was the structure of government. Radicals drew heavily at first on Paineite republicanism for their political language, but were soon forced in part to transcend it.

Despite the fact that many American radicals shrank from a full acceptance of his religious views, Paine's contribution to the three variants of American radicalism was profound. This is not a question of individual "influence" — a difficult thing to measure in any case — but the way Paine helped to shape the modes of thought and expression that became characteristic of the American radical tradition. In his writings both in America and Europe, Paine helped to create the language of revolution of the late eighteenth century and transformed the meaning of the key words of political discourse. In *Common Sense*, he was among the first writers to use "republic" in a positive rather than a derogatory sense. In *Rights of Man*, he abandoned the old classical definition of "democracy" as a state where each citizen participated directly in government, and created its far broader, far more favorable modern meaning. Even the word "revolution" was transformed in his writing, from a term derived from the motion of the planets and implying a cyclical view of history, to one signifying vast and irreversible social and political change.

It was *Common Sense*, that remarkable pamphlet advocating the independence of the American colonies from Britain, which more than any other document impressed Paine's language on the American radical tradition. Through his attack on the monarchy, and upon the entire principle of hereditary rule and aristocratic privilege, Paine helped make republicanism a living political issue and a utopian ideal of government. Paine's savage attack on "the so much boasted Constitution of England" contained the most striking passages in that pamphlet. His description of the accession of William the Conqueror would become one of his most frequently quoted passages: "A French bastard landing with an armed banditti and establishing himself king of England against the consent of the natives, is in plain terms a very paltry rascally original . . . The plain truth is that the antiquity of the English monarchy will not bear looking into," or, again, his assault on the principle of hereditary rule: "Of more worth is one honest man to society . . . than all the crowned ruffians that ever lived."

By the way, the phrase "plain truth" is interesting because—according to Benjamin Rush, who claimed to have given Paine the title, *Common Sense*—Paine originally planned to call the pamphlet *Plain Truth*. In both those, the key word is plain or common, both of which in the eighteenth century meant coming from ordinary people. The notion of plain truth or common sense in the eighteenth century was a radical idea. Whatever it means today, it was the idea that you did not need a classical education. You did not need familiarity with law books, with Latin phrases, with Greek philosophy to understand government. "Com-mon" means something that anyone can understand; it's a democratic idea that common sense is all you need in order to be part of the political nation. All that was then required was a nation that symbolized liberty, in contrast to a world otherwise overrun by oppression.

Instead of the debased constitution of England, Paine proposed the establishment of republican government in America, based on new state legislatures with broad suffrage, popular representation through frequent election, and a written constitution guaranteeing the rights of person and property. He pictured an inde-pendent America, trading freely with the entire world, pursuing a policy of friendship with all nations, promoted by a strong continental government. In lyrical rhetoric, he outlined a breathtaking vision of the meaning of American independence: "We have it in our power to begin the world over again . . . The birthday of a new world is at hand." Paine transformed the struggle over the rights of Englishmen into a contest with meaning for all mankind: "O! ye that love mankind! Ye that dare oppose not only tyranny but the tyrant, stand forth! Every spot of the old world is overrun with oppression. Freedom hath been hunted round the globe. Asia and Africa have long expelled her. Europe regards her like a stranger and England hath given her warning to depart. O! Receive the fugitive and prepare in time an asylum for mankind."

A recent book by Lee Ward, *The Politics of Liberty in England and Revolutionary America* [Cambridge University Press, 2004], devotes an important chapter to Paine, showing how *Common Sense* popularized "a potent blend of distinct radical Whig republican ideas," grounded in the idea of popular sovereignty—political liberty meant not simply defense of individual rights but popular control of government. "Paine more than any other thinker ensured that the result and goal of the revolution in America would be emphatically republican." He was the first to propose a national constitution—a Charter, he called it—establishing the manner of elections, parliamentary rules, and federal-state relations, and securing "freedom and property to all men." Unlike Britain, America would have no monarch: "In America," he wrote, "the law is king." To put it another way, the people would take the place of the King as the foundation of the law's legitimacy.

Common Sense, as is well known, had an astonishing success. It went through 25 editions and reached literally hundreds of thousands of readers in 1776. Paine's antagonist John Adams always resented the fact that *Common Sense* was credited with having contributed so much to the movement for independence and republicanism. Its discussion, he insisted, was simply "a tolerable summary of the argument which I had been repeating again and again in Congress for nine months." Nothing in it was new, Adams believed, except "the phrases, suitable for an emigrant from New Gate . . . such as 'the Royal Brute of England.'" Adams may have been ungrateful, but to some extent he was right. What was unique in Paine was not simply his ideas, but his mode of expressing them. Paine was the conscious pioneer of a new style of political writing, one designed to extend political discussion beyond the narrow bounds of the eighteenth century's "political nation." His savage attacks on kinship and his careful exposition, in language common readers could understand, of republicanism were two sides of the same coin: both were meant to undermine the entire system of deferential politics.

In *Common Sense* and his subsequent writings, Paine outlined a vision of republicanism that had a profound impact on the American radical tradition. He never felt the need to describe precisely what he meant by a republic. It was simply a government devoted to the public good. Its hallmarks were equality among its citizens and a devotion to the common good rather than any particular social interest. Class conflict was, in a sense, incompatible with the essence of republicanism that, Paine believed, "does not admit of an interest distinct from that of the nation." Although during his American career Paine often found himself expressing the immediate political aims and concerns of the radical artisans of Philadelphia — the city where he spent most of that American career — his republicanism was not the ideology of a specific social class. Rather, it was rhetoric of exclusion; the people, when set against their rulers and a narrow, non-productive aristocracy, were a homogeneous body with a definable common interest.

The key characteristic of republics, according to Paine and other thinkers of the revolutionary era, was not so much a particular structure of government but a set of qualities among the citizenry. The key terms in republican discourse were "virtue," the willingness to subordinate one's selfish interests to the good of the entire society; "equality," which encompassed not only equality before the law and in political rights, but a fairly equitable distribution of private property so that vast disparities of wealth would not upset political stability; and "independence," the ability to resist outside coercion, which was usually seen to rest on the possession of private property. Most republican thinkers believed that only property provided the autonomy that enabled men to exercise their political rights freely. The Pennsylvania constitution of 1780 expanded suffrage to include all male taxpayers, including nearly all free men. But even Paine, while in America, believed personal servants should not have the right to vote. (Later, in England, he came to advocate universal manhood suffrage).

America, Paine believed, because of its relatively equal distribution of wealth (always excepting, of course, black slavery), was uniquely fitted to possess a republican government. In such a circumstance, governmental structure should be extremely simple. Americans did not need a large government, expensive and complex, such as existed in England. A central axiom of Paineite republicanism was the distinction between society and government. In the opening section of *Common Sense*, he explained, "Some writers have so confounded society with government, as to leave little or no distinction between them; whereas they are not only different, but have different origins. Society is produced by our wants and government by our wickedness . . . The first is a patron, the last a punisher. Society is in every state a blessing, but government, even in its best state, is but a necessary evil."

This distinction between society and government helps to explain Paine's vision of a republic without class conflict or economic oppression. Paine was, to be sure, an eloquent and scathing critic of the social order of Europe. He could comment in moving terms on the "mass of wretchedness" lying "hidden from the eye of common observation," which had "scarcely any other chance than to expire in poverty or infamy." But the cause of this wretchedness was political, not economic: the existence of poverty implied that "something must be wrong in the system of government." Paine singled out oppressive taxation, aristocratic privilege, and monarchy-inspired wars as the cause of poverty in Europe—all examples of the destructive effects of excessive and unjust government. While he outlined a pioneering and far-reaching program of social welfare measures in Chapter 5 of *Rights of Man, Part II*, Paine never suggested that such measures needed to be applied in America (and many of his proposals we still have not adopted today, more than 200 years later). His remedy for economic injustices was the establishment of republican government.

Paine thus did not attribute inequalities of wealth to economic oppression, although his views on this subject did change during his lifetime. In *Common Sense*, he explicitly rejected the idea that poverty was the result of "the harsh, ill-sounding names of oppression and avarice," a belief he repeated in virtually the same language twenty years later in *Dissertation on the First Principles of Government*. Only in *Agrarian Justice*, written in 1796 in France, did Paine suggest that economic inequality might have a fundamental root outside the political system.

In that pamphlet, Paine noted that private property in land deprived millions of men their natural right to a portion of the soil. Yet cultivation of private property was essential for the onward progress of civilization. Unlike Babeuf, who used similar logic to demand the outlawing of private property in general, or Thomas Spence, who demanded an end to property in land, Paine proposed that each individual reaching age of 21 be given a sum of fifteen pounds (which was worth considerably more at the time than it is now) as compensation for "the loss of his or her natural inheritance." Spence considered the pamphlet a "dire disappointment," and condemned Paine's "poor beggarly stipends" as "contemptible and insulting" substitutes for "our lordly and just pretensions to the soil of our birth." But because it linked poverty not simply to bad government but to the alienation of land to private individuals, *Agrarian Justice* established Paine as a pioneer of the land reform tradition that stretched in America down to Henry George almost a century later.

In his American writings, then, Paine enunciated themes that would come to dominate eighteenth-century American radicalism: a commitment to social and political egalitarianism, a division of society into producing and non-producing classes, a hostility to monarchy and hereditary privilege, and an American nationalism coup-led with a concern for the fate of liberty overseas. All were embodied in the ideal of the Paineite republic. Yet within Paineite republicanism there lay a crucial ambig-uity, or, perhaps, a tension between the liberal and republican elements.

On the one hand, as we have seen, Paine exalted the common good and rejected the notion of a republic divided into competing social classes. James Madison, in a sense, was much more realistic than Paine, more attuned to the dangers of class conflict in a republic—for that reason he wrote into the Constitution an elaborate system of checks and balances to prevent a property-less majority from seizing control of the reins of government in order to despoil the rich. On the other hand, Paine's exaltation of commerce as the cement of the natural order of society, and his general optimism about economic change, led him as well in a liberal, individualistic direction. There was a natural affinity between the new political economy of Adam Smith and the republicanism of Thomas Paine—both were based on the harmonious workings of society. Perhaps we might simply conclude that Paine's republicanism contained within it the common origins of the divergent streams of radical thought of the eighteenth century. Republican, individualist, and socialist radicalism all had common origins in the radicalism of the Age of Revolution, but under the later impact of the industrial revolution, their unity was shattered, and they came to be developed in distinct directions.

Having contributed so much to the American Revolution, Paine departed for England in 1787. But even while Paine pursued his checkered career as a founding father of British working-class radicalism in the 1790s and as an unhappy participant in revolutionary France, Paineite republicanism remained alive in America. In 1793 and 1794 the Democratic-Republican societies—formed to combat the politics of the Washington administration, promote the party of Jefferson, and defend the French Revolution— distributed copies of *Rights of Man* and drank toasts to Paine as a symbol of opposition to aristocratic tyranny.

The ranks of Paineites were reinforced by an influx of British Jacobins in the 1790s and early eighteenth century. These included Joseph Gales, a Sheffield newspaper editor and leader of the Sheffield Corresponding Society, who fled that city one step ahead of the law and later became a newspaper editor and Jeffersonian leader in Raleigh, North Carolina; John Daly Burk, a United Irishman who became a lawyer, historian, and playwright in Virginia; William Duane; John Binns; and other Paineite newspaper editors. These men formed a distinct group in American politics; they knew and assisted one another and, despite personal success, did not abandon their democratic, Paineite ideas. Some joined Elihu Palmer's deistic Columbia Illuminati, a society of secularists for whom Paine did some writing on his return to America in 1802. Others pursued a host of humanitarian concerns: the abolition of slavery, reform of debtor laws, the defense of freedom of the press. Yet as a group, their radicalism did not extend to economic matters. Only one Jacobin-Jefferson editor, Philadelphia's William Duane, defended the journeyman shoemakers who were convicted in a famous conspiracy trial in 1806. The others, drawing on one side of Paine's outlook, viewed any organizing for the interests of a specific class as incompatible with republican government.

It was not until the 1830s that the possibilities of merging republican radicalism with the grievances of the working class became fully apparent in America. In the rise of the early labor movement, Paine's memory and legacy played an important part. In response to the early manifestations of industrialism in America and the rapid decline in the skill and autonomy of the traditional artisan class, there appeared the first workingmen's parties in any nation, as well as a class-conscious unionism that conducted the first extensive wave of strikes in American history. The key to their social outlook was Paineite republicanism, adopting Paine's strident language as a critique, not of European aristocracy, but of an emerging American aristocracy. American society, they believed, was being divided into antagonistic classes, opportunities for the workingman were declining, and wealthy nonproducers now accumulated the lion's share of economic and political power.

For the early labor movement, Paine emerged as a hero and symbol. By the 1830s, dinners celebrating the anniversary of Paine's birth were being held in Boston, Philadelphia, Cincinnati, and Albany, and in 1834 some 70 men and women attended a ball following the New York Paine birthday dinner at the City Saloon. While the organizers of these dinners tended to be emigrant English labor leaders, for whom Paine's memory seems to have been stronger than their American counterparts, many native-born artisans were among the celebrants. However, some labor leaders refused to attend—for an acceptance of *The Age of Reason* was still required to associate oneself with the memory of Paine. The toasts and speeches at the Paine dinners dealt as often with religious questions as social concerns, and the Paineites denounced not only threats to the dignity of labor, but what they perceived as attempts to unite church and state—the movement to halt Sunday mail deliveries, for example. For the men and women who celebrated his birthday, Paine was above all a symbol of the evil effects of clerical persecution, and of the virtues of the free intellect, unfettered by "superstition."

Parenthetically, in 1987 on the 250th anniversary of Paine's birth, Sean Wilentz and I organized a reenactment of a Paine birthday celebration dinner at Fraunces Tavern in New York, attended by fifty or so historians. Modeled on one the dinners held by the New York Working Man's party in the 1830s, we repeated the many toasts that had been published at the time. Some of the toasts sound rather arcane today ("to the liberators of Haiti"), but some sound very much up to date ("may women achieve their rights"). Parts of this actually were broadcast on National Public Radio.

But even if some labor leaders were reluctant to identify themselves too closely with Paine as an individual, Paineite ideology permeated the movement, not only inspiring it, but also setting limits to its outlook, for the essentially political basis of Paineite republicanism left little room for a comprehensive analysis of the causes of labor's economic discontents. While the labor movement was convinced that nonproducers were somehow appropriating far too large a share of the products of labor, they found it difficult to explain this situation within the old republican paradigm. Just as in the 1790s, they continued to seek political reforms to achieve economic ends. Their major demand was for free, universal public education, which would not only level social distinctions but enable the laborer once again to take his rightful place as an active republican citizen. They demanded an end to imprisonment for debt so that people would not be jailed for owing some small amounts of money.

Even the 10-hour day, demanded by the trade unions, was seen not simply as an economic measure, but as a way of revitalizing the republican tradition by providing more time for labor to participate in public affairs. Education and the 10-hour day were "the great lever by which the Working Men are to be raised to their proper elevation in the republic. It will make but one class out of the many that now envy and despise each other." Note the traditional republican goal of transcending class conflict in the name of social unity. When the labor movement did search for economic remedies to the problems of labor, they remained within the Paineite tradition. It was distortions caused by government that disrupted the natural and harmonious functioning of the economy. Some blamed government-granted monopolies for enriching non-producers; others pointed to paper money issued by hands under government charter. The Paineite tradition was not well suited to an analysis of the rapidly modernizing economic order.

There were, however, two leaders of the labor movement who, while strongly influenced by Paine, sought to adapt Paineite republicanism in more economic direction. Thomas Skidmore, a machinist and teacher in New Jersey, published *The Rights of Man to Property*—a title suggesting both a tribute to Paine and the need to move beyond his analysis, to extend political equality that had been achieved in America into the economic realm. Skidmore's program called not simply for political change, but for the abolition of inheritance. All property would revert to the community at a person's death, and each person on reaching maturity would receive an equal stipend. The idea clearly derived from Paine's program of government grants in both *Rights of Man* and *Agrarian Justice*, but Skidmore extended this to a critique of all inequalities of property. As long as wealth was unequal, he insisted, attempts to end other inequalities would fail (and he included, by the way, blacks and women as recipients of governmental grants). Yet Skidmore could not escape the competitive individualism inherent in Paine's vision of the natural functioning of the economy, for once individuals received their equal grants, they could accumulate as much wealth as they were able. They would simply not be allowed to pass it on to their children. Yet even in this focus, Skidmore's ideas were too radical for the bulk of the labor movement, which dropped his program after briefly embracing it in 1829. His vision of an active government constantly redistributing property contradicted the more general republican belief that government intervention should be kept to a minimum.

More popular was the English immigrant radical, George Henry Evans, who also sought to make republicanism relevant to the changed economic conditions in America, this time by drawing on Paine's *Agrarian Justice*. In conjunction with Horace Greeley of the *New York Tribune* and the remarkable Irish Chartist emigrant Thomas Devyr (author of the intriguingly-titled memoir *The Odd Book of the eighteenth Century*), Evans demanded that the government supply free homesteads on the public land for any individual who desired to escape the bonds of wage labor. Combining Paine's argument that men had a natural right to the soil with the view that an oversupply of laborers in the East depressed the wage level, Evans warned that if something were not done, "European" conditions of poverty would soon emerge in America. Land reform was the certain way to avoid unrepublican class conflict while at the same time providing access to the property ownership that was the only guarantee of republican independence, equality, and virtue. The homestead law, Evans argued, would give "thousands and tens of thousands, who are now languishing in hopeless poverty . . . a certain and speedy independence." With Evans, land reform emerged as a central theme in the transAtlantic radical tradition, finding expression in the Free Soil and Republican parties in the United States and the Chartist movement in England, and later in Irish nationalism and the movement inspired in the 1880s by Henry George.

With the decline of the early labor movement after the 1830s and 1840s, the memory of Paine receded somewhat from American radical movements. In 1859, the *Atlantic Monthly* described Paine as "only an indistinct shadow" to most Americans. Yet among English radical immigrants and German refugees of 1848, Paine's legacy survived. It was at a meeting of English-born "infidels" in Cincinnati that Moncure D. Conway, who was later to write the first modern biography of Paine, was introduced to Paine's writings. After the Civil War, the great American orator Robert Ingersoll (most famous for his great speech characterizing James G. Blaine, Republican standard bearer of 1884, as "the plumed knight") gave numerous lectures on Paine, but Ingersoll too was a notorious atheist, a fact that helps explain the frustration of his political ambitions. Ingersoll's brother served as Congressman from Illinois, but he himself failed in numerous attempts to obtain the governorship or a seat in the Senate. At Paine's birthday celebration in San Francisco in 1884, Miss Eva Ballou read a poem specially composed for the occasion:

> Among the dear immortal names,
> The names that ne'er shall perish,
> Whose honor, genius, worth and fame
> Americans should cherish,
> None is more worthy of their love

> More free from taint or stain,
> Or more entitled to endure
> Than that of Thomas Paine.

Miss Ballou went on to lament, poetically, that Paine's memory was the subject of "bitter hate, and shame, and obloquy."

Perhaps she overstated her case. While Paine as an individual had faded from view, that peculiar phenomenon which I have been describing—Paineism without Paine—continued to flourish among American radicals. In the years after the Civil War, the labor movement emerged as the inheritor of the ante-bellum radical tradition. Resurrecting the notion of wage slavery and the republican hostility to the wage system, organizations like the Knights of Labor returned once again to Paine's utopian vision of a republican society without class conflict. The Knights' "cooperative commonwealth" was based, not on class warfare, but on the harmony of interests among producers and the arbitration of their differences with employers. Their aim was classically republican—the abolition of the wage system. "We complain," said one Knights leader, "that our rulers, statesmen and orators have not attempted to engraft republican principles into our industrial system, and have forgotten or denied its underlying principles. . . . There is an inevitable and irrepressible conflict between the wage system of labor and the republican system of government."

Even after the decline of the Knights, Paineite radicalism continued in the 1890s. The key elements of Populist thought harked back to the radical republicanism of a century before: hostility to banks and middlemen, belief that class divisions were a symptom of the Europeanization of American society, emphasis on the key element of economic independence for the citizen, and the unity of "the people" against the non-productive aristocracy. The ideal of "the republic" as a vision of a better world retained its resonance. The rallying cry of Tom Watson, one of the greatest of Populist orators, attempted to link classical republicanism with a critique of the modern industrial order: "Day by day the power of the individual sinks. Day by day the power of the classes, of the corporations rises. And every loss to the individual is a loss to the Republic. . . . In all essential respects . . . the Republic of our fathers is dead."

Equally dead, perhaps, was the radicalism based on

the ideal of a small producers' republic. For the next major expression of American radicalism—socialism— marked a final break with the Paineite tradition, with its emphasis on the political causes of economic discontents. The great socialist leader, Eugene V. Debs, hailed Paine as a founder of the radical tradition, but in socialist thought there was little that could be directly linked to Paine's writings. Paine remained now primarily as a symbol, a personal inspiration, the man who had said, "a share in two revolutions is living to some purpose." As such, he would continue to inspire various individual radicals claiming his legacy: anarchists, free thinkers, non-conformists of every variety.

So often in American history, if one looks into the background of an individual who sought to supersede the conventions of his or her society, one finds evidence of Paine's legacy. To take just one further example, from a realm perhaps far afield from our discussion today: that pioneer of American modern dance, Ruth St. Denis, was the daughter of an English immigrant who spent his evenings in a Somerville, New Jersey, tavern with a group of deistic admirers of the "good old anti-christians" Tom Paine and Robert Ingersoll. (I might add that St. Denis's mother, a devoutly religious woman and teetotaler, heartily disapproved of her husband's activities.)

We return to the paradox with which we began—the general exclusion of Paine from the list of revolutionary forebears celebrated in American popular culture, and his apparent neglect even among American radicals. Despite this, as I have argued, Paine's influence was indeed profound. More than any other individual, he not only created the language for radical politics but set an example of the radical cast of mind in America—his revolutionary internationalism and defiance of existing institutions, his rationalism and faith in human nature, his belief in casting off the burden of the past and remaking institutions so as to "bring forward, by a quiet and regular operation, all that extent of capacity which never fails to appear in revolutions." As a political writer and as a scientist (he helped design the iron bridge), Paine helped to usher in the modern world, yet at the same time he provided a body of ideas and a personal example that would continue to inspire those who believed that the modern world had betrayed, not fulfilled, the high hopes for a just social order raised during Paine's Age of Revolution.

To conclude, we have never had a greater need for a sort of Paineite frame of mind than today. I want to refer back to the idea of the Radical Enlightenment. I often feel that we are living now at the end of the Enlightenment, at the end of a two-century or so great movement in human history. Partly this is because of the crimes committed in its name, the misuses of "science" in support of racism, colonialism, and so on. But equally it is because scientific knowledge, expertise, and reason are being denigrated. Blind loyalty is now exalted over knowledge. Science is increasingly subordinated to political ideology, faith, and dogmatism. Fundamentalism, asserting that you do not have to actually think deeply about anything, seems to be dominant in many areas of this country. We need to recapture the Enlightenment belief—as represented by Thomas Paine—in the power of people to remake society and the ability of reasonable men and women to understand and change the world. Thank you.

Question (partly audible): . . . I have read Paine over the years and have taught him. The things you said today resonated in an interesting way in terms of common sense of the people. I think that Paine lives today, the common sense of the people lives, but it's on the right side of the spectrum. You know, we are the new aristocrats who have the knowledge that people do not need, because their knowledge comes from the gut, not from our heads, so I feel Paine does live, except he's come back in a way we may not recognize.

Eric Foner: That's an interesting comment. I'm not sure I totally agree with it. This very notion of common sense has meant many different things at different points in history. When Tom Watson and such people talked about the elite, they meant corporations, big industrialists, power brokers. Today when politicians talk about the elite, they mean people who watch public television or something, so I agree with you; there can be something very anti-intellectual in the notion of common sense, the notion that you don't actually have to have any expertise to discuss something.

When Paine used that concept, however, it was very different. It was a critique of any tiny group of educated, self-appointed people. In the 18th century, before *Common Sense*, most pamphlets sold (if they were lucky to sell) two- or three-hundred copies. They were addressed to a very, very small audience of those who were the power brokers in society. Paine shattered that notion of the boundaries of acceptable political discourse. It was a highly democratic thing to do.

Question: I agree with you that Paine was a publicist, brilliantly, for ideas that were held by many people, in the same way that Thomas Jefferson was. But as John Adams said in his dying words, Thomas Jefferson survives, and Tom Paine appears not to have. Is he a victim of popular interpretation, that Paine became a kind of embarrassment?

Eric Foner: Adams also said, this is the age of Paine (and Adams disliked Thomas Paine very much). Harvey Kaye's new book, which is well worth reading, demonstrates a very robust tradition of recognition for Paine in American history, more robust than I had thought existed when I did my book. I'm sure Harvey would agree that Paine is not as revered as Jefferson in our culture, but it's probably not correct to say that Paine virtually disappeared.

But I do think in this society, at various points in our history, Paine's forthright attack on revealed religion, on the Bible, on organized Christianity, alienated a lot of people. In Europe, most radicalism of the 19th and even into the 20th century had an anti-clerical side to it, because the established church could be seen as a bastion of the social order. In America, so much of our radicalism comes out of evangelical Protestantism, whether it's abolitionism or civil rights movements, so that that poses a problem for the legacy of Paine. People either forget about *The Age of Reason*, or they are embarrassed by, it as you suggest.

Also remember, Paine also didn't stick around in America. He didn't hold public office except as Secretary to the Committee on Foreign Affairs for a bit. Jefferson was a President, Adams was a President, Franklin sat in the Second Continental Congress, and so on, so Paine doesn't appear as a maker of the government, so to speak. Paine was not a person who took part in governmental processes the way some of these other people we remember did. That's another part of the story. But I still think Paine's limited reputation is a paradox—which, by definition, just means you have to scratch your head and say, hmm, that's hard to explain.

Question: Your very last comment, about the end of the Enlightenment—does it apply in Europe, for Europeans, too, or just the United States?

Eric Foner: Fundamentalisms are rife in many countries in the world today, as you all know. It's not purely confined to the United States, but I think Western Europe is less influenced by this tendency than many other parts of the world. They have problems of their own, obviously. Regarding the value of science and reason, for example, this is the only country in the world that doesn't believe there's global warming; at least that's the official position of the government. There are certain areas where I think we are unique, in simply allowing faith or political self-interest to just override science and reason. It's not a question in Europe, or in Japan or even in China. We just happen to be at a rather peculiar moment in our political culture.

Question: As a historian, would you say something about whether the Declaration of Independence, in that time, was a revolutionary act based on a revolutionary proposition? If so, how does the Declaration of Independence—its aims, ideas, and visions—create America, not as revolutionary America, but America as a continual revolution?

Eric Foner: Yes, of course the Declaration of Independence is a revolutionary document. George III certainly thought it was. It is a justification for revolution; that's why it was written. Indeed, it was written, as the author says, to demonstrate a decent respect for the opinions of mankind, to explain to mankind why this revolution is taking place. That's a concept that seems to have faded out of our political culture, a decent respect to the opinions of mankind.

With the Declaration, I was thinking this morning, there's a phrase in there which is quite well related to this notion of common sense, and that is "self-evident"—we hold these truths to be self-evident. That's another way of putting the notion of common sense. They don't need to be demonstrated. They don't need to be argued. Anybody can see that this is true, self-evident.

As a revolutionary document, it has inspired revolutions in many countries, in many places, at many times, for the hundreds of years since. People seeking to throw off tyranny of one form or another have frequently cited the Declaration of Independence because it gives the intellectual and political justification of the right of revolution.

Question (continued): I want to follow up regarding the revolutionary character of the Declaration of Independence, for I don't consider the Declaration to be revolutionary at all. Revolution truly was in the notion of common sense, itself. It was a revolution of rationalist thought and ideas. Independence was a proclamation by the new colonial ruling elite to the rest of the world saying, we are preparing our defense because of the usurpations of the King, and we have a right to do this, and we want France's help in particular. As far as revolutionary thought goes, most of the revolutionary thought was already there. It's just reiterated, as self-evident to the colonists.

Eric Foner: The Declaration, however, was a justification of revolutionary action, which is sometimes considered more dangerous by people than revolutionary thought.

Question: As a historian, and with what you cited as changes in the meaning of different words throughout the centuries, how do you interpret the Constitution? Is it a living document?

Eric Foner: The question is based on the debate in jurisprudence between those who argue that the way to think about the Constitution is through this concept of original intent, hat is, that you must go back to the purposes in light of the people who wrote it, so that the job of the Justice is to probe the minds of the founders and figure out what they meant by such words as "due process" or "cruel and unusual punishment." Opposed to this is the idea of a living Constitution, with meaning changing over time, so what was not considered "cruel and unusual punishment" in 1787 may seem quite cruel and unusual to us today, 200 and some odd years later.

Of course, the Constitution is a living document. That's what we have to go by, our society, not what they were thinking back then. Individual freedom is an evolving idea, and more and more groups are brought into it. One of the best statements of the living Constitution view was in Justice

Kennedy's majority opinion in *Lawrence v. Texas*. That was the case that overturned the Texas sodomy law outlawing homosexual acts. Basically, he said the founding fathers might have thought that homosexuality was bad. It wasn't really what was on their mind when they were writing the Constitution. But that's irrelevant to us today in our modern society, when our concept of liberty and personal autonomy has evolved.

There is a similar argument about original intent regarding *Brown v. Board of Education*. The people who wrote the 14th Amendment were not thinking about school segregation. But, as Justice Warren said, the role of education in American society had changed so much in the centuries since the 14th Amendment was ratified that today to segregate people by race in schools is a violation of their equality. Maybe it wasn't in 1866, but it is today.

If you really want an original intent issue, my favorite is, what about the view that corporations are entitled to be treated as persons under the 14th Amend-ment? The people who wrote the 14th Amendment did-n't have that in mind. Believe me; I've read all the Congressional debates. Not a single person said a word about this having anything to do with corporations. That wasn't what they were interested in. They were interested in the rights of the former slaves who had just been emancipated. Now, let's see if the original-intent advocates think we should strip corporations of all the protections they have developed under the Constitution in order to go back to the original intent. My view is that justices can often be rather flexible in how they apply what seem to be rather irreconcilable doctrines. Anyway, that's a very short answer.

THOMAS PAINE: GIVING CAUSE FOR AMERICA AND FREEDOM TO MANKIND

Brian McCartin

Michael Kreizenbeck

My name is Michael Kreizenbeck, and I am the staff coordinator for this symposium. It is probably impossible to exaggerate the importance of Thomas Paine to Brian McCartin. Brian is President of the Thomas Paine National Historical Association. He and his family reside in the Thomas Paine Museum. The museum is located in New Rochelle, New York, on land that was once part of the farm of some 300 acres given to Paine in 1784 by the State of New York in recognition for his services in the Revolutionary War. The estate currently houses the historic Thomas Paine Cottage and a monument.

Brian is the author of *Thomas Paine: Common Sense and Revolutionary Pamphleteering*. He has worked passionately to advance public recognition of and appreciation for the life and achievements of Paine, focusing especially on educational outreach. In addition to his voluntary service to the Paine Association, Brian's full-time day job is lead teacher at an alternative high school in a place that has long been known to try men's souls, the South Bronx. His devotion to Thomas Paine, his works, and his legacy is impressive. Will you all please welcome Brian McCartin.

Brian McCartin

Thank you for the kind introduction. On behalf of the Thomas Paine National Historical Association, I would like to thank our hosts at San Diego State University for their vision and generosity in sponsoring this symposium. The Association would also like to thank all the historians, educators, and authors present for their contributions to the scholarship on Paine. By providing a venue for our discourse about the ideas of Thomas Paine and their relevance today, this symposium gives honor to Paine's belief that "when opinions are free . . . truth will finally and powerfully prevail."

The Thomas Paine National Historical Association is an independent, non-partisan, and non-profit organization dedicated to the historical legacy and enduring relevance of Paine's life and ideas. Founded on January 29, 1884, in New York City, the Association provides public access to research materials, programs, exhibitions, and events that disseminate his works and illuminate the significance of Thomas Paine. It endeavors to serve as a historical and educational resource that may better secure a culture of peace, justice, and dignity for ourselves and our posterity.

In November, 2005, we will be having the centenary anniversary of our dedication of the Thomas Paine Monument to the City of New Rochelle. The monument was first erected in 1839 by Gilbert Vale, editor of the *Independent Beacon* in New York, a freethinker and ex-patriot from England who decided that Paine's burial plot was not substantial enough for such a prestigious person. The sculpture was done by John Frazee, America's pre-eminent sculptor at the time. In 2006, we will be hosting the grand re-opening of the Museum, which is presently undergoing renovations. It was founded by Association President William Vander Weyde and Vice-President Thomas Alva Edison on the former site of Paine's farm, and was first opened in 1926. The Museum serves as a historical community resource center and as a visible national symbol for America's pre-eminent Founding Father.

The focus of my presentation today will be Thomas Paine, his life in England and his times in America. I see constant references in my readings to people like Francis Oldys (a pseudonym for Chalmers) and James Cheetham regarding Paine's life. Although certain things that they report are true, there are also many misrepresentations. After discussing Paine's early years, I will turn to *Common Sense* and how this seminal work on political liberty created a revolution in thought so profound that it gave cause for American independence. The pamphlet continues to set the standard for human rights in the modern political state and to provide a philosophy of political empowerment and social justice for today. As Paine wrote in *Common Sense*, "The cause of America is in a great measure the cause of all mankind." At the end of my talk, I will segue to the exhibit we brought to this conference, which also puts into focus Paine's experiences in Europe, his coming to America, and his legacy.

Although born of humble origins, Thomas Paine rose to become the most influential political figure and best-selling author of the eighteenth century transatlantic world. English by birth, French by decree, and American by choice, he left an impact upon all three countries. In his greatest works, including *Common Sense*, *Rights of Man*, and *The Age of Reason*, Paine proposed a political and social system based on liberty, justice, and equality. His ideas shocked, challenged, and inspired inhabitants of both the New and Old Worlds to seek revolutionary change. General Charles Lee once remarked that Paine "burst forth upon the world like Jove with thunderbolts." From Philadelphia to Paris, London to Dublin, and Warsaw to Santo Domingo, Thomas Paine's revolutionary philosophy radically altered the political landscape of his times — and ours.

Seventy-five miles north of London, in the county of Norfolk, is the small town of Thetford. It is located on the banks of two rivers, the Thet and Little Ouse. For most of the eighteenth century, Thetford was a farming community lying in the heath, or countryside, rich in meadows, wildlife, and forests. With its small manufacturing and trade economy, Thetford served as a market town and trading center for the surrounding towns and villages. In the year of Paine's birth, Thetford's small population of 2,000 people included a wide range of social classes. Wealthy lawyers and merchants formed the upper level of an expanding middle class, shopkeepers and artisans formed its lower middle class, while Thetford's number of poor remained low for most of the eighteenth century. Dominating the surrounding countryside were the estates of the wealthy aristocracy and landed gentry. At a time when land meant wealth and wealth meant power, these land-owning nobles and untitled country squires were members of the ruling class that rose to power at the end of the previous century.

Like many rural towns and villages in the England of Paine's childhood, Thetford was ruled by a wealthy aristocrat. Through patronage and bribery, nobles often exercised domination over towns and boroughs throughout the eighteenth-century English countryside. As part of this "rotten borough" system of government, Thetford and several other small villages and hamlets fell under the control of the Duke of Grafton. With an estate almost forty miles in circumference, the Grafton family maintained influence over the political and social affairs of Thetford for generations. In Parliament, the Duke and his chosen representative to the House of Commons allied with the ruling Whig political party.

In the era of Paine's birth, the majority of Englishmen could not participate in government. Men without property or an annual income of 40 pounds could not vote or hold office. Controlling the House of Lords through inheritance and the House of Commons with patronage and bribery, the Whig ruling class denied representation for the majority of English citizens. Out of a population of five million Englishmen, only 6,000 could vote for members of Parliament. Despite growing national wealth and power, economic conditions for the lower classes of English society continued to grow worse. As a result of the system of enclosure, agricultural laborers, peasants, and tenant farmers were denied access to common grazing lands. Cites became overcrowded with an expanding class of poor and dispossessed. Labor unrest caused by poor working conditions and food riots caused by shortages spread through English cities. Partly in response, the government advanced the great myth that all free-born Englishmen were equal before the law, an idea that would make its way to British-America in the 1700s. Parliament also enacted almost 200 capital crimes in order to maintain "liberty and property" for the English ruling classes. For committing such minor offenses as stealing bread, women and children were sent to the gallows. This was England at the time of Thomas Paine's birth on January 29, 1737.

Paine's literary talent was evident at an early age. He was eight years old when he wrote the following:

>Here lies the body of John Crow
>Who once was high but now is low;
>Ye brother crows take warning all,
>For as you rise, so must you fall.

Exposed to injustice and inequality almost from birth, young Thomas was as familiar with the arrogance of crows towards smaller and less powerful birds, as he was with the arrogance of the wealthy and powerful towards the suffering lower classes. This simple yet profound reminder about equality and justice became a major theme throughout all of Paine's future writings.

Located in a section of town called "the Wilderness," the Paine cottage overlooked Gallows Hill, an execution site. In the spring of each year, Thetford hosted the civil and criminal court sessions for the county of Norfolk. Every

March during the Christian season of Lent, hundreds of visitors from the surrounding countryside swelled Thetford's inns and taverns to see this spectacle of state justice. The majority of criminal cases involved the poor over the stealing of food, money, or property. With few murders and no real criminal culture existing among England's poor, most crimes were committed out of need and desperation. Nevertheless, punishments for crimes against property were quite severe and included hanging, exile to America, the ducking stool in the river Thet, the town pillory, a whipping, branding, or imprisonment.

For the first nineteen years of his life, Thomas Paine was an eye-witness to the brutality and injustice executed by the state in the name of English law. He saw from his house the local goal, with its dungeon, and the prisoners as they marched up Gallows Hill with their hands and feet shackled on execution day. He saw their eyes covered by a black handkerchief, and he saw their bodies dangle in the cold spring air for the customary hour. The injustice and brutality of English law made a strong impression on his young mind and gave him an early understanding of the nature of power and wealth and its use of state brutality to maintain that power. This understanding was expressed by Paine years later, when he wrote:

> When, in countries that are called civilised, we see age going to the Workhouse and youth to the gallows, something must be wrong in the system of government. It would seem, by the exterior appearance of such countries, that all was happiness; but there lies hidden from the eye of common observation, a mass of wretchedness, that has scarcely any other chance, than to expire in poverty or infamy. Its entrance into life is marked with the presage of its fate; and until this is remedied, it is in vain to punish . . . Civil government does not exist in executions; but in making such provision for the instruction of youth and the support of age. Instead of this, the resources of a country are lavished upon kings, upon courts, upon hirelings, impostors and prostitutes; and even the poor themselves, with all their wants upon them, are compelled to support the fraud that oppresses

them. Why is it that scarcely any are executed but the poor?

Closer to home Paine witnessed another form of injustice, that of religious intolerance. He was the child of a mixed-religious household, for his mother was Anglican and his father Quaker. Baptized and confirmed an Anglican, Paine learned the Bible and Anglican catechism at home, school, and church. He would later quote passages of the Bible by memory in his own works. However, Paine grew to doubt a church that scared him with its sermons of a vengeful God, and he witnessed the intolerance displayed by the Anglicans towards the Quakers in Thetford. This early lesson in the power of the established church would later influence Thomas to write on behalf of freedom of religious thought and the separation of church and state.

At the age of seven, Paine began his formal education, at the Thetford Grammar School down the road from his house. Founded two centuries earlier, the Puritan-run school was free to the children of freeborn Englishmen of Thetford. As the son of a freeman, Thomas attended the school for the next six years. Limited in his formal education to arithmetic, science, accounting, and English, Paine excelled at mathematics and showed a strong interest in science and poetry. His readings of Shakespeare and Milton helped develop his unique insight into human nature. His decision not to take Latin, most likely because of his Quaker upbringing, prevented him from becoming a professional.

In 1750, when he was thirteen years old, Thomas left school to begin serving as an apprentice to his father. Seven years was the standard term of apprenticeship for most trades, and Joseph Pain's staymaking trade was no different. It is still uncertain whether Joseph was the type of staymaker who produced stays for ships masts or was the maker of corsets. We do know, however, that after six years as an apprentice staymaker, an occupation imposed more by his social class and a limited education than by personal choice, Thomas Paine left home. Spurred on by his readings of Daniel Defoe's *Robinson Crusoe*, and Jonathan Swift's *Gulliver's Travels*, he left Thetford for London and adventure.

Reading advertisements calling for seamen to serve as British privateers, he signed on the *King of Prussia* and served for nearly a year, arriving back in London in August, 1757.

Stimulated by his observations of navigation and astronomy, he decided to pursue his interests in science. Apart from browsing London's bookstores and devouring newspapers, pamphlets, and broadsides, Paine's formal introduction to the newly opening world of eighteenth-century science and philosophy came from attending London's Royal Society. As Paine later recalled, "The natural bent of my mind was to science. As soon as I was able, I purchased a pair of globes, and attended the philosophical lectures of Martin and Ferguson."

These men were part of the scientific revolution in England that began in the previous century after Isaac Newton discovered the universal laws of gravity. They emphasized empirical study based on observable data, believing that nature served as a grand analogy for all human activity and that human society could be brought into harmony with nature. As the center of expression for these new ideas, members of the Royal Society examined topics that ranged from Newtonian philosophy to the behavior of comets, reflection of light, properties of air, and phases of the moon. Lectures at the Royal Society attracted large groups of self-educated shopkeepers and artisans, including many of those who rejected traditional notions of the power of the state and church. Paine's public exposure to these ideas not only aroused his passion for science but introduced him to new political and social ideas that equated science and reason with liberty. His critical attitude toward the power of state and church was now joined to a positive alternative. By understanding the natural laws that operated in the human world, through reason and scientific inquiry, man could develop a science of government that would improve and reform society. Paine was thus drawn to the intellectual movement of the Enlightenment, and would later take his place among those thinkers who passionately asserted that through reason and science men could create a better world.

Over the next several years, Paine continued to develop his political and social ideas through what I like to call his experiential self-study program. After leaving London, he briefly worked again as a journeyman staymaker in Dover. Paine had moved to Sandwich by 1759 and set himself up in a small shop as a master staymaker. During his time there, Paine found himself influenced temporarily by the Methodist movement under the leadership of John Wesley. Encouraging literacy and education for the common masses, Methodism influenced Paine's developing sense of egalitarianism. Sandwich also provided Thomas with his first love in life, Mary Lambert. Married in the fall of 1759, the couple left town following Mary's pregnancy, and Thomas began another business in the seacoast town of Margate. Unfortunately, both wife and baby died in childbirth in the summer of 1760.

Shortly after his wife's death, Thomas returned to Thetford and decided to study for the excise office. Following his appointment, he spent the next few years working in small towns around England, leaving the excise under a cloud of corruption in 1765. He was accused of stamping without seeing the products that he was stamping for taxes. Paine then returned to London, working as an artisan, teacher, and professional student. Recalling this period of his life to his friend Rickman, Paine remarked: "Here I derived considerable information; indeed I have seldom passed five minutes of my life, however circumstanced, in which I did not acquire some knowledge." Now thirty years old, Paine had acquired a substantial understanding of political oppression, religious intolerance, and poverty. Imbued with a natural genius and taught by the leading natural philosophers of the day, Paine was now almost ready to begin his role as leader of this "enlightened" age.

The next step in formalizing Paine's political and social principles came from his role as a community and labor activist. He petitioned the government for reinstatement as an exciseman in 1767 and in the following year was appointed to the town of Lewes, England. He owed the appointment to his friendship with George Scott, head of the Excise Office, the former tutor to George III but later a radical Whig leader of the opposition. Living in Lewes from 1768 to 1774, Paine became an active member in the community. Marrying Elizabeth Ollive, the daughter of a prominent local official, in 1771, he eventually took over the family business as well as keeping his job as an excise officer. As the leading political debater in the local tavern known as the White Hart Inn, Paine developed a reputation as a "shrewd and sensible fellow with a depth of political knowledge." This same club member dubbed Paine "General of the Headstrong Club," and for his vigorous defense of liberty and justice wrote the following ode:

    Immortal PAINE! While mighty reasoners jar,

> We crown thee General of the Headstrong War;
> Thy logic vanquish'd error, and thy mind
> No bounds, but those of right and truth, confined.
> Thy soul of fire must sure ascend the sky,
> Immortal PAINE, thy fame can never die;
> For men like thee their names must ever save
> From the black edicts of the tyrant grave.

His reputation as a spokesman and civic reformer persuaded the overworked and underpaid excise officers to commission Thomas Paine to petition Parliament for a wage increase. In the summer of 1772, he authored his first public pamphlet, entitled *The Case of the Officers of the Excise*. Writing with simplicity of style and force of reason that would mark all his future work, Paine argued that higher salaries were necessary to prevent the excise men from falling into poverty and possible corruption. "Poverty," Paine said, "in defiance of principle, begets a degree of meanness that will stoop to almost anything . . . Nothing tends to a greater corruption of manners and principles than a too great distress of circumstances." This sociologically based attack on poverty, quite courageous at the time, has become a standard argument used by advocates for social reform, and it remains valid today. Paine spent the next several months in London lobbying members of Parliament with his petition. Although unsuccessful, the arguments that Paine used in this petition indicated his attempt to use reason and justice as the foundation of law. This would become the cornerstone of all of Paine's future works.

When he returned to Lewes in 1773, both the family business and his marriage began to fall apart. In the spring of the following year, Paine received a dismissal notice from the Excise office while agreeing to separate from his wife. Giving her all their belongings, Thomas left Lewes and headed for London. There he reacquainted himself with Benjamin Franklin, who recommended he sail to America. In the autumn of 1774, Thomas sailed for America on the *London Packet* with little more than letters of introduction from Franklin and a suitcase of clothes. Ironically, Thomas Paine's revolutionary career in America almost ended before it began. Paine and most of the ships' passengers were stricken by an epidemic of typhus during their two-month-long voyage. More dead than alive when he arrived in Philadelphia in November of 1774,

Thomas had to be carried off the ship by stretcher. Fortunately for Paine, his friendship with Philadelphia's great Franklin brought him to the attention of Dr. Kearsley, who attended to him for the next six weeks.

By the time of Paine's arrival, British-America was a thriving, dynamic, and rebellious country. A population of three million included a variety of European nationalities and about 750,000 African slaves. In many ways, however, British-America must have appeared much like England to Paine. Criminal justice was cruel, and capital crimes were many. Property in the colonies as in England determined voting rights, and, like their British counterparts, the lower classes in America were excluded from political participation and sometimes resorted to mob actions to voice their complaints. British-America replaced an English ruling aristocracy with a colonial ruling class of southern planters, northern landlords, and wealthy merchants. Forming the political and social leadership of colonial America, these ruling elites, like their English cousins, prided themselves on English liberties while denying those liberties to others. Below this ruling class yet closely connected with them, as in England, were the middle-class lawyers and clergy followed by the working-class shopkeepers and artisans, and then farmers, laborers, and the poor.

Still, significant differences between Britain and her American colonies did exist. Wealth was more widely dispersed in America than in England. Religious diversity created a more tolerant attitude throughout the colonies. With a relatively free press, an abundance of newspapers, pamphlets, and broadsides, and access to scientific and political literature, Americans had the highest literacy rate in the eighteenth-century world. American political thought embodied to a considerable degree the ideas of self-determination and individual liberty, stemming from their concrete experience in creating a society from the wilderness and managing their own affairs at a considerable distance from England. Most importantly, suspicious of a corrupt Parliament, the American colonists had begun their resistance against Britain's attempt to increase its control. This colonial resistance had escalated into open rebellion by the time of Paine's arrival in Philadelphia in late 1774. Finding himself at the center of the emerging American conflict, he later confessed to Franklin, "I thought it very hard to have the country set on fire about my ears almost the moment I got into it." Barely one year later, Paine's own inflammatory words in *Common Sense* would help set America free and establish the Age of Democracy.

Paine started writing for the *Pennsylvania Magazine*. By November, 1775, he authored a major essay, "A Serious Thought," openly calling for independence. It was during this time that Paine developed his revolutionary philosophy of democratic republicanism. The essential word here is "revolutionary." Much of my dispute with traditional thought about the War of Independence concerns the meaning of this word. We are all familiar with the phrase on a dollar bill: *Novus Ordo Seclorum* (A New Order of the Ages). This was the true American Revolution, not merely the successful war for political separation, and it was Paine, more than anyone else, who argued that the new nation should rest upon new foundations, establishing a new political and social system based on radical republican principles and a rights-based representative democracy.

Paine linked together reason and justice in defense of the democratic system of government, calling for a constitution guaranteeing equality of rights and protection of those rights under the law. This simple yet profound expression of the political process allowed common folk to theorize for themselves what was reasonable and proper, politically and socially. His image of republican society consisted of several things—groups of associations working independently, cooperatively, and collaboratively; government of people, connected by interest and trust to their directly elected representatives; and representatives who protect the people against the usurpation of power by either external or internal threats.

To Paine, equity took on a distinct meaning. Dominant in British political thinking was the notion of proportional equality. Not all would have the same equality because of their various stations in life—class, gender, wealth. By contrast, Paine asserted a formal equality inclusive for all, assuring to everyone basic rights and dignity. Similarly, freedom to Paine went beyond so-called negative freedom, which gives us the capacity to not to be interfered with by government. He defended a notion of positive freedom based on the empowerment of individuals in society. To Paine, equal empowerment among free individuals represented the spirit of the American character.

Paine, as a visionary, imagined a society built on the power of the people who were morally good and who, through useful education, would understand the issues, the political practices and principles of government, and who would enact laws through representatives directly concerned with the same interests. It would be a society based on the notion of common sense—the idea that ordinary people have basic and innate perceptions about what is right and what is wrong. (Whether or not Benjamin Rush gave Paine the name for his famous pamphlet is uncertain. Rush said that he did, but by then he had changed political sides and joined with the Adams faction.)

Common sense is the understanding that it is the people who have to have sovereignty. Thus, Paine wanted to rid America not just of British soldiers, but of the entire British system. It was a system of imperialism, of colonialism, of tyranny and slavery. He wanted to start anew, with a new system based on justice and rights, equality and reason. Give power to the people, and establish a government that ensures the adequacy of people to be what they can be. Do not merely give people rights; give them the idea of using those rights.

There's a scene in Mel Gibson's movie *The Patriot* (not to say that it has any real historical legitimacy) where the main character makes a statement opposed to independence, saying, "What's the difference between having a tyrant 3,000 miles away and having 3,000 tyrants a mile away?" That's how many people felt. What did *Common Sense* do? *Common Sense* enlightened the masses and told them: this system that controls you, that denigrates you, that has kept you down—it's not justifiable to keep this system any longer. Have the power to change things, and the courage to change. The alternative to the status quo is a democratic ideal, grounded on the power of ordinary citizens. To the masses of people who never experienced such basic respect, that was very inspiring. It was very motivating. It was worth fighting for, and people fought and died because of Thomas Paine's ideas.

It is important to contrast Paine with certain others among the Founding Fathers, people like Adams, Madison, Jay, and Hamilton, who wanted independence from Britain without getting rid of much of the British system. One can imagine a conversation between John Adams and Paine after the publication of *Common Sense* in February, 1776. Adams would say, "Hey, Tom, independence is a good idea. But democracy? Democracy is mob-ocracy. You can't give power to the people. The people are ruled by their emotions. They're ruled by irrationality. You can't do that. Power has got to stay within a small group, and they will know what to do with it." Although Adams advocated for Paine's position as Secretary to the Committee on Foreign Affairs a year later, he definitely and defiantly contradicted Paine's ideas regarding the foundations of government, and although Adams did at times ascribe responsibility for the American Revolution to Paine, he advanced a very different notion of that revolution and its historic meaning.

Paine's vision was radically different from that of many of his contemporaries in American politics. He saw the Declaration of Independence as a necessary tool that, as he mentioned at the end of *Common Sense*, would be used as a vehicle for revolution. Adams saw the Declaration primarily as a document of propaganda written to win support for American independence from the European powers. To Paine, independence was not the revolution. The real American Revolution was a revolution in thought. One must remember that, at the time of the Constitutional Convention of 1787, Shay's Rebellion in Massachusetts and the regulators in North Carolina were demonstrations that many who fought in the war were losing their farms to powerful economic speculators. The revolution that Paine had hoped for didn't begin to emerge at the national level until Jefferson became President, after he had returned to Europe. Reflecting on the constitution 1789, in a letter to Kitty Few, Paine wrote that he hoped never to see the day, 1,000 years from now or sooner, when America would become like England, with a loss of virtue, a loss of freedom, and a loss of reputation.

I will contend, although some will disagree, that Paine started the independence movement itself. Many might say that people had been talking about independence for years. Sam Adams mentioned separation and independence. John Adams said that he sought independence all the time. But in reality, there had been no sustained independence movement. The resistance movement that started after the Stamp Act and the Stamp Act Congress and the formation of the Sons Of Liberty, and later on the Committees of Correspondence and Safety — these were all extra-legal agencies, but never was there a systematic call for a sustained independence movement for the entire set of British colonies. But within a six-month period of time, *Common Sense* persuaded, motivated, inspired people to fight and die for this new movement.

In a sense, Paine was the ultimate re-inventor. He not only reinvented himself when he came to America, but he reinvented America. He gave us a new direction. He gave us principles for government, although not entirely adhered to. He helped to define the American character. He gave us the ideas that we are still talking about 230 years later. Nevertheless, I am always quick to say that it is not Thomas Paine who is important. It is the ideas that are important. We must never confuse the cult of personality with what's really important. Unfortunately, in our country today, because we are not connected to the principles and practices of government as it should be, we have taken refuge in celebrity-ism and status rather than understanding that the true heroes are those people who work for justice on a daily basis.

Paine is not dead as an American symbol. The fact that we are here today, talking about Paine at this university, shows that the ideas of Paine are alive and well. But we need to get those ideas out to the public, to let people know that there is a better way, a better society to be built. We need to change our government, not through revolutionary arms but by changing ourselves. We need to take control of our destinies by becoming involved in the political system. Paine believed that the key relationships were political associations, and that the unity of interest and principle will direct us to a better life. These are the ideas we have to keep.

Let me just repeat the two things that I want to emphasize. First, according to Paine, the War of Independence was not the American Revolution. Second, Paine viewed the American Revolution as a revolution in thought, as the vehicle for the establishment of a society based on equality and justice. Inspired by the Declaration of Independence and, more so, by *Common Sense*, the American colonists fought not just for political autonomy, but for a new system of freedom and equality that would rest upon and enhance the life of common people. Paine, more than anyone else, justified war on the basis of principles—principles that had already been within the mind-set of the colonists: self-determination and liberty. He elevated these ideals and placed them directly in the center of the struggle for a new America. He argued for a concept of revolution that entailed a profound shift in thought and practice. His was a different, more radical practical philosophy than had existed in the past, and it's something that we have yet to attain today. We have the power to reinvent ourselves and to reinvent and change a system that continues to oppress and tyrannize many. It is important for us, as educators and historians, to facilitate this process.

With that being said, let me quickly describe some of the artifacts that I brought with me. It is a little exhibit of things from our museum—nothing of great value, but still of interest. First, there are several early editions from the 1800s. Included among them are: "Case of the Offices of Excise," stating Paine's prominent ideas on poverty as being the producer of crime, and the "Crisis" essays that helped keep the revolution going, informing the people about what was going on and reminding them of the importance of the struggle. We mentioned Oldys/Chalmers before. Here is an early 1800s edition of his biography of Paine's life. Oldys, of course, was subsidized by the English government to write a derogatory biography of Thomas Paine. Unfortunately, many historians today still go back to Chalmers and Cheetham, his earliest biographers, to use as a source. *The Age Of Reason,* which we must note is not a denunciation of religion per se, gives an alternative to established religions: deism. It is an attack on the institution of religion, not religion itself. Paine believed that religion has only one purpose, to teach morality. If it doesn't do that, what's the sense of having it? In *Rights Of Man*, Paine enunciates the principles already started in *Common Sense*. He adjusts them to a European audience and therefore gives more power to governments in order to eradicate poverty. Also, here are his famous letters to George Washington. Most people think they were just degrading Washington because he didn't help him get out of prison, but really they were an attack on the Federalist policies of the day. These were followed up by the "Letters to the Citizens of the United States," when he comes back from England.

Next, I have a couple of facsimiles of Paine's smokeless candles. Paine believed that, by limiting the amount of smoke going up, candles would work better. He was an artist and scientist. For example, he thought about a combustion engine with Fitch in Pennsylvania, as early as 1786. His idea of combustion was to use gunpowder. Of course, it didn't work too well, but it gives you an insight into Paine's ideas. He saw scientific technology as a positive boon for mankind.

Rather than use gunpowder to kill people, he wanted to use gunpowder for the betterment of mankind. That was Paine's mind-set, to use technology to enhance people's lives, not to destroy them.

Here is the Big Apple Classical Award we won several years ago from New York State. We developed a curriculum with a high school, an integrated curriculum using computer technology and a variety of strategies that invoke Paine's ideas—from English to social studies to science and math.

This is the bust of Paine by Malvina Hoffman that presently resides in the Hall of Fame of what used to be the University Heights section of NYU, but is now Bronx Community College, and this is a copy of his death mask taken, I believe, shortly after death. There was another death mask that I didn't bring with me, the one that Cobbett had done after he disinterred Paine ten years later. I decided not to bring it with me because people sometimes get a little squeamish; it doesn't quite look as good as this one.

Here are some pictures of Paine's gravesite, near where I live. He didn't have many people there— Madame Bonneville, her two sons, a couple of black servants, and few others. Here are some other pictures of Paine's alleged deathbed scene, in which people are trying to convert him to Christianity. Also I have brought some pictures of the places where Paine resided during the last few years of his life. Paine left his house in New Rochelle, from about 1806 to 1809, and lived in various residences in New York City, Greenwich Village, in particular.

This is a caricature of Paine. You have to remember that the English were so afraid of him that Paine became the first enemy of the state. After *Rights Of Man, Part I* appeared, the government was not too scared. The book was a little expensive, most people had not seen it, and basically it was a lot like *Common Sense*. *Common Sense* was freely published in London during the American War of Independence. Trouble began with *Rights Of Man, Part II*, with its talk about economic equality, taxation of the rich, and programs to get rid of poverty. The price of *Rights Of Man, Part II* was very low. It became widely distributed, disseminated even in Ireland and Scotland, and there was political worry particularly about Ireland.

This, I think, is particularly interesting. As I said, *Rights Of Man, Part II* really got the British government worried. In order to suppress Paine, they sent government provocateurs to his meetings to start riots and protests. Along with hiring Oldys to write a derogatory biography, they also actually minted coins. Although these coins aren't worth much, they're very interesting. On one side it says "The Rights Of Man," and the other side has Paine hanging in effigy. Aristocrats of the day would take these and nail them to their heels so they could walk and stamp on the *Rights of Man* on the cobblestone streets of London.

Last but not least of these exhibits—comic books. Even in 1946, there are comic books about Thomas Paine.

Thomas Paine's legacy has not left us. Thomas Paine's words have not left us. The very fact that we are here today shows that his ideas are not only relevant, but important. History does not really repeat itself. It evolves, it changes, and it is now up to us to make it better. Thank you.

THE RELIGIOUS RADICALISM OF THOMAS PAINE: WHY THE AGE OF REASON STILL THREATENS UNREASON

Susan Jacoby

William Weeks

My name is Bill Weeks, from the History Department at SDSU. This morning we have before us Susan Jacoby, the author of the very well-received recent book, *Freethinkers: A History Of American Secularism*. Ms. Jacoby is an independent scholar and writer. Her book, *Freethinkers*, was selected by the *Los Angeles Times* in 2004 as a notable book. It was also cited as an outstanding international book of 2004 by the *Times Literary Supplement* from London and by *The Guardian*.

A former reporter for the *Washington Post*, Ms. Jacoby is the author of a number of other books, including *Wild Justice: The Evolution of Revenge*, which was finalist for the Pulitzer Prize. She is currently Director of Public Programs at the Center For Inquiry in Metropolitan New York, a research and advocacy organization for secular humanism.

Her articles and essays have appeared in a wide variety of national publications, including the *New York Times, Los Angeles Times, The Nation, Vogue,* and *The American Prospect*. Susan Jacoby is currently working on a new book, about the relationship between anti-intellectualism and political polarization in America. Without any further ado, let me introduce to you Ms. Susan Jacoby.

Susan Jacoby

First of all, I want to thank you all for coming out so early on this rather gloomy morning. My whole life people have told me that the sun always shines in San Diego, which is clearly not true. I was originally unhappy that I had neglected to bring my bathing suit, but I would have had no use for it. Onto the subject of Thomas Paine, rather than my discontent at there not being sun.

Shortly after my book, *Freethinkers*, was published last year, I received an e-mail from a University of Georgia faculty member whose subject was early American intellectual history. He told me that, although he did include excerpts from

Thomas Paine's *Rights Of Man* in his freshman course, he had dropped *The Age Of Reason* from the syllabus because it so deeply antagonized the devout religious fundamentalists among his students, that they simply closed their minds to everything else he was trying to teach them.

This, of course, tells us something about the power of the most reactionary forms of religion in American culture today. In the only country in the developed world where evolution is not accepted as scientific truth by a majority of the public, an eighteenth-century book challenging the literal truth of the Bible — and the Koran, by the way — is considered too hot to handle by a young college instructor in the Bible Belt.

This small anecdote also explains why a writer whose unparalleled capacity to move both hearts and minds on behalf of the revolutionary cause has never quite (as Eric Foner said yesterday) made it into the pantheon of American revolutionary heroes. Thomas Paine's face appears on no coins. You almost never see his name on a public building, and he is still an un-person in the ever-metastasizing body of statuary and monuments in Washington, D.C.

My views are a bit different from some of the other panelists, because I don't think that this neglect of Paine has much to do with the radical economic views that so outraged Federalists in the 1790s. I seriously doubt that one American college graduate in a thousand has the slightest idea that Paine ever wrote anything about economics. I do think this relative obscurity has everything to do with the fact that the memory of Paine, the patriot, has been eclipsed by the memory of Paine, the religious heretic. Paine has the honor of being the first American free-thinker to be labeled an atheist (inaccurately as it happens), denigrated both before and after his death, and deprived of his proper place in American history.

In 1776, Paine's clarion call for steadfast patriotism in dark times, "the times that try men's souls," inspired his countrymen in every corner of the former colonies. But by the 1790s, Paine's role in the Revolution had been eclipsed by denunciations of his infidel views on religion. In *The Age Of Reason*, he set forth the astonishing idea that Christianity and Judaism, like all other religions, were inventions of men rather than the revealed word of God, and in 1809 Paine died a pauper, either reviled or ignored by all of the revolutionary leaders whose cause he had served so ardently and effectively, with the notable exception of Thomas Jefferson.

As this conference itself indicates, Paine is enjoying something of a renaissance at the moment. One of the more annoying aspects of this renaissance, to me, is the fondness of ultra-conservative intellectuals for quoting the Paine who described government, even in its best state, as a necessary evil. Paine was, of course, writing at a time when the divine right of kings had been only slightly abridged—a little detail conveniently ignored by his modern right-wing acolytes in their highly selective quotations. I would absolutely love to hear Paine's reaction to Justice Antonin Scalia's rationale for the death penalty in America, which is that all governments, including ours, derive their power from God, and since God has the power of life and death, so too should governments.

But Paine has never quite satisfied true believers in the left, either, because he had this most inconvenient tendency to look at what was actually going on around him in terms of its impact on individual human beings. If he disapproved of what he saw, he revised his thinking. An unintentionally comical example of the dogmatic left's attitude recently appeared in the snotty review in *The Nation* of Harvey Kaye's fine new book, *Thomas Paine And The Promise Of America*. In the opinion of this reviewer, Paine was something of a disappointment, not quite perfect in spite of his radical views on economics and religion. Why? Because during his stay in revolutionary France, he consorted with both liberal French aristocrats, without whom by the way the American Revolution probably would never have been financed properly, and with American Francophiles. He even opposed the execution of Louis XVI—what a despicable thing. Paine was actually such a bourgeois humanist, as a later generation of revolutionaries would have put it, that he opposed the death penalty for both princes and paupers. He was soft on death.

Indeed, Paine's greatness is magnified by his membership in the select—and it is very select—company of political idealists who did not take refuge in fantasy and denial and illusion when they saw that their ideals had been betrayed. In Part II of *The Age Of Reason*, written after his release from prison, where he had landed because he had opposed the execution of the King, Paine recalled his many friends who were not so lucky, who were sent directly from jail to the guillotine. He declared flatly that, "The intolerant spirit of church persecution had transferred itself into politics; the tribunals, styled Revolutionary, supplied the place of an Inquisition; and the Guillotine of the Stake." It was the same quality, which I would call absolute moral clear-headedness, that made Paine a religious radical and has prevented him from receiving his full due in American history.

No one has better described the fate of Thomas Paine than someone I don't think has been mentioned yet—Robert Greene Ingersoll—who in the last quarter of the nineteenth century did more than any other man to revive Paine's reputation in the country whose revolution he had so greatly served. Ingersoll, who deserves a renaissance of his own, by the way, was known as the Great Agnostic, and was the most famous orator in late nineteenth-century America. Here is how he explained to his fellow Americans of the Gilded Age why so many of them were ignorant of Paine's true importance. "At the close of the Revolution," Ingersoll said,

> no one stood higher in America than Thomas Paine. The best, the wisest, the most patriotic were his friends and admirers; and had he been thinking only of his own good, he might have rested from his toils and spent the remainder of his life in comfort and in ease. He could have been what the world is pleased to call 'respectable.' He could have died surrounded by clergymen, warriors and statesmen. At his death there would have been an imposing funeral, miles of carriages, civic societies, salvos of artillery, a nation in mourning, and, above all, a splendid monument covered with lies.

Paine chose instead to benefit mankind, Ingersoll said. He went on.

> He had spent his life thus far in destroying the power of kings, and now he turned his attention to the priests. He knew that every abuse had been embalmed in scripture—that every outrage was in partnership with some holy text. He knew that the throne skulked behind the altar, and both behind a pretended revelation from God. By this time, he had found it was of little use to free the body and leave the mind in chain . . . He had dug under the throne,

and it occurred to him that he would take a look behind the altar.

The title of that look behind the altar was, of course, *The Age Of Reason*. A few words about the conditions under which *The Age Of Reason* was composed, which I'm sure most of you know, but indulge me. Part One was written in Paris in 1793, in great haste because, as I mentioned earlier, he placed his life in danger by opposition to the execution of Louis, even though he had originally and rightly been lionized by the French as a true comrade in the cause of liberty, equality, and fraternity. Arrested on Robespierre's orders, Paine was able to deliver the manuscript to his friend, Joel Barlow, one of those American Francophiles with whom it was so terrible to have associated and who was also a close friend of Jefferson. He placed it in his hands while being escorted to the Luxemburg Prison, on December 28, 1793. Apparently, the people taking him to prison were considerate enough to let him drop off his manuscript on the way.

In one of the more disgraceful manifestations of ingratitude by any American government, Paine was left to rot in prison for more than nine months—rot literally because he almost died of an infected ulcer after he was released. Gouverneur Morris, the American Minister to France at the time, detested Paine's views on both religion and politics, and misled the French by telling them that the United States did not recognize the British-born Paine's claim to American citizenship. At the same time, Morris also may have mislead President Washington, who, though he too disagreed with Paine's economic views, did recognize his debt to the man whose writings had inspired widespread support for the revolutionary cause. Anyway, there's a good deal of evidence that Morris told Washington that everything possible was being done to obtain Paine's release. By the way, this was the same Gouverneur Morris who became the subject of an admiring 1898 biography by Theodore Roosevelt, who took that occasion to describe Paine as "a filthy little atheist . . . that apparently esteems a bladder of dirty water as the proper weapon with which to assail Christianity." The bladder of dirty water was, again, of course, *The Age Of Reason*.

Now this is a book that everyone with any interest in history has heard about, but I dare say that the text has actually been read from beginning to end by very few people. I am going to read a few passages verbatim. I'm sure that those of you who are familiar with them will enjoy hearing them again, and those of you who have missed or forgotten the passages will be reminded of what the fuss has always been about. You may judge for yourselves how well these thoughts would be received in America in today's political and cultural climate. I don't think that the good folks, as our President would call them, at the Heritage Foundation, the American Enterprise Institute, or the Christian Coalition will be quoting these passages from Paine any time soon. Here goes:

> Every national church or religion has established itself by pretending some special mission from God, communicated to certain individuals. The Jews have their Moses; the Christians their Jesus Christ, their apostles and saints; and the Turks, their Mahomet, as if the way to God were not open to every man alike. Each of these churches show certain books, which they call revelation, or the word of God. The Jews say that their Word of God was given by God to Moses, face to face; the Christians say that their Word of God came by divine inspiration; and the Turks say that their Word of God (the Koran) was brought by an angel from heaven. Each of those churches accuses the other of unbelief; and for my own part, I disbelieve them all.

Further, on revelation:

> It is a contradiction in terms and ideas to call anything a revelation that comes to us at second-hand, either verbally or in writing. Revelation is necessarily limited to the first communication—after this, it is only an account of something which that person says was a revelation made to him; and though he may find himself obliged to believe it, it cannot be incumbent on me to believe it in the same manner; for it was not a revelation made to me, and I have only his word for it that it was made to him. When Moses told the children of Israel that he'd received the two tablets of the commandments from the hands of God, they were not obliged to believe him, because they had no other authority for it than his telling them so;

and I have no authority for it than some historian telling me so. The command-ments carry no internal evidence of divinity within them; they contain some good moral precepts, such as any man qualified to be a lawgiver, or a legislator, could produce himself, without recourse to supernatural intervention.

(I would really like it if even one of the Supreme Court Justices in the recent Ten Commandments cases had cited this paragraph in their opinions.)

Paine was not an atheist, although many of his contemporaries—Theodore Roosevelt may have picked up this notion from their writings—said he was. Paine made himself absolutely clear on this point in *The Age Of Reason*, where he states unequivocally: "I believe in one God, and no more; and I hope for happiness beyond this life." But then Paine goes on to list all of the things in which he does not believe, from the savage punishments of the Old Testament to the virgin birth and the resurrection of Jesus in the New Testament. Those who called him an atheist either hadn't read his book, or simply found it politically useful to call him an atheist, and tar Jefferson with the same brush. It is rather like those who tar liberals with the dreaded S-word, for "secularism," today.

The radicalism of Paine's religious beliefs lay not in militant atheism, but in his absolute rejection of any form of religion that conflicted with nature: "The Laws of Nature and Nature's God," as the Declaration of Independence puts it, or that relied on the supernatural. Paine, by the way, doesn't even bother with the "loony tunes" book of Revelation in his discussion of the New Testament. But I think we can safely say that if he were alive today, he would not be a fan of the "Left Behind" books. Paine not only rejected the supernatural, but rejected all religious authority over human opinion, not only when combined with the power of the state, but when exerted by the church on the beliefs of any individual.

Middle-of-the-road historians, today as well as in the nineteenth century, have tended to dismiss the idea that Paine's anti-religious arguments in the eighteenth century had any real impact on the public. *The Age Of Reason*, it has often been said, was more often denounced by anxious clerics than read by ordinary people. I find that viewpoint suspect, because it reflects the customary scholarly—as well as journalistic—denigration of free-thinkers and their role in American history. *The Age Of Reason* was reprinted 18 times in five American cities between 1794 and 1796. It is impossible to determine how many people read the book, but the total number certainly had to be many times more than the 25,000 printed copies. (By the way, I should point out that fewer than two percent of all hard-cover books today, as those of you who are authors all too unfortunately are familiar, sell more than 20,000 copies.)

On this point, the testimony of Paine's contemporaries, including scholars working in the early years of the Republic, is far more persuasive than that of later historians who pooh-poohed his influence. John W. Francis, a New York City physician and historian born in 1789, and no admirer of Paine's religious philosophy, declared flatly that no work had a demand for readers comparable to that of Paine. *The Age of Reason*, Francis went on to lament, was printed in America as: "an orthodox book by orthodox book publishers, doubtless deceived by the vast renown which the author of *Common Sense* had obtained, and by the prospects of sale." By orthodox, Francis of course meant respectable and commercially solvent.

Nathan Bangs, a chronicler of the early Methodist Church in America, wrote in 1845 that Paine's arguments against the truth of the Bible were received with great avidity by Americans on account of the eminent services he had rendered to his country during the War of Revolution. But, Bangs said, Thomas Paine as a politician and Thomas Paine as a theologian were very different men. Wrong. Paine the theologian and Paine the political writer were one and the same. The anti-monarchal and anti-ecclesiastical Paines were united in their belief that there could be no legitimacy in any form of government or religion that defied reason. Hence, in *Common Sense*, Paine argued that "One of the strongest natural proofs of the folly of the hereditary right of kings is that nature disproves it, otherwise she would not so frequently turn it into ridicule, by giving mankind an ass for a lion." In *The Age of Reason*, Paine envisions a God who reveals himself not through miracles and mysteries, but only in a manner consistent with nature. "When men, whether from policy or pious fraud, set up systems of religion incompatible with the word or works of God in the creation, and not only above but repugnant to human comprehension, they were under the necessity of inventing or adopting a word that should serve as a bar to all questions, inquiries and speculations. The word mystery answered this purpose . . . As mystery answered all general purposes, miracle followed as an occasional auxiliary. The former served to bewilder the mind, the later to puzzle the senses. The one was the lingo, the other the legerdemain." Wouldn't you have liked to have written that wonderful sentence? It is one example of what a great, great polemical writer Paine was.

To this day, the received opinion about Paine, except among scholars specializing in the history of radicalism, is that he was an important revolutionary propagandist but a fairly unimportant thinker about economics, politics, and religion. You won't find that at this conference, but you will find it among a lot of middle-of-the-road historians. In 1859, the *Atlantic Monthly* magazine, from its lofty perch in intellectually infertile and intellectually pretentious Boston, described *The Age of Reason* as a "shallow, deistical essay," while nevertheless calling for the restoration of Paine to the canon of revolutionary heroes. Ladies and gentlemen, the idea that moral truth can be sought and found only in accordance with reason and nature is not shallow, but merely controversial. As we've seen repeatedly in our political and cultural life during the past twenty years, it is no less controversial today than it was in Paine's time. It seems to me that American politicians today are as frightened of the words "reason" and "rational" as they are of "secularism" and "atheism." The revolutionary secularists of Paine's generation were united in their belief that if God existed, in whatever form, he would endow man with the gift of reason as the supreme instrument for devising a rational government and a rational society.

The story of Paine's last years in American is a very painful one. In 1802, he returned to America from Paris at the invitation of President Jefferson. Most of Paine's old friends, embarrassed by his anti-Christian writings, had deserted him. Jefferson, being the exception, received him in the White House and took his lumps in the press for doing so. In 1802, the American press reaction to Jefferson's encouragement of Paine's return was scathing. The commentary portrayed Jefferson himself as an atheist. One Federalist journal, the *Philadelphia Portfolio,* embodied the tone of all of these attacks, noting that,

If during the present season of national abasement, infatuation, folly and vice, any portent could surprise, sober men would be utterly confounded by an article current in all of our newspapers, that the loathsome Thomas Paine, a drunken atheist and a scavenger of faction, is invited to return in a national ship to America by the first magistrate of a free people, a measure so enormously preposterous we cannot yet believe has been adopted, and it would demand firmer nerves than those possessed by Mr. Jefferson to hazard such an insult to the moral sense of the nation.

Among the words applied to Paine in the popular press were Judas, reptile, hog, mad dog, souse, arch-beast, brute, liar, and of course, the ever-useful infidel. Paine was refused a seat on a stagecoach from New Jersey to New York after he left Washington. In the city itself, an admirer of Paine's was suspended from church membership for having publicly shaken hands with the arch-beast. As Paine sat in his farmhouse in New Rochelle on Christmas Eve, 1802, a bullet fired by an unknown assailant narrowly missed his friends. He was chastised by old friends and allies, like the revolutionary firebrand Samuel Adams, who told Paine that his association with Jefferson had done the president great political harm. What, Paine replied to Adams, "is this thing called infidelity? If we go back to your ancestors and mine, three or four hundred years ago, for we must have had fathers and grandfathers or we should not be here, we shall find them praying to Saints and Virgins, and believing in purgatory and the transubstantiation; and therefore all of us are infidels according to our forefathers' belief." In conclusion, Paine reiterated his belief in a god of nature, a god who is served by helping others in this life rather than by obeisance to churches that promise eternal life. Humans "can add nothing to eternity," Paine asserted, but it is within the power of men to render a service to their God, "not by praying, but by endeavoring to make his creatures happy."

There's no doubt that the constant attacks on Paine and his abandonment by many old friends took a considerable emotional toll in his final years. Paine died on June 8, 1809, at the age of 72. Like so many other famous skeptics, he would be pursued beyond the grave by false reports that he had asked for a minister and recanted his anti-religious views on his deathbed. In fact, he died in his sleep, in rented lodgings, in the vicinity of what is now Grove Street in Greenwich Village. For much of the nineteenth century, however, Grove Street was called Reason Street in honor of Paine. The name was changed after immigrants began flooding into the area in the 1880s. Mishearing the word, they called it Raisin Street, which the older local residents considered a silly name for a street, and so they changed it, for unknown reasons, to Grove Street.

Paine had expressed a wish to be buried in a Quaker cemetery—the Quakers being the one religious sect of which he'd always approved. But the local elders decided that they did not want to be associated with such a notorious character. He was buried on his farm in New Rochelle, his interment witnessed by fewer than a dozen people. Among them were Marguerite de Bonneville, a friend of Paine's from his time in France and a refugee from the Napoleonic government, and her two sons. Madame de Bonneville described the unceremonious burial as a scene "to wound any sensible heart." Looking around at the small group of spectators, who included none of Paine's old friends from his Revolutionary years, she said, "Oh! Mr. Paine! My son stands here as a testimony of the gratitude of America, and I for France."

In a final indignity, Paine's corpse was dug up and his bones spirited away in 1819 by William Cobbett, the Englishman who had published a slanderous biography of Paine in 1797 but apparently changed his mind after actually reading Paine's books. Cobbett, who also had a general political change of heart, had spent some years in America but returned as a social reformer to England, where he supposedly intended to bury Paine. For whatever reason, it didn't work out. Cobbett apparently kept the bones in a box in his house. His heirs failed to keep track of the remains, probably something that would not have struck the author of *The Age of Reason* as an immense catastrophe.

In America in the 1820s and 1830s, Paine's memory was kept alive only by small, marginalized groups of freethinkers. In the early nineteenth century, Americans who cherished similar political and religious views affirmed their common values by celebrating the birthdays of their heroes (not by the visits to the shopping mall that have become a customary celebration of Presidents Day in our era). Jacksonian Democrats observed Jefferson's birthday, free-thinkers honored both Paine and Jefferson, and everyone celebrated Washing-ton's birthday. The British-born free-thinker, Benjamin Offen, organized the first formal Paine birthday celebration in 1825 in New York City. The practice of annual commemorations—including dancing, eating, and drinking, as well as serious speeches—soon spread to other Eastern and then Midwestern communities with nests of free-thinkers. When Offen had arrived in New York from England, where Paine's writings were—given his relations with England—ironically much better known in the 1820s than they were in America, he was astonished at the general denigration of Paine and attributed it to the sheer religious bigotry, together with thousands of falsehoods uttered from the pulpits respecting his moral character.

During this period of Paine's general eclipse, his writings nevertheless had quite an influence on a number of significant Americans. The great editor, William Lloyd Garrison, born in 1805, was raised by a fanatical Baptist mother, who warned him against going near the ocean (because, should you be drowned, your soul must go to God to be judged) and advised him to confine his reading to the scriptures. He disobeyed his mother's injunction about reading, and he was particularly fond of the poetry of Byron. But he did not read Paine until he was nearly 40 years old. In the November 21, 1845, issue of *The Liberator*, Garrison confessed to his readers that until a few days earlier, he had never read so much as a paragraph by Paine because he had been raised to regard the author of *The Honor of Reason* (sic) as a monster of iniquity. Reading *The Age of Reason* crystallized Garrison's rejection of literal interpretation of scriptures (many of which at the time were used to justify slavery) and his opposition to ecclesiastical authority (many northern churches at the time refused to provide a platform for anti-slavery speakers because it might offend their religious brethren in the south—their White religious brethren, that is). In a famous passage, Garrison wrote that the Bible, like any other book written by man, "should be judged by its reasonableness and utility, by the probabilities of the case, by the facts of science, the intuition of the spirit. Truth is older than any parchment." Garrison also embraced Paine's belief in absolute separation of church and state. The connection between the two men is most fitting because Garrison was, in fact, the most effective political polemicist since

Paine, and both men's writings actually changed the course of American history.

It was not until the golden age of free thought, in the last quarter of the nineteenth century, that Paine's reputation was truly revived with a larger public. Ingersoll deserves a good deal of the credit for that, because he spoke before millions of Americans, more than any public figure in his era, including presidents. One of his most frequent lectures was on the writings of Thomas Paine. Unfortunately, no champion has emerged from the twentieth century to do for Ingersoll, who is now forgotten, what Ingersoll did for Paine. In 1892, Moncure Daniel Conway, a minister turned free-thinker, finally gave both the revolutionary and the religious skeptic his due, in a magisterial two-volume biography that is still required reading for anyone who wants to write about Thomas Paine. Conway concluded his book with these words. "There is a legend that Paine's little finger was left in America, a fable, perhaps, of his once small movement, now stronger than the loins of the bigotry that refused him a vote or a grave in the land he so greatly served. As to his bones, no man knows the place of their rest to this day. His principles rest not."

There has never been a better concluding line to a biography in my view, and I intended to end this lecture with Conway's quote. However, we should take a closer look at that line, and its description at the end of the nineteenth century of free thought as a once small movement, now stronger than the loins of bigotry. Moncure Conway, like Robert Ingersoll and all of their contemporaries in the free-thought movement, assumed that free thought and rationalism would be the dominant forces in the American future, that the most retrograde forms of religion and their influence on government and the minds of human beings would wither away in the light of scientific truth. I think Paine himself probably would have been astonished if anyone had told him that, two-hundred years in the future, his writings would still be considered controversial by large numbers of the American public. But then, Robert Ingersoll, who died in 1899, would have certainly been astonished that two-thirds of Americans in 2005, according to a recent poll conducted by the Pew Forum on Religion and Public Life, believe that both evolution and the biblical story of creation should be taught in public-school science classes. The fact is that nearly a third of Americans, as indicated in repeated opinion polls, do believe that every word in the Bible is literally true. The reasons why this is so here, and not in any other developed country in the world, are perhaps a subject for another conference.

As he wrote in *The Age of Reason,* Paine believed that the American Revolution in the system of government would be followed by a revolution in the system of religion. "Human inventions and priestcraft would be detected; and man would return to the pure, unmixed and unadulterated belief in one God, and no more." We know this revolution didn't happen, certainly not in the sense that Paine intended and hoped for. We also know that people are being slaughtered around the globe today because of a quarrel over which of the descendants of the two sons of Abraham have the right to occupy the same supposedly God-given piece of land, so what the *Atlantic* called "a shallow deistical essay" in 1859 still speaks powerfully to our time—because much of the world, and a huge segment of the citizenry of our own nation, which prides itself on being blessed (a word I've come to hate), still rejects any rational examination of religion. The separation of church and state, which Paine regarded as the foundation of everything potentially good in the new American government—as America's founding gift, not only to its own citizens but the world—is denigrated as a lie of the left by many of the most influential figures in every branch of our government.

One of these figures is Justice Scalia, who, in his minority dissent in one of the Ten Commandments cases I mentioned earlier, had the sheer chutzpah to write that the court was mistaken in its decision to prohibit in-your-face displays of the tablets in Kentucky courthouses. Why was the court majority wrong? Because, according to Scalia, the U.S. Constitution clearly, clearly permits "disregard of polytheists and believers in unconcerned deities, just as it permits the disregard of devout atheists." The Constitution, of course, prohibits no such thing. It has nothing to say about God, Gods, or any form of belief or not, believer or non-believer, apart from the first amendment's familiar Establishment Cause, and Article IV in the body of the Constitution, which prohibits all religious tests for public office. Justice Scalia, who certainly knows better, can get away with this bold-face lie because so few Americans know anything about the secular side of our history and the reasons why the founders deliberately omitted the word "God" from the Constitution and instead gave supreme governmental authority to "We the People."

We surely need a new Thomas Paine to explain all this once more. But the old Thomas Paine continues to speak powerfully to these issues. Here is the line that appears in the Preface, in which Paine entrusts his arguments in the *Age of Reason* "To my fellow-citizens of the United States of America" (that really ought to be chiseled on every courthouse and schoolhouse wall): "The most formidable weapon against errors of any kind is Reason. I have never used any other, and I trust I never shall." Thank you.

Question: I'm interested in your Center For Inquiry. I understand that you have some sort of channel to the United Nations. I'm wondering what is it that the Center For Inquiry does.

Susan Jacoby: I want to make clear that I'm not the director of the Center For Inquiry; I just organize their public programs in New York. We have a Thomas Paine lecture and an annual Darwin Day lecture. But the Center For Inquiry is a very large organization serving as a rationalist think tank. It is based in Buffalo. If you want to learn more about it, the website is centerforin-quiry.net. It publishes magazines, *Free Inquiry* and *The Skeptical Inquirer*. Its focus now is very heavily on attacks against science. The Council For Secular Humanism, which some of you know about— the Center For Inquiry is the umbrella organization for that.

Question: My name is Jim Underdown, Director of the Los Angeles office for the Center For Inquiry. Susan, I have a loaded question that calls for pure speculation on your part. If Thomas Paine were alive and had the benefit of a century and a half of the theory of evolution and all the science that we now know, would he be an atheist today?

Susan Jacoby: That does call for pure speculation. Yes, I imagine he would. All of these people were writing in light of the geological discoveries of the eighteenth century, which greatly influenced them. Intelligent people then knew that the earth wasn't just 4,000 years old. But, of course, the theory of evolution was far in the future. I think he probably would be an atheist today.

However, that isn't my requirement for considering Paine a great man. One of the things that is most annoying to me is that conservatives are always trying to portray the founders as deeply religious men. At the same time, there are many people on the left who insist that they must have been atheists. What I always say, especially when I talk with right-wing religious people, is that you can read the writings of Jefferson and Adams, and they wrote so much that you can find almost anything in them. They're like the Bible in that respect. I'm more interested in terms of our government—not in what they truly believed inside, but in what they did regarding church and state. The thing that stands as an immense obstacle to these right-wingers is that the Constitution doesn't mention God. They try to get around this by saying everybody was such a devout believer that mentioning God would have been superfluous. This, of course is a lie, because the admission of God was thoroughly debated in all of the state ratifying conventions in 1787 and 1788. The religious right lost its battle then. It lost, and it's never gotten over it. There have been several attempts to put a Christian amendment into the Constitution, and they all have failed.

Question: It may sound like we're ganging up on you, but I'm also affiliated with the Center For Inquiry, as program chair for the San Diego Association for National Inquiry. (So much for the commercial.) It might be of interest to you that one of our talk-show hosts has adopted the idea—in defending a cross on public property—that the First Amendment gives us permission to do things in the name of religion, thereby standing the Constitution on its head. A real quick question: where would Mark Twain fit in your golden age of free thought?

Susan Jacoby: Mark Twain fits into my golden age of free thought very well. He's in the book. When you look at the golden age of free thought, you also should look at what was happening in the arts. You have both Walt Whitman and Mark Twain, who obviously fit into the golden age of free thought, not just in terms of their thinking, but as artists. There is certainly a reason why Mark Twain's anti-religious writings were not too well-known until much later. The executor of his estate wanted to keep them close by, because she was afraid that he would lose fans. But Twain and Whitman are very important figures in the golden age of free thought. By the way, one of the most beautiful eulogies ever written was Robert Ingersoll's eulogy for Walt Whitman. Also, Whitman and Twain both had an influence on foreign-born radicals who lived here, like Emma Goldman. Emma Goldman discovered Whitman when she was in prison on what is now Riker's Island, and also Paine, I believe, as well. She had a lot of time to read, and the prison had a good library, so there were some connections between various kinds of radical movements.

Question: If you compare Paine's Biblical scholarship with the academics who are studying the Bible and have dug out old manuscripts, the conclusions are identical. They all say that the books weren't written by Matthew and Mark and Luke. There were no miracles. It is just impressive that his stuff agrees with the academics who are studying the Bible from a rational viewpoint.

Susan Jacoby: You might say Paine was just judging it by virtue of common sense, even though he didn't speak Hebrew or read Greek or anything like that. A few weeks ago, I was at a conference titled "Is Secularism Dead?" at the New School in New York. There was a participant on the panel who has a new book out called *The Secular Bible*. The thesis of this book is, the reason that secularists are having such trouble in America today is because they don't know anything about religion and can't contradict the Bible because they can't read the original scriptures in their original language. I think this gentleman's argument is incorrect. Paine didn't have any learning in original Biblical languages. You certainly don't need to be able to read Aramaic, Hebrew, or Greek to realize that the Bible was a book written by men.

Question: I wanted to ask your thoughts about the irony, as I understand it, that one of the reasons we have separation of church and state is actually due to the first Great Awakening and the antagonism of the people in that Awakening toward the Congregationalists and the Anglican Church. As I understand it, this stirred them up to be rebellious against the crown. One of the first things that seems to have happened after the Revolution, although it took until 1820 to go through all the states, was the disestablishment of religion.

Susan Jacoby: It is ironic that the first state constitution to definitively separate church and state was Virginia's. It was in response to a proposal by Patrick Henry to tax people for the support of Christian teachers of religion. James Madison came back with his famous "Memorial and Remonstrance," and the Virginia separation of church and state—the 1786 "Act For Establishing Religious Freedom"—came about as a result of a coalition of enlightenment rationalists and evangelicals who were then the minority in Virginia and wanted the privileges of the state-established Anglican Church to be eliminated, so that is a real irony.

The right-wingers are correct today to say that the religious people who were in favor of separation of church and state were concerned almost entirely with the protection of religion from government, as well they might have been given recent history. The rationalists were concerned with the protection of government from religion, and they achieved the kind of coalition that seems absolutely impossible in our day.

One of the things I've noted when I speak before religious audiences is that Evangelicals in the eighteenth century would have been horrified at the idea of the federal government giving money to faith-based programs. They would have understood and instinctively recoiled at something that certainly will be true today if the faith-based bandwagon and money roll on—that there is no free lunch. Government money doesn't come attached without strings. I have a good friend who is an African-American minister in Washington, who is also the executive director of the Religious Coalition for Reproductive Choice. He has a great many arguments with his fellow Baptist African-American ministers because he is totally opposed to faith-based funding, and they want it mainly because their churches are poor and they need it. The point he always makes is, how free would the Black churches of the South have felt in the 1950s—to be the spearhead of the Civil Rights Movement—had they been dependent on government money at the time? That is a really good point. He who feeds at the government trough lives by government rules. One of the real ironies is that religious people don't see that. I think that some of them, organizations like the Christian Coalition, think they're so powerful that they own the government.

Question: I am curious why the intellectuals in the press criticized Paine, attacked him as an atheist even though in writing he said he believed in God and an afterlife. Did he contradict himself in his writings, or in public and in speeches, or was there a different definition of atheism back then that basically meant if you defy orthodoxy and fundamentalism, then you're an atheist?

Susan Jacoby: Actually, unlike Jefferson and Adams, Paine did not contradict himself on issues of religion. He never claimed to be an atheist. But at that time, free-thinkers were often called atheists. There were free-thinkers and infidels, and they were all lumped together. You're right. Not believing in orthodox religion, not believing the truth of the Bible, was just lumped together with atheism, all as a bad thing. It wasn't that Paine contradicted himself, for all of those things in the mind of right-wing orthodox ministers went together.

Although there weren't very many ministers who had a good word to say for him, there was one. Among the effects of free thought—I think it's one of the reasons that the orthodox churches hated people like Paine so much—is that it converted people from an orthodox form of religion to a more liberal form of religion. Half of the Congregationalist churches in New England between 1780 and 1825 turned into Unitarian congregations, which from the perspective of religiously orthodoxy was as bad as being an atheist. One of the ministers who, when Paine died, had a good word to say for him was a great Unitarian pastor of the church in Salem, Massachusetts (which, by then, had left witchcraft behind). He said Mr. Paine was indeed a wonderful man, and he is despised because he saw in Christianity those flaws that the most sensible (meaning sensible in the eighteenth-century sense) Christians have seen. One of the reasons Paine was so hated by the religious right of his day was not that he made converts to atheism, but that he diverted people from their preferred form of religion.

Question: Was there a big disparity between those who hated Paine in the press versus the general public? Did they have sympathies for him, or was the *Zeitgeist* basically orthodox at that time?

Susan Jacoby: The religious structure in America was much looser. For example, a majority of people in colonial America, and until the early 1820s, didn't belong to churches at all. It didn't mean that they weren't religious, as the spirit of religion being between you and your God was very strong in America. There were other people, like Elihu Palmer, for instance, who had very little circulation and influence on the public at large. Paine had much more effect because *Common Sense* was known to everybody who could read a word or had a brain in their head in the colonies, and that meant *The Age of Reason* would have been given a look by more people, and I think that Paine had an influence because he was interested in education for ordinary people, for obvious reasons. When you look at Paine's writing, although it looks so polished by today's standards, he wrote in words that could be understood by every person who spoke the English language. He didn't write in words that could be understood only by theologians who had gone to Harvard or Oxford.

PAINE AND AMERICA'S UNFINISHED REVOLUTION

Harvey Kaye

Ronald King

I hope you all have been taking pleasure from this conference on Thomas Paine. My daughter commented this morning that taking pleasure from Paine sounds like an S&M conference. She thinks that attendance would be even better had we advertised this as an S&M conference, and the costumes would be a lot more interesting.

Something happened in the United States in the decades following the Revolution. Political legitimacy shifted from the people to institutions. The source of authority moved from the consent of the governed to the mechanical processes of government. As a political scientist, I don't find this surprising. But it was not a trivial event, politically. Many might celebrate the change—the creation of orderly, balanced, temperate governmental processes. But something was also lost, especially the idea of the engaged and powerful citizen. Thomas Paine as a historical figure spoke on behalf of popular power and against institutions. His legacy within the American democratic discourse, widely adapted in many forms, is used to remind us of the popular alternatives to the status quo.

That thought serves as a fitting introduction to the speaker for this session. Harvey Kaye is the Ben and Joyce Rosenberg Professor of Social Change and Development at the University of Wisconsin, Green Bay. He is the author of a number of books, but the latest one is probably most relevant for this afternoon. *Thomas Paine and the Promise Of America* is clearly divided into two distinct sections, representing the two sides of Paine studies—the historical person and the continuing legacy for American democratic politics. I gather that the book is not quite selling at the rate of *Common Sense*, but it is generating considerable interest. It is with such interest that I welcome Professor Kaye.

Harvey Kaye

In contrast to many of the speakers, I don't have bifocals, so I'll put my glasses on to start, and then I'll take them off in order to stay close to my text. I want to thank our hosts and conference organizers for handling all the logistics for this event. Before actually beginning my talk, I'm going make a preface-like comment. I want to tell you something about how I came to write *Thomas Paine and the Promise Of America*. It might help you understand my talk and the motivation for the words I have. As we are in California, it seems only appropriate that I start by acknowledging my intellectual debt to Ronald Reagan—and I do mean Ronald Reagan.

Thomas Paine had been my hero ever since I was a child (due, probably to my grandfather's influence—for my grandfather, a young socialist and New York trial lawyer, really admired Paine and kept volumes by and about him in his at-home book collection, volumes that I explored as a boy).

In fact, however much other historical figures may have inspired my youthful political progressivism, Paine did so most of all. Thus, it naturally shocked me—as it did so many others, on both the left *and* the right—when Reagan, of all people, took to quoting him during the 1980 presidential election campaign. Anyhow, the thought of Reagan with his arm around Paine haunted me, and I eventually responded, first, by writing about Reagan's use and abuse of the past and then—hoping to reclaim my hero—by authoring a young adult biography, *Thomas Paine: Firebrand of the Revolution*.

Yet I still felt the need to do more (not to mention, I was really enjoying myself and did not want to give up Tom for another subject). I knew we didn't need another full-scale treatment of his life, for we had two truly excellent adult biographies in those by John Keane and Jack Fruchtman, as well as Eric Foner's outstanding *Tom Paine and Revolutionary America*.

Still, I felt we needed to hear more about Paine's contributions, memory, and legacy, so I proposed to write a short book of three parts: in part one I planned to recount Paine's life and labors; in part two, to relate the story of the suppression of his memory; and in part three, to resurrect Paine and reflect on what he might have to say to Americans today, the last of which led a friend of mine, a Lutheran minister, to suggest that I follow the fashion of those young evangelicals who wear bracelets bearing the letters "WWJD" ("What Would Jesus Do?"), and create a line of jewelry engraved with the letters "WWTPD."

Yet the new book turned into something else, something quite different and something quite more than I had expected, for I discovered that I was very much mistaken—that we were all very much mistaken—about Paine's afterlife. No, I did not discover that the nineteenth-century spiritualists, who loved to "channel" Paine more than anybody else, had been right all along. Rather, I kept encountering evidence that contradicted the long-told tale of Paine's exile from public life. In fact, what I came across indicated that Americans had never forgotten Paine. Truly, never! Yes, efforts continually were made to suppress appreciative remembrance of him. Yes, lies were told, and crude things were said of him, and yes, he was both effectively banished from "official" memory and sadly despised in orthodox religious circles.

However—with the aid of archivists, librarians, and colleagues—I found that Paine actually had remained very much alive in American memory. More importantly, I found that he had remained very powerfully engaged in the making of American freedom, equality, and democracy, so I ended up telling a critically different story than I had projected. Indeed, I ended up re-telling the story of America itself—not a Jeffersonian or Hamiltonian story, but rather, a Painite story. Moreover, it's a story that, if Paine has anything to say about it, is far from over.

Today I speak—historically and, as requested, politically—about "Thomas Paine and America's Unfinished Revolution." In that spirit, I will ultimately ask, not only, "Why do we, too, turn so eagerly to Paine?" but also, "What Would Thomas Paine Do?"

On July 17, 1980, Ronald Reagan stood before the Republican National Convention and the American people to accept his party's nomination for President of the United States. Most of what he said that evening was to be expected from a Republican. He spoke of the nation's past and its "shared values;" he attacked the incumbent Carter Administration and promised to lower taxes, limit government, and expand national defense; and invoking God, he invited Americans to join him in a "crusade to make America great again."

Yet Reagan had much more than restoration in mind. He intended to transform American political life. He had constructed a new Republican alliance—a New Right—of corporate elites, Christian evangelicals, con-servative and neoconservative intellectuals, and a host of right-wing interest groups in hopes of undoing the liberal programs of the previous 40 years, reversing the cultural changes of the 1960s, AND establishing a new national governing consensus.

All that is well known. But that night Reagan startled many a listener by calling forth Thomas Paine and quoting his words of 1776, from *Common Sense*: "We have it in our power to begin the world over again."

American politicians have always drawn upon the words and deeds of the Founders. Nevertheless, in quoting Paine, Reagan broke emphatically with long-standing conservative practice. Paine was not like Washington, Franklin, Adams, Hamilton, and Jefferson. Paine had never really been admitted to the most select ranks of the Founding Fathers. Recent presidents, mostly Democrats, had referred to Paine, but even the liberals had generally refrained from quoting Paine the revolutionary. When they called upon his life and labors, they usually conjured up Paine the patriot, citing the line with which he opened the first of his *Crisis* papers: "These are the times that try men's souls."

Conservatives certainly were not supposed to speak favorably of Paine—and for 200 years they had not. In fact, for generations they had publicly despised Paine and scorned his memory, and one can understand why. Endowing American experience with democratic impulse and aspiration, Paine had turned Americans into radicals, and we have remained radicals at heart ever since.

Contributing fundamentally to the American Revolution, the French Revolution, and the struggles of Britain's Industrial Revolution, Thomas Paine was one of the most remarkable political writers of the modern world and the greatest radical of a radical age. Yet this son of an English artisan did not become a radical until his arrival in America in late 1774 at the age of 37. Even then he had never expected such things to happen. But struck by America's startling contradictions, its magnificent possibilities, and its wonderful energies— and moved by the spirit and determination of its people to resist British authority—Paine dedicated himself to the American cause.

Through his pamphlets, *Common Sense* and the *Crisis* papers—and by way of words such as "The sun never shined on a cause of greater worth," "We have it in our power to begin the world over again," and "These are the times that try men's souls"—he emboldened Americans to turn their colonial rebellion into a revolutionary war. Paine not only encouraged his fellow citizens-to-be to declare their independence, but he also inspired them to create a republic; defined the new nation in a democratically expansive and progressive fashion; and articulated an American identity charged with exceptional purpose and promise.

At war's end Paine was a popular hero. Yet he was not finished. The story is told of a dinner gathering at which Paine, on hearing his mentor Benjamin Franklin observe, "Where liberty is, there is my country," cried out, "Where liberty is not, there is my country."

Truly, America's struggle had turned Paine into an inveterate champion of liberty, equality, and democracy, and after the war he went on to apply his pen to fresh struggles. In *Rights of Man* he defended the French Revolution, challenged Britain's political and social order, and outlined a series of public initiatives to address the material inequalities that made life oppressive for working people. In *The Age of Reason* he criticized organized religion, the claims of Biblical scripture, and the power of churches and clerics, and in *Agrarian Justice* he proposed a democratic system of addressing poverty that entailed taxing the landed rich to provide grants to young people and pensions for the elderly.

Reared an Englishman, adopted by America, and honored as a Frenchman, Paine often called himself a "citizen of the world." But the United States always remained paramount in his thoughts and evident in his labors. Yet, as great as his contributions were, they were not always appreciated and his affections were not always reciprocated. His democratic lines, style, and appeal—as well as his background, confidence, and single-mindedness—antagonized many among the powerful, propertied, prestigious, and pious and made him enemies even within the ranks of his fellow patriots.

Elites and aspiring elites—New England patricians and ministers, Middle Atlantic merchants and manufacturers, Southern slaveholders and preachers—feared the power of Paine's pen and the implications of his arguments. In reaction, they and their heirs sought to disparage his character, suppress his memory, and limit the influence of his ideas. According to most accounts, they succeeded. For much of the nineteenth century, and well into the twentieth, Paine's pivotal role in the making of the United States was effectively erased in the official telling.

Writing in the 1880s, Theodore Roosevelt believed he could characterize Paine with impunity as a "filthy little atheist" (though Paine was neither filthy, little, nor an atheist). Not only in the highest circles, but also in various popular quarters—particularly among the religiously devout—Paine's name persistently conjured up the worst images, leading generations of historians and biographers to assume that memory of Paine's contributions to American history had been lost. In the early 1940s, the historian Dixon Wecter observed that, "To trace the curve of Paine's reputation is to learn something about hero-worship in reverse." As recently as 1995, scholar of the Revolution Gordon Wood could state that Paine "seems destined to remain a misfit, an outsider."

Yet those accounts were wrong.

Paine had died, but neither his memory nor his legacy ever expired. His contributions were too fundamental and his vision of America's meaning and possibilities too firmly imbued in the dynamic of American political life and culture to be so easily shed or suppressed. At times of crisis—political, military, and economic—when the Republic and the nation's very purpose and promise seemed in jeopardy, Americans almost instinctively would turn to Paine and his words. Even those who apparently disdained him and what he represented could not fail to draw on elements of his vision. Moreover, there were those who would not allow Paine and his arguments to be forgotten.

Contrary to the ambitions of the governing elites—*and* to the presumptions of historians and biographers—Paine remained a powerful presence in American political and intellectual life. Recognizing the persistent and developing contradictions between the nation's ideals and reality, rebels, reformers, and critics—both native-born and immigrant—continually rediscovered Paine's life and labors and drew ideas, inspiration, and encouragement from them as they struggled to defend, extend, and deepen freedom, equality, and democracy.

Some honored Paine in memorials. Many more honored him all the more by adopting his arguments and words as their own. Workingmen's advocates, free-thinkers (as well as democratic evangelicals!), abolitionists, suffragists, anarchists, populists, progressives, socialists, labor and community organizers, and liberals have repeatedly garnered political and intellectual energy from Paine, renewed his presence in American life, and served as the prophetic memory of his radical-democratic vision of America. The roster of Painites is lengthy, so I will be selective.

As we know, Paine had departed Philadelphia for Europe in 1787, hoping to secure funds to erect his projected iron bridge. Yet even in his absence he would remain a radical presence in 1790s America, not simply by way of his earlier writings. Thrilling Jefferson and his allies, *Rights of Man* played a critical role in the emergence of both the Democratic-Republican Societies and the Republican Party. Those same texts not only inspired many an English, Scottish, Welsh, and Irish radical to challenge Crown and Constitution in the British Isles, but also, when royal repression ensued, to seek refuge in Paine's beloved "asylum for mankind," where they continued to serve the cause of republican democracy as periodical editors and writers. Moreover, Paine's literary assault on organized religion fomented a short-lived, but vibrant Deist movement that included— from Cambridge to the Carolinas—both working people *and* college students.

Yet there's more. Undeniably, *The Age of Reason* shocked the Christian faithful. Nevertheless, many an evangelical—from the Baptist revivalist John Leland to the peripatetic Methodist preacher Lorenzo Dow—continued to draw upon Paine and his arguments as they themselves challenged Church Establishments and clerical power structures. One might even say that Paine himself contributed to the Second Great Awakening (at least, that is, to its more democratic dimensions).

For all of his ranting, John Adams was quite perceptive and prescient about modern history when he wrote:

> I know not whether any man in the world has had more influence on its inhabitants or affairs for the last thirty years than Tom Paine. . . . For such a mongrel between pigs and puppy, begotten by a wild boar on a bitch wolf, never before in any age of the world was suffered by the poltroonery of mankind to run

through such a career of mischief. Call it then the Age of Paine.

Eager to limit the power of the people, the powers that be did their best to squelch recognition and remembrance of democracy's greatest champion. Yet, just as Paine had expected, Americans would not easily fall into line. They would make the first half of the nineteenth century not only a time of economic and geographical expansion, but also of "militant democracy" — and they would affectionately carry Paine with them as they did.

Intent on embalming the Revolution more than celebrating it, orators at official Independence Day commemorations glorified Washington and, depending on the state wherein they spoke, Adams, Hamilton, Franklin, or Jefferson. Those who wielded power and purse did not want to hear of Paine, and they figured others should not either, at least not in any appreciative way. Nevertheless, from Boston and New York to the burgeoning towns and cities of what we now call the Midwest, radicals and liberals staged their own commemorative events. Gathered together, they joyously recalled Paine's life and labors to redeem the nation's revolutionary heritage and, therewith, empower workingmen, create egalitarian communities, secure the separation of church and state, speak freely, and revere the creation free-mindedly. Still others turned to Paine as they pursued the liberation of black Americans from bondage and the establishment of women's equal rights as citizens.

Utopians and free-thinkers like Robert Owen and Fanny Wright, "Workies" like William Heighton and Thomas Skidmore, land reformers like George Henry Evans, abolitionists like William Lloyd Garrison and Wendell Phillips, suffragists like Elizabeth Cady Stanton, Ernestine Rose, and Susan B. Anthony, along with armies of others, read Paine, recited his words, and spurred themselves and their comrades into action.

Paine also fired the imaginations of Spiritualists — most of whom were rather progressive on matters of class, race, and gender — *and* of Transcendentalists. Ralph Waldo Emerson himself would write that, "Each man . . . is a tyrant in tendency, because he would impose his ideas on others. Jesus would absorb the race; but Tom Paine . . . helps humanity by resisting this exuberance of power."

Concurrently, the early Young Americans—a prominent cohort of New York political and literary figures associated with the Democratic Party—both embraced Paine's progressive and expansionary vision of America's future *and* cultivated his memory in their magazine, *The United States and Democratic Review*. Admittedly, several of their leaders, such as John O'Sullivan, who actually coined the term Manifest Destiny, would turn into jingoists and worse. But the movement also shaped the thinking of two of America's greatest democratic writers, Herman Melville and Walt Whitman, who, as their writings attest, remained Painites for the rest of their entire lives. Forever hoping Americans would absorb him as affectionately as he had absorbed them, Whitman not only wanted to "help set the memory of Paine right," he also apparently wanted to become Paine. While Whitman did not know it, Abraham Lincoln, the man who tragically would become Whitman's fallen "Captain, had embraced Paine, as well.

We now acknowledge the young Abe as a Deist. But he apparently learned more than skepticism from Paine. Roy Basler, the editor of Lincoln's *Collected Works*, noted that Paine was probably Lincoln's "favorite author," from whom the future President received his "most important literary education" and in whose writings he found his "model of eloquence." Though Basler himself did not pursue the matter, if we listen carefully, we can definitely hear Paine's words regarding freedom and America's extraordinary purpose and promise echoing through Lincoln's finest speeches.

Examples abound of those who turned to Paine, increasingly so as civil war threatened. But here I'll simply cite the testimony of the Unitarian minister and abolitionist Moncure Conway. In an 1860 Paine birthday address in Cincinnati, Conway observed that "Thomas Paine's life up to 1809 . . . is interesting; but Thomas Paine's life from that time to [now] is more than interesting – it is thrilling!"

Conway's observation would also aptly describe the later decades of the century. Undergoing phenomenal growth and development, Gilded Age America witnessed intensifying exploitation, widening inequalities, and new forms of oppression. But as much as the governing classes might have wished it otherwise, the nation would also see vigorous struggles to extend and deepen freedom, equality, and democracy, *and*, just as their predecessors had, the new generations of radicals and reformers would find ideas, inspiration, and encouragement in Paine.

A host of intellectuals honored Paine's life and memory. Against the grain of his own class interests, Republican business lawyer Robert Ingersoll, the foremost lecturer of his day and leading advocate of religious skepticism, so admired Paine, he defended and promoted him everywhere he went. Raised in the old artisan quarter of Philadelphia, Henry George, the printer-turned-political economist, registered Paine's tutelage in his movement-making book, *Progress and Poverty*. Outfitted with Painite ideas about freedom and human possibilities, Lester Ward, the father of American sociology, challenged the Social Darwinism of Herbert Spencer and William Graham Sumner, and, convinced that Paine was one of the most important men in history, Mark Twain, America's greatest story-teller, read Paine on the Mississippi and proceeded to incorporate Paine's religious and political arguments into his fiction and commentaries, most evidently so in *A Connecticut Yankee in King Arthur's Court*.

Even as Teddy Roosevelt was scribbling stupidities about Paine, smarter scholars were recovering and recounting his contributions. Cornell professor Moses Coit Tyler delivered a talk on Paine at the very first American Historical Association meetings in 1884 and later devoted entire chapters to Paine's work in his pioneering *Literary History of the American Revolution*. In that same year, the aforementioned Moncure Conway became the first president of the Thomas Paine National Historical Association and, not long after, published a magnificent two-volume biography of Paine and a four-volume collection of his writings.

Yet far more than the literati attended to Paine. Confronting the Robber Barons and their ilk, labor leaders like William Sylvis of the 1860s National Labor Union, Thomas Phillips of the 1880s Knights of Labor, and Eugene Debs of the 1890s American Railway Union found strength and energy in Paine's life and labors.

Paine empowered American- and European-born alike. In the wake of the Revolutions of 1848, cohorts of liberal and radical German refugees, like their British and Irish predecessors, came to Paine's "asylum for mankind" hoping for the best, but prepared to continue the fight for the good society, and fight they did. Joining with native-born unionists and social democrats, they and those who followed them to

America actively served in the campaign for the eight-hour day and improved living conditions. Moreover, they never forgot their hero. Every January 29th, German-American workers and intellectuals from New York to Chicago and Milwaukee celebrated Paine's birthday with drinks, dining, and dancing.

Having studied Paine's works, the Haymarket Martyrs, as well as later anarchists such as Voltairine de Cleyre and Emma Goldman, clearly saw themselves advancing America's Revolutionary tradition. Populists, Progressives (Teddy Roosevelt excepted), Suffragists, and Socialists—all, to varying degrees, admired Paine and joined him to their movements. Plains-state and southwestern politicians such as Kansas Congressman Jeremiah Simpson and Texas Judge Thomas Nugent appealed to farmers, miners, and other laboring folk with Paine's words. Crusaders such as the attorney, editor, and advocate of labor and racial equality, Louis Freeland Post, and the muckraking journalist George Creel were motivated by Paine's life and labors. Feminists, from the radical Victoria Woodhull in the 1870s to the reformer Dr. Mary Putnam-Jacobi in the 1890s, quoted Paine at length on equality and the right to vote as they demanded the enfranchisement of their sex. More than any on the left, socialists—most notably, Julius Wayland, the publisher of *The Appeal to Reason*, Clarence Darrow, the renowned "attorney for the damned," and, again, Eugene Debs, the party's leader and presidential candidate—promoted Paine's memory as they cam-paigned for a cooperative commonwealth.

Indeed, given our venue, I should not fail to note how the San Diego Baptist minister, the Reverend George Washington Woodbey, who was born a slave in 1854, proudly pronounced, "I stand on the declaration of Thomas Paine when he said 'The world is my country'" as he urged the Socialist party's 1908 national convention to oppose the exclusion of Asian immigrants from the United States.

No less so, twentieth-century radicals and liberals would also reach back and grab hold of Paine's life and labors, though, sadly, they would hardly do so in unison. In fact, all too often they would do so in conflict with each other, as in 1917-1918, when the Wilson Administration, even as it was suppressing antiwar dissent and jailing many a Paine-inspired radical for sedition, was enlisting Paine's words in support of a war intended to make the world safe for democracy, and the President himself was deriving critical elements of his famous Fourteen Points from Paine's internationalist republican vision.

Still, for all of their efforts, pro-war liberals would not easily monopolize Paine. Arrested for sedition, Eugene Debs eloquently testified to a patriotism alternative to, if not grander than that of the Wilsonians by summoning a host of great American radicals to stand alongside him in the courtroom at his trial in Canton, Ohio, Paine positioned in front of all the rest.

Though capitalism, conservatism, racism, and anti-Semitism dominated 1920s America, progressive-minded scholars and public intellectuals such as William Dodd, Vernon Parrington, and Gilbert Seldes, not to mention the infamous debunkers in their own sly way, celebrated Paine's career and contributions as a means of challenging the right-wing tenor of the times.

Then, in the 1930s, responding to both Great Depression crises and New Deal possibilities, left-wing historians, writers, artists, and composers made Paine a popular literary, visual, and lyrical reference as they advanced the cause of labor and pressed for further government initiatives on what one scholar has dubbed the "Cultural Front." (If I had the time, and a tenth of Paul Robeson's talent, I would sing *Ballad for Americans* for you right now.)

The passion for Paine would continue to grow as Americans anxiously witnessed the rise and expansion of European Fascism and Japanese imperialism and then had to deal with them head-on in the wake of Pearl Harbor. Dramatically attesting to Americans' deep and persistent affection for the radical and patriot, President Franklin Delano Roosevelt urgently called Paine back to military service in a Washington's Birthday "fireside chat" of February 23, 1942, a speech considered one of Roosevelt's greatest ever.

Confronting the nation's most severe crisis since the Civil War, FDR made clear the demands of global warfare, laid out a vision of a world shaped by the Four Freedoms ("Freedom of Speech, Freedom of Worship, Freedom from Want, and Freedom from Fear"), and called upon his fellow citizens to work and fight energetically in favor of victory and peace. Finally, realizing full well that he had to inspire and encourage his fellow citizens, not antagonize or alienate them, Roosevelt concluded by proclaiming:

"These are the times that try men's souls." Tom Paine wrote those words on a drumhead, by the light of a campfire. That was when Washington's little army of ragged, rugged men was retreating across New Jersey, having tasted naught but defeat. And General Washington ordered that these great words written by Tom Paine be read to the men of every regiment in the Continental Army, and this was the assurance given to the first American armed forces: "The summer soldier and the sunshine patriot will, in this crisis, shrink from the service of their country; but he that stands it now, deserves the love and thanks of man and woman. Tyranny, like hell, is not easily conquered; yet we have this consolation with us, that the harder the sacrifice, the more glorious the triumph." So spoke Americans in the year 1776. So speak Americans today!

Americans responded as never before. Moreover, they took Paine with them into every front of the war. They named an "ugly ducking" Liberty Ship and a B-17 Flying Fortress after him. They produced national radio programs about him, and they published new Paine biographies and anthologies. In fact, they turned Howard Fast's 1943 novel, *Citizen Tom Paine*, into a national bestseller.

I could go on to relate the continuing conflicts and struggles over Paine's memory and legacy through the years of Cold War consensus and anxiety, Korea, McCarthyism, Civil Rights, Vietnam, Great Society, student antiwar movement, urban upheavals, recession, stagflation, and malaise, and the rise of the New Right. But, given the time (and hoping you'll pick up and read my book), I'll move directly to Paine and us, today.

Heartened and animated by Paine, we Americans have pressed for the rights of workingmen; insisted upon freedom of conscience and the separation of church and state; demanded the abolition of slavery; campaigned for the equality of women; confronted the power of property and wealth; opposed the tyrannies of Fascism and Communism; fought a second Revolution for racial justice and equality; and challenged our own government's authorities and policies, domestic and foreign. We have suffered defeats, committed mistakes, and endured tragic and ironic turnabouts. But we have achieved great victories and far more often than not, as Paine himself fully expected, we have in the process transformed the nation and the world for the better.

Now, after more than two centuries—facing our own "times that try men's souls"—it seems we have all become Painites. Today, references to Paine abound in public debate and culture, and in contrast to the past, not only the left but also, in the wake of Reagan, the right claims him as one of their own.

Indeed, in these years of conservative ascendance and the retreat of liberalism and the left, we have witnessed—rather ironically, it would seem—an amazing resurgence of interest in Paine, extending all the way across American public culture. His writings adorn bookstore shelves and academic syllabi. References to him appear everywhere, in magazine articles, television programs, Hollywood films, and even in the work of contemporary musical artists, from classical to punk rock. While Paine's image may not have become iconic, the editors of American Greats, a Hall-of-Fame-like volume celebrating the nation's most wonderful and fascinating creations, enshrined his pamphlet *Common Sense* as popular Americana, alongside the baseball diamond, the Brooklyn Bridge, the Coca-Cola recipe, and the Chevrolet Corvette. Media critic John Katz dubbed Paine the "moral father of the Internet."

Paine has definitely achieved a new status in public history and memory and has come to be admired and celebrated almost universally. Nothing more firmly registered the change than the decision in October, 1992, by Congress to authorize the erection of a monument to Paine in Washington, D.C. on the Mall, for the lobbying campaign for the memorial involved mobilizing truly bipartisan support, from Ted Kennedy to Jesse Helms. More recently, in 2004, while Howard Dean and Ralph Nader were issuing pamphlets modeled on *Common Sense*, and *TomPaine.com* was publishing liberal news commentary, Republicans and Libertarians were quoting Paine in support of their own political ambitions.

Paine's new popularity truly has seemed nothing less than astonishing, leading Paine biographer Jack Fruchtman to muse, "Who owns Tom Paine?" The very extent of it has made it seem as if it had never been otherwise. Reporting on a campaign to have a marble statue of suffragists Susan B.

Anthony, Elizabeth Cady Stanton, and Lucretia Mott moved into the capitol Rotunda, a Washington-based journalist wrote, "Imagine a statue of Benjamin Franklin shoved into a broom closet in the White House. Or a portrait of Thomas Paine tucked behind a door. That would never happen." In Columbus, Ohio, a reporter noted without reservation: "Some politicians evoke Abraham Lincoln or Thomas Paine to express Middle America's ideal of honesty and patriotism."

Undeniably, Paine's attraction is related to the recent wave of "Founding Fathers Fever." But saying that simply raises the questions: why have we become so intent on re-engaging the Founders, and, in those terms, why Paine in particular?

Historically, we have turned to our Revolutionary past at times of national crisis and upheaval, when, as I said at the outset, the Republic and the very purpose and promise of the nation were at risk or in doubt. Facing wars, depressions, and other travails and traumas, we have sought consolation, guidance, inspiration, and validation. Some of us have wanted to converse with the Founders, and others to argue or do battle with them, all of which is to be expected in a nation of grand political acts and texts. As historian Steven Jaffe has noted, "The Founders have come to symbolize more than just their own accomplishments and beliefs. What did [they] really stand for? This is another way of asking, What is America? What does it mean to be an American?"

We find ourselves in similar circumstances today. That is, events and developments have led us to ask ourselves once again, "What does it mean to be an American?" Commitment to the "American creed of liberty, equality, democracy," the "melting-pot theory of national identity," and the idea of American exceptionalism endure. We continue to comprehend our national experience as entailing the advancement of those ideals and practices, and we still want that history taught to our children. Nevertheless, globalization, immigration, expanding corporate power, intensifying class inequalities, the enervation of civic life, and domestic and international terrorism have instigated real anxiety and trepidation about the nation's future and the political alternatives available. In the 1990s those very concerns fomented "culture wars" and a discourse of crisis reflected in works with titles like *The Disuniting of America* and *America: What Went Wrong?*

Of course, in the wake of September 11, many of those titles no longer seem relevant. The Islamic terrorists' attacks on America and the nation's ensuing wars in Afghanistan and Iraq dramatically refashioned the prevailing sense of crisis and danger. However, they did not resolve the critical questions of American identity and meaning. Not at all. They simply posed them anew and in a more urgent manner.

Today we sense that America's purpose and promise are in jeopardy, and we wonder what we can and should do. Like other generations confronting national crises and emergencies, we have quite naturally looked back to the Revolution and the Founders in search of answers and directions.

Still, why have we become so eager to reconnect specifically with Paine? Perhaps because, when we compare him to the other Founders, he has come to look so good. He was no slaveholder or exploiter of humanity, nor did he seek material advantage by his patriotism.

But that explains his popularity in an essentially negative manner. Besides, as admirable as Paine was, the answer lies not in his life alone. It also has to do with our own historical longings. However conservative the times appear, we Americans remain—with all our faults and failings—resolutely democratic in bearing and aspiration. When we rummage through our Revolutionary heritage, we instinctively look for democratic hopes and possibilities, and there we find no Founder more committed to the progress of freedom, equality, and democracy than Paine. Moreover—as our ancestors did, and probably on account of them, as well—we discover that no writer of our Revolutionary past speaks to us more clearly and forcefully than Paine. In spite of what might have seemed a long estrangement, we recognize Paine and feel a certain intimacy with his words.

Yet appearances and rhetoric can deceive, for if we all truly revered Paine, then for a start we surely would have built the promised monument to him on the Mall in the nation's capital. We would have placed his statue where it belongs, near the memorials to Washington, Jefferson, Lincoln, Roosevelt, and the veterans of the Second World War, whose lives and acts he so powerfully informed and motivated. We would have engraved Paine's words in marble to remind us of how it all began and to keep us from forgetting that "much yet remains to be done."

But the truth is that not all of us are Painites. For all of their many citations of Paine, conservatives really do not, and truly cannot, embrace him and his arguments.

Bolstered by capital, firmly in command of the Republican Party, and politically ascendant for a generation, they have initiated and instituted policies and programs that fundamentally contradict Paine's own vision and commitments. They have subordinated the Republic and the public good to the marketplace and private advantage. They have furthered the interests of corporations and the rich over those of working people and overseen a concentration of wealth and power that—recalling the Gilded Age—has corrupted and debilitated American democratic life and politics, and they have carried on culture wars that have divided the nation and undermined the wall separating church and state.

Moreover, they have pursued policies that have made the nation both less free and less secure: politically, economically, environmentally, and militarily. Even as they have spoken of advancing freedom and empowering citizens, they have sought to discharge or at least constrain America's democratic impulse and aspiration. In fact, while poaching lines from Paine, they and their favorite intellectuals have disclosed their real ambitions and affections by declaring the "end of history" and promoting the lives of Founders like John Adams and Alexander Hamilton, who, in decided contrast to Paine, scorned democracy and feared "the people."

Still, conservatives do, in their fashion, end up fostering interest in Paine. It's not just that, aware of his iconic status, they insist on quoting him. It's also that their very own policies and programs, by effectively denying and threatening America's great purpose and promise, actually propel us, as in crises past, back to the Revolution and the Founders, where once again we encounter Paine's arguments and recognize them as our own.

Arguably, the heightened popular interest in Paine that we have witnessed these past several years reflects anxieties and longings generated not simply by the grave challenges we face, but also by the very triumph of right-wing politics and the threat they pose to freedom, equality, and democracy, and yet progressives—those of us who might make the strongest historical claim on Paine—have yet to properly re-appropriate his memory and legacy. In the course of the late sixties and early seventies the left not only fell apart, but it also lost touch with Paine. While we continue to cite him and his words, we have failed to make his vision and commitments once again our own.

In contrast both to the majority of our fellow citizens and to generations of our political predecessors, liberals and radicals no longer proclaim a firm belief in the nation's exceptional purpose and promise, the prospects and possibilities of democratic change, and ordinary citizens' capacities to act as citizens, not subjects. In short, we have lost the political courage and conviction that once motivated our efforts.

Electrified by America and its people, and the originality of thought and action unleashed by the Revolution, Paine argued that the United States would afford an "asylum for mankind," provide a model to the world, and support the global advance of republican democracy. But many on the left have eschewed notions of American exceptionalism and patriotism and allowed politicians and pundits of the right to monopolize and define them. Furthermore, whereas Paine declared that Americans had it in their power to "begin the world over again," too many of us seem to have all but abandoned the belief that democratic transformation remains both imperative and possible. We must rediscover and reinvigorate the optimism, energy, and imagination that led Paine to aver that "We are a people upon experiments" and "From what we now see, nothing of reform on the political world ought to be held improbable. It is an age of revolutions, in which everything may be looked for."

Finally, while Paine had every confidence in working people and wrote to engage them in the Revolution and nation-building, we, for all our rhetoric, have remained alienated from, if not skeptical of, our fellow citizens. Committed to cultivating democratic life, progressives must assure that Democrats not only commission expert panels, draft plans, and line up legislative votes in a top-down fashion, but also engage American aspirations and energies and enhance public participation in the political and policy-making process.

Paine himself would assure us that the struggle to expand American freedom, equality, and democracy will continue, for as he proudly observed of his fellow citizens after they turned out the Federalists in 1800, "There is too much common sense and independence in America to be long the dupe of any faction, foreign or domestic."

Indeed, those of us who think of ourselves as Painites have good reason not only to hope, but also to act. For Americans' persistent and growing interest in and affection for Paine and his words signify that our generation, too, still feels the democratic impulse and aspiration that he inscribed in American experience. Responding to those yearnings, we might well prove, as Paine himself wrote in reaction to misrepresentations of the events of 1776, that, "It is yet too soon to write the history of the Revolution." Thank you.

❧ ☙

Question: You said that Paine was left out of Fourth of July celebrations, the official ones. Is that why he's left out of our textbooks and standards in schools? One more part to the question: where do you envision Paine in a public school classroom? How do you envision him being presented? Where is his role in public education?

Harvey Kaye: The first part about the exclusion—the folks who ran the Fourth of July celebrations were also, of course, the folks who sat on the school boards that chose the texts. Not every text left Paine out. I've actually found a few that include Paine, some include Paine and scorn him, some include Paine and say that he made the contribution to the American Revolution but he was the anti-Christ so we'll forget him. But it took an awfully long time for official inclusion.

But do you want to hear something ironic? The most popular textbook in American history teaching, from 1911 all the way through the twentieth century, was by David Muzzey. Muzzey was a Paineite; he adored Thomas Paine, and he reinserted Paine into these official books. Muzzey was regularly in attendance at the Thomas Paine National Historical Association gatherings. He became a professor at Columbia University and was a lecturer in the Ethical Culture Society in New York, and held the Gouverneur Morris Chair of History at Columbia University. (Talk about an irony.)

You also asked about schools, where we should use Paine in the schools. Obviously, we should use him in literature classes and American history classes. When we teach the American Revolution—Adams and others lay claim to a Massachusetts legacy for the Revolution—it's not a Revolution until *Common Sense*. By the way, *Common Sense* is so readable.

You can't take students under 21 years old to a tavern and re-enact *Common Sense* being read in the taverns. But it would be fun to imagine these students reading *Common Sense* out loud, or *The Crisis* out loud, to hear the words, let them feel it physically. I think that would be a good place to start.

Then I would talk to them about those many Americans who continued to quote Paine, including Ronald Reagan (since we are here in California) and also Barry Goldwater. By the way, I'll tell the Barry Goldwater story quickly. One of the most famous lines in American politics of the twentieth century is from Barry Goldwater's 1964 speech, "extremism in the defense of liberty is no vice." But I bet you didn't know those are Thomas Paine's words. Harry Jaffa, who is the godfather of the Claremont Institute, is one of those rare conservative Republicans who really liked Thomas Paine. He wrote Goldwater's speech. I interviewed him. He couldn't remember where he found the words (I actually re-found them for him). The words are: "moderation in temper is always a virtue, moderation in principle is a species of vice" and are from Paine's "Letter to the Addressers on the Late Proclamation Against Seditious Writings." Jaffa took the phrase and made it, "extremism in the defense of liberty is no vice." For all the courage that the Goldwater-ites seemed to have, they couldn't actually bring themselves to quote Thomas Paine's name in front of the Republican convention, probably because they imagined it would have turned off the entire crowd.

Question: I agree with you. I don't think there is any great contradiction between Paine and the Second Great Awakening. That supports the idea that Paine was actually respectful of religion. There is a paper, in one of the *Prospect* papers. *The Prospect* was a deistic journal edited by Elihu Palmer. There is one short piece by Paine on the religious revival. I think that Paine actually saw in the Second Great Awakening, in religious revival, something that must have pleased him, because it was a way for a number of people to shape Christianity in the way they wanted. You said that some text by Paine had been reproduced in one of those Evangelical journals during the early 1800s. Which journal?

Harvey Kaye: It was the *Herald Of Gospel Liberty*. The text was *Common Sense*. I'll add (as long as you've asked about the 18-teens, when Paine was supposedly forgotten) in Kentucky,

Unitarians and Baptists and Presbyterians argued about the future of Transylvania College, and they were all quoting Thomas Paine in their letters to the editors. If Baptists and Presbyterians were quoting Paine, it means they were reading him. It's not the case that Paine was ever forgotten in the 18-teens. Michael Wallace, in his Pulitzer Prize-winning history, *Gotham*, has a line saying, when Evangelicals or missionaries came down to the New York waterfront in the early 18-teens to try to convert the longshoremen, longshoremen would reach in their back pocket and pull out *The Age Of Reason* as if a vampire had just approached, saying "stay away." The problem is that it is very hard to document anything more than this kind of anecdotal moment. I mean, how many people sat down or did oral histories with longshoremen in the 18-teens? We do not know the actual extent of things.

Question: I was glad to hear all the citations of people tapping into Paine over the last couple hundred years, but it still seems like the average person knows his name but really doesn't know anything about him. Do you have any thoughts about how to resurrect his memory among the average person?

Harvey Kaye: I'm glad you asked that question because one of the reasons I began this book project is every time I would mention that I had written a young adult biography or that I was working on Thomas Paine, someone would say, "I have a brother who loves Thomas Paine, or my sister, or my father." In fact, I decided to write the book because I felt that Americans knew Paine, but didn't know him. In other words, I figured that Americans had a deep cultural memory of Thomas Paine, but didn't have a formal academic memory of Thomas Paine. Furthermore, for those of us who are Liberals or Progressives, if we're ever going to reclaim American public and political life, what we need to do is tap into that deep cultural memory, not so that people can pass a test on Paine's life, but so that they can see for themselves just how deeply imbued with that democratic spirit they are. I would argue it's true for Evangelicals as well. I wanted to do this book to remind Americans of what they felt, but didn't necessarily know in a deliberate and conscious way. The analogy is that Paine wrote *Common Sense,* not because he didn't think Americans knew what was going on, but because he knew that inside they had these sensibilities.

    I will close with one more story. There was a Vermont minister, Samuel Williams, who in a 1790s work on the history of Vermont said (I wish I had the exact words with me) that Paine taught to Americans what he learned from them. What a great thought. What a brilliant way of putting it. Paine would have agreed exactly.

PANEL 1:
TRICKS OF TOM'S TRADE: LANGUAGE USE AND RHETORICAL DEVICES

Introduction: Elsie Begler

Good morning, and welcome to San Diego State University. A particular welcome from the College of Arts and Letters, the host of this symposium. I am Elsie Begler, Director of the International Studies Education Project at SDSU, and the organizer of this symposium. I am not a historian. My doctorate is in anthropology, and the project I direct works primarily with K-12 teachers, trying to improve international education and expand global perspectives in teaching. My first experience with Thomas Paine—an experience that left a lasting impression—was when I was in high school and read Howard Fast's *Citizen Tom Paine*. Ever since, I have thought of Paine as "a citizen of the world," so my role as symposium organizer is not as far afield for me as it may initially seem.

We have a full program and a tightly packed schedule for the next two days, with stellar speakers and wonderful panelists. I hope that all of you will actively participate as citizens in the coming discussions about Paine and his writings, and will have a good time as well. If you have any logistical questions or problems, there are a number of staff people around who can help. At this point, I'm going to pass the microphone to Dr. Tony Freyer, who will be moderating our first panel.

Moderator: Tony Freyer

I was an undergraduate here almost 40 years ago, and this symposium is a real testament to the continuing tradition of excellence at SDSU that inspired me to pursue a career as a historian. I am grateful to be able to participate in this example of how that tradition has continued. This first panel can be seen as an introduction to the subject of the symposium in general. In examining the "Tricks of Tom's Trade," we will see that Paine was, above all, a brilliant wordsmith. We are going to see how he used language in many ways to change the course of social conflict. Yet language is never uncontroversial, for it helps to construct the reality it describes, and those who use language skillfully themselves often sit at the center of that controversy.

Our first speaker is Seth Cotlar from Willamette University. He is the author of a forthcoming book on transatlantic radicalism in the early American republic, and he will talk about Paine's readership and the effect the works had upon them. Second is Timothy Killikelly from the City University of San Francisco, who will use insights from the great theorist of radical consciousness, Antonio Gramsci, to inform his interpretation of Paine's ideas about popular culture and its use as a political force. Finally, we will turn to Hazel Burgess. Her Ph.D. is from the University of Sydney in Australia, although I gather she is originally from Melbourne. She focuses upon Paine as a paid propagandist, in a paper that is quite controversial and is likely to be contested by some others at this conference. In addition, joining the panel for our discussion is Sophia Rosenfeld from the University of Virginia.

TOM PAINE'S READERS AND THE MAKING OF DEMOCRATIC CITIZENS IN THE AGE OF REVOLUTIONS

Seth Cotlar

Let me start by drawing attention to one word in my title, "Readers." There are two very different yet related ways in which I've been thinking about reading in the eighteenth century. One is methodological. I have been very influenced by the work of French cultural historian Roger Chartier, a pioneer in writing what we might call the history of the book, expanding the subfield to include the history of reading. The fundamental insight of his work is that the meaning of any particular text resides not solely (or even primarily) in the intention of the author or within the actual words in a text, but in the meanings that readers produced during their interaction with and subsequent use of a text.[1] We might call this a history of reception rather than a history of publication. Such an approach opens the door to an intellectual history told from the bottom up, putting the consumers of ideas at the center of the story.

When we locate the production of meaning at the point of reception rather than the point of authorship, it requires us to know a wide range of things that historians of ideas never cared much about in the past. Who read a particular text and who didn't? How did the text get where it did? What was the physical form in which someone encountered a body of ideas? Were they excerpted in newspapers, read aloud in a tavern, or read silently and alone in someone's study? What did readers do with the ideas they encountered in a text? Did they select certain features for particular emphasis, features that perhaps were not central to the author? How, in other words, did the context in which people read a text shape their response to it and the meanings they got out of it? Seen in this way, the intellectual history of something like Paine's *Rights of Man* becomes less about what Paine did, and more about how this text was reproduced, circulated, received, and contested. What I am about to say is based on reading thousands of newspapers over the course of years. I hope to show that viewing Paine through the eyes of his newspaper readers produces insights about his historical significance that we could not arrive at by merely reading Paine's text itself.

Yet one need not be a French cultural historian to think reading is important, for the politics of reading was an explicitly thematized aspect of 1790s political theory, especially among the community of democrats that gathered around Paine and his writings. This is the second point regarding my study of "readers," that there was in history a late eighteenth-century conversation about the politics of popular reading. Everyone in this room, I assume, knows the story about how *Common Sense* was read by almost every American and how Paine's style was unprecedented in its ability to communicate political ideas to an audience that was not formally educated or used to thinking of itself as part of the political class. But we have barely begun to learn about what became of that new community of people who were ushered into political consciousness by *Common Sense*. Paine himself commented on how revolutionary moments transform those who live through them, expanding ordinary citizens' sense of the politically possible: "There is existing in man, a mass of sense lying in a dormant state, and which, unless something excites it to action, will descend with him, in that condition to the grave. As it is to the advantage of society that the whole of its faculties should be employed, the construction of government ought to be such as to bring forward, by a quiet and regular operation, all that extent of capacity which never fails to appear in revolutions."[2]

Democratic printers and activists in America and throughout the Atlantic world took up Paine's charge in the 1790s as they created new outlets for these popular political energies, and that place was in the newspapers and popular pamphlet market that exploded in the 1790s. What I want to stress about these popular political reading practices is how new and experimental they were, and how self-conscious Paineite authors and newspaper editors were about their efforts to transform both the consciousness of individual citizen-readers and the broader society they inhabited. Rather than focusing on formal, electoral politics, these activists saw widespread reading as the best way to make politics more literally about self-rule, for it could break the monopoly that a constricted political class continued to have on political opinion and policy-making.

These utopian hopes about the power of popular reading partly explain why the 1790s witnessed an explosion of print. The number of newspapers almost tripled in that decade, and the rate of expansion in newspapers was four times greater than the rate of population increase. Also, pamphlets, especially European ones, began flooding the American print market at unprecedented rates due to the economic recovery of the decade and the expanded ability for American booksellers to get credit from their British counterparts. Virtually every European who visited America in the 1790s seconded the Duke de La Liancourt Rochefoucault's observation that "every one here . . . takes an interest in state affairs, is extremely eager to learn the news of the day, and discusses politics as well as he is able." He was astonished to find that "from the landlord down to the house-maid they all read two newspapers a day."[3] British traveler Henry Wansey was likewise amazed to find himself in a carriage with two men who were reading a pamphlet that had been printed only a week before he had left London. He described the ordinary citizens he met on his travels as "great politicians" who were "ready to ask me more questions than I was inclined to answer, though I am far from being reserved."[4] In sum, both the statistics and the accounts of European travelers suggest that the 1790s witnessed a dramatic expansion in popular reading, much of which was oriented around the international political events of that tumultuous decade.

To understand the political significance of this reading explosion, it is important to take into account how differently people read in the eighteenth century. Historians of reading have argued that the eighteenth century was still dominated by public or social reading practices, rather than the private reading that would become the norm by the last half of the nineteenth century. Newspapers in particular, especially the ones most likely to sympathetically reprint portions of Paine's works or pieces by his democratic compatriots, were more likely to be read aloud to others in taverns or family homes than read silently and in isolation. They were also read in workshops. Many workers would get together and buy a subscription to a newspaper. They would keep it in the workshop, and occasionally one person would read it to the others as they were working.

The majority of the news in these newspapers was about foreign affairs, and the democratically-oriented newspapers spun that foreign news in very particular ways. The editors of these newspapers seemed particularly drawn to stories that showed how the organized and increasingly assertive ordinary citizens of Europe were forming political societies to bring about reform and to educate laborers about political theory. These newspapers thus created face-to-face and imaginary communities of readers, and then introduced these readers to models of how ordinary citizens could organize themselves to accomplish political goals.

The Americans who were most excited about this new emerging world of reader-citizens saw the publication of the *Rights of Man* as a crucial turning point in the history of popular reading. In May of 1791, for example, several democratic papers reprinted the same story from a London paper about the "immense" demand for the *Rights of Man*: "Upon publication of the first edition, upwards of twelve thousand copies were sold off in sheets, wet from the press; and the remainder of that edition entirely disposed of in a few hours after its first appearance. Upon the coming out of the second edition, it was found almost impossible to supply the orders; and at the date above mentioned, the third edition was already in press."[5]

These inspirational stories about democratic readers scurrying home with ink-stained hands to read Paine's latest work served the interests of American printers quite well. Not only were they themselves reprinting, selling, and hoping to profit from Paine's latest tracts, but they also sought to create a citizenry animated by the same sense of political urgency that drove ordinary Europeans to flock to the print shops. A March, 1793, essay in the *National Gazette* crisply summarized the hopes that American democrats invested in Paine's reemergence on the political scene: describing a wave of popular politicization in Ireland, the author of the piece noted that "since Paine's *Rights of Man* has made its appearance: almost every one is turned politician."[6]

By consistently presenting foreign news in this manner, democratic editors encouraged their readers not only to remember, but also to reconceptualize the role they had played and eventually could play in generating historical change. The Americans who advertised their 1791 reprint of a radical pamphlet by Englishman David Williams, for example, trumpeted his new democratic theory of historical change as one of the pamphlet's primary selling points. They acknowledged that readers might find the author's bottom-up account of the American Revolution "strange" because it ascribed the success of the revolution to "the spirit of the people" rather than "the mere personal merit of the few." This new conception of historical causality was important for American readers to comprehend, however, for only then could they grasp the full meaning of Europe's "REVOLUTION *without leaders*," an event that they considered "unexampled in history."[7] In sympathetic pamphlet and newspaper accounts of the early 1790s, the democratic protagonists were rarely great military or political leaders like George Washington or Lafayette. Rather, they were usually organizations that identified themselves as representatives of the people that worked toward their goal in part by holding public meetings, but mostly by disseminating their ideas in printed form.

Democratic editors in America identified this new vision of print as one of the principal ways in which the French Revolution marked a radical break from the political past. As reported in American democratic papers, the story of the French Revolution was a radically new one about an ongoing process of democratization through dissemination. Editors framed the French Revolution as a "new scene . . . in the Theatre of human affairs" in which politics ceased to be "the study and benefit of the *few* to the exclusion and depression of the *many*." Since no one could deny that a portion of the national sovereignty resided "in the breast of every individual," it was now clear that all legitimate political decisions must flow from "the actual information of all" and not the wisdom of a chosen few.[8]

In the 1790s no one symbolized this emerging world of potentially revolutionary, plebeian reader-citizens more than Thomas Paine. Paine was a useful figure for these advocates of democratic reading, since his reputation as an American patriot rendered him fairly unassailable at first. As an enemy of aristocracy and monarchy, he said little that was threatening to an American leadership class that had abandoned these ascriptive forms of power and inequality. Indeed, it is almost impossible to find a critique of Paine until 1793 and into 1794. It did not take long, however, before democratic newspapers started using stories about Paine as a way to criticize an emerging American elite, consistently framing Paine as an advocate for the poor and someone who espoused policies that would benefit them and cultural practices that would politicize them. This popular appropriation of Paine, I would argue, is largely what turned him into an increasingly polarizing figure over the course of the 1790s. As long as it was aristocrats and kings he was lambasting, American elites could concur. But once Paine became a symbol for plebeian assaults on the economic, social, and political power of the American leadership class, then he became inspirational for some, dangerous for others. In sum, the democratic editors and readers of the 1790s transformed Paine's public image from that of an American patriot into that of an international working-class hero. While there is little evidence that Paine himself sought to play that role, it was eventually what his readers, both sympathetic and hostile, turned him into.

As soon as the *Rights of Man* appeared in 1791, Paine became a regular topic of discussion in newspapers, especially those that identified themselves as democratic. Paine's emergence as an inspirational polestar for American democrats in the 1790s marked a major reversal in his public career, for he had fallen into relative obscurity preceding the publication of the *Rights of Man,* Part I in 1791. Paine's reputation had suffered badly during the Silas Deane affair in 1778-79, and for the next decade his writings on political affairs were far less influential than *Common Sense* and *The Crisis* papers had been. While many newspapers commented upon Paine's departure from the country in 1787, almost none done did so in such a way as to suggest that Paine would be missed. I collected data from newspapers, searching for hits on the name "Paine." They show that the publication of the *Rights of Man* quickly brought Paine back into the center of the American popular imagination. While the data are imprecise in a number of ways, it seems reasonable to claim that Paine's name appeared in the average American newspaper only once every four or five months in 1790, while in 1791 and 1792 a newspaper reader would encounter a story about him at least once a month.[9] One historian has estimated that between 50,000 and 100,000 copies of the *Rights of Man* circulated in America, a remarkable number considering that few pamphlets were printed in multiple editions and the usual print run was smaller than 2000.[10] Throughout the 1790s, everything Paine published in Europe was re-printed in America, usually in multiple editions. Meanwhile, three different versions of his collected writings were produced in Albany (1794), Baltimore (1796), and Philadelphia (1797). Based on publication as well as citation statistics, over the course of the 1790s Paine rapidly moved from the periphery of American discourse back into the center.

As the figure of Tom Paine became more prominent in the 1790s, it also became more radical. Most of the newspaper articles that discussed him and his work linked him explicitly to the ongoing struggle to give ordinary citizens a greater voice in public debate. Democratic newspapers played up Paine's background as a staymaker, and they drew particular attention to the sections of his writings where he aggressively asserted his right, as a non-elite and non-elected citizen, to voice his opinions on political matters. An anonymous newspaper essayist in Philadelphia defended his right to participate in public debate by noting that "It is well enough in England to run down the rights of man, because the author of those inimitable pamphlets was a *stay-maker*; but in the United States all such proscriptions of certain classes of citizens, or occupations, should be avoided."[11]

This Paineite style of plebeian assertion suffused not only the newspapers but also the growing number of democratic pamphlets that were printed in the 1790s, such as the *Democratic Songster* and *Paine's Jests*, the latter being an inexpensive British pamphlet reprinted in two American editions in 1794 and 1796. The editor of this collection of radical songs, jokes, and anecdotes introduced them by mimicking the words of anti-Paineite elites: "Beware of that fatal error of judging for yourselves. What! think for yourselves! O let me intreat, nay let me insist upon it, that you never think of *thinking for yourselves*; for the more you *think*, the more you will differ from [your betters] in your way of thinking: Think also, how many mild, happy and glorious Constitutions have been ruined by men thinking *for themselves*! Let your betters, therefore, think for you; because it stands to reason, they must think *best*."[12] The songs and jokes in this 100-page pamphlet focused almost exclusively on the injustices of British society, framing both the law and the current political system as corrupt means by which gross inequalities of wealth and power were perpetuated. The pamphlet ridiculed the pretensions of elites, and celebrated the wisdom of ordinary people and their new unwillingness to accept their status as second-class citizens. As democratic printers in America tried to inspire their readers to embrace such a self-assertive style of citizenship, Tom Paine served as an effective legitimizing symbol for such practices. This perhaps helps us explain why they would entitle the pamphlet *Paine's Jests*, when it contained nothing that was actually written by Paine.

Much as he had done in 1776, Paine set the terms of public political debate for much of the 1790s, and just as George Washington had become an iconic symbol of the American Revolution, Paine quickly emerged as the figurehead of the new revolutionary movements now sweeping the Atlantic world.[13] That said, Paine was a figurehead of a very different sort. Whereas Washington was a man to be idolized and followed, Paine was someone to emulate. The figure of Washington hovered in the unreachable distance, for his greatness lay in his uniqueness. Paine, on the other hand, embodied a new popular political assertiveness that was accessible to everyone and seemed to be percolating to the surface around the Atlantic basin, at least according to the newspapers of the 1790s. Indeed, the stories that both his detractors and his supporters told about him implied that Paine's writings worked like a virus, entering into the mental world of readers and then replicating Paine's political subjectivity over and over again.

By the time of the Alien and Sedition Acts of 1798, it became common to refer to Paineite tracts as forms of contagion that diseased the minds of readers, but even as early as 1791 when the *Rights of Man* was published many people feared the political effect that Paine's writings were having on the political attitudes of their social inferiors.[14] A Frenchman traveling in Virginia in that year, for example, provoked a hysterical response from a gout-ridden old planter when he mentioned Paine's name. "The Virginian, at the mere mention of Payne, moved his bad leg, looked steadily at me with angry eyes, and interrupted me, exclaimed furiously: 'I wish that Thomas Payne and all the people like him had been hanged before the American Revolution.'" In the eyes of people like this Virginian, Paine and "the people like him" symbolized a threatening new world of politically assertive commoners. His only response was to eye Bayard "from head to foot" and then leave "without saying another word." Bayard took his parting shot by walking away whistling the revolutionary tune, "Ça Ira," thus suggesting that people like Paine were all around and not about to be intimidated into silence.[15]

Paine's unique place in the public discourse of the 1790s suggests that he was not just one writer among many with whom one could dispassionately choose to agree or disagree. Rather, he embodied a social type that was perceived as threatening by some and inspirational by others. Indeed, the figure of the assertive, plebeian reader became a prominent trope in 1790s political discourse throughout the Atlantic world, deployed by both opponents and supporters of democratization, though to different ends. The British government twice put Thomas Paine and his publishers on trial—in December of 1792 for the *Rights of Man, Part 2* and in June of 1797 for *The Age of Reason*—and both times the state's argument focused not on the content of the texts, but rather on the effect they would have on ordinary readers. The prosecutors conceded that Paine made few arguments that hadn't already appeared in print, print that did not approach the boundary of the treasonous. Even the first part of *Rights of Man* did not merit prosecution because "it was ushered into the world in that shape, that it was likely to fall only into the hands of tolerably informed persons." The second part of *Rights of Man* differed, however, for it "appeared in a smaller size, printed on white brown paper, and thrust into the hands of all persons, of all ages, sexes, and conditions: They were even wrapped up with sweet meats for children."[16]

The fear was not just that the lower orders would be deluded, but that they would be inspired by what they read in Paine's works. The very name "Tom Paine" gained a remarkable degree of infamy amongst those who thought themselves uniquely entitled to power and deference. It conjured up memories of disobedient servants, rebellious slaves, insouciant children—in sum, social subordinates who refused to play their assigned role. Ironically enough, these fears themselves then became a source of greater inspiration for the Atlantic world's democrats as the transcripts of Paine's trials—as well as the trials of seven other Paineite activists who sought to disseminate democratic tracts—were printed in numerous editions in Britain and America.[17] The trial transcripts expressed the fears of the British government about the dissemination of Paine's ideas. In turn, the transcripts became more fodder for the democrats, who pointed to them and said, "Look how these people are afraid of you and what you are reading."

The democratic editors of the 1790s frequently printed anecdotes that dramatized this mode of self-assertive citizenship, thus translating abstract ideas about citizenship into concrete examples of how a politically energized person could find the confidence to challenge local authority figures. One of my favorite stories is from the trial of Thomas Muir. It's a story of a woman who works for him, whose job was to go out and buy Paine's tracts and then deposit them in local barbershops and other places. She herself says: Oh yes, of course I read them. The prosecutor is shocked and appalled that this working-class woman had read Tom Paine, and the democratic newspapers then print this. Similarly, for example, at the same time that New York's leading democratic printer, Thomas Greenleaf, was advertising *Paine's Jests* for sale in his shop, he inserted the following dialogue between a Tory and a young republican in his *New York Journal*:

> While watching a procession honoring William Keteltas, a lawyer who had defended Irish laborers who had been insulted by a city official, the young republican overheard the Tory sniff, "What a set of raggamuffins are these . . . there is not a man of respectability among them!" / I doubt, sir, answered the young man, if you are perfectly right in pronouncing so freely concerning these men. Is money, sir, or merit, the object of your respect? / T. Why both, to be sure. / R. I beg leave to dispute your opinion then — Those who follow here, may be the most meritorious men; good husbands, good fathers, and good citizens; men by whose mechanical labours the necessaries and conveniences of life are produced in abundance, and by whose courage and sufferings the pride of an invading foe may be humbled . . . / T. Tut, tut man, you want a little more experience in the world to be a judge of this matter. / R. This is evading the question, sir; however, I confess that my experience has not been so great as some others, but it has been sufficient to convince me, that although the possession of riches is in itself no crime, yet that it is the consequence of many . . . The RICH, generally speaking, have always made a party against the poor. / T. I have nothing more to say, your ideas are so incongruous, that I find it impossible to argue with you. A good day, sir. / R.

> I cannot but wish you a change of sentiment, and that the triumph of reason may be complete. A good day, Sir."[18]

By repeatedly dramatizing social encounters where non-elite citizens refused to defer to their supposed social betters, democratic editors sought to model a new, class-inflected form of citizenship that put Paineite egalitarianism into daily practice.

How effective were these newspapers and other forms of print in producing an army of assertive Paineite citizens in America? We have a wealth of evidence from British archives, that are filled with reports from that government's extensive network of counter-revolutionary spies and voluntary informers who documented in great detail the evolution of radical groups around the country, including information about the taverns and workingmen's clubs teeming with Paine's readers. For example, one worried Sheffield magistrate informed his local MP that the poor of his town believed "that the *Rights of Man*, can justify an opposition to the usual and Reciprocal Duties of Masters and Servants, in so much that I fear the former will be in subjection to the latter who will constantly dictate all the terms of their Connections."[19] Put another way, the workers were casting off their traditional deference and refusing to play their allotted role as social inferiors.

Unfortunately, such detailed evidence does not exist for the American reception of Paine's ideas. It is not unreasonable, however, to assume that his work had similar effects on American readers. In the *Rights of Man*, Paine himself noted how revolutionary eras can have a transformative effect on the consciousness of ordinary people: "One finds oneself changed, one scarcely knows how." From my reading of the newspapers and pamphlets of the 1790s, it is clear that this phrase of Paine captured one of the key, yet often overlooked dimensions of what happened in that decade—people found their political consciousness changed, but it was still unclear what the consequences of these changes would be.

I would like to end with an overly brief and intentionally provocative set of assertions about this new political consciousness that Paine's example encouraged, and which his readers tentatively began to embrace in the 1790s. Many of Paine's modern interpreters have seen Paine and his admirers as bourgeois radicals—people who thought of themselves not as members of a structurally disadvantaged working class, but rather as independent, liberal subjects capable of making what they wanted of themselves once the artificial barriers of aristocracy, monarchy, and mercan-tilism were pushed aside. From this perspective, Paine's writings appear as straightforward endorsements of the laissez-faire economy and representative democracy that have come to define what we might call "the dominant American ideology" of the post-World War II era. There is much ammunition to be found in Paine's writings for the claim that he imagined a future that resembled Ronald Reagan's vision of America. In the 1770s and 1780s he distanced himself from the rough and tumble working-class culture that was emerging around him in Philadelphia, rejecting the crowd action and popular appeals for price controls that informed the moral economy of the early American laboring class. Like Reagan, he pronounced government a "necessary evil" in *Common Sense* and called for an end to all governmental interference in the free market. He was a scathing critic of entrenched power, but in his eyes it was primarily aristocratic and monarchical privilege that lay behind these unjust forms of power. Until the 1790s, the privilege of the moneyed few did not concern him; indeed, he saw the distinction between the rich and the poor as a natural result of people's different abilities.

Yet, despite the fact that he did not set out to become a working-class hero, that is precisely what he became in the 1790s, in the eyes of both his laboring-class supporters and his elite detractors. Paine is partly responsible for the increasingly class-inflected nature of his popular support. At the very end of the *Rights of Man, Part 2*, written in 1792, Paine sketched out a set of institutional remedies for systemic poverty, and these passages became the most oft-quoted and referred to sections of this tract that was probably the largest-selling book of the decade. In 1796 Paine expanded these ideas in *Agrarian Justice*, garnering him even more support from those people in Britain and America who saw economic inequality as an issue that was just as important as (if not more so than) political equality. The message was this—political change, the expansion of the right to vote, and the creation of republican governments were not sufficient to create a just society. A rough degree of economic equality was also essential, and a freely operating market was not able to ensure this.

For Paine, these insights were important but not central. Yet for his readers throughout the Atlantic world, this critique of economic inequality became one of the key things that Paine stood for. Paine became a working-class hero, in other words, in some part because of his own transformation in the 1790s, but primarily because the increasingly independent working-class movement that emerged in Britain (and to a lesser extent in America) adopted Paine as their central figurehead, and they selectively chose aspects of his writings that resonated with their emerging critique of the growing economic inequality that accompanied the expansion of commerce.[20]

In many ways, Paine was a follower as much as a leader in this transformation of his ideas about the relationship between economics and politics. None of his ideas was profoundly original, and many of his arguments had appeared in newspaper articles and pamphlets produced by plebeian radicals who were his contemporaries. But originality was never Paine's strong suit—it was his ability to take ideas that were emerging on the streets, in the homes, and in the taverns surrounding him, and render them in print as serious political theory. Throughout the 1790s in America, Paine played the role of the bard who gave public voice to the highest aspirations of his democratically-minded readers. He had the capacity to take ideas that were percolating about, organize and focus them, and cast them out loudly with his microphone.

By the time he returned to America in 1802—long after the utopian excitement of the age of revolutions had passed and in the midst of the ascendancy of a Jeffersonian party eager to demonstrate its respectability by purging itself of the more Jacobinical elements of its coalition—Paine had been transformed into a figure of discord and danger, an infidel and a Jacobin who polluted the minds of Americans with French-inflected poison. It is telling of just how dangerous Paine was perceived to be that the two months when he was most frequently and fervently discussed in America's press were November and December of 1802 when he returned to the United States. Paine's name was mentioned more than once for every newspaper that was printed in this period, and almost all of those mentions are negative. The stories were no longer about Paine the staymaker turned political theorist—they were about Paine the drunkard, Paine the atheist, Paine the bloodthirsty Jacobin. He had become a magnet for vilification. A few true believers welcomed Paine back to America, but for the most part, the nation banished Paine and his followers to the supposedly irrelevant radical fringe of the political nation. Generations of children were weaned on stories about Paine the pathetic drunkard. It would take much hard work, as Eric Foner discussed earlier in this conference, for the radical democrats of the nineteenth and twentieth centuries to teach American readers to re-conceive of Paine as an inspiration, rather than as a threat to what America could be. Thank you.

Notes

[1] Roger Chartier, *Cultural History: Between Practices and Representations*, trans. Lydia G. Cochrane, (Ithaca: Cornell University Press, 1988). The theme is developed more fully in my forthcoming book, *Making Democracy Safe for the New Nation: The Rise and Fall of Trans-Atlantic Radicalism in the Early American Republic*, to be published by the University of Virginia Press.

[2] Thomas Paine, *Rights of Man* (New York: Hugh Gaine, 1792) Part the Second, Ch. 3.

[3] *Travels through the United States of North America: The Country of the Iroquois, and Upper Canada, in the Years 1795, 1796, and 1797; with an Authentic Account of Lower Canada.* Vol.1, (London: R. Phillips, 1799), pp. 25, 399.

[4] Henry Wansey, *Journal of an Excursion to the United States of North America in the Summer of 1794.* (Salisbury: J. Easton, 1796), pp. 56, 61. This paragraph offers just a small sampling of travelers' descriptions of newspapers and politics. See also Pierre Dupont de Numours comment in 1800 that "a large part of the nation reads the Bible, all of it assiduously peruse[s] the newspapers. The fathers read them aloud to their children while the mothers are preparing breakfast." Quoted in Donald Steward, *The Opposition Press of the Federalist Era.* (Albany, N.Y.: State University of New York Press, 1969), p. 630.

[5] *New York Journal & Patriotic Register* (May 21, 1791). The same piece also appeared in the [Philadelphia] *Independent Gazetteer* on May 28, 1791.

[6] *National Gazette* (Philadelphia, Mar. 13, 1793).

[7] James Mackintosh, *Vindiciae Gallicae* (Philadelphia: Will-iam Young, 1792), p. 65.

[8] *American Daily Advertiser* (Philadelphia, Jan.3, 1795).

[9] These numbers are based on averages, and I suspect that the frequency of hits for Paine in self-consciously democratic newspapers would be significantly higher than in other newspapers. Also, Paine's ideas were often discussed in newspaper without reference to his name, so the extent of his presence in public discourse after the *Rights of Man* is probably severely understated by these statistics.

[10] On the printing history of the *Rights of Man* in America see Alfred Young, "Common Sense and the Rights of Man in America: The Celebration and Damnation of Thomas Paine," in *Science, Mind, and Art: Essays on Science and the Humanistic Understanding in Art, Epistemology, Religion, and Ethics in Honor of Robert S. Cohen*, eds. Kostas Gavroglu, et. al. (Dordrecht: Kluwer Academic Publishers, 1995), pp. 411-38.

[11] *National Gazette* (Philadelphia, Dec. 12, 1792).

[12] *Tom Paine's Jests* (Philadelphia: Mathew Carey,1796).

[13] Although Paine was the central figure of this cosmopolitan movement, many other European authors garnered significant attention from American readers. In 1791, James MacKintosh, the author of a scathing anti-Burke pamphlet entitled *Vindicae Gallicae*, was named in many toasts in tandem with Paine. After Joel Barlow's *Advice to the Privileged Orders* appeared in 1792, his name began to appear with great regularity as an important friend to Paine and the rights of man. Likewise, when printers Francis Childs and John Swaine brought out an American edition of David Williams's *Lessons to a Young Prince* in 1791 they made the case for its signifi-

cance by explicitly linking it to Paine's work: "the quiet and unmolested, and unmenaced publication and circulation of this book, Mr. Paine's Rights of Man, &c. through Great Britain, evidently proves that a Revolution has already been effectuated on the minds of the people there" (New York: Childs and Swaine, 1791). This is just one example of how American printers capitalized on Paine's fame in order to sell the works of other European radicals. The result was that American democrats quickly became familiar with a wide range of European texts which, had they not been linked to Paine's political project, would never have found a market of American readers.

[14]For a discussion of the demonization of Paineites in during the Alien and Sedition crisis, see Seth Cotlar, "The Federalists' Transatlantic Cultural Offensive of 1798 and the Moderation of American Democratic Discourse," in Jeffrey L. Pasley, Andrew W. Robertson, and David Waldstreicher, eds., *Beyond the Founders: New Approaches to the Political History of the Early American Republic* (Chapel Hill: University of North Carolina Press, 2004), pp. 274-99.

[15]Ferdinand Marie Bayard, *Travels of a Frenchman in Maryland and Virginia*, trans. Ben C. McCary, (Ann Arbor: Edwards Brothers, 1950), p. 61.

[16]*The Trial of Thomas Paine, for a Libel, contained in the Second Part of Rights of Man*, (Boston: I. Thomas and E. T. Andrews, 1793).

[17]The following trials of British Paineite radicals were reprinted in America between 1793 and 1796: Tom Paine for the Rights of Man (3 editions); London bookseller Daniel Isaac Eaton (1 edition); Scottish lawyer Thomas Muir (4 editions); United Irishman Archibald Hamilton Rowan (1 edition); English lawyer and former resident of Philadelphia Joseph Gerrald (1 edition); English reformers Thomas Watt and David Downie (2 editions); Thomas Walker and five other Manchester radicals (2 editions); and Scottish radical Maurice Margarot (2 editions).

[18]*Greenleaf's New-York Journal, & Patriotic Register* (Apr. 19, 1796).

[19][Unknown author] to the 4th Early Fitzwilliam (May 29, 1792), Sheffield Archives, Wentworth Woodhouse Muniments, F. 44 (a) p. 29.

[20]This argument is more fully developed in Seth Cotlar, "Radical Conceptions of Economic Equality and Property Rights in the Early American Republic: The Trans-Atlantic Dimension." *Explorations in Early American Culture*, vol. 4 (2000), 191-219.

EXAMINING COMMON SENSE: A GRAMSCIAN ANALYSIS OF THOMAS PAINE

Thomas Killikelly

This is an analysis of Thomas Paine's "common sense," not only his famous pamphlet with that title, but also as the concept was developed by Antonio Gramsci. It is an attempt to see Paine's work through the lens of Gramsci's common sense. Gramsci's common sense is a tool for the critical analysis of change, how it occurs, and what are its obstacles and limits. In examining common sense, Gramsci focused on folklore, language, and people's everyday beliefs.

Thomas Paine's dilemma can be summed up in the question, "What is a revolutionary intellectual to do?" On the one hand, to move society forward in a progressive direction you need to critique the existing common sense among the masses, although this may be unpopular. On the other hand, to succeed you need to employ parts of that accepted common sense to challenge the existing hegemonic rule and create a basis for a new alternative hegemony. When Paine wrote *Common Sense*, he was speaking to the mass to bring them into politics so as to increase the likelihood of creating a progressive new common sense and hegemony. Seen through the ideas of Gramsci, over the course of his revolutionary career in England, France, and the United States, Paine grappled with this dilemma to which there is no one correct solution. Throughout, he sought to articulate a previously unspoken mass voice, expressing it in a way that resonated with the mass.

Gramsci was a leader of the Italian Communist Party (PCI) during the 1920s. In 1926, after the failure of the Communist Party in Italy to spark a workers' revolution and Mussolini's rise to power, he was arrested and spent most of the rest of his life in jail, until his death in 1937. In his *Prison Notebooks*, Gramsci tried to understand why revolution did not sweep the industrial West. "In the developed capitalist countries, the ruling class possesses political and organizational reserves that it did not possess in Russia."[1] Merely seizing state power in the advanced industrial nations could be an important step in transformation, but it would not create a new hege-mony and society. "Civil society" was where the battle for the West would occur. Gramsci defined civil society as the collection of all of the private institutions that influenced the running of society: the businesses, the media, the church, unions and civic organizations, and so on. The power of "civil society" in the West created a need for different revolutionary strategy, a strategy he called a "war of position." Civil society also creates its own complex set of accepted beliefs, its own common sense. This is why addressing and understanding common sense is so critical, playing a pivotal role in Gramsci's overall world view.

The use of the term "common sense" in everyday life usually means something that everyone knows, or should know. It is what most of us believe to be real and hold to be natural. It is a way of looking at the world that seems obviously correct. For Gramsci, however, common sense is neither good sense or bad sense alone, although his connotation usually emphasizes bad sense.

> "Common sense" is 'the "philosophy of the non-philosophers", or in other words the conception of the world which is uncritically absorbed by the various social and cultural environments in which the moral individuality of the average man is developed. Common sense is not a single unique conception identical in time and space. It is "the folklore of philosophy."[2]

Common sense is where the legacy of the past and human agency meet in a piecemeal and contradictory fashion. It is the primary mode of thinking a society shares and employs.

Common sense to Gramsci is not some mere manipulation of the powerless by the powerful. It has implications that are far-reaching and can actually be used against the rulers in revolutionary ways. But as one surveys an entire set of common sense ideas, rulers must have some important elements of popular, common sense on their side if they want to maintain and create the intellectual and moral hegemony that is key to the public's acceptance of their rule as legitimate. The ruling class has an advantage in gaining mass consent. Gramsci writes, "this consent is 'historically' caused by the prestige (and consequent confidence) which the dominant group enjoys because of its position and function in the world of production."[3]

While Gramsci saw common sense as primarily an obstacle to revolutionary change, it was not unambiguous in its effects. Philosophy, to Gramsci, is lived. He is not referring to an isolated world of ideas; philosophy is integrated into everyday life. He writes, "every man finally, outside his professional activity, carries on some form of intellectual activity, that he is a philosopher, an artist, a man of taste, he participates in a particular conception of the world, has a conscious line of moral conduct, and therefore contributes to sustain a conception of the world, or to modify it, to bring into new modes of thought."[4] For Gramsci, practice is theorized after it has reached a level of common sense. The dialectical dialogue around common sense can lead to a degree of resistance to, as well as of acceptance for the hegemony of the ruling classes. Since it can create different practices, it is a realm central to political activity.

As a revolutionary, Gramsci's attack on Stalinist "economism" and "mechanism" recast the relationship between the Marxist conception of the base and super-structure, between the economic component and the social and political components. He wanted a politics where the modern political party was the vehicle for a dialectical dialogue between the common sense of the masses and the philosophy of intellectuals, who would be connected "organically" to the working-class. "Every social group, coming into existence on the original terrain of an essential function in the world of economic production, creates together with itself, organically, one or more strata of intellectuals which give it homogeneity and an awareness of its own function not only in the economic but also in the social and political fields."[5]

Gramsci used the term "intellectual" quite broadly. It does not mean only academics and philosophers, but refers to anyone whose primary function is to organize, lead, direct, or educate others. He contrasted "organic" with "traditional" or "crystallized" intellectuals, left over from older social formations who still operate as a new social order is emerging. It was the historic role of organic intellectuals to highlight the contradictions within existing common-sense consciousness and to articulate an alternative vision. The object is to challenge key elements of the dominant hegemony, in order to create a new and liberating hegemony.

To examine Gramsci's concept of common sense in relationship to Thomas Paine's *Common Sense*, one must begin with the world that Paine inhabited. Louis Hartz, for example, understands American liberal individualism as a common sense, as the "natural" perception of a nation that exceptionally escaped the feudal stage in history.[6] Similarly, Enrico Augelli and Craig Murphy identify three major aspects of American common sense: liberalism, denominational religion, and faith in science.[7] All three play a significant role in the arguments that Thomas Paine makes in *Common Sense*. Those familiar with Paine's ideas may easily see how liberalism and faith in science are part of his worldview, but knowing his anti-biblical views, they may doubt that denominational religion fits. Augelli and Murphy argue that a central element of American nationalism is the idea that America is a special place in the world and a sanctuary of liberty and opportunity, which comes from the evangelical spirit of Northeastern Puritanism. God had chosen them among all others to come to a new land, establishing the new Israel. It was a view common among liberals and radicals in England and Europe with whom Paine associated. As Paine wrote, referring to America, it is "as if the Almighty graciously meant to open a sanctuary to the persecuted in future years."[8] While this view lost its strictly religious connotations, it did not lose its missionary zeal. In the same missionary tone, Paine professes that "the sun never shined on a cause of greater worth" than the American call for independence.[9] He also made direct references to the Bible to support his arguments, which will be discussed later.

Paine articulated a sense of missionary destiny that connected the cause of American independence to a faith in science and reason. Reason became connected to support for a liberal view of the concept of individual freedom that, in turn, was seen as central to a new, barely regulated, market economy. This interrelated set of ideas became American "common sense." Further-more, the phenomenon of his bestselling *Common Sense*, its widespread dissemination and popularization, con-nected these ideas to the mass in a new way.

Because common sense is often peculiar to a particular time and place, it does not often easily translate across cultures and nations. In the case of Thomas Paine, we can examine a common sense that maintains its local particulars, but that also translates across the transatlantic world of the late eighteenth and early nineteenth centuries. Where exactly was

Thomas Paine's common sense from? Ultimately, it is more American than British, and more British than French. Paine was expressing the British liberal-radical Whig ideology that had developed from the Leveller politics of the 1640s. This view represented the London radicalism of a particular class of artisans and skilled wage-earners in the middle class who believed that the British system, particularly its hereditary politics, was keeping them down.

These views were certainly not the common sense of British society in the 1770s, but they had a more receptive audience in colonial America in the 1770s, especially in the cities. In Philadelphia, when Paine arrived in 1774, Benjamin Franklin was its emblematic hero. It was an ideology fascinated with anything scientific and painted an Enlightenment world in which science could understand what was natural. It applied this view to politics as well. It was reform-minded and supported an egalitarian and democratic politics and sought to create a republican form of government. This middle class also had strong admiration for the entrepreneurial spirit and, at least on the level of argument, supported free-trade and free-market con-cepts as central to individual freedom.

These ideas became the core of a new hegemonic thought that Paine articulated and popularized so effectively. Paine became a leader in articulating what Gramsci called a new historical bloc[10] between the middle and working classes. Colonial American politics of the 1770s saw the emergence of a less deferential artisan class. These middle-class artisans transmitted their "Ben Franklin" values to the lower-class artisans and fellow citizens. There was a spirit of egalitarian participation that was to become central to the common sense developing in America. They promoted literature, literacy, and interest in science along with values of the Protestant work ethic and prosperity. Middle-class values of hard work, prosperity, social mobility, and an ideal of an "autonomous" individual became, and remain, the moral center of American common sense. Work-ethic politics, deeply ingrained in American beliefs, is a morality tale in which the individual learns to become an effective and autonomous self, learning not to burden those around him or her, or society at large. As a hegemonic idea, it has been at times turned against the rich, as idle, arrogant, and detached for not having earned their way in the world. It has also, in ways Paine would not have recognized, been used against the poor, as lazy parasites leeching off society and unwilling to take advantage of its opportunities.

Paine's effectiveness in *Common Sense* rested upon his ability to use part of the established common sense in the culture to attack and defeat other parts of that common sense. He was using one element that people had hooked onto, merging it into the worldview he was supporting, and distancing it from the other parts of the world that he wanted to destroy. His arguments were not new, but his style helped give these ideas a popular voice, and in turn he became known as the principal articulator of the newly emerging American common sense.

An example of Paine's argumentation is seen in his critique of the hereditary monarchy and the idea of a "perfect balance" presumed among the Crown, Lords, and Commons in Britain. According to Paine, mankind is originally equal in birth; only oppression and avarice create the distinction between ruler and ruled, rich and poor, King and subject. He asks, "What do Kings do?"[11] This question suggests the emerging bourgeois work ethic of the class for which Paine speaks. Moreover, Paine wrote that the British system was comprised of two parts tyranny, one part republican.[12] The republican part, centered in the House of Commons, is the basis of his attack on the monarchy and the development of a new system. Paine's rhetoric, seen through Gramsci's concept of common sense, shows how common sense often changes. Some element of the established common sense is challenged, using part of the old idea as the basis for the new. The purpose of the House of Commons, to Paine, was to check the King who cannot be trusted because the thirst for absolute power is a natural disease of monarchy. The King and the House of Lords exist arbitrarily, tend toward the tyrannical, and add nothing to the freedom of the people. The essential flaw in the British system was that the checking relationship was reversed; it was the King who was assured an absolute check over commoners. Paine called this an absurdity, which it was from the standpoint of pure republican principles.

A widely used form of argument is to string together and connect a series of interrelated common sense ideas. This can be done even when one is making an argument against a particular common sense in order to create a new common sense. Paine's argument against hereditary succession and monarchy essentially follows a variety of interrelated, emerging common senses dealing with liberalism and its central themes: individualism, a strong work ethic, an egalitarian relationship of rulers to ruled, an affinity for finding what is natural, and using reason and science in justification.

Paine argues that the acceptance of monarchy is a lessening and degradation of ourselves, individually and collectively. Hereditary succession gives someone an honor that they do not deserve. Honor can only belong to the individual and can not be given to an heir. Hereditary succession is unnatural, falsely assuming that the original King was honorable. Later on, stories and fables were developed to justify and legitimize this succession. Those who think of themselves as born to rule become insolent and are poisoned by their own self-importance, nor, he shows, does hereditary succession bring stability and order; Britain had eight civil wars from the time of the Magna Carta until the American Revolution.[13]

It is important to note how Paine uses religious citations as part of his anti-monarchial treatise in *Common Sense*. Considering the anti-Christian rhetoric in Paine's *The Age of Reason*, it might seem ironic that he was so concerned with making sure that his points were supported by Scripture. Paine's foray into Biblical text highlights his understanding of the common sense of the colonies. He understood that an appeal to Protestant evangelical elements was important in building and articulating the broad coalition in creating this historic bloc that could bring a new vision of power and a new hegemony into existence. It was recognition of the importance of religious dissent as one stream of the American Revolution,[14] and in particular of the perceived and unwanted potential imposition of an Anglican Bishop in America. Although Paine could be seen here as manipulative, his behavior accords with what Gramsci wrote about Machiavelli, as someone who identified the real in democratic politics, applicable to a specific historical time and place.[15]

Paine was certainly familiar enough with the Bible for his own purposes. The Bible stories he chooses make the same points as he made with reason, although some of his arguments employ a creative interpretation of these Scriptures. The first story in *Common Sense* is of Gideon defeating his enemies and protecting the Jews. The Jews ask Gideon to be King and for his son to be King. Gideon replies, "I shall not rule over you, my son shall not rule over you, the Lord shall rule over you."[16] Gideon's point, according to Paine, is that there is no such right as a hereditary monarch, although the supremacy of the Lord seems more to the point. The other Bible story Paine uses is Samuel warning the people against monarchy. The Lord has told Samuel, the patriarch, that there will be no King, but the people insist and forsake the Lord and Samuel, following the practice of the Heathens to create a King.[17]

Paine comments that these stories are often kept from the laity in the interest of both King and Priest. Monarchy, he says, is "the Popery of government."[18] The term "popery" was not meant as a strictly anti-Catholic attack. It was a term also used at the time with direct reference to the official Anglican Church.[19] Paine was partaking in the ideology of dissent that linked denominational Protestant religions with egalitarian, republican politics. Acting as an organic intellectual, by Gramsci's definition, for the new American revolutionary consciousness—even though he was barely living in America when the Revolution began—Paine was articulating one religious stream from the prevailing popular consciousness, and integrating into it his own views based primarily in the rationalist and Enlightenment part of the stream. The result was effective politics. The American Revolution never had the anti-clericalism that the French Revolution did. Thus, no mention had to be made of his generally anti-clerical and anti-establishment attitudes—which after the publication of *The Age of Reason* were used so effectively to stain his reputation in this country.

Paine's *Common Sense* is filled with many American common sense ideas. For example, he writes of America that, "resolution is our inherent character."[20] Existing in America, as Paine envisions it, just waiting to be fully unleashed, there is faith that science and an experimental approach will achieve results. There is a belief in freedom, necessary for these experiments to flourish. There is a related belief about the naturalness of liberalism and the moral superiority of the work ethic. It is only a matter of time that progress is inevitable, given hard work and perseverance. There is also a belief in toleration. The new American social contract would establish a sense of obligation in each citizen to support the rights of the different parts of the society, as a precondition for secure national unity. It would be egalitarian in social structure, with no aristocratic notions separating those of "better sort" from those of "middling" or "meaner sort."

Paine also called for an egalitarian republican form of government. He proposed elections every year for a President who would be elected by the Congress. The Presidential candidates could only come from the state that was selected by lot that year. This way, each state would be assured a President from its territory over a 13-year period. He called for a 3/5's majority to pass laws. He wanted to include specific provisions guaranteeing freedom of speech in a new constitution. The law, and no person, would be King.[21] These ideas were to be the core of the developing American nationalism. Already supposed to be the experience of everyday life in the colonies, it was merely necessary—in Paine's political vision—to articulate them and to indicate firmly their condition in the received wisdom from England.

Thomas Paine's adventure into the French Revolution can help us understand how common sense ideas from one area can overlap and influence other areas while also revealing significant differences. The French Revolution's slogan of "liberty, fraternity, and equality" reflects the same liberal ideals prominent in America and in Britain during this time. Also in France it was the same middle-class ideology that spawned a coalition of middling and poorer elements, particularly in the cities, to change society. But the differences with America are clear. Revolutionaries in France needed to destroy the power of the monarchy and an aristocratic class on their own soil. This created in France and in Europe a revolutionary spirit. According to Hartz, the Americans, lacking the need to destroy an aristocratic class, tended to view liberalism as natural, existing without the need for revolutionary creation or institutionalized defense. The American working class was thus less attracted to a socialist vision of the future. Furthermore, the increasing outlets for political participation for the lower and middle classes throughout the early nineteenth century in the United States reinforced the individualistic characteristics of American society.[22]

Importantly, Paine the historical figure did not speak with only an American voice. The American version of common sense liberalism emphasizes the individualist ethos. The European version generally has a stronger ethos of social responsibility. Paine's work reflects both. There is a tension within liberalism between the individual's freedom from the government and its repressive apparatus, and the call for a collective, cooperative responsibility that each member of society has to the community. When is collective cooperation just another form of repression? When is the call for individual freedom just a shirking of social responsibility? Although Paine generally rejected or ignored this tension, we can see that the typical American version of common sense is the central element to *Common Sense*. But his more European versions of liberalism came to the fore in other writings.

In *Rights of Man*, in 1791, Paine writes glowingly of America, "the poor are not oppressed, and the rich are not privileged. Industry is not mortified by the splendid extravagance of a court rioting at its expense. Their taxes are few, because their government is just."[23] But his experience in France brought out a more radical version of liberalism that dealt with the class distinctions that were growing as the market economy spread. In *Agrarian Justice*, for example, he argues that civilization creates benefits and evils, and one of the first objects of legislation is to deal with those evils. Poverty is not just created by government, but by the entire course of civilization as it proceeds. The object, he argues, is to remedy the evils while preserving the benefits. He elaborates some of the ideas first suggested in *Rights of Man* regarding the development of the welfare state and the equitable distribution of land.

Although Paine's analysis is consistent with nineteenth-century radicalism, he was no Leveller. Paine "went out of his way to deny that equality of property was either possible or desirable."[24] Yet his views are far from the individualist defense of freedom against the state, and far from the Protestant idea of private charity as a solution to poverty. He writes, "There are, in every country, some magnificent charities established by individuals. It is, however, but little that any individual can do, when the whole extent of misery is to be relieved is considered. He may satisfy his conscience, but not his heart."[25] Personal property is an effect of society. Individuals cannot make money without society, and thus part of that money is owed back to the community. In further recognition of the class nature of capitalist society, Paine argues that the accumulation of personal property often is the result of paying too little for labor. It is not quite Marxism, but it reflects ideas still somewhat strange to American consciousness.

Antonio Gramsci described common sense as "the conception of the world which is uncritically absorbed by the various social and cultural environments in which the moral individuality of the average man is developed."[26] We return to the question, what is the revolutionary intellectual supposed to do? On the one hand, s/he has to create a unity among the people, which entails appealing to their "natural" common sense. On the other hand, it is also necessary to challenge that common sense, destroying a certain part of what people already believe to the extent that it works to support existing oppressions and prevent just remedies. As Gramsci argued, when a new class surges toward power, it brings organically into the forefront an entire group of intellectuals to develop and justify its emerging hegemony. Thomas Paine, seen in this way, was the articulator of an emerging American ideological hegemony based on a new historical bloc.

Paine, writing in the midst of a revolutionary era, sought to create a new language from elements appearing within the old. He gave voice to the people's new common sense in a way that moved the masses. During his time in America, he articulated an American version of radical liberalism, much of which Americans have come to view as natural. Using the lens of Gramsci's concept of common sense to examine the life and work of Thomas Paine helps to illuminate the radicalism of the transatlantic world in the late eighteenth and early nineteenth centuries. Through Paine's common sense, we can examine the process of ideological change, see its obstacles, and understand how similar ideas play themselves out differently in differing historic places and contexts. Thank you very much.

Notes

[1]Christine Buci-Glucksmann. *Gramsci and the State*. Lawrence and Wishart: 1980, p. 249.

[2]Antonio Gramsci. *An Antonio Gramsci Reader*. Ed. David Forgacs. Schocken Books: 1988, p. 343.

[3]Ibid., p. 307.

[4]Marcia Landy. *Film, Politics and Gramsci*. University of Minnesota Press: 1994, p. 79.

[5] Antonio Gramsci. *An Antonio Gramsci Reader.* Ed. David Forgacs. Schocken Books: 1988, p. 301.

[6] Louis Hartz. *The Liberal Tradition in America.* Harcourt Brace: 1955.

[7] Enrico Augelli and Craig Murphy. *America's Quest for Supremacy and the Third World.* Pinter Publishers: 1988.

[8] Thomas Paine. *Common Sense*, in *Collected Writings.* Ed. Eric Foner. The Library of America: 1995, p. 25.

[9] Ibid., p. 21.

[10] "Historical bloc" refers to more than a governing coalition of social groups or classes. It is an idea that expresses "the dialectical unity of base and superstructure, theory and practice, intellectuals and masses." (See David Forgacs, in *An Antonio Gramsci Reader.* ed. David Forgacs. Schocken Books: 1988, p. 424).

[11] Thomas Paine. *Common Sense*, in *Collected Writings.* ed. Eric Foner. The Library of America: 1995, p. 19.

[12] Ibid., p. 9.

[13] Ibid., pp.15-19.

[14] Patricia U. Bonomi. *Under the Cope of Heaven: Religion, Society and Politics in Colonial America.* Oxford University Press: 1986. p. 188.

[15] Benedetto Fontana. *Hegemony and Power: On the Relation Between Gramsci and Machiavelli.* University of Minnesota Press: 1993, p.1.

[16] Thomas Paine. *Common Sense*, in *Collected Writings.* ed. Eric Foner. The Library of America: 1995, p. 13.

[17] Ibid., p. 12.

[18] Ibid., p. 15.

[19] Patricia U. Bonomi. *Under the Cope of Heaven: Religion, Society and Politics in Colonial America.* Oxford University Press: 1986. p. 191.

[20] Thomas Paine. *Common Sense,* in *Collected Writings.* Ed. Eric Foner. The Library of America: 1995, p. 41.

[21] Ibid. pp. 32-34.

[22] Louis Hartz. *The Liberal Tradition in America.* Harcourt Brace: 1955. Also, Seymour Martin Lipset and Gary Marks. *It Didn't Happen Here: Why Socialism Failed in the United States.* W.W. Norton: 2000.

[23] Thomas Paine. *The Rights of Man, Part Two,* in *Paine: Collected Writings.* Ed. Eric Foner. The Library of America: 1995, p. 555.

[24] Eric Foner. *Tom Paine and Revolutionary America.* Oxford University Press: 1976, p. 250.

[25] Thomas Paine. *Agrarian Justice,* in *Paine: Collected Writings.* Ed. Eric Foner. The Library of America: 1995, p. 406.

[26] Antonio Gramsci. *An Antonio Gramsci Reader.* Ed. David Forgacs. Schocken Books: 1988, p. 343.

THOMAS PAINE: THE GREAT PHILOSOPHER UNVEILED

Hazel Burgess

With a background in anthropology, I was lead by a personal interest in Thomas Paine to research the man himself, first as the subject of a doctoral thesis and then beyond. Within the socio-religious context of retribution or payback, I sought the unknown person behind the enigmatic historical figure portrayed by his biographers. I made no attempt to find intellectual meaning in his philosophical, political, social, or religious writings. My research was rewarded in the uncovering of formerly unrecorded information on Paine. Some of that information, together with accepted details of his life, led to my having to revise much of my planned writing. I had approached the project from a position of determined impartiality somewhat clouded by a leaning towards admiration of Paine. My position has not changed. I should like to make it clear that, despite my irrefutable findings and questionable speculations, I cannot help but respect the author whose powers of persuasive writing left an indelible mark on the modern world.

Paine, once referred to as a "mere adventurer *from England*, without fortune, without family or connexions [*sic*] ignorant even of *grammar*,"[1] is frequently hailed as one of the great thinkers of his time. Yet his name as such is known to relatively few. Why? By examination of the circumstances behind just two of his major works, *Common Sense* and *Rights of Man*, of necessity brief, this paper endeavors to explain the most probable reason for Paine's lack of recognition. I will demonstrate that this general lack of recognition of Paine as a major player in the break of the American colonies from Britain is due to the fact that, in writing *Common Sense*, he was an author hired and manipulated by those set upon independence. Evidence of the circumstances behind his writing of *Rights of Man* suggests that in Britain also his role was solely that of a scribe.

Nothing is known of Paine's early life other than the little imparted by his first biographer, Francis Oldys, whose work is suspect; he was commissioned by the government of the time to discredit the author of *Rights of Man*, a fact admitted by the writer himself.[2] All biographers since have relied upon that work. I have dealt in detail with the problem of Paine's background elsewhere;[3] it is of little relevance to this paper, but the problem is not peculiar to Paine. There is scant knowledge of the early years of many men and women whose deeds have brought them fame. Two examples, both acquaintances of Paine, are Oliver Goldsmith and George Washington. It is often the case that it is the essence of fame that the circumstances that create it are not recorded until it manifests itself.

On January 9, 1776, a momentous pamphlet named *Common Sense* hit the streets of Philadelphia.[4] The acclaim with which it was greeted defied superlatives. Its author was unknown. Benjamin Rush, who became acquainted with Paine soon after his arrival from England, later declared that he had already written a similar piece in an attempt to illustrate to loyalists the futility of remaining under British rule. (The colonists had no rights of representation; there had for some time been murmurs of discontent and skirmishes; and the king had declared the colonies to be in a state of rebellion.) Rush told that he feared to publish his text because it might jeopardize his medical practice and lose the friendship of his loyalist associates in Philadelphia. He also told of how he exhorted Paine, who had nothing to lose, to embrace the cause.[5] Paine, "the adventurer from England," did. The pamphlet went through several reprints, anonymously. It was only three months later, in April, 1776, that the author of a series of articles signed "The Forester" then revealed himself as the author of *Common Sense*. He did not name himself, but told that he then only disclosed himself as both the writer of "The Forester" letters and the best-selling pamphlet at the request of certain gentlemen who honored him with their acquaintance.[6]

Many people thought that Benjamin Franklin had written the piece; others ascribed it to John Adams, who had been putting similar ideas before the Congress for some time. Several years later, in a letter to James Cheetham, a denigrating, much disparaged yet significant biographer of Paine, Benjamin Rush claimed that the drafts of *Common Sense* had been read by himself, Franklin, and Samuel Adams. They all, according to Rush, reassured the author that they advocated similar opinions. Rush even took credit for the title of the work that Paine wished to name *Plain Truth*.[7] Questions arise: Why did these radical colonists need to read the drafts? Why did Rush name the treatise? All of these men had a vested interest in independence, as their places in history have shown. Why did such men have such say in an independent work that did not bear the name, or even a pseudonym, of the author? These facts suggest that the work was commissioned. In my view, the interest of these men and their influence on the writer went beyond friendly concern. They appear to have advised and possibly dictated the contents of the piece.

Moreover, just three years later, Paine himself said he made no profit on *Common Sense*.[8] Yet, at the time of its writing, he was without work and did not appear to be well off.[9] It is difficult to understand how a man of little substance could spend several months without income, writing for a cause of which, so far as is known, he knew little, and was less well schooled or well supported than the men with a vested interest. Paine served the young nation well. However, he never allowed those in power to forget his "services." He wrote of having always given his writings free of charge except for costs of printing and paper, and sometimes not that.[10] Celebrated as a generous benefactor who gave his services to the nation, it must be asked, who did he charge for the costs, and why? It is apparent that the expenses he paid from his own pocket were recoupable expenses from an interested source. Paine was a master of words who wrote for masters of radical ideas. I believe it was as their scapegoat that he delivered his manuscripts, expressive of their sentiments, to the printers.[11]

When Paine was appointed as Secretary to the Committee of Foreign Affairs in April, 1777, he continued to write persuasive, patriotic articles of propaganda under his adopted pseudonym of "Common Sense." His salary was set at $70 per month, yet, despite having been paid during his tenure,[12] an entry in the *Journals of the Continental Congress* for March 6, 1778, noted that in consequence of an adjustment by the Commissioners of Claims, the Auditor General had reported that the amount of $700 was due to Paine for his services from April 17 of the previous year to February 17 of the current year. It was ordered that the "account" be paid to him. His salary had doubled. He was in a position of seeking, and being given, reward. He sought more, well beyond the end of the war with Britain. He even resorted to threats, writing to George Washington in 1784 that he had two reasons for begging for more: one was his "own interest and circumstances," and the other his concern about not wishing to reveal, unless they forced it from him, the selfishness with which those in power had treated him.[13] His requests concerned matters of which much was "not publicly known."[14] Paine, the prolific writer, wrote nothing at all that year, but was well repaid for his erstwhile labors by the states of New York and Pennsylvania;[15] the first favored him with a fine property and the second with £500 in specie, "a snug little fortune."[16]

In April of 1785, he wrote to Congress of his intention to return to Europe in about two months' time. He had matters he wished to place before the members. Congress formed a committee to study his case, which resulted in the decision that he was "entitled to a liberal gratification from the United States."[17] Still in the country in September, not in receipt of his "liberal gratification," Paine again wrote to Congress giving an estimate of his needs, at least $6,000.[18] The Congressional committee recommended that he be paid the sum of $6,000, but the motion was defeated; they had considered the sum of $4,000, but he was finally awarded $3,000.[19] He was content; he was now a man of wealth; he had money in the bank, and was able to plan a trip to Europe. He left eighteen months later, in April, 1787, well reimbursed for his wartime services. The penman of the revolution had been paid off and bought out by his employers, themselves then cleared of being revealed as the real authors of the pamphlet that possibly beyond all else had persuaded the colonists to rebel. Incontrovertible evidence of Paine's requests and payments made to him exist in the records of Congress.

It is worth mentioning that no complete manuscript of *Common Sense* exists. There are, however, at the American Philosophical Society, some few fragments of paper on which Paine wrote notes for the piece—just notes.[20]

On November 4, 1789, to celebrate the anniversary of the Glorious Revolution of 1688, the London Revolution Society held a dinner.[21] Richard Price, a Unitarian minister, was invited to give the customary morning sermon prior to the meal. His address told of how the Revolution had reinforced the rights of Englishmen under their Constitution. Those rights entitled individuals to liberty of conscience, liberty to challenge abuses of power, and the right to choose their own rulers. In light of recent events in France, Price suggested that the Society should send a message of congratulation to the

French National Assembly. He and the London Revolution Society were looking to reform in Britain.

On reading Price's sermon, Edmund Burke, the Anglo-Irish statesman, was horrified. Having been a friend to the American cause, he seemed to have changed his mind on revolution, possibly in favor of a more conservative approach than a radical remaking of the establishment. Price's sermon confirmed his fears that the British radicals might emulate the French. Burke's response came in the form of a pamphlet, *Reflections on the Revolution in France*, an eloquent defense of the *status quo*, and an upholding of the Constitution in its historic context against the possibilities of its being cast aside by the "swinish multitude.[22]

As *Common Sense* had burst upon the American colonies in 1776, Paine's *Rights of Man* was published in England in February, 1791, with similar effect. Written as a reply to Burke's *Reflections*, it has frequently been described as the most vigorous and lucid exposition of fundamental human rights ever written. More than he had in *Common Sense*, Paine criticized monarchy and the traditions so strongly defended by Burke. *Rights of Man* was dedicated to George Washington, and the title page named Paine as the author.

It is known that William Godwin, writer and member of the Revolution Society, had attended the 1789 dinner at the London Tavern and heard Price's sermon. He wrote of having dined with Paine, Horne Tooke, Joseph Priestley, Thomas Brand Hollis, and others.[23] On the following day, Godwin again dined "with the Revolutionists," and noted in his diary meeting with others including Hollis.[24] It was Godwin who composed the congratulatory message that Price suggested be sent to the French revolutionaries.[25] Available evidence suggests, but to my knowledge nowhere explicitly states, that Paine was employed by the Society to expound their views in the work known as *Rights of Man*. This answer to Burke's *Reflections* was probably already conceived by members of the Revolution Society, who jointly provided the mastery of the subject, as it gestated, to the writer who put his name to it.

Members of the Revolution Society took great personal interest in the work as it was being written. It can well be assumed that they replied as a body, none of them wishing to be known as the author. The first publisher of *Rights*, Joseph Johnson, refused to publish further editions; it is not known why, but it seems obvious that he feared the consequences. Three weeks after it first appeared in bookstores, the second edition, published by J.S. Jordan, became available. Members of the Revolution Society were delighted with the results. One of them, Thomas Holcroft, quickly obtained a copy and made a comparison of the Johnson and Jordan editions. He wrote to Godwin:

> I have got it—If this do not cure my cough it is a damned perverse mule of a cough—The pamphlet—From the row—But mum—*We* don't sell it—Oh, no—Ears and Eggs— Verbatim, except the addition of a short preface, which, as you have not seen, I send you my copy—Not a single castration (Laud be unto God and J.S. Jordan!) can I Discover—Hey for the New Jerusalem! The Millennium! And peace and eternal beatitude be unto the soul of Thomas Paine![26]

Holcroft's excessive excitement suggests personal rather than general interest. In his *Reflections*, Burke had written of the Revolution Society, or the Society for Constitutional Information, being the "subject" of his "observations," so it is reasonable to assume that certain members replied as a body. It is also reasonable to assume that the first publisher, Johnson, had refused to republish without "castration" of parts of the work. Following the three-day sellout of the second edition, Paine took it upon himself to print a large number of the work under his own direction. Again, questions arise: why did he, himself, not direct publication of the work in the first place, and why was the Revolution Society so extremely interested? I suggest because Paine was their scribe, taking full responsibility for further editions. They had provided the material for the book.

As early as 1783, when John Adams first took up his appointment as Minister Plenipotentiary representing the United States at the Court of St James, he noted that when living in the house of a publisher, he had the opportunity to learn the current state of literature in England. He found it "in the hands of hirelings." These were the same men, "both in Paris and London, who preached about the progress of reason, the improvements of society, the liberty, equality, fraternity, and the rights of man."[27] He quoted the situation as told to him by an eminent printer and bookseller:

> There are in this city at least one hundred men of the best education, the best classical students, the most accomplished writers, any one of whom I can hire for one guinea a day to go into my closet and write for me whatever I please, for or against any man or any cause. It is indifferent to them whether they write pro or con.[28]

Thomas Paine was one such "accomplished writer."

When *Rights of Man* was published, Paine expected to be prosecuted,[29] which might explain his being in Paris on the day of publication. Officers of law considered whether the author could be prosecuted, but Paine's clever use of language could not be found to be seditious. He traveled between England and France regularly, writing of causes dear to the hearts of French radicals. He had been approached by the Marquis du Chastellet, who persuaded him to "offer his services" to the publishers of a new republican journal. He did, but let the publishers know that he was obliged to spend part of that summer in England.[30] It was in France that he began work on the sequel to *Rights of Man,* which was to be named *Kingship,* but it appears obvious that he was constrained to consult with his English masters.

In response to the King's flight from Paris on June 21, 1791, Paine wrote a manifesto, born of his association with the Marquis de Condorcet, a supporter of revolution and one of the editors of the new republican journal, the radical Abbé Emmanuel Sieyès, and the young Achille François du Chastellet, who had sought his services. The manifesto, which advocated the proclaiming of a republic, and had been plastered by Paine and Chastellet on the walls of Paris, was published the following day. On the same day, a leading article by Paine was printed in the new journal of the Republican Society for which he was writing. Paine admitted to being the author of the manifesto, which evoked the ire of the National Assembly. He returned to England, leaving behind a small line-up of writings recently published or about to be published in France.[31]

Paine's arrival in England on July 13, 1791, was noted in the press. On July 26, *The Times* featured the first of four parts of a satirical article on the death of a metaphorical, "holy hypocritical Old Maid" named "Miss Presbyterea Democracy." She had expired at a dinner she gave to celebrate the first anniversary of the French Revolution. Her "body" had been conveyed to the house of Dr. Priestley where it was "laid out in the Library on some corrected proofs of *Rights of Man*," before being conveyed to lie in state at a public house. It is evident that the writer was aware of the interest that members of the Revolution Society took in Paine's *Rights of Man*, and was suggesting that they edited the work. The fourth installment, on July 30, concluded with the burial of "the deceased" at Runnymede where King John had sealed Magna Carta, known as the great char-ter of liberties, in 1215. From this I infer that Paine was publicly exposed as a hired pen. At the annual dinner of the Revolution Society on November 4, 1791, Paine, who was an honorary member,[32] was one of the 250 guests. A toast was proposed thanking him for his defense of the rights of man.

According to Oldys, almost our only source for this time, as his piece neared completion, Paine conversed only with Horne Tooke in a location known only to the proposed printer, Thomas Chapman.[33] The new book was intended "to go further" than *Rights of Man* because Paine saw "that *great rogues* escape by the excess of their crimes, and, perhaps, it may be the same in honest cases."[34] It is possible to suggest that Paine conceived of himself as a "rogue" and the Crown of England as an "honest case" because, just three years earlier, in a letter to an acquaintance, he had written in glowing terms of the position of the King as the true representative of commoners.[35] Paine, in private correspondence oblivious to the fact that such writing would ultimately be available to those who wrote about him, defended popularly based "kingship." Extraordinarily, his stance has been simply, and unquestioningly, described as "remarkable."[36] It seems clear that Paine's opinion on kingship then was not as it appeared to be in his published writing. He had once maintained that his pen and his soul had "ever gone together," but that was a published statement under his pseudonym of "Common Sense."[37]

On completion, Paine's work was named *Rights of Man*, Part II. Apparently, even the title was not his to decide. (It will be recalled that his *Plain Truth* was renamed *Common Sense* by Benjamin Rush.) After printing part of the piece, Chapman backed out, and the manuscript was sent to J. S. Jordan, who had taken over publication of *Rights of Man*, Part I. On the day of publication, February 16, 1792, Paine wrote two letters to Jordan. It seems probable that he requested the second, or that Paine had been instructed and was recompensed by one or more of the reform societies for making the claim therein. The first letter, a cover note, for both Jordan's and Paine's own "satisfaction," freed Jordan of any responsibility and directed him, if he had need of the enclosure, to send for Paine immediately. He was also to send for Horne Tooke.[38] The enclosure read:

> Sir, —Should any person, under the sanction of any kind of authority, inquire of you respecting the author and publisher of the *Rights of Man*, you will please to mention me as the author and publisher of that work, and show to such person this letter. I will, as soon as I am acquainted with it, appear and answer for the work personally.[39]

Paine was expecting trouble, and the fact that he involved Tooke suggests that he was to witness Paine's claim.

On May 18 Paine presented a letter to the Revolution Society. Finding it "incumbent" upon him-self and due to their "patronage," words indicative of an obligation or duty to the Society's authority, he wrote of having received numerous letters from all over England begging that the first and second parts of *Rights of Man* be printed in a cheap edition that would make it more affordable. He informed the Society that he had taken means to comply with the requests, and was proceeding with the work as he had been informed that he was to be prosecuted.[40] The Society "resolved to give him thanks and to support him. They also resolved to inquire into the rumor of his prosecution.[41] Unless members had an interest, Paine had no need of keeping the Society informed because *Rights of Man* and its author were the talk of Europe. It is obvious that they paid the costs of the cheap editions. The vast profits from the book were "donated" to the Revolution Society to use as members saw fit.[42] Again questions must be raised: Why did this body of men have so much influence upon an independent author, and why were the profits donated to the Society? It appears obvious that the profits were not Paine's for the keeping; he had been well paid.

Jordan, the printer, was prosecuted for publishing *Rights of Man* well before Paine was issued with a summons for seditious libel, because, according to the Attorney General, his name on the title page would not stand up in court as proof of authorship. However, the summons he had been expecting was delivered to his lodgings on May 21, the day that the government issued a proclamation against seditious writings, a proclamation designed specifically to contest the effects of *Rights of Man*. It was also the day upon which Jordan pleaded guilty. Paine wrote to the Home Secretary on June 6, answering arguments that had been put before the House of Commons and, in effect, pre-empting his own defense.[43] The trial was postponed until December, but Paine had fled to France, and was tried in absentia. In France, as has been shown, he had already taken up a cause which was to lead to his writing of *The Age of Reason*. The circumstances behind its writing also suggest that it was a commissioned work; I have dealt with the complications of that story in another piece.[44]

Thomas Paine may have been a great thinker, but it is fair to say that the accepted philosophy of Paine through his writings was merely the combined thoughts, or philosophies, of bodies of men who sought change. This is not to say that he disagreed with their aspirations. He might or might not have done. It is impossible to know from this distance in time. Paine's contemporaries seem to have known him as a man with a pen for hire—a brilliant, useful scribe with a need to earn a living. To my way of thinking, he has no real place in the history of ideas, and it is only as the result of his resurrection by hagiographic biographers that some few afford him one. Those eulogists have done both Paine and history a disservice. Beyond study of his use of language as a literary device, always suited to the causes his works embraced, it is doubtful whether he is of any relevance to common sense for the modern era. He was a man of his own time, employed in working for reforms of that time. Each era is a period unto itself, occasioning the need for meeting and dealing with its own exigencies. There is, and always will be, a demand for writers of persuasive, simply written "truths." Propaganda is ever present. Forcefully produced, its power can be tremendous. It was the strength of Paine's arguments that carried him, as "Common Sense," on the crest of a wave in the newly united States of America and the same that led to his being outlawed in Britain. I have given examples of two works only, but the same can be said with confidence of other important pieces.[45]

Question: This is, I guess, directed toward all of you. I would like to know more about Paine's education (self-education, I presume) and what kind of materials he had read. In particular, was he familiar with any of the early philosophers of ancient Greece?

Thomas Killikelly: I will make one comment, as I am certainly not an expert on his education. It has been written that Paine would brag that he really hadn't read very much. In some books about Paine, people have commented, when they were referring to some writer at the time, that he seemed unfamiliar about that writer, so he was a real popularizer in that sense, but that's my extent of my knowledge on it.

Sophia Rosenfeld: There's obviously a large body of literature debating exactly what he did read, didn't read, might have read, could have read, could have seen, and which versions. I think there are several people at the back of the room who might want to address that question more specifically.

Tony Freyer: The one, simple answer is that classicism was a basic mode for the educated, as well as people who were self-educated and well-read. They would use references to classical thinkers because it was part of educated discourse.

Hazel Burgess: May I comment that we know very little about Paine's education, only what we were told by Francis Oldys. Based on what I have said, you will realize that he could have been educated by the men with whom he associated. But we don't really know. We have no real records. I will tell you that there is no single record of Paine in Thetford, England, at that school he is supposed to have attended.

Harvey Kaye (from the audience): I was just going to say that in reply to your question that there actually is fairly good evidence, based on the things he wrote and even some of the lines that he used, that Paine was familiar with Shakespeare and Milton from his education. The big question about Paine's literary background is only whether he might or might not have read Locke. Although there may not be the primary evidence of what he read, in terms of his transcript from school, we can pretty much derive what he would have read based on his own writings and the kinds of references he makes.

I will add that one should not trust anything Francis Oldys said about Paine. I can't imagine anyone would, and especially I couldn't imagine using that as my primary reference. You really have to be careful about sources regarding Paine, especially the early sources, because many are not fair. Hazel Burgess talked about paid propagandists—that's where the real paid propagandists are, in the critics hired to insult and misrepresent Paine. Oldys, quite obviously, was paid to slander, to intentionally injure Paine and his reputation. It is not good history to use the paid propagandists of the British as the source to draw conclusions about Paine as a possible paid propagandist of the revolutionaries. I would have to look over Hazel Burgess' paper in detail, but beyond the fact that some of her sources are biased and suspect, I think that the interpretations and inferences she makes are really quite stretched—indeed, foolish and wrongheaded.

Question: I have a question for Seth Cotlar. Kind of tangential to Thomas Paine, but we talk about how people in America today do not read political stuff. It strikes me, whenever I open up the newspaper and I see the bestseller list, how many political works are listed. The problem is, with a couple of exceptions, most of those are crap, so I was wondering, since you've done work on political pamphlets in eighteenth century and nineteenth century, how sophisticated are those? Paine obviously is unassailable, especially in this room. But how sophisticated were those pamphlets compared to the things you find in Barnes & Nobles and Borders today in the current events section?

Seth Cotlar: I could get my historian's card revoked for answering this question in too detailed of a fashion. I didn't start off this project thinking I was going to be working predominantly with newspapers. Once I started reading the newspapers, I became quite enthralled by how sophisticated they were. I came to realize that these newspapers were creating a community of readers, and that the stories continued through them. References would start—for example, the story of Thomas Muir—and his name would be misspelled, and they would get some of the details wrong, and they would have to explain the context of what was going on in Scotland. Then, in the same newspaper three months later, they would just say, "like the case of Muir," and then go on.

Clearly what had happened — or what the editors assumed had happened, and I presume they were probably right — is that the community of people who had gathered around their newspapers had come to adopt a set of ideas and a way of understanding what was going on around the world that could be referred to within a shorthand way. It would conjure up a whole set of associations amongst a particular community, whereas for another community it would fall on deaf ears; it would mean nothing. In that sense, the newspapers are sophisticated in their attention to the community of people who were reading them.

In addition, these democratic newspapers were aimed at ordinary readers. This was not an elite phenomenon. They included excerpts from Voltaire, and they included excerpts from very long and learned treatises on banking policy, for example, that you wouldn't even find in the *New York Times* today. I'm not going to make value judgments about relative sophistication or not. But as someone coming from the twenty-first century back into the 1790s, I was amazed by that. Also, there's a lot of acerbic, sarcastic wit. That wit, in the context of an incredibly hierarchical society, had a function in legitimizing the grievances of people who were reading it, basically saying to them, "we know that you hate these people and you resent them, and that's okay, and so do I, and let's laugh at them together." That function of print, which today we take for granted as part of our politics, was something really experimental and new in the 1790s, and it gives these writings of the 1790s a real vibrancy and creativity, because it was so new.

Question: I would like to ask about the notion of common sense. The term seems to have multiple uses, both in Paine and in the world today. I somehow suspect that the common sense of Americans in this era is quite opposed to the kinds of principles that Paine held dear.

Sophia Rosenfeld: If you look at contemporary political discourse, you will find that the use of the term "common sense" appears probably with equal frequency on the right and on the left. It's a buzz word of contemporary politics. It appeared in the most recent "State of the Union" address. You could do a nice Lexis search ,and you'll see how often it comes up, and it comes up for Democrats as much as Republicans.

However, what interests me is the various functions it plays in contemporary political discourse. It can be used in a genuinely populist spirit, to encourage the idea that what ordinary people think can matter. It can empower people who are outside of the inner circle of expertise, whether they be marginal people of any kind or just simply ordinary people, to have opinions that matter. It is the idea that those opinions actually, collectively, could be the basis of a political movement.

Conversely, though, common sense often functions in quite a different way, to cut off debate, to say there is nothing to be discussed because there is a common sense on this. It can work in an anti-intellectual fashion, and it can work strangely to polarize debates. It is to say there is nothing that we reasonably need to debate; there is something like common sense out there, which then heightens the stakes in any political contest and provides you with two opposing sides, both of which claim to have some absolute ideological construct on their side. Hannah Arendt famously argued that common sense is essential to democracy; it's the ground on which democracy forms and maintains itself. But there have been plenty of recent commentators who have shown also the way in which debate is constantly limited by our kind of knee-jerk recourse to talk about common sense. I do think that we live with that dualism as part of our political landscape.

Seth Cotlar: I've been thinking about this common sense issue, too, and I wonder. Not to defend Paine, but there are two registers in which people use common sense. One is in terms of idealism. We have a body of ideas that we hold as common-sensical, and then we have the world of reality, and you have people saying, "Come on; common-sensically, we all know that it doesn't work that way." That's an appeal to common sense in the real world as opposed to the uncommon sense of the ideal world. Paine, it strikes me, doesn't use common sense in that register of the real world. He seems to pitch it at the level of ideals. That is, we take common-sensical ideals and look at how the reality doesn't match up. This tradition, in American radicalism right throughout the eighteenth and nineteenth and twentieth centuries, is at the level of "all men are created equal"; it's your fundamental, foundational principles. The claim that radicals make is that their ideals are common-sensical. The conservatives use it differently, as empirical against ideas. I believe there might be a useful distinction to make, a distinction between ideality and reality in thinking about common sense.

Sophia Rosenfeld: I would say that two kinds of common sense do exist in Paine, especially in the pamphlet, *Common Sense*. On the one hand, he offers a number of small maxims or precepts which seem to be ideals that govern the world across time and across place—small things shouldn't rule bigger ones; simple things are better than more complicated ones—kinds of trite truisms that can be applied to a variety of circum-stances and seem to be universal. In this realm, he is suggesting that obvious trans-historical wisdom comes directly from certain natural principles, so obvious they are hardly worth stating. On the other hand, he also uses common sense to cut through things that ordinary people believe but he insists are simply prejudices. Common sense is also the thing that reveals what's gone amok in contemporary thinking.

I'm not sure I would follow Seth's distinction exactly. But if you want to take this in terms of real world/ideal world, I think common sense operates for him in both ways. He could say, I'm representing the common sense of all people, and it's obvious to all of us and should be. Simultaneously, it argues for something extremely subversive and radical.

Thomas Killikelly: The way I think about common sense, it is something not usually questioned or thought about. There may be some idealized idea that people have about the world, that it should be a certain way. But I would even say that the ideas that you just mentioned, the one like about equality, at some level, it's an idealized notion that the world should be equal. At another level, people in daily life get really worked up about this stuff, so I don't think it is a proper contrast, idealized out there and not real. That distinction—I don't think that's always what's going on. I think com-mon sense most of the time is invisible to people. It's just, everybody agrees on this, so there's nothing to discuss.

Question (Brian McCartin): Just a response to the question about Paine's educational experience. I agree with Harvey Kaye; if you read Paine, you'll understand that his influences are great. They are from Milton, from the rationalist philosophers of the continent and the empiricist philosophies of Hobbes and Locke. You'll see this in his writings.

Common sense would be an interpretation of a linguistic tool by Paine. It refers obviously back to the common school sense of Scotland and to others, but Paine is relating it to the string of events that occurred over the last so many years in America. It is related to the thought in America, and is about how governments should be structured. It is common sense not only in that way of thinking, but in the way that we should interpret things in the future, about independence and self-determination and individual liberty. This is common sense. It is the philosophy that had been circulating in the colonies since the early 1700s, influenced by theorists and also by the civil strife going on in England. Paine knows this, and he sees this as common sense, things that the American colonists will know. He will flip that around, turning his whole philosophy against the ruling elites, even in ways that diverged from other so-called founding fathers.

Therefore we see two things. One, his educational experience is grounded in philosophy going back to Plato. Two, he is versed in the modern philosophies of the continental rationalists, the English empiricists, and the American enlightened thinkers of the day, and so, therefore, he had a whole slew of educational experience. Yet his conclusions are predicated also on his own philosophical ideas and interpretation of things like common sense.

Hazel Burgess: Paine himself insisted he had never read Locke. Yet it is very obvious he had.

Brian McCartin (from the audience): That's exactly my point.

Tony Freyer: I would say this fulfills the idea of what a symposium is supposed to do. Everyone stayed within the time boundary, and we had great audience response. It was overall an educational, positive experience, real nourishment of the mind. We look forward to maintaining this same high-level conversation throughout the rest of the papers. Thank you.

Notes

[1] Gouverneur Morris's speech to the Continental Congress during the second day of a debate on Paine's authorship of a piece printed in the *Pennsylvania Packet* of January 2, 1779 under the title of "Common Sense to the Public, January 7, 1779. Quoted from the papers of Morris in Jared Sparks, *The Life of Gouverneur Morris*, 3 Vols. (Boston: Gray & Bowen, 1832), vol. 1, p. 202, Morris's emphasis. Paine never forgot nor forgave the speech, which was not recorded in the *Journals of the Continental Congress*. In 1808, in a letter to the Committee of Claims, he referred to his enemy as "prating Gouverneur Morris." "Claim of Thomas Paine," *Annals of Congress*, 10th Congress, 2nd Session, p. 1782.

[2] W.T. Sherwin, *Memoirs of the Life of Thomas Paine* (London: R. Carlile, 1819), pp. iv-v.

[3] Hazel Burgess, *The Disownment and Reclamation of Thomas Paine: A Reappraisal of the "Philosophy" of "Common Sense,"* unpublished doctoral thesis, University of Sydney, 2002.

[4] The date of publication is often given as Jan. 10, 1776, but, as noted by Moses Coit Tyler, there was an advertisement in *The Pennsylvania Evening Post* of Jan. 9, which indicated that the pamphlet was out that day. *A History of American Literature: 1607-1783*, ed. Archie H. Jones (Chicago: University of Chicago Press, 1967), n., p. 271.

[5] Benjamin Rush to James Cheetham, July 17, 1809, in James Cheetham, *The Life of Thomas Paine* (New York: privately printed, 1809), p. 38. See also George W. Corner, ed., *The Autobiography of Benjamin Rush: His "Travels Through Life" together with his Commonplace Book for 1789-1813* (Princeton: Princeton University Press for The American Philosophical Society, 1948), pp. 113-14.

[6] Thomas Paine, "Reply to Cato's Eighth Letter," in Eric Foner, ed., *Thomas Paine: Collected Writings* (New York: Library of America, 1995), pp. 84-85.

[7] Rush to James Cheetham, op. cit., pp. 37-38.

⁸Thomas Paine, "To the Honorable Henry Laurens," in Philip S. Foner, ed., *The Complete Writings of Thomas Paine*, 2 vols. (New York: Citadel Press 1969), vol. 2, p. 1163.

⁹Soon after his arrival from England Paine was employed by Robert Aitken to work on his new *Pennsylvania Magazine; or American Monthly Museum*. That employment probably ended in June, 1775. See Burgess, op. cit., pp. 50, 56-60. Lyon Richardson suggested that Paine might have terminated his employment with Aitken about September of the same year as his last contribution to the magazine appeared in the August issue. (*A History of Early American Magazines: 1741-178* [New York: Thomas Nelson & Sons, 1931, p. 177].) That contribution would have been "An Occasional Letter on the Female Sex," frequently attributed to Paine, which Frank Smith proved to have been the work of Antoine Léonard ("The Authorship of An Occasional Letter on the Female Sex," *American Literature*, vol. 2, 1930-31, pp. 278-80). It appears that Paine was not gainfully employed from June.

¹⁰Thomas Paine, "The American Crisis II," in Philip S. Foner, ed., *The Life and Major Writings of Thomas Paine*, 2 vols. (New York: Citadel Press, 1945), vol. 1, p. 72.

¹¹See Paine, "To the Honorable Henry Laurens," op. cit., p. 1162.

¹²Paine himself wrote of his salary being $800 per year, which would have been less than $70 per month. "To the Committee of Claims of the House of Representatives," *Complete Writings*, vol. 2, p. 1494. Paine resigned from the position within ten months of having been appointed.

¹³"To His Excellency General Washington," ibid., pp. 1248-49.

¹⁴"To Honorable General Irwin, Vice President, ibid.," pp. 1249-50. Paine's letter to Irwin should be read in conjunction with his letter to Washington of Apr. 28, 1784. See note 12.

¹⁵Paine had been advised by men of influence to seek reward from the individual States as they thought that if he applied to Congress alone his claim might be rejected. See "To His Ex-

cellency General Washington," *Complete Writings*, vol. 2, p. 1248.

[16]Moncure D. Conway, *The Life of Thomas Paine*, 2 vols. (New York: G.P. Putnam's Sons, 1892), vol. 1, p. 209.

[17]Worthington C. Ford, *et al.*, eds., *Journals of the Continental Congress, 1774-1789*, Washington, D.C., 1904-37, vol. 29, pp. 662-63, http://memory.loc.gov/ammem/amlaw/lwjc.htmll.

[19]"To the Congress of the United States," *Complete Writings*, vol. 2, p. 1252.

[20]Ford et al., op. cit., pp. 774-75, 796. Due to the complexities of interconnecting Paine's letters of demand — which poured into Congress while the committee considered his case — with the brief and confused notes in the *Journals of the Continental Congress*, in presenting this paper at San Diego in 2005, I overrated the amount paid to him. It was not $7,000 as then indicated, but $3,000. This matter is clarified in a source of which I was then unaware, that is, "Claim of Thomas Paine," *Annals of Congress*, 10th Congress, 2nd Session, p. 1781, http://memory.loc.gov/ammem/amlaw/lwac.html.

[21]See "Thomas Paine Papers," http://www.amphilsoc.org/library/mole/p/paine.xml.

[22]Fear of Roman Catholic tyranny during the short reign of James II (1685-88) had then united both the Church of England and nonconformists, an event which brought about the deposition of James and put his daughter, Mary, and her husband William, on the throne.

[23]See Edmund Burke, *Reflections on the Revolution in France and on the Proceedings in Certain Societies in London Relative to that Event*, 5th ed. (London: privately printed, 1790), p. 117.

[24]Alfred Owen Aldridge, *Man of Reason: The Life of Thomas Paine* (London: The Cresset Press, 1960), p. 135.

[25]C. Kegan Paul, *William Godwin: His Friends and Contemporaries*, 2 vols. (London: Henry S. King & Co., 1876), vol. 1, pp. 61-62.

[26]Ibid., p. 62.

[27]Ibid., p. 69. For an interesting interpretation of this "lyrical note," see Aldridge, op. cit., pp. 134-35.

[28]Charles Francis Adams, *The Works of John Adams, Second President of the United States: With a Life of the Author*, 10 vols. (Boston: Little, Brown & Co., 1856), vol.1, p. 404.

[29]Ibid.

[30]Thomas Paine, "Letter Addressed to the Addressers on the Late Proclamation," *Complete Writings*, (New York: Citadel Press 1969), vol. 2, pp. 486-87.

[31]"To Messieurs Condorcet, Nicolas de Bonneville and Lanthenas," *Complete Writings*, (New York: Citadel Press 1969), vol. 2, p. 1315.

[32]The works for publication in France were "To the Conductors of a Parisian Print, entitled, *The Republican*," "Answer to Four Questions on the Legislative and Executive Power," and "To the Abbé Sieyès," published respectively in *Le Républicain, ou le Défenseur du gouvernement representative; par une société de républicains, Chronique du Mois*, and the *Moniteur*.)

[33]Paine is recorded as having attended seven meetings of the Society in 1791 and 1792. "Trial of John Horne Tooke," in *A Complete Collection of State Trials and Pro-ceedings for High Treason and Other Crimes and Misdemeanors from the Earliest Period to the Year 1783, with Notes and Other Illustrations* (London: T. C. Hansard, 1818), vol. 25, pp. 102, 114, 137, 139, 147, 152, 154, 161. In a letter from the Revolution Society in London to the Society of Friends of the Constitution at Bordeaux, the secretary wrote "Dr. Priestley and Mr. Paine are neither of them Members of our Society; but they decorate other Societies whose principles are the same." Revolution Society (London, England), *The Correspondence of the Revolution Society in London, with the National Assembly, and with Various Societies of the Friends of Liberty in France and England* (London: n.p., 1792), p. 217. *Eighteenth Century Collections Online*, Gale Group,

http://galenet.galegroup.com. At the trial of Thomas Hardy for high treason the Attorney General told of Paine and Thomas Clio Rickman being members of the London Corresponding Society. *Bell's Reports of the State Trials for High Treason* (London: n.p., 1794), p. 41, *Eighteenth Century Collections Online*.

[34] Francis Oldys [George Chalmers], *The Life of Thomas Pain, the Author of the Seditious Writings, Entitled Rights of Man*, 6th ed. corrected (London: privately printed, 1793), p. 23, Eighteenth Century Collections Online.

[35] "To William Short," *Complete Writings* (New York: Citadel Press 1969), vol. 2, pp. 1321.

[36] "To Thomas Walker, Esqr.," ibid., pp. 1279-80. Paine expressed this opinion following a speech by the Prime Minister, William Pitt, on the occasion of the illness of George III. The Opposition had proposed that the Crown should pass to his son, but the Pitt Ministry insisted that the Prince of Wales had no right to rule as Regent while his father lived.

[37] See Moncure D. Conway, ed., *The Writings of Thomas Paine*, 4 vols. (New York: AMS Press, 1967), vol. 4, p. vii.

[38] "The American Crisis II," op. cit., p. 72.

[39] "The Whole Proceedings on the Trial of An Information Exhibited ex-Officio by the King's Attorney-General Against Thomas Paine," in *The Complete Works of Thomas Paine, Political and Miscellaneous, Including a Complete Report of His Trial in the Court of King's Bench, Dec. 18, 1792, with the Eloquent Speech of His Counsel (Erskine) in His Defence* (London: E. Truelove, n.d. [1878?]), appendix, p. 758.

[40] Ibid.

[41] "To the Chairman of the Society for Promoting Constitutional Knowledge," *Complete Writings*, vol. 2 (New York: Citadel Press 1969), pp. 1324-25.

[42] Society for Constitutional Information, *At a Meeting held this Day, the following Letter was received, addressed to the Chairman*

of this Society, London, 1792, *Eighteenth Century Collections Online*, Gale Group, http://galenet.galegroup.com.

[43]Thomas Paine, to the Society for Constitutional Information, July 4, 1792, printed at Paine's request in the Philadelphia *Aurora* (Dec. 11, 1802).

[44]"To Mr. Secretary Dundas," *Complete Writings*, vol. 2 (New York: Citadel Press 1969), pp. 446-57.

[45]Burgess, op. cit., pp. 234-44.

[46]According to an agreement signed by George Washington, Robert Morris and Robert Livingston on Feb.10, 1782, Paine secretly wrote for those three. See "Agreement with Robert R. Livingston and George Washington," in E. James Ferguson, et al., eds., *The Papers of Robert Morris 1781-1784* (Pittsburgh: University of Pittsburgh Press, 1973/1995), vol. 4, p. 201. See also Burgess, op. cit., p. 137. It is known, too, that Paine was rewarded with a considerable share holding and, it was rumored, 12,000 acres of land for his writing of *Public Good*. See Arnold Kimsey King, "Thomas Paine in America, 1774-1787," unpublished doctoral dissertation, University of Chicago, 1951, pp. 260-62. The rumors were confirmed by Paine himself in an article he placed in the *Pennsylvania Journal* of Mar. 27, 1782. See Alfred Owen Aldridge, op. cit., pp. 92, 329. Paine placed another article on the same matter in *The Freeman's Journal* of May 1, 1782. "Response to an Accusation of Bribery," in Eric Foner, op. cit., pp. 318-24.

**PANEL 2:
PAINE, POLITICAL IDEOLOGY, AND
DEMOCRATIC REFORM MOVEMENTS**

Moderator: Dawn Marsh Riggs

I was invited by Dean Paul Wong of the SDSU College of Arts and Letters to help organize this conference a number of months ago, and I guess I was ultimately instrumental in selecting the variety of speakers that we have here today and tomorrow. I was just asked by a reporter what it was that helped shape the conference vision. I said, basically, there were two things. First, we wanted something interdisciplinary. Second, we wanted to go beyond Thomas Paine as a historical figure, Paine as a literary figure, Paine as somebody whose name is found on bumper stickers and in slogans. We wanted to bring together people who thought that Thomas Paine was critically relevant to us today. Relevance is a major reason we are holding this conference.

One of the recurring themes about Thomas Paine is that his importance has sometimes been celebrated in history by groups that seem despairingly different from one another, and sometimes that importance has been subverted, intentionally or unintentionally, often by those not wishing us to be inspired by his ideas. A number of the papers in this panel speak to this topic and also speak to the internationalism and relevance of his ideas today.

This panel focuses on Paine and the democratic political movements that he inspired. Our speakers include Kenneth Burchell, President of the Thomas Paine Institute, University of Idaho, who will talk about the political significance of nineteenth-century birthday celebrations and commemorations for Thomas Paine. (As we heard, Eric Foner and friends have sought to duplicate such a celebration.) Bryson Clevenger from the University of Virginia will consider the impact of Paine's ideas on the reaction among British ultra-radicals to the Irish reform movement. Finally, David Robinson, Director of the Center for the Humanities at Oregon State University, will explore the ideas embedded in Paine's *Agrarian Justice* and their implications for poverty, land ownership, and social welfare.

BIRTHDAY PARTY POLITICS: THE THOMAS PAINE BIRTHDAY CELEBRATIONS AND THE ORIGINS OF AMERICAN DEMOCRATIC REFORM

Kenneth W. Burchell

Let's brighten things up and talk about a party, a birthday party. First, though, thanks are due to the university and the organizers of this event. Perhaps because of my own childhood in a Baptist pastor's home, various kinds of impulses come to mind whenever I stand on a podium or lectern. One of them is confession, the cleansing of the soul. There was something in Paine that liked confession, because confession is based on honesty, so let me be honest with you and share a confession: I am a Paineite. I admire Paine's life, his wit, and his willingness to influence the world far beyond what would have been expected from his birth in a way matched by few, even among the founders far better remembered than he. I admire the Whig in the early Tom Paine, who viewed history as a struggle to maintain liberty against militarism, corruption, and power. Moreover, I admire Paine the democrat, whose faith in the inherent goodness of mankind was matched by few in his time or ours. But perhaps above all stands my admiration of Paine the smasher of idols, the iconoclast who attacked established superstition with little else than his mind and the nib of his pen, and subsequently liberated more people from bondage to the false claims of established religion than any man or woman in history.

That said, let me also explain what sort of Paineite I am not. There is a class of Thomas Paine enthusiast who believe him responsible for everything from the authorship of the Declaration of Independence to the creation of the American abolitionist movement. No claim seems too far-fetched. One day, I am certain, we shall see the claim that he designed the great pyramid of Cheops. The record of Paine's achievements is not advanced by attribution to that which he demonstratively did not do or by the kind of history that ignores his context. Paine's enormous achievements stand realistically on their own merit.

The present paper concerns the celebration of Paine's birthday and its relationship to the history of nineteenth-century democratic reform. The idea grew out of research on the New York City publisher and equal rights activist Gilbert

Vale (1788-1866), who published a scientific and literary journal called the *Beacon*. That journal and related periodicals frequently contained detailed announcements of Paine birthday celebrations. A long-standing interest in Paine scholarship was motivation enough to catalogue them. The catalogue's contents and its impressive growth suggested a case that the Thomas Paine birthday celebrations played a greater role in the history of nineteenth-century democratic reform than historians have yet acknowledged.

The celebration of Thomas Paine's birthday, though widely overlooked today, is a tradition of central historical importance to movements for democratic reform in the U.S. and around the world. With the exception of the Fourth of July, perhaps no other political celebration was commemorated with more constancy and attended by a more stellar array of political and social reformers than the natal day of Thomas Paine. Inaugurated shortly after Paine's death and honored ever since, Paine's birthday served to provide unification and inspiration for generations of reformers throughout the nineteenth and twentieth centuries. This paper first surveys the origins of the first known Thomas Paine birthday celebrations in England and then narrows to a focus on the history of the event in nineteenth-century America. A review of the personalities who organized or participated in the celebrations demonstrates the event's close relationship to American democratic reform and its centrality in efforts to reconstruct and vindicate Paine's reputation in the wake of the defamation campaign waged by his political and religious detractors.

The first known Paine birthday celebrations took place undercover in London, at a time when the need for secrecy was acute. In 1812, just three years after Paine's death, the printer Daniel Isaac Eaton was pilloried and imprisoned for printing Paine's works. *Habeas corpus*, first suspended in the disturbances of 1794-95, was again set aside in 1818 with a new Seditious Meetings Act that banned all protest meetings. The 1819 Blasphemous and Seditious Libels Act and Newspaper Stamp Duties Act allowed printers and writers of "seditious materials" to be imprisoned on the mere allegation of libel and were designed to ensure that all ". . . Societies and Clubs . . . should be utterly suppressed and prohibited as unlawful combinations and confederacies." Within a year virtually every prominent reform leader was rounded up, transported, or imprisoned. The first three decades of the nineteenth century were days of struggle for democratic activists in Britain.[1]

The nature and dates of the first Paine birthday celebrations are still somewhat obscure, but they began soon after Paine's death in 1809, perhaps as early as the following year. In a note to his *Popular Freethought in America, 1822-1850,* historian Albert Post claimed that "the first Paine celebration was held secretly in London in 1818," a slightly later date for which he unfortunately provided no source. The claim that Lancashire radicals held regular Paine birthday dinners as early as 1820 is made in Professor James A. Epstein's *Radical Expression: Political Language, Ritual and Symbol.* He cites a January 29, 1820 article in the *Manchester Observer.* In his *Thomas Paine: Social and Political Thought,* Gregory Claeys claimed that the event "may have been initiated by [Thomas] Wooler early in 1818," but was likely to have been celebrated more or less continuously since Paine's death "at least in London, where its fourteenth anniversary was proclaimed in 1823." Claeys referenced his account to the early radical periodicals the *Republican,* the *Lion,* and the *Black Dwarf.* Professors Epstein, Edward Royle, and William H. Wickwar point variously to William Sherwin, Richard Carlile, Thomas "Clio" Rickman, Henry Hunt, James Watson, John Cartwright, Robert Taylor, and others as likely instigators or participants in these early and necessarily secretive celebrations.[2]

While the precise dates and participants remain obscure, all sources are in agreement with respect to the importance and centrality of the Thomas Paine birthday celebrations for the history of nineteenth-century British reform. In *Radical Expression,* Professor Epstein described them as "the highlight of the political year for these advocates of Enlightenment reason." Albert Post observed that the event reached cult status and that freethinkers and reformers celebrated Paine's birthday with an enthusiasm equal to that of Christians on the holy days of their calendar. Professor Claeys pointed to the over 500 in attendance at the 1823 London event and noted that the celebration had spread to cities and halls throughout England. Historian Edward Royle recounted the wide range of reform groups represented by participating radicals. The relationship of the Paine celebrations to the beginnings of the British Forum and the participation of Spenceans and Watsonites are further detailed in Iaian

McCalman's *Radical Underworld: Prophets, Revolutionaries and Pornographers in London, 1795-1840*. Later nineteenth-century labor leaders and freethinkers like Henry Rowley, George Foote, George Jacob Holyoake, and Charles Bradlaugh were all enthusiastic participants in their time. The commemoration of Paine's birthday is integrally connected to the widest possible representation of British reform and free thought well into the twentieth century.[3]

The earliest known American celebration was organized in 1825 by British émigré Benjamin Offen, a shoemaker. Perhaps no other phenomenon demonstrates the acknowledged connection between radical British émigrés and the development of early nineteenth-century American reform movements as explicitly as the genesis of the Paine birthday celebrations. Offen and others were aware of the earlier London meetings, so the two events were directly related. The most visible attendees in 1825 were fellow British émigrés, many of whom fled to America after the Panic of 1819 left England in disastrous economic and social condition. Some fled England's restrictive laws, and many imported their radicalized temperament with them. The same wave of immigrants that brought Offen included influential reformers Robert Owen, Robert Dale Owen, George Henry Evans, Gilbert Vale, Frances Wright, Ernestine Rose, and George Houston. These and others less well known became leaders and activists in the labor, equal rights, abolition, and agrarian reforms that arose during the first half of the nineteenth century.[4]

In their descriptive bibliography of the movement, entitled *Freethought in the United States*, historians Gordon Stein and Marshall G. Brown claimed that the celebration in 1825 represented the rebirth of organized free thought in the United States. The claim is reasonable, but the relationship between participants in these celebrations and movements for democratic reform was far more extensive than Brown and Stein's limited association with free thought indicated. Key participants in these events played prominent roles in all of the great nineteenth-century reform and equal-rights movements. Workingmen activists, land reformers, equal-rights proponents, free soil, free labor, abolitionists, labor reformers, suffragists, and universalists met to commemorate the reformer they all claimed as a progenitor of their respective movements.[5]

Thanks to Offen and his close associate, Gilbert Vale, scholars have a bit more information with regard to the first Paine birthday celebration in America than we do for that in England. Offen remembered the event in a letter written in 1844 and published in Vale's *Beacon*, an educational and literary journal.

> I arrived in New-York, April 27, 1824, and found, to my surprise, that with whomsoever you might converse, with few exceptions, the name of Thomas Paine was treated with contempt, and his services to the cause of American liberty in "the time that tried men's souls," were not known; or, if known, entirely disregarded. I then saw clearly the reason why his name was so offensive to the ears of almost every person to whom it might be mentioned.
>
> It was sheer religious bigotry, together with the thousands of falsehoods uttered from pulpits respecting his moral character, that had poisoned the minds of the rising generation against him. The Liberals of New-York met together and determined to celebrate, for the first time, his birthday in the United States.[6]

Offen added that his decision to organize the Paine birthday celebration was inspired in part by the reaction of New Yorkers to the visit of the French patriot and Revolutionary War ally, the Marquis de Lafayette.

> A fortunate circumstance occurred that gave spirit to the determination. It was the arrival of Lafayette from France in August 1824, to visit that country for whose liberties he had, when young, fought and bled. From the place of his landing, up Broadway, to the City Hall, I followed in the train of thousands of the citizens who gave the old veteran hearty welcome, and the demonstration of joy and gratitude exceeded every thing I had ever before seen, convincing me that the Americans were a grateful people, and that if the services of Mr. Paine were fully known, they would be highly valued.[7]

In this letter, Offen revealed an additional concern overlooked in the few existing accounts of the event. The birthday celebration was to be more than a simple commemoration of Paine's natal day. He and his allies were motivated by a desire to counteract and refute the campaign of defamation waged against Paine's memory by his old Federalist enemies and their evangelical allies. This concern would still be paramount in celebrations at the end of the nineteenth century, when participants would include Paine's most important biographer and the two men who, after Vale and Offen, contributed most to the rehabilitation of Paine's reputation.

The 1825 celebration established another pattern that continued throughout the history of the Paine birthday celebrations; the participants were central figures in the seminal reform movements of the era. There were forty of them in 1825. Offen himself was perhaps the most widely traveled lecturer on the free-thought circuit. The subscribers of George Houston's *Correspondent*, one of the earliest journals of Biblical criticism in the United States, sponsored and funded Offen's 1828 lecture tour through the Mohawk Valley. George Houston, a prominent participant in the 1825 birthday event, was a close friend of the radical British publisher Richard Carlile. Houston fled to the United States after he served two years imprisonment in Newgate Prison and paid a 200-pound fine for publication of Baron d'Holbach's *Histoire de Jésus Christ* under the title of *Ecce Homo*. Houston was close to the commun-itarian Robert Owen and co-founded the Franklin Community in Haverstraw, Rockland County, New York in 1826. Robert L. Jennings was an Owenite activist who co-edited the *Correspondent* and later the *Free Enquirer* with Robert Dale Owen and Frances Wright. Owen and Wright themselves regularly extolled Paine's contribution to reform from lecture platform and printing press. Thomas Paine's colleagues John Fellows and William Carver were probably there, though their names do not appear in the 1825 newspaper accounts. Fellows and Carver were intimate associates of Offen, served as lecturers within the group, and were prominent participants in the entire range of free-thought and reform activities in New York City.[8]

Two years later, on January 29, 1827, when the same group of individuals established the Free Press Association, birthday participant and attorney Henry A. Fay was the central figure. Historians remember Fay in the context of the debate over Sunday or Sabbath Laws. Fay defended the dry-goods seller Miles Chambers, who was charged with selling clothing on Sunday. The Free Press Association was initially created for the defense of George Houston's *Correspondent*. Authors and publishers were still prosecuted for blasphemy in 1825. The Unitarian minister Abner Kneeland was tried, convicted, and jailed for blasphemy as late as 1834-38. Houston, who was himself imprisoned prior to emigration, pulled no punches.[9]

> According to Jesus, we can only be happy by being *poor in spirit*. Immediately after, he bids us be perfect as our heavenly father is perfect. To say the least of these notable maxims, it would seem that the Christians believe God to be a senseless being, destitute of all spirit; and that perfection, by which we are to attain heaven, consists in being equally stupid . . . It is a maxim which paralizes (sic) our reasoning faculties, and renders us the fit instruments of despots, to perpetuate slavery, crush science, and prevent the diffusion of knowledge.[10]

The reactions from pulpit and press were shrill. The *Times* and the *National Gazette* commended Houston's publication to the bonfire. For the *National Advocate*, it was "to the flames" with anything that attacked the church. Owing to the frequently short distance between yelling "riot" and the breakout of riot itself, the concerns of Houston and supporters in the Free Press Association were doubtless justified.[11]

The Paine birthday celebrations spread throughout continental North America in the wake of the New York City event. Every major city in the United States had its own event, and the custom spread westward with the growth of the nation. While enthusiasm ebbed and flowed from time to time, as during the Civil War, when records seem to fall off for a few years, reformers and freethinkers enthusiastically celebrated Paine's birthday throughout the nineteenth century.[12]

The celebrations in 1838 were characteristic, if not archetypal, for both the early period and subsequent celebrations throughout the nineteenth century. At the 1838 New York City event, Gilbert Vale served as presiding officer. Vale was a multi-talented educator, publisher, author, and lecturer whose *Beacon*, a "scientific and literary" journal, was the longest running periodical of its kind in the period prior to 1850. An enthusiastic Paineite and Equal Rights Democrat,

Vale organized the construction of the Thomas Paine Monument in New Rochelle, New York. Vale's *Life of Thomas Paine* was an important milestone in Paine scholarship and nineteenth-century social history. He was also a political activist who served as a delegate from the 4th Ward of New York City to the 1836 Equal Rights/Loco Foco convention. Benjamin Offen, with whom Vale often shared the lecture podium, was again in attendance. So was Joseph Lawton, who served a dual vice-presidency of the event with Thomas Thompson. Lawton was a publisher and agent for George Henry Evans' *Working Man's Advocate,* the *Free Enquirer* of Frances Wright and Robert Dale Owen, and the works of Richard Carlile. Thomas Thompson was treasurer of both the Paine Monument project and the United States Moral and Philosophical Society (USMPS), a membership that he shared with George Henry Evans, himself a perpetual attendee. George Purser was a Tammany Hall Democratic activist and veteran freethinker who, with Benjamin Offen, took on a distinguished champion of Christianity, Dr. W. W. Sleigh, member of the Royal College of Surgeons, in a controversial 1835 religious debate of fifteen days' duration. Edward Webb, a prominent workingmen's activist and later an influential member of the General Trade's Union and Mechanic's Institute, recited two ribald poems, "Calvin's Ghost" and "The Garden of Eden." A deist and close friend of socialist Robert Dale Owen, Webb also served as chairman of the Paine Monument subscribers committee. John Frazee was the architect of the Customs House in New York, a recognized classic of American Greek Revival style and a national monument today. Frazee, perhaps also the most famous American sculptor of his period, was a political activist who stood for state office on the Workingmen's ticket, an ally of the cause of equal rights, and a freethinking skeptic. Frazee also donated his talents to the design and construction of the Thomas Paine Monument. George W. Matsell, who co-owned a popular liberal bookstore, was a Justice of the Police Court and the first Police Chief of New York City just seven years later, in 1845.[13]

The opposite of somber, these were gala, exuberant, and occasionally tipsy affairs. The New York City festivities featured an elaborate banquet at the Knickerbocker Hotel catered by Alex Welsh and attend-ed by 114 persons. Vale reported that Welsh was "famous" in the city for this sort of event. Many standing toasts were offered, occasionally ribald, like one proposed by James Armsten ". . . to the church-going ladies of the United States—walking poles to exhibit British dry goods on." Toasts were almost always accompanied by a song from the proponent, often original, bold, and *a capella*. After a banquet of many courses and many a round of toasts, the revelers retired to the ballroom where an orchestra kept them dancing late into the night.[14]

Celebrations elsewhere in America, like that hosted by Abner Kneeland and his associates in Boston, were not necessarily bibulous. The Boston group had strong temperance leanings. Vale, who periodically mocked them for their abstemiousness, reported a "dinner, from which all intoxicating liquors were excluded, as usual, but in lieu of which coffee and tea were substituted." Though less ribald than that of New York, the Boston event was nevertheless well attended and included a speech by pioneer birth control advocate Dr. Charles Knowlton and the participation of J. P. Mendum and Horace Seaver, both later important abolitionists. The latter two men printed a greater volume of Paine's works and related materials than any other publisher in the second half of the nineteenth century.[15]

The 1838 Paine celebration in Cincinnati, Ohio (the West, at that time) was a fiery affair. From a report in the *Boston Investigator*:

> The anniversary of the birthday of Thomas Paine had never been celebrated in the Queen of the West [Cincinnati]; and when the proposal was made, alarm and consternation seemed to have seized the enemy's camp. The Bankocrats stirred in their corruption, and their foulness dirtied the pages of their journals . . . many were frightened and alarmed, for the very idea of Paine's birthday being celebrated by the firing of cannon, eating, drinking, and speaking, music and dancing, was like giving an invitation to the devil himself to come and preside over the ceremonies. Nay, no doubt something would happen; for the Mayor would stop the firing—he had received orders to do so; and there would be a mob, that there would, it could not be otherwise, for Fanny Wright would be there.[16]

Frances "Fanny" Wright was perhaps the first woman to publicly lecture on political and social topics in America. Contrary to the more demure fashion of the period, Wright kept her hair bobbed short and wore a flowing white pantsuit with strong Greek revival overtones. Equally notorious were her appeals against slavery, for women's rights, and her Tennessee communal experiment with African-American freedmen that ended in failure and scandal. This so-called "High Priestess of Infidelity" arrived at the Cincinnati celebration and spoke for equal rights. Despite the characteristically histrionic alarms, however, the event appears to have been both successful and peaceful, notwithstanding that twenty-five rounds of cannon were indeed fired in Tom Paine's honor to cheers of approval (now *that* would be a worthy goal for Eric Foner and company at one of their future celebrations!).[17]

The 1838 celebrations in New York, Boston, and Cincinnati were representative of the many hundreds of Paine birthday celebrations throughout the nineteenth century. Participants included prominent members of the American equal rights, labor, and agrarian reform movements and, consonant with the founder's original hope, attendees at the birthday events were prominent contributors to the reconstruction of Paine's reputation and the record of his accomplishments.

While an extended review of nineteenth century celebrants is beyond the scope of this paper, an abbreviated list suggests the merits of the case for the celebration's close relationship to nineteenth-century democratic reform. In 1853, Ernestine Rose was the first woman to be elected president of the New York Paine birthday celebration. Rose was arguably the founder of the women's suffrage movement in America. She was the exemplar and mentor of Susan B. Anthony, who kept a giant portrait of Rose over her desk. Walt Whitman delivered the principal address at the 1877 Philadelphia celebration. Thomas Edison, who deeply admired Paine, was an enthusiastic participant who turned the first spade of earth for the Thomas Paine Museum, built near the Thomas Paine Monument in New Rochelle, New York. Dr. Edward Bond Foote presided over the 1892 celebration held at the Manhattan Liberal Club in Chickering Hall, New York. He and his father, Dr. Edward Bliss Foote, were perhaps the most outstanding proponents of birth control and sex education in the nineteenth century. The elder Dr. Foote developed the women's cervical cap birth control device. The two doctors Foote, father and son, bankrolled the legal defense of Whitman's *Leaves of Grass*, Ezra Heywood's *Cupids Yokes*, D. M.

Bennett for mailing Heywood's book, and many other victims of Anthony Comstock's censorship campaign. Moncure Daniel Conway, the prominent and unconventional Virginia abolitionist, was the author of *The Life of Thomas Paine*, still the most influential Paine biography. D. M. Bennett, who officiated or participated at many Paine birthday events, was the editor and publisher of *The Truth Seeker* and a key participant in the campaign to vindicate and honor Paine. His free press contest with Comstock led to the Supreme Court in *The United States v D. M. Bennett*, a case that established the Hicklin Standard, the foundation for American obscenity jurisprudence until the middle of the twentieth century.[18]

Robert Green Ingersoll, one of the greatest reform crusaders in American history, was highly visible. Brown and Stein called him "the greatest active freethinker America produced . . . by far the greatest freethinker of the period" and "one of the most brilliant orators of all time." In her recent popular survey of the era, *Freethinkers,* author Susan Jacoby claimed, "Ingersoll did more than anyone to restore Americans' memory of their country's secular and rationalist tradition." Ingersoll's *Vindication of Thomas Paine* was reprinted scores of times, and he campaigned throughout his life for the recognition and commemoration of Thomas Paine's life and works. With Gilbert Vale and his associates at the beginning of the century, Conway, Ingersoll, and Bennett were the greatest contributors to the reconstruction of Paine's reputation and career in the latter half of the nineteenth century. Their work laid the foundation for all subsequent Paine scholarship.[19]

Though widely overlooked today, the celebration of Thomas Paine's birthday is a tradition of central historical importance to movements for democratic reform in the U.S. and around the world. Few political celebrations have been commemorated with more constancy and attended by a more stellar array of political and social reformers than the natal day of Thomas Paine. Attendees viewed Paine as the father of modern reform and cooperated towards their mutual goal to correct the record and remove the slanders heaped upon Paine's memory by his political and religious enemies. Moreover, this symposium and its contributors are the heirs and successors of that first Paine birthday celebration and the scholarship of Vale, Conway, Ingersoll, and Bennett.

The celebration of Paine's birthday, while still observed

in homes and meeting places throughout the United States and Britain, is now at a low ebb historically. For the most part, the sparsely attended events take place out of the public eye. We have forgotten one of the most important events in American reform history. Will the celebrations die out with the inexorable distancing effect of time, or will they flare up again in the midst of present or future crises? More than likely, the Thomas Paine birthday celebrations will stand or fall on the democratic and egalitarian ideology that Paine advocated. The celebrations will likely persist for as long as people admire the ideology and its distinguished proponent.[20]

Notes

[1]For the British prohibitive acts and good treatment of early eighteenth-century British reform, see Edward Royle and James Walvin, *English Radicals and Reformers, 1760-1848* (Lexington, Kentucky: The University Press of Kentucky, 1982), pp. 77-78. The classic in-depth study is still E.P. Thompson, *The Making of the English Working Class* (New York: Pantheon Books, 1963). For the case of Daniel Isaac Eaton, see Ian Dyck, ed., *Citizen of the World: Essays on Thomas Paine* (London: Christopher Helm, 1987), p. 104.

[2]See Albert Post, *Popular Freethought in America, 1825-1850* (New York: Ferrer, Strauss, and Gould, 1974), p. 76n; James S. Epstein, *Radical Expression: Political Language, Ritual, and Symbol in England, 1790-1850* (New York/Oxford: Oxford University Press, 1994), pp. 122-23, 157-58, and 160-61; Gregory Claeys, *Thomas Paine: Political and Social Thought* (Boston: Unwin Hyman, 1989), p. 211; Edward Royle, *Victorian Infidels* (Manchester, England: Manchester University Press, 1974), pp. 36-37; and William H. Wickwar, *The Struggle for Freedom of the Press.* (London: George Allen & Unwin Ltd., 1928), pp. 55-75.

[3]Ibid. See also Epstein, p. 158; Post, p. 155; Claeys, p. 211; Royle, p. 95; and Iaian McCalman, *Radical Underworld: Prophets, Revolutionaries and Pornographers in London, 1795-1840* (New York/Cambridge: Cambridge University Press, 1988), p. 197.

⁴For Offen, see Post, p. 32, and pp. 76-77; DeRobigne Mortimer Bennett, *The World's Sages, Infidels, and Thinkers* (New York: D. M. Bennett, 1876), p. 695; Marshall G. Brown and Gordon Stein, *Freethought in the United States: A Descriptive Bibliography* (Westport, Connecticut: Green-wood Press, 1978), pp. 31-33. For British immigration, see Post, pp. 7-33; McCalman, p. 214; Royle, *Victorian Infidels*, p. 173; and John Ashworth, *'Agrarians' and 'Aristocrats': Party Political Ideology in the United States, 1837-1846* (London: Royal Historical Society, 1983), pp. 179-93; Michael Durey, "Transatlantic Patriotism: Political Exiles and America in the Age of Revolution," in Clive Emsley, ed., *Artisans, Peasants, and Proletarians, 1760-1860: Essays Presented to Gwyn A. Williams* (Dover, New Hampshire: Croom Helm, 1985), pp. 7-311; Mark Lause, "Unwashed Infidelity: Thomas Paine and Early New York City Labor History," *Labor History* 27: 3 (Summer, 1986), 385; and Sean Wilentz, *Chants Democratic: New York City and the Rise of the American Working Class, 1788-1850* (New York: Oxford University Press, 1984), pp. 48n, and 100-10. An excellent work on New York City immigration and settlement patterns is Robert Ernst, *Immigrant Life in New York City 1825-1863* (New York: Octagon Books, 1979).

⁵Brown and Stein, pp. 34-45. The first and most valuable scholarly attempt to document and explain the extent of Paine's influence on nineteenth- and twentieth-century democratic reform is Harvey J. Kaye, *Thomas Paine and the Promise of America* (New York: Hill and Wang, 2005).

⁶*Beacon*, August 10, 1844. Like the newcomer, Benjamin Offen, scholars generally interpret the campaign of character assassination carried out against Paine as the result of his 1794 publication of *Age of Reason*, a cutting attack on established religion and the inerrancy of the Bible. The attacks on Paine, however, began much earlier than his writings on deism. The British government, for example, secretly paid Scottish writer George Chalmers for the hidden authorship of a 1791 pseudo-biographical attack on Thomas Paine. Chalmers' work, written under the alias Dr. Francis Oldys, MA of the University of Pennsylvania, was the first biography of Paine. Unfortunately, its intentionally slanderous errors have since been replicated both by uncritical scholars and venal partisans. While religionists were certainly threatened by *Age of Reason*, it is important that historians remember that Paine's religious

important that historians remember that Paine's religious views were used as a cudgel by Federalists (and their later descendants, the Whigs) to discredit his democratic-republican political ideology. His religious views were, after all, no more heterodox than those of Thomas Jefferson, Ethan Allen, George Washington, John Adams, and many others from the founding era. Paine's enemies hoped to reduce his considerable political influence by way of lurid attacks on this religious views and slanders on his personal life.

[7] Ibid.

[8] Ibid. Offen's tour is in Waterman, p. 146n and Post, pp. 148-49. For the Franklin Community, see Wilentz, p. 163; Henry J. Fay is in Post, p. 80 and Wilentz, p. 163. Robert L. Jennings is Post, pp. 39 and 181.

[9] For the Free Press Association, see Post, pp. 76-80. Kneeland's trials are recounted in Post, pp. 215-18.

[10] *Correspondent*, March 24, 1827.

[11] *Correspondent*, February 10, 1827.

[12] Many early celebrations are surveyed in Post, pp. 155-59. The author of this paper has also archived notices, programs, and other information relative to many more such throughout the nineteenth century.

[13] Details of the 1838 New York celebration *Beacon*, January 13, 1838, and February 3, 1838. The Cincinnati event is in *Beacon*, February 24, 1838. Vale's biography is justifiably called the "first honest and conscientious biography" of Paine in Audrey Williamson, *Thomas Paine: His Life, Work, and Times* (New York: St. Martin's Press, Inc., 1973), p. 281. Vale's early biography thoroughly refuted the campaign of character assassination by Paine's opponents and supplied the foundation for all later Paine scholarship. The best short treatment of Gilbert Vale is in Gordon Stein, ed. *The Encyclopedia of Unbelief*, 2 vols. (Buffalo, New York: Prometheus Books, 1985), pp. 709-10. See also Post, pp. 48-49; Brown and Stein, pp. 31-33; Bennett, pp. 698-99 and, the most extensive treatment to date, Kenneth W. Burchell, "New York Beacon: Hidden Influence in the Life

and Works of Gilbert Vale" (MA thesis, University of Idaho, 2005). For Vale's Loco Foco candidacy, see Fitzwilliam Byrdsall, *The History of the Loco-Foco or Equal Rights Party . . . its Movements, Conventions, and Proceedings with short Characteristic Sketches of its Prominent Men* (New York: Clement and Packard, 1842), p. 55. Joseph Lawton is in Post, pp. 112 and 126. For Thomas Thompson, see Brown and Stein, p. 35 and *Beacon*, March 24, 1837. George Purser is in Post, p. 138. For Edward Webb's labor activism, see Wilentz, p. 272. His deism and affiliation with Owen are in Wilentz, p. 196. For his recitation of two poems, see *Beacon*, February 3, 1838. See also *Beacon*, December 23, 1837. For John Frazee and his various involvements, the best sources are Linda Hyman, "From Artisan to Artist: John Frazee and the Politics of Culture in Antebellum America" (Ph.D. dissertation, City University of New York, 1978), pp. 85, 87, and 113; and Frederick S. Voss, *John Frazee: Sculptor, 1792-1852* (Boston: The Boston Athenaeum, 1986). George Matsell is in Post, pp. 125 and 161. For his public safety offices, see Augustine Costello, *Our Police Protectors, History of the New York Police* (New York: Published by the Author, 1885); available as an internet resource at http://www.usgennet.org/usa/ny/state/police/ch4pt2.html , and http://www.usgennet.org/usa/ny/state/police/ch5pt1.html .

[14]*Beacon*, February 3, 1838, and March 27, 1841.

[15]*Beacon*, February 17, 1838.

[16]From the *Boston Investigator* reprinted in the *Beacon*, February 24, 1838.

[17]For Fanny Wright, see William Randall Waterman, *Frances Wright*. New York: Columbia University, 1924); Celia Morris Eckhardt, *Fanny Wright: Rebel in America* (Cambridge: Harvard University Press, 1984); and Susan S. Kissel, *In Common Cause: The "Conservative" Frances Trollop and the "Radical" Frances Wright* (Bowling Green, Ohio: Bowling Green State University Popular Press, 1993).

[18]Ernestine Rose is from Carol Kolmerton, *The American Life of Ernestine Rose* (Syracuse, New York: Syracuse University

Press, 1999), p. 102. Whitman's participation in the 1877 Philadelphia celebration is in George E. Macdonald, *Fifty Years of Freethought,* vol. 1 (New York: The Truth Seeker Company, 1927), p. 194. Edison at the Paine Museum is from Macdonald, vol. 2, p. 614. For Foote and the 1892 Manhattan Club celebration, see Macdonald, vol. 2, p. 65. The doctors Foote, junior and senior, are covered in the superlative work by Hal D. Sears, *The Sex Radicals: Free Love in High Victorian America* (Lawrence, Kansas: The Regents Press of Kansas, 1977). Additional information on the Footes and Ezra Heywood is from Marin Henry Blatt, *Free Love and Anarchism: The Biography of Ezra Heywood* (Urbana: University of Illinois Press, 1989), pp. 111-13. Conway is in Macdonald, p. 991, and Moncure Daniel Conway, *Autobiography, Memories, and Experiences of Moncure Daniel Conway* (New York: Houghton, Mifflin, and Company, 1904). A useful biography of Conway is John D'Entremont, *Southern Emancipator: Moncure Conway, the American Years, 1832-1865* (New York: Oxford University Press, 1987). Information on D. M. Bennett is from Roderick Bradford, *D. M. Bennett: The Truth Seeker* (Am-herst, New York: Prometheus Press, 2006).

[19]The best biography of Ingersoll is Frank Smith, *Robert G. Ingersoll: A Life* (Buffalo, New York: Prometheus Books, 1990). Quotations about Ingersoll are in Brown and Stein, pp. 47-50, and Susan Jacoby, *Freethinkers: A History of American Secularism* (New York: Henry Holt and Company, 2004), 184.

[20]Information on current and past Thomas Paine birthday celebrations can be found at www.tompaine.org.

PAINE, THE BRITISH LABOR MOVEMENT, AND IRISH POLITICS

Bryson Clevenger, Jr.

My paper actually is not really about Thomas Paine. There is a little shock here. I was not intending to work on Paine, but Paine sort of insinuated himself into my work, and made his presence known, intruding into it. I am currently working on a project on the development of British working-class ideology in the early nineteenth century, using one special focus, looking at one problem and developing insights from that. The problem is the Irish Question. The goal is not just to understand the Irish Question, but to see how the British working class looked at the Irish Question. My object is to understand how they thought about things in general, and about themselves in the world, and I found that Thomas Paine set the framework for the development of British working-class ideology, especially the development of the British labor movement's reaction toward internationalism and nationalism, at least in the first half of the nineteenth century.

During this time, a unified working-class movement with a coherent philosophy or ideology did not yet exist; the English working class was only beginning the process of identifying itself. What I do is study the developing English working class and its developing political ideology, tracing how they look at the Irish Question in this period of time. Following E. P. Thompson's methodology, I seek to characterize the ideas and inclinations of those who would influence the birth of the later labor organizations, trades unions, and international workers movements. Many of these ideas are derived from those who spoke for the interests of the workers, from at least the formation of the London Corresponding Society in the last decade of the eighteenth century. This paper refers to these figures as "ultra radicals," a phrase from their own literature, to distinguish them from others who identified with the goals of the middle classes.

The Irish Question was the question that dominated the British scene over that period of time. It's one of the liveliest controversies of the nineteenth century. Governments fell because of their Irish failures. In the beginning, Ireland appeared to pose a threat to British security. In fact, during the war with Napoleonic France, the government feared a French landing in Ireland that might prompt an Irish rebellion against the British. This threat played no small role in the formation of a Union between Britain and Ireland in 1800. The French threat passed, although the Irish did stage a rebellion in 1798 with the apparent sympathy of the British ultra radicals. But Irish unrest remained, and would remain for the greater part of the nineteenth century and a considerable portion of the twentieth (if one includes the Ulster Question).

Some historians argue that there was a clear alliance between the ultra radicals of the British labor left and the Irish throughout the first part of the nineteenth century. Other historians have thought that the British labor left was not really interested in the Irish Question during that period of time. What I try to do is look at the writings of the British labor left—at their pamphlets, letters, and newspapers page by page. I found a number of interesting things. One is that they do seem to be developing an ideology, a way of looking at the world, a way of formulating their beliefs in some kind of coherent political thought. This is long before the era of Marx. The second thing I found is that they were looking to Tom Paine. Paine insinuates himself into the ideology at a very high level.

As was mentioned earlier in this conference, there is a paradox in Paine, using the idea of common sense to challenge an established way of looking at the world that was commonly accepted. The writings of the people within the labor left were using Paine's ideas, through their own reasoning processes, to challenge the existing order. I was often surprised; when I thought that they would take one kind of common-sense approach or political tack, they took another, and the tack that they took was in line with the general ideas of Paine and with Paine's rationalist critique of society. His notions of society tempered, at different points in time, what could have led them to see the world through more prejudice, using their common sense in a coarser, more anti-intellectual way. Surprisingly enough, they don't do that. Throughout my readings of the British ultra radicals, I find very little of what we call a negative prejudice in these writers, and I attribute a lot of that to Paine, the way Paine formulated his ideas on the subject.

I want to talk a little bit about the people I'm focusing upon. I call them the ultra radicals, a word that they used to describe themselves. The terms can be complicated. There was a group of people called the "radicals," who would become more of a middle-class left, the followers of Bentham and Mill who become utilitarians in the 1830s, for example. By contrast, the ultra radicals are a strange mixture of labor leaders, some Tory democrats, people who support very radical suffrage—all of whom see themselves as self-consciously working in the interest of the working classes. They see themselves as consciously different from the middle classes. By the late 1830s, we see them coming together in a very large movement, the Chartist movement, that calls for political reform in the Paineite tradition, especially universal manhood suffrage. Even when they consider economic problems, political reform is the key point of their philosophy. Everything revolves around the political solution.

James Epstein in his *Radical Expression*, Gregory Claeys in his *Thomas Paine*, and of course E. P. Thompson in his *Making of the English Working Classes* point to the centrality of Paine's ideas, especially in the early period.[1] Epstein argues that the ultra radicals followed two traditions of expression: the rights of Englishmen as expressed in their understanding of historical rights, and the natural-rights theory of Paine. They were likely to see English policies in Ireland, and the Irish response to those policies, in light of those traditions. I argue, even further, that the British ultra radicals generally supported the Irish in their struggles, and that the appreciation of Irish rights was founded not only on the idea of the "rights of Englishmen" traceable back to Locke, but even more on Thomas Paine's *Rights of Man* and on the reflected experience of both the American and French Revolutions.

Ireland was a land of poverty, a land of unrest, and a land where people were very unhappy. For the British, the problem of governing Ireland was known as the Irish Question. But, during this time, there were really three Irish Questions. Should Ireland's resources, especially land, be managed differently? Should Ireland have freedom of religious choice? Finally, should Ireland be a nation separate from Great Britain, or at least enjoy some form of self-government? When we examine the rhetoric of the British working-class advocates and leaders, we find some aspects of their rhetoric that appear to have been engaged with the Irish Question and other aspects of the same rhetoric that were distanced, or even detached, from Irish causes. The aspects of that rhetoric that supported the Irish causes largely came from Paine. His ideas informed the

British working classes' ideological position on the Irish Question long before incorporating the Irish workers into the Chartist movement became a practical political matter.

As noted, the Irish Question may be separated into economic, religious, and political (or national) components. In a period where the English working classes and their often middle-class leaders formed the great national trade unions, gained a measure of factory reform in terms of shorter hours at least for children, attempted to secure poor relief, and extended the suffrage, the Irish achieved Catholic Emancipation, secured repeal of the tithe in Ireland, and began to build a movement for national self-determination. We shall look at these components one at a time, looking at how the ultra radicals addressed each issue.

The first of these Irish Questions — the economic fact of Irish underdevelopment and poverty — corresponded with the efforts of the ultra radicals to improve their own economic fortunes. As the ultra radicals organized for political reform, they began to form organizations or combinations to fight for the rights of workers. They won this right in 1824 with the repeal of the Combination Acts of Pitt the Younger, meant to keep workers and critics of the government from meeting and organizing.. They began work immediately, even founding a newspaper to express their programs and beliefs, the *Trades Newspaper*, edited by John Gast, a shipwright. These combinations, nascent unions, in fact, reached a climax in 1834 with the Grand National Consolidated Trades Union. Throughout the 1830s, into the 1840s and beyond, the workers and their leaders pressed for the ten-hour day and for better working conditions. In the late 1830s. The Dublin trades unionists followed suit. Their strikes drew the support of the English ultra radicals and drew the opposition of the chief Irish leader, Daniel O'Connell.

The labor and political reform leaders, following Paine, emphasized the natural rights of the individual, such as freedom from hunger and access to the fruit of one's own labor. Those interested in the role of immigration in affecting wages, those interested in addressing and improving the condition of the poor (including the work-ing poor), and those interested in new rational solutions for society could and did look to Ireland in this period for examples of their principles.

The ultra radicals looked to political reform to take care of economic reform. The pressing concern was the extension of the suffrage. They saw Parliament as the tool of the propertied interests, primarily the landlords. This view, of course, is consistent with the Paineite tradition. British workers should look not to the same government that ruled Ireland for relief, but to the possibility of a reformed government that would better represent them. In 1819, parliamentary reformers such as Henry Hunt believed that the struggle of the English, Scots, and Irish for "Universal Liberty" in the form of universal suffrage would do the most to end the sufferings of the Irish as well as the British. [2] The ultra radicals would hold to this course throughout the first half of the nineteenth century.

Yet, observing that Ireland was in much worse shape than Britain, they began to see that Ireland's economic situation had to be studied within its own context. There is a story about working-class leaders going to Ireland and seeing an old naked woman walking down the street, frail and gaunt, and they reported their horror, especially that it seemed to be a normal sight. They compared the situation of Ireland to that in southern Europe, especially southern Italy, rather than with northern Europe. Despite the differences in Irish and British economic development, the British ultra radicals clearly saw the Irish as fellow sufferers and as fellow victims of the insensitivity of both the British government and the dominant economic interests in Britain. They began to analyze the economic aspect of the Irish Question using the same ideological positions, derived largely from Thomas Paine, as they used to address their own issues.

One concern for many ultra radicals, clearly in the Paineite tradition, was high taxation coupled with corruption. Those who denounced high taxation and corruption as burdens for the poor in England saw them as equal burdens for the Irish. High taxation was seen to support what Paine would call the non-producers of society. They were paid by the mass of the people, the direct producers of wealth, and those who could not pay were driven into poverty. For example, an article in *The Gauntlet* defending O'Connell's call for a tax on fund-holders, argued that the British government "machined" the people "by taxation into serfs and slaves" to support the luxuries of the "aristocracy and priesthood."[3] This analogy resembled the oppression of the Third Estate by the other two Estates in eighteenth-century France.

The ultra radicals were also impressed that Ireland had no outdoor poor relief in the early part of the nineteenth century. Englishmen had been guaranteed the right of poor relief since Tudor times, but these rights were in question in the

1830s. The Whig reformers, now the government, determined to end what they regarded as an inefficient system that discouraged free contracts between capital and labor by encouraging the latter to seek relief in the protection of the poor laws. The government's solution was to make relief available only in workhouses, and then only by making it more onerous than the lowest paying and most odious job. Demonstrations and even violent disturbances erupted. The British ultra radicals, outraged, argued that taxation in general and not the poor rates were at the core of national misery.

The outcry of the ultra radicals was extraordinary. But the ultra radicals even earlier supported poor laws for Ireland. In its argument in favor of tax reform and poor relief for Ireland, the *Black Dwarf* in 1817 restated Paine's argument in favor of outdoor relief when necessary. The English lower orders had poor laws but were crippled by taxation; the Irish poor, on the other hand, had no state welfare mechanism yet paid taxes to the state. Thus the British ultra radicals argued not only for outdoor relief in Britain but also for outdoor poor relief in Ireland.

Some workers worried that the Irish poor would naturally come to England and compete for their jobs because they could not get relief in Ireland. However, the really poor of Ireland were not in the cities, but in the countryside. Irish tenants drew the sympathy and the support of the ultra radicals, who thought it a disgrace that people could live in such squalor and desperation within the United Kingdom. In addition, the Irish suffered from the precariousness of their land tenure. Tenants who raised the value of their own land by improvements were then obligated to pay a higher rent, known as "rack rents." Often they could not afford these higher rents; the landlord then would lease the land to someone who could pay, and the former tenants became beggars.

All of this shocked the ultra radicals. Using the rhetoric of "old corruption," the working-class leaders looked to the traditional enemy, the aristocracy, as the chief villain. The enemies of the French Revolution were still the enemies of the British workers and the enemies of the Irish poor. Irish misery came not just from the failures of British policy, but primarily from the practices of Irish landlords. The twist on this issue, making it much worse, was the Irish landlords' status as absentee landlords. They not only collected exorbitant rents, but also usually spent their gains in England rather than in Ireland. They not only took from the poor but also from their own "country."

This war of the landlords, primarily Anglican or British landlords, against the people had a long history. William Cobbett, the great popular journalist, traced this history back to Elizabeth I, who found conquering and then ruling Ireland to be a trial. She "had constant *war* in Ireland; constant *pretended rebellion;* constant *confiscation* and *bloodshed*" (see note 4 below). In the end, according to this account, Elizabeth gave Ireland "as a spoil to her rapacious courtiers" (see note 4 below). This policy continued under the Stuarts. He traced present Irish miseries directly to the Irish past. "Out of these confiscations, forfeitures, seizures, grants, and appropriation[s] . . . have grown *tenures* as numerous as the stars in the sky."[4]

In 1832, *The Poor Man's Advocate*, claiming to speak for the trade union movement in Manchester, declared that misery in Ireland came from the "harsh-ness of landlords towards their starving tenantry."[5] Recognizing the Irish Question as a question of class struggle, the paper feared that the same "sword" being used on the Irish might be used on the English working classes.[6] As a group, the ultra radicals wanted to see the development of an Irish economy freed from the self-serving interests of the British and the Irish absentee landlords. The conflict in Ireland continued the class struggle against the feudal system along the principles of the French Revolution.

Their language comes from Paine's characterization of the aristocracy as a burden on society. Paine, in his *Rights of Man*, best expressed this—in words appearing over and over in the writings of the British labor radicals: "The aristocracy are not the farmers who work the land, and raise the produce, but are the mere consumers of the rent; and when compared with the active world, are the drones, a *seraglio* of males, who neither collect the honey nor form the hive, but exist only for lazy enjoyment."[7] In this case, they were a burden that actually stole from one society and took it to another society. Until the 1830s and 1840s, the central character in the sympathy for the Irish and the Irish poor was Paine. Other figures come into play—Robert Owen and social thinkers were adding their voices to the discussion—but the ideas of Paine provide the central focus of this economic criticism on the Irish Question

The second part of the Irish Question—and a primary issue for many of the Irish—concerned religious establishment and the discrimination against Irish Catholics. The English Reformation, that had made England and Scotland Protestant, left Ireland Catholic. Queen Elizabeth I settled Protestants in Ireland; Oliver Cromwell carried this much further in the seventeenth century, especially in Ulster where the Orangemen remained in the ascendancy even after Ireland gained independence in the twentieth century. The restoration of Charles II explicitly excluded Catholics and other non-Anglicans from political office. The Glorious Revolution of 1688 put William and Mary on the throne. A battle still commemorated today, in which the Protestant troops of William III defeated a largely Catholic army of James II, confirmed the exclusion. Later, enlightened British leaders, including William Pitt the Younger, tried to undo this situation and to ensure Irish Catholics their political liberties in return for their support for the Act of Union in 1801. But this attempt failed in the face of determined old-guard opposition, led by the King. Thus, Ireland's place in the United Kingdom after the Napoleonic Wars was predicated still on the exclusion of Catholics from political office.

In the 1820s, in the aftermath of the repeal of the Combination Acts, and following the successful repeal of the provisions excluding other non-Anglicans from official office, Irish and English Catholics under the leadership of Daniel O'Connell began to press for Catholic Emancipation, as they put it, the end to these acts of exclusion. The government defended its policy of excluding Catholics on the premise that Catholics would exclude or oppress others if they had the chance.

Interestingly enough, Thomas Paine, the hero of the ultra radicals, had long before refuted this argument:

> Persecution is not an original feature in any religion; but is always the strongly marked feature of all law religions, or religions marked by law. Take away the law establishment, and every religion resumes it original benignity. In America, a Catholic Priest is a good citizen, a good character, and a good neighbour; an Episcopalian Minister is of the same description.[8]

Paine's refutation and the reference to the American example would appear often in the arguments of the ultra radicals, both on this question and on the question of Irish independence. The *Republican*, for example, which reprinted portions of the *Rights of Man*, noted the American example where the most "dangerous tenet [of religion was] becoming perfectly harmless." The answer, as the *Republican* saw it, was to "let opinion look for assistance to argument, not law; and where reason cannot determine, let authority learn to hold its peace." The paper reasoned from this that the "claims of both Dissenter and Catholic to full participation in the rights of civil government must be admitted."[9]

The ultra radicals supported Catholic Emancipation as a victory for general liberty. Their understanding of Irish religious freedom particularly owed a debt to Paine's *Rights of Man* (as well as to his *The Age of Reason*) in its call for religious liberty,[10] its preference for scientific reasoning,[11] and its opposition to an established church.[12] The Religious Question was subsumed under the general question of rights. Paine wanted men to be liberated from the domination of political and religious institutions founded on tradition and unquestioned authority. He had emphasized the relationship of the individual to his creator, despising the idea of a state church, or "law church." We often think of Paine as anti-religion and anti-church. But he had a strong belief in the liberty of conscience and the freedom to be clear in one's religious consciousness. For Paine's successors, the imposed Anglican Church of Ireland was an easy enemy. But the ultra radicals wanted to emphasize the liberating nature of Catholic Emancipation as a principle of general emancipation rather than merely as a victory for Catholicism.

This state church, warned against by Paine, was an ally of the British ruling classes in the same way as the Catholic Church had been the ally of the French monarchy. Thomas Paine had emphasized religious liberty, secularism, and opposition to a hierarchical autocratic church. Following Paine, with very few exceptions, the ultra radicals consistently supported the Irish Catholic's rights to political equality and freedom from religious bigotry. Even Cobbett, an Anglican through and through, found it relatively easy to see the Catholic poor and their tyrannical Protestant oppressors as analogous to the British poor and their oppressors.

The Catholics—with the support of the radicals, the Whigs, and the ultra radicals—gained their emancipation in 1829. The ultra radicals, while celebrating with them, never tired of reminding them of two things: that the British workers had supported the Irish Catholics, and that Catholic Emancipation would not solve all of Ireland's problems.

In fact, this victory did not settle the question of Irish Catholic rights. The Anglican Irish Church, as an institutionalized state church, still required the payment of tithes for its support. In Ireland this meant that Catholics would be paying to support a Protestant church. As it happened, most of the Irish Catholics were also the poor tenants. This controversy electrified the ultra radicals, who nearly without exception supported the Irish Catholics' right to refuse the tithe, with some going so far as to urge disestablishment of the church. The Irish, in this view, could not pay tithes without undergoing severe economic hardship. Tithes represented for the British ultra radicals the robbing of the Irish poor by the English establishment, in this case by the most politically conservative element of the British establishment, the Anglican Church. The issue prompted them to reflect on the history of its establishment. William Cobbett, for example, accused Queen Elizabeth of attacking Ireland and then dragging the Irish "into the churches by force."[13] Again, as with the issue of civil liberty and of resistance to the authority of the Church, the theme had been set forth by Thomas Paine.

The fierce resistance by the Irish to tithe payment resulted in disorder and violence. The state responded by passing what Dorothy Thompson, the great historian, referred to as the most brutal measure of coercion ever passed by a British government.[14] This bill of coercion further committed the ultra radicals to the Irish cause. They saw the struggle against the tithes as not merely a struggle for religious liberty but as a struggle against the arbitrary use and abuse of force.

The ultra radicals in two of the biggest conflicts involving religion supported the Irish Catholics, seeing both Catholic Emancipation and the revocation of the tithes in Ireland as a victory for general liberty. This is a kind of irony, because they were mostly English Protestants, supporting Irish Catholics against the Irish Orangemen. Because they saw the issue as a matter of prejudice and religious oppression, there was a consistent position over time on the part of the British radicals. Yet the position did cause them problems. They always felt much more comfortable with the democratic, rather than the religious, aspect of the struggle. They especially disliked the Pope, who was seen as a monarch, a political figure almost in the same way as a Hapsburg king or a Russian czar. There were also concerns about a Catholic Holy Alliance across Europe.

For the most part, secularism had been an important theme for the ultra radical thinkers, going at least as far back as Paine's *The Age of Reason*, although Paine had put forth his own form of deism. The secular British ultra radicals associated superstition and arbitrary government with organized religion. They mistrusted both Protestant and Catholic priests. Thus, these ultra radicals were unlikely to sympathize with any notion that religious and cultural differences expressed the national identity, even a Catholic identity for the Irish.

In the 1850s, when Protestants and Catholics fought in the streets over the question of the Papacy, the ultra radicals were to condemn the violence of both sides, albeit showing a little more sympathy for the Irish, especially when the latter were outnumbered. Religion itself was clearly not the important issue in their eyes. In the 1850s, *Cooper's Journal* supported secular education against its enemies, among which it included Roman Catholicism as well as the chief Protestant groups. The paper called for a system of education that would "preclude the peculiarities of any religious creed."[15] The Irish were able to count on British ultra radical support throughout this period, but the same ultra radicals despised the hierarchy of the Catholic Church, represented in Italy by the Pope, a church that clearly represented the state Church earlier opposed by Paine.

The third issue in the Irish Question was repeal of the national union, the idea of Irish national liberation. It was fairly easy for the working-class Left to sympathize with the Irish poor, to support Irish trade unions, and to oppose the interests of an aristocratic state Church. But, in a more imaginative recognition, the ultra radicals also began to see Ireland as an oppressed nation. The Act of Union in 1801 had created the United Kingdom, putting the Parliament at Westminster supreme over the British Isles as a whole. The Irish, again led by O'Connell, fought for a measure of independence and self-government in the 1830s and 1840s.

The ultra radicals recognized that Ireland, in the words of *Northern Star*, the most important Chartist publication, needed "equal laws, equal rights, and equal liberties."[16] Here again, we see here that the strength of the British ultra radical position was in Paine's *Rights of Man*. E.P. Thompson, treating an earlier period, and Dorothy Thompson, writing about the Chartists, also saw Paine as a central figure for the ultra radicals. The ultra radicals believed that liberty was the right of all subjects of the empire, not just of one class or ethnic group. Tyrannical rule over another country, moreover, could accustom the English government to autocratic rule at home. Early on, the ultra radical *Black Dwarf*, writing about the Irish Catholic peasant, asked whether the man could be "content, who finds himself governed by a system from which he is proscribed, and considered as an alien in his own country."[17] It was a consistent step from the recognition that the Irish were oppressed as a national group to the opinion that the Union of Ireland and Great Britain had been a true disaster for the Irish.

A meeting of the National Union of the Working Classes in London went further, raising the issue of separation of Ireland from the United Kingdom. In a petition to Parliament in 1831, during the tithe wars in Ireland, the N.U.W.C. warned that, should their pleas for Ireland be ignored, the "long sufferings of Erin will, ere long, shake off the cruel yoke of English bondage and cease to be part of the British Empire."[18] In the same meeting, an English delegate said that before the English Conquest Ireland had a great culture that had even influenced the development of England.[19] At the next meeting, an Irish delegate continued by arguing that Irish immigration "took food out of English mouths." This same delegate was reported as speculating that the English working class would benefit if the Union between England and Ireland were repealed.[20] All of this was reported favorably in the ultra radical press.

Even Thomas Sadler, the famous Tory democrat, recognized that Ireland suffered from British rule. In 1829, the year of Catholic Emancipation, Sadler compared Ireland with England in that both "shared the fate" of "having been a conquered country." Ireland, however, was "more unfortunate" because it had been more "frequently subdued;" the descendants of the Normans continually re-conquered Ireland. There have been "few generations . . . without witnessing the confiscations of large portions of property of the Island."[21] This historical misfortune had a cultural impact on Ireland: "genius," "dignity," "merit," and "elegance" went unrewarded in the absence of wealth.[22] Richard Carlile, the Paineite secularist, attacking the government of the Whigs and aristocrats, chose as his ally the Great Liberator, Daniel O'Connell of Ireland. Asserting that the "House of Commons . . . [even after Reform, was] still but the lower-house of the aristocracy," he argued that the government in power had "no sanction but that of hereditary power, usurped by conquest and supported by military power."[23]

Carlile, in fact, called for an end to the Union. He saw the Union in actuality as a "conquest" of Ireland by England. According to Carlile, the Union was "a Union by force only; it is not a Union of interests, of love, or of necessity in mutual defence." It was not a Union of peoples but merely a "Church and State Union." The Union, according to him, was "founded by corruption." Repeal was "a justice," which would be in the interest of the people of England as well as the people of Ireland." Both countries were "degraded as well as otherwise injured by the Union." Carlile thought that the Union could, should, and would "be overthrown."[24]

Both Ireland and England had been conquered by the Normans, according to the theory prevalent during this period. Paine, of course, had referred to the beginning of modern British government coming from the sword of William the Conqueror.[25] If the "Norman" ruling class was still allowed to treat the Irish as a conquered people, then they might be encouraged to see the English — Anglo-Saxon — common people in a similar light.

In 1833, the year of the Whig Coercion Act against Ireland mentioned above, the *Pioneer* recommended that the working classes unify against the oppression of the "Norman Yoke" and ridiculed any attempt to use English patriotism as a club against the Irish; the paper wondered why anyone should thank his country for a "life of ceaseless toil."[26] The "Norman Yoke" idea was taken from Paine, and brought home to British workers the notion that Ireland was a conquered country   The oppression of the Irish, to the ultra radicals, resembled the enslavement of Poland by the Russians and the Hapsburg rule in Italy. Reacting along with the other radicals to the concert of Europe and the old heads of state — the old international aristocracy — the ultra radicals supported many national movements almost unconditionally, especially if a republic was possible. They supported the Canadian grievances against the British and even took a stand against the British government in the Opium Wars against China in the early 1840s. The irony of fighting a war for opium was not lost on them. The Chinese in this instance were seen as an oppressed nation. The Irish, with this surprising British ultra radical support, constructed a new Irish national identify consistent with radical national movements throughout Europe. The idea of Ireland as an independent nation in the same connection as the nationalist movements in Italy, Poland, and Hungary among others is interesting in that the ultra radicals were caught somewhat in a dilemma, although that is too strong a word. An Ireland governed by an Irish aristocracy, by Irish landlords, or even by Irish Whigs was not to their liking. An independent Ireland should be a Chartist, a republican, Ireland. Ireland should have a better government than England. They believed that there should be greater unity between the working classes of both countries in support of the larger aims of the ultra radicals. They explicitly feared an independent Ireland that would be governed as badly as the British were governing themselves. These criteria, almost detailed depictions of an acceptable independent nation, were not usually conditions they placed on a Mazzini in Italy or a Kossuth in Hungary.

The ultra radicals' insistence on the superiority of class solidarity and the superiority of a republic as a form of government at times led to unusual conflicts. The most interesting perhaps was their later support for Garibaldi, the greatest republican hero, but also a serious enemy of the Pope, offending Catholics in England and in Ireland. They did not perceive this as a conflict at the time, and their bewilderment is the subject of another paper.

In conclusion, E. P. Thompson has written of the continuous alliance between the Irish and British working classes during this time period. This was true, at least in the eyes of the ultra radicals. They devised economic proposals that they hoped would benefit Ireland, kept a close eye on Irish political liberties, opposed land policies that required the Irish to pay high taxes to absentee landlords, promoted religious liberty for the Irish Catholics, defended the latters' refusal to pay tithes, opposed the domination of the Protestant Anglican Church over the Catholic Irish, and supported Irish independence. The ultra radicals insisted on the brotherhood among workers—including the Irish rural poor—in all countries. Their successors would support the French in the 1870 Commune, and some of them would refuse to fight in the First World War against their fellow workers.

My main point today is that they looked at Ireland consistently from the perspective of their own political ideology. That ideology, as it developed, took a lot from

Thomas Paine. Paine also served as a positive influence to temper prejudices, to support religious liberty, to support political liberty, and to support the national self-determination of all people. His insistence on the basic rights of all men encouraged the belief that the workers and poor people of both England and Ireland were brothers and part of the same struggle. Paine's notion of indigenous national classes under the thumb of an international ruling class (for example, the Norman aristocracy) now lives mainly in the lore of the Left and in old songs of the laying on of hands. But some day it may serve to inform a debate over developing nations in the grip of global forces.

Notes

[1] James Epstein, *Radical Expression: Political Language, Ritual, and Symbol in England, 1790-1850*, (New York: Oxford, 1994), pp. 5-11; Gregory Claeys, *Thomas Paine: Social and Political Thought*, (London: Unwin Hyman, 1989), pp. 210-15; and Edward P. Thompson, *The Making of the English Working Class* (New York: Vintage, 1963), pp. 754, 755, 762-64.

[2] *Black Dwarf*, 3:30 (July 28, 1819), 494-95.

[3] *GAUNTLET*, 56, (Mar. 2, 1834), 881.

[4] *Cobbett's Political Register*, 87:5 (Jan. 31, 1835), 266-70.

[5] *Poor Man's Advocate* (Sep. 15, 1832), 6.

[6] *Poor Man's Advocate* (October 13, 1832), 1.

[7] Thomas Paine, *The Rights of Man*, in *The Rights of Man, Common Sense and Other Political Writings,* ed. Mark Philip. (Oxford: Oxford University Press, 1995), p. 279.

[8] Thomas Paine, from the *Rights of Man*, as quoted in the *Republican*, 11, 212.

[9] *Republican*, 1, (Jan. 16, 1812), 4.

[10] Thomas Paine, *The Rights of Man*, in *The Complete Writings of Thomas Paine*, Philip Foner, ed. (New York: Citadel Press, 1945),

vol. 1, p. 274. Also see Thomas Paine, *The Age of Reason*, in *The Complete Writings of Thomas Paine*, vol. 1, p. 506.

[11]Paine, *Rights of Man*, vol. 1, p. 276. See also Paine, *Age of Reason*, vol. 1, pp. 498, 499, 601.

[12]Paine, *Rights of Man*, vol. 1, pp. 290-93. See also Paine, *Age of Reason*, vol. 1, p. 586.

[13]*Cobbett's Political Register*, 87:2, (January 10, 1835), 67-70.

[14]Dorothy Thompson. "Ireland and the Irish in English Radicalism before 1850," in *The Chartist Experience: Studies in Working-Class Radicalism and Culture, 1830-60*, James Epstein and Dorothy Thompson, eds. (London: Macmillan, 1982), p. 137; Edward P. Thompson, *The Making of the English Working Class* (New York: Vintage, 1963), pp. 92-94.

[15]*Cooper's Journal*, 1:19 (May 11, 1850), 289-90.

[16]*Northern Star*, (Jan. 13, 1938), 7.

[17]*Black Dwarf*, 1:5 (Feb. 26, 1817), 74.

[18]*The Poor Man's Guardian*, (Sep. 10, 1831), 79.

[19]*The Poor Man's Guardian*, (Sep. 10, 1831), 78.

[20]*The Poor Man's Guardian*, (Sep. 17, 1831), 88.

[21]Michael Thomas Sadler, *Ireland: Its Evils and Their Remedies: Being a Refutation of the Errors of the Emigration Committee and Others, Touching that Country*, 2d. ed. (London: Murray, 1829), p. 46.

[22]Sadler, p. 54.

[23]*Gauntlet*, 56 (Mar. 2, 1834), 881.

[24]*Gauntlet*, 56, (Mar. 2, 1834), 882.

[25] Thomas Paine, *The Rights of Man*, in *The Complete Writings of Thomas Paine*, Philip Foner, ed. (New York: Citadel Press, 1945), vol. 1, pp. 285-86.

[26] *Pioneer*, (Oct. 5, 1833), 39; (Nov. 30, 1833), 99; and (Dec. 7, 1833), 106.

AGRARIAN JUSTICE: PAINE, JEFFERSON, CRÈVE-COEUR, AND ECONOMIC EGALITARIANISM IN THE NEW REPUBLIC

David M. Robinson

  The concept of agrarianism had a powerful and shaping effect on the Enlightenment, both in France and in the American colonies and the early republic. We do not usually think of Thomas Paine, who represents a kind of quintessence of Enlightenment thought, as an agrarian. He is urban, at least in his general sense of audience and connections—artisans, skilled laborers, small merchants, and so forth—the incipient American blue collar and lower middle classes and eventually middle classes to whom he spoke. But one of his last works, and I would argue one of his most significant works, was entitled *Agrarian Justice*. My paper is an inquiry into the context and meaning of that work and its title, in which I hope to put Paine into dialogue with two recognized American agrarian thinkers, Jefferson and Crèvecoeur, author of *Letters From An American Farmer*.

  In the winter of 1795-96, a year after his release from prison in France and a narrow escape from execution during the Terror, Paine wrote a political pamphlet, *Agrarian Justice*, that confirmed his continuing belief in the principles of the French Revolution and added a significant dimension to his egalitarian theories. *Agrarian Justice*, published in 1797, has been somewhat overshadowed in Paine's oeuvre by his powerful advocacy for the American Revolution, and his masterworks, *Rights of Man* and *The Age of Reason*. But it is worthy of our attention because of its amplification of the consideration of economic rights that Paine had broached in *The Age of Reason*. Linking the concept of human rights to the question of land ownership, Paine forwarded the concept that the legitimacy and the progressive development of civilization depend upon the recognition that "the earth" is "the COMMON PROPERTY OF THE HUMAN RACE" (AJ, p. 398).[1]

  Both the title of Paine's work and its key assumptions connect it with a tradition of agrarian thought, which was influential in both the French and American political contexts. Paine, himself more an urban and cosmopolitan figure than a pastoral type, is typically not counted with either the physiocratic school of agrarian economic theorists that emerged in France in the late eighteenth century, or the American form of agrarian social theory best represented by Thomas Jefferson and Michel-Guillaume de Crèvecoeur. Paine's turn to the terminology and some of the fundamental concepts of agrarianism, however, is significant. Paine and Jefferson were correspondents who held a mutual respect, but who also had their differences. Paine, too, may have read or at least had an acquaintance with Crèvecoeur's book, which had currency in England in the early 1780s and was published in two editions in France in the middle 1780s, but this is only speculative. What is significant about *Agrarian Justice* is Paine's employment of a key agrarian assumption to formulate an early version of public welfare philosophy, and to link that policy to the discourse on human rights in which Paine had been, and continues to be, so influential. His use of this framework of thought in this stage of the emergence of the new French republic can be usefully compared with the important articulations of an agrarian myth in the American context by Jefferson and Crèvecoeur.

The agrarian philosophy of the French physiocratic school, most notably articulated by François Quesnay in his *Tableau Économique* (1759), emphasized the importance of the cultivation of land as the primary source of wealth.[2] The surplus value created by a nation's farmers through the cultivation of crops was the key determinant of a nation's economic well-being. In the new American republic, these theories took on a wider dimension and influence as they were articulated by Jefferson and Crèvecoeur, who hailed not only the economic value of land cultivation, but its personal and societal values as well. The farmer was not only the source of a nation's wealth, the American agrarians contended, but the anchor of its stability and its moral values. Jefferson and Crèvecoeur transformed agrarianism from an economic theory into a cultural myth, one which spoke to the direction that the rapidly developing new nation would take.

The best-known statement of this conception of the virtues of farming is Jefferson's discussion of "Manufactures" in the nineteenth query of his *Notes on the State of Virginia*, written in 1781-82 and published in 1787. Rejecting the ideas of "the political œconomists of Europe . . . that every State should endeavour to manufacture for itself,"[3] Jefferson argues that the "immensity of land courting the industry of the husbandman"[4] creates a different set of circumstances in America. "While we have land to labour then, let us never wish to see our citizens occupied at a work-bench, or twirling a distaff."[5] Such work estranges them from the conditions that nurture lives of virtue and fulfillment. "Those who labour in the earth are the chosen people of God, if ever he had a chosen people, whose breasts he has made his peculiar deposit for substantial and genuine virtue."[6] Jefferson uses the term "virtue" here in its fullest sense, not restricting it to a narrow moralism, but including in it a sense of living and active power. The farmer is close to the fundamental and originating energy of nature, and also becomes in essence a part of that energy. The work of farming, Jefferson writes, "is the focus in which [God] keeps alive that sacred fire, which otherwise might escape from the face of the earth."[7] The virtuous energies generated by agricultural labor guarantee, Jefferson believes, a morally whole culture. "Corruption of morals in the mass of cultivators is a phænomenon of which no age has furnished an example," Jefferson concludes, maintaining that the best path for America is to build a society grounded in the work of farmers on their own land.[8]

Jefferson's assumptions about the values and virtues of the agrarian life were given literary form in Crèvecoeur's *Letters from an American Farmer*, a work built from a series of sketches written in the 1770s and early 1780s and published in 1782, when Jefferson was completing his Virginia *Notes*. Crèvecoeur's farmer James, who narrates the text as a series of letters to an English correspondent (Jefferson's *Notes* were written in reply to queries from "a Foreigner of Distinction"), describes an idyllic life on a Pennsylvania farm from which an egalitarian and mutually supportive society was beginning to emerge. Mixing a close knowledge of the detail and cycles of nature with a hymn to the disciplined labor of farm life, James paints a utopian picture of the new American republic. Although Crèvecoeur undercuts this idyllic vision in the later part of the text, and left unpublished manuscripts that cast further shadows on his initial bright images of farm life, it is those optimistic early portraits of the farmer content in his calling and secure in his community that have left the deepest impression on American culture.[9]

"Where is that station which can confer a more substantial system of felicity," James asks, "than that of the American farmer possessing freedom of action, freedom of thoughts, ruled by a mode of government which requires but little from us?"[10] Most notably, Crèvecoeur described a process of almost complete transformation or rebirth that follows upon a European peasant's acquisition of a farm in North America, an early and influential articulation of the agrarian version of the American dream. "From nothing to start into being; from a servant to the rank of a master; from being the slave of some despotic prince, to become a free man, invested with lands to which every municipal blessing is annexed! What a change indeed! It is in consequence of that change that he becomes an American" (p. 83). As Crèvecoeur's depiction of American life suggests, the agrarian myth was a formative one for the American consciousness, and it reinforced the cherished image of many French intellectuals of America as a rustic paradise.[11]

Paine and Jefferson were friends and correspondents who held each other in mutual respect and shared in the experience of the American Revolution. But Paine was far from being an agrarian in the Jeffersonian sense, and his difference from Jefferson is instructive. He did not reject the theory that agriculture is a basic source of social wealth; indeed, he would embrace it in a sense in his late work. But his milieu and his audience differed from Jefferson's. The first 37 years of his life were spent mostly in smaller English towns, learning a trade as a stay-maker, shopkeeper, and government revenue officer, and he seems to have come alive only after emigrating to Philadelphia. It was Franklin who helped him come to Philadelphia, and his experience and orientation are in many ways akin to Franklin's. Paine lived the life, and understood the people whom Jefferson distrusted, a nonagrarian working class who were beginning to demand a larger role in the institutions that governed them, and a larger share of the economies to which their labor contributed. The social image of the virtuous farmer that we find in Jefferson and Crèvecoeur did not resonate with Paine. He spoke instead to the discontent of the artisan and laboring class as he found it in the American colonies, and then in England, and with less success in France. *Agrarian Justice* can best be understood as Paine's adaptation of agrarian economic assumptions to the situation of this growing population.

In his preface to *Agrarian Justice*, Paine tells us that this new consideration of human rights and the progress of civilization was spurred by one of his theological critics, Bishop Landaff, who had entitled a sermon "THE WISDOM AND

GOODNESS OF GOD, IN HAVING MADE BOTH RICH AND POOR" (AJ, p. 396). God did no such thing, Paine responded: "he made only Male and Female; and he gave them the earth for their inheritance" (AJ, p. 396). Poverty, Paine goes on to argue, is not in the natural state of things; it "is a thing which is created by that which is called civilized life" (AJ, p. 397). If humans have created poverty through their social arrangements, Paine believes, they can begin to alleviate it through social processes as well. He thus outlines a plan of taxation that guarantees every citizen a small initial sum of money at age 21, an inheritance so to speak, and a small maintenance after the age of 50, and, he insists, "it is a right and not a charity that I am pleading for" (AJ, p. 400).

Paine's advocacy of tax policy as a response to inequalities in the distribution of income has clear relevance to political practice and public policy in our era. His argument is grounded in his concern about the extremes of wealth and poverty that had emerged in the evolution of modern society, and their resulting social wreckage and personal devastation. These are the very conditions, it should be noted, that were fundamental to the outbreak of the French Revolution. "The most affluent and the most miserable of the human race are to be found in the countries that are called civilized" (AJ, p. 397), Paine observes, a situation that calls into question the equation between civilization and progress. Paine argues that it is not at all clear whether what we refer to as civilization "has most promoted or most injured the general happiness of man" (AJ, p. 397). What has been granted to some has been denied to many others. "On the one side the spectator is dazzled by splendid appearances; on the other he is shocked by extremes of wretchedness" (AJ, p. 397). Both of these conditions, Paine writes, "he has erected" (AJ, p. 397), as a member and beneficiary of civilization.

As we can see from his formulation, Paine is interested not only in portraying the great divide between rich and poor, but also in implicating his imagined spectator (and of course his readers) in the construction of this state of affairs. As men and women who function within the society, they must assume responsibility for it. Paine intends to show those who are the beneficiaries of civilization that they have a corresponding responsibility to address its costs to others, to begin a process of rebalancing a system of human distribution and consumption that has lost its equilibrium. Civilization is the result of human choice and will, Paine suggests, a constructed or artificial condition. That is a crucial recognition, for what has made by men and women can be unmade or remade. Paine's experience in the American Revolution, and more dramatically in the French Revolution, had confirmed for him both the artificiality and the fragility of human social constructs. In *Agrarian Justice* he hopes to employ that essential truth in the progressive betterment of the poor, and as he sees it, of civilization as a whole.

But in order to define and describe civilization as a construction, he must differentiate it from a prior state of affairs that he calls the "natural state," or the "natural and primitive state" (AJ, p. 397), that mythical original condition in which humans initially existed on the planet. Here we find that Paine, like many of his eighteenth-century philosophical colleagues, had to resort to some questionable anthropological and ethnological analysis. That original condition of the natural state is lost to us in time, except for the glimpse of it that Paine believes we can find in the peoples of the North American continent. "To understand what the state of society ought to be," Paine explains, "it is necessary to have some idea of the natural or primitive state of man; such as it is at this day among the Indians of North America" (AJ, p. 397). He finds that the "spectacles of human misery which poverty and want present to our eyes" in Europe are not found among the Indians, nor do we find among them "those advantages which flow from Agriculture, Arts, Science, and Manufactures" (AJ, p. 397). Paine sees the Indian as a kind of mean for the vastly different conditions of civilized men and women—neither as degraded by poverty as the European poor, nor as enriched by the elements of civilized progress as the European middle and upper classes. "The life of the Indian is a continual holiday, compared with the poor of Europe; and, on the other hand, it appears to be abject when compared to the rich" (AJ, p. 397).

We cannot, perhaps, blame Paine too severely for sharing some of the preconceptions of his time and place, nor for failing to understand the enormous diversity of Indian cultures and situations. Suffice it to say that, like many others, he found in the peoples of North America a new way to conceptualize Europe and to recognize its form of society not as an inevitability but as an alterable product of human history, nor did Paine unqualifiedly pronounce European civilization superior to the kind of life he imagined among the Indians, wryly commenting that civilization was perhaps "erroneously" named, and that the assumption of its superiority is "a question that may be strongly contested" (AJ, p. 397). Paine uses the Indian to represent a kind of egalitarianism that he can associate with the "natural" state. This allows him to depict the extreme poverty of modern society as a distortion of the natural order of things, a disequilibrium that should, and inevitably will, be righted. We might speculate here that Paine's sensitivity to such a distortion was sharpened by the recent events of the French Revolution, where the severity of the economic imbalance generated a violent social calamity. Paine writes now, as his title tells us, less as a revolutionary than as a maker of public policy offering a plan for "Meliorating the Condition of Man" (AJ, p. 396).

If there is an egalitarian principle underlying the natural order of things; if, as Paine emphasizes (with capitals), the earth is "the COMMON PROPERTY OF THE HUMAN RACE" (AJ, p. 398), then those in civilized society who have been relegated to poverty have been denied a fundamental right. This is a crucially important point, one which Paine elaborates with great emphasis.[12] Paine was by no means the first to broach such a concept, we should note. Eric Foner has explained how Paine tapped into a set of ideas implicit in Locke's theory of property, which was expanded by William Ogilvie and Thomas Spence in England, and by François Babeuf in France. This line of thought claimed that the universal right to land existing in the state of nature overrode existing laws and systems of private land ownership.[13] While Paine was cautious in his policy recommendations concerning the redistribution of property, his vivid and persuasive explanation of the concept of a universal right to the natural resources of the earth makes Paine's text an important point of reference in the history of property theory.

"I have entitled this tract *Agrarian Justice*, to distinguish it from *Agrarian Law*" (AJ, pp. 399), Paine writes. A system of absolute justice would provide for an equal stake in the earth's resources for all individuals as they were born, but existing law, which protects the private holding of land, excludes most men and women from this inherent legacy in the earth. "Nothing could be more unjust than Agrarian Law in a country improved by cultivation," Paine writes, underlining "the hard case of all those who have been thrown out of their natural inheritance by the introduction of the system of landed property" (AJ, pp. 399-400). Such dispossession is a violation of the fundamental order of things, or the state of nature. "There could be no such thing as landed property originally," Paine argues in a way that brings out the powers of striking illustration and the sardonic edge that gives his prose such bite: "Man did not make the earth, and though he had a natural right to occupy it, he had no right to locate as his property in perpetuity any part of it: neither did the Creator of the earth open a land-office, from which the first title deeds should issue" (AJ. p. 399).

While Paine did not believe that the whole course of human history can be redone from the beginning, he felt that this basic recognition could guide future social policy. Those who have not been born to landed property must be treated as if they had a right to landed property. In practical terms, this meant that a portion of the wealth generated by property should be directed to them as part of their inalienable rights as human beings.[14] But what principle should guide such a transfer? Paine again referred to the concept of a state of nature to propose a rationale: "The first principle of civilization ought to have been, and ought still to be, that the condition of every person born into the world, after a state of civilization commences, ought not to be worse than if he had been born before that period" (AJ, p. 398). Civilization, Paine believes, can only justify its worth if it does not harm those who comprise it. Civilization must include all men and women in the benefits that it produces.

Two important implications flow from this principle. First, those who require economic assistance from society are entitled to such assistance as a right, not as the objects of charity. Paine recognizes that it is not advisable to leave it "to the choice of detached individuals, whether they will do justice or not," and underscores the necessity of invoking "a principle more universally active than charity" in righting the wrongs of civilization (AJ, p. 406). The reclamation of the poor must be recognized as essential to the very nature of civilization. "It is a right and not a charity that I am pleading for" (AJ, p. 400), Paine insists.

The second implication, closely related to the first, is that the owners of land owe to the larger community a portion of the value of the land that they legally hold, while others, equally entitled, are excluded from ownership. "Every proprietor therefore of cultivated land, owes to the community a ground-rent" (AJ, p. 398). Paine proposes this rent as essentially a ten per cent inheritance tax on land, with some supplementation. He does not want to dispossess the landowners of property (which also reflects added value that they or their ancestors have produced), nor does he want to disrupt or overturn the benefits that the cultivation of land has generated for the human race as a whole. Civilization, he feels, does have its unquestionable value. What must now be done, he argues, is "to remedy the evils, and preserve the benefits, that have arisen to society, by passing from the natural to that which is called the civilized state" (AJ, p. 398). The rent or tax that he proposes is not the confiscation of private property, but the reclamation of value that has always been, by rights, a common possession.

Paine's argument for the rights of the dispossessed is the core of *Agrarian Justice*, but this basic contention is supplemented by another important consideration. He maintains that righting the economic balance of civilization is not only just in principle, but will generate advantages to civilization as a whole. We might say that he proposes a measure that will lead to a true civilization, a civilization that will fulfill the promise that its name carries. The rent that Paine advocates would create a national fund from which all persons would be paid, at the age of twenty-one, fifteen pounds "as a compensation in part for the loss of his or her natural inheritance by the introduction of the system of landed property" (AJ, p. 400). An annual payment of ten pounds per year would also be guaranteed to the blind and physically disabled, and to those aged fifty or over. As Paine argues, this system would "immediately relieve and take out of view . . . the blind, the lame, and the aged poor" (AJ, p. 406). That such a measure would relieve some of the suffering of the poor is clear, but what Paine also finds appealing about it is that it would take their suffering "out of view." (AJ, p. 405) Those who suffer would be helped, and those who must witness suffering would also benefit. In one of his most arresting images, he writes that "the contrast of affluence and wretchedness continually meeting and offending the eye, is like dead and living bodies chained together" (AJ, p. 405). Paine believes that removing the shadow of the poverty of others would actually enhance the benefits that the well-to-do draw from their wealth. "The sight of the misery, and the unpleasant sensations it suggests, which though they may be suffocated cannot be extinguished, are a greater draw-back upon the felicity of affluence than the proposed 10 per cent upon property is worth" (AJ, p. 406).

At first encounter it seems as if Paine is more concerned with relieving the sensibilities of the well-to-do than we might expect. Closer examination, however, suggests that at least implicitly he is invoking a form of moral-sense ethical theory by suggesting that the exploitation and suffering of others inevitably creates a moral revulsion. Human happiness and fulfillment, he suggests, can never be achieved in a society in which inequalities extreme enough to create suffering in others are allowed to exist. What might he have thought, we can wonder, if he could tour the major American cities in the early twenty-first century? But whether or not we concur with Paine's implicit moral-sense assumptions, his image of the living and dead bodies chained together is a powerful one, that repays close reading. The living body is itself dead in a fundamental sense, severely hampered physically and, no doubt, traumatized psychologically. So it is with society weighed down by an impoverished class. It cannot progress as it should in material terms, nor can it flourish in its citizens' sense of worth, achievement, and well-being.

Paine is also confident of another benefit from his ground-tax proposal. The provision of a small legacy to each citizen at the achievement of adulthood would be a benefit to the larger society by providing the necessary means for a productive life. "When a young couple begins the world, the difference is exceedingly great whether they begin with nothing or with fifteen pounds apiece" (AJ, p. 406). Such a legacy would increase the likelihood that they would become "useful and profitable citizens," self-sufficient and productive rather than "burthens upon society" as they began their family life (AJ, pp. 406-7). The enactment of justice through the provision of these legacies is in addition, Paine argues, an economically fruitful strategy, one that empowers the young who receive this support and also benefits society through their enhanced self-reliance and productivity.

Paine is one of the great theorists of the progressive impulses of the modern age, a thinker who struck important blows against feudalism and aristocracy, and who articulated an egalitarianism that is still potent in its implications. Nowhere is this more dramatically true than in *Agrarian Justice*, a pamphlet written in the heat of political and policy debates, but a work grounded on ideas that are very far-reaching. In summary, I would underline two principles of this work that are of particular importance as we consider it today, principles that are very much alive and at work in contemporary progressive political thought. The first of these, as we have seen, is Paine's extension of the doctrine of individual rights into the economic sphere through his contention that landed property is an illegitimate form of disenfranchisement for the mass of humanity, who are entitled by their very birth to a stake in the common property of humanity. Paine understands the importance of conceiving this claim as a right, rather than as the basis for a call on charitable action. Those without landed property are also rightful owners of the earth. It should be noted that Paine takes a very moderate approach to the policy implications of this claim. He did not advocate extensive land distribution for the France of the 1790s, but a system by which this right could be addressed in a way that he believed was productive to society as a whole. His aim was not to destabilize the social order further, but to balance and ultimately strengthen it, both materially and morally. He sets forth the broad outlines of a plan of taxation and modest income redistribution that he believes will accomplish that.

The second principle, not yet remarked upon—as far as I have read—in the critical literature, is Paine's linkage of universal ownership and universal rights to the fundamental productive capacities of the earth. I doubt if anyone in the 1790s, no matter how far-sighted they might have been, could have imagined that in two-hundred years, humans would have gained the power to endanger the earth's productivity through environmental defilement. It would not be accurate to label Thomas Paine an ecologist, but his declaration that "the earth" is "the COMMON PROPERTY OF THE HUMAN RACE" (AJ, p. 398) has powerful implications for environmental policy. Unsustainable overproduction in farmlands, excessive harvesting of the ocean and other natural areas, pollution of water and air, emission-produced climate change—all of these environmental problems come face-to-face with the principle that no particular government, corporation, or group of people have rightful control over what must be understood as humanity's "common property."

It is here, I think, that we can most clearly see the influence of the agrarian tradition of thought in Paine's work.

Paine employs the agrarian assumption that all value and wealth originate in the land. While he is not inclined to sentimentalize the agrarian life and the figure of the farmer in the mode of Jefferson and Crèvecoeur, he understands the importance and the power of the concept that the earth is the source of wealth, and he recognizes the crucial role that the cultivation of land has played in the growth of civilization and in its continuance. This principle, adapted of course to the technological conditions of our age, continues to be a vital assumption in addressing our building environmental crisis.

Question: I have a question about the birthday celebrations. Except for the recent notorious event at Fraunces Tavern in New York, when did they sort of tail off? Can you guess why that sort of happened, and when would be the next one, as I'd like to attend?

Kenneth Burchell: That's a great question. I think they really tailed off at the end of the nineteenth and beginning of the twentieth century. It probably had a lot to do, from the best I can tell, with the beginnings of World War I and what we now call the Red Scare. The history of the United States, or really the history of any country in the world, is a pattern of action and reaction, forming the constant cycles of history, and the reaction that occurred in the early twentieth century, which we now collectively group under the term Red Scare, was a doozy. It was a big one, and it suppressed an awful lot of the people who tended to be the real progressives, the real reformers of their day — the birth-control advocates, the labor reformers, the anarchists during that period of time, who were big Paine fans also. The celebrations also had recurrences periodically in a kind of wave pattern, though nothing today like their size in the nineteenth century.

As far as information, go to TomPaine.org. There's now a Thomas Paine birthday celebrations location where we're posting all of the celebrations that occur both here in the United States and around the world, giving contacts for people who might want to participate or, if you wanted to establish one yourself, you could place an announcement there.

Harvey Kaye (from the audience): There were, in the nineteenth century, the German communities that established themselves in the wake of 1848 that regularly celebrated Thomas Paine's birthday. There was a church established in Sauk City, Wisconsin—a German free church, 1850 or 1852 is the founding—and they have had a continuous Thomas Paine birthday festival to this very day, the closest Sunday to January 29th they can get. They are now a Unitarian, Universalist church, but very active and proud. (I have to admit, I haven't been able to make it to the celebration—it's tough to get from one side of Wisconsin to the other in the wintertime.) They also have some kind of statue or monument or bust, so it has continued, and there is also the birthday celebration that takes place around New Rochelle.

Kenneth Burchell: The bust is actually in the church. Thanks for recalling that, Harvey.

Question: Dr. Clevenger, I wonder if you could say something about how the ultra radicals propagated their ideas and furthered their program.

Bryson Clevenger: The ultra radicals is a term that I use for the very early British working-class left. They were the forerunners of the Chartists in the late 1830s. But in earlier periods, they were led by people like Henry Hunt, who organized a great universal-suffrage event that ended in the Peterloo massacre of 1819. They also organized around trying to end the repressive Combination Acts or restrictions against meetings that had been put in by William Pitt in the 1790s. A lot of their concern is political liberties. They also were involved in labor organizations, after the Combination Act was ended in 1824, organizing large unions, which climaxed in 1834 with the Grand National Consolidated Trades Union. They also took a strong stand against the poor laws. The Whig government wanted a poor law system where, if you could not prove that you could find a job, you were put in regimental, barracks-like conditions. Of course, Dickens writes a lot about that in his works. They support the Reform Bill in 1832 from a more radical direction; they wanted to carry it further to universal suffrage. This sort of reaches a climax in the late 1830s. Moving toward the 1840s—these are the same people—all these different groups form together into something called the

Chartists. Their central measure is a political reform, a Paineite reform, to force the British govern-ment to give universal suffrage.

At the same time, the Irish are moving toward their own rebellion in 1848, and the point of what I'm doing is that these British ultra radicals—the people who are Chartists by this time—carry on this support of the Irish in their own struggles through the 1830s and 1840s. There's an issue that I don't talk about in this paper too much. The Irish had their own leader, Daniel O'Connell, who saw it as a better deal to make alliances with the Whig government and with the other governments, so the courtship between the British ultra radicals and the Irish leadership was very stormy. But they still kept sending flowers and candy throughout this whole period of time.

Question: In the spirit of confession, I must admit that I hardly knew anything about Thomas Paine until today, and I appreciate the information that I have learned through the presenters about Paine and his works, and I wonder, in light of his grandiose and radical and revolutionary ideas, is there an element of hypocrisy in it, because I haven't heard anything about the issue of colonialism during that period, or does it take Karl Marx to really influence people about social and human conditions in other areas? I wonder if you can [say] anything about the lack of imperialism in Paine's thought.

Bryson Clevenger: There is a kind of Paineite criticism of colonialism, the notion of big nations influencing small nations. There's a very strong defense for the nations in Europe that had been under the influence of the Hapsburgs and under the influence of the Russians. This is a very strong element in the 1830s and the 1840s. Also, among Paineites, some of this is translated into concern with the Chinese in the Opium Wars, that there was a serious miscarriage and a serious breach of British power. What we think of as colonialism, in an economic context, is more of a Marxist thing. Within the Paineite tradition, we have the criticism of political oppression.

Seth Cotlar: Paine was a real advocate of national self-determination, which would cut against colonialism in that context. That's how he understood what the French Revolution was about, and he celebrated what was happening in Poland and various other places around Europe at that time. He saw these as wars of national self-determination, much like the American Revolution was. Also, he was very opposed to war. He was part of a community of English radicals who saw warfare as the product of monarchies and aristocracies, and the kind of voraciousness of these monarchies and aristocracies. It would be interesting to know what he said about what was going on in India in the 1790s. But I know the community of which he was a part was pretty critical of English colonial behavior in India at that time.

Bryson Clevenger: A lot of foreign news shows up in the ultra radical publications in the early part of this period, and even within Ireland, there's a strong sentiment that the Irish are not only oppressed politically and religiously, but they're being exploited in a sense. These absentee landlords are taking Irish goods out of Ireland and taking them back into Britain, which is a kind of colonialism.

Kenneth Burchell: Sometimes we can't see the forest for the trees, using an old expression. After all, the United States was a former colony, and the revolution was about the rejection of colonialism from the beginning. Even though you may not see the same terminology or keywords—like imperialism, Marxism, anti-colonialism—if you take the time to read the original works, you'll see very clearly anti-colonial sentiment running through all of those early reformers.

Question: I just wanted to respond to the birthday celebration comments. We had a birthday celebration on January 29th of 2005, and we had over 200 people—we had to turn people away, so there is a resurgence of interest, and that was in Pasadena, California, which is not a hotbed of radicalism. We had a grand buffet, it was in a beautiful ballroom, and we had a theater with actors portraying Thomas Paine, Thomas Jefferson, and Benjamin Franklin. We're having another one on Sunday, January 29th of 2006, and we're including Abigail Adams (speaking for her husband).

Question: This is particularly for David Robinson. Why did Thomas Paine advocate the collection of rural ground rent from the public, because urban land, area by area, could have been more valuable?

David Robinson: The context Paine is responding to is France after the Revolution, where new public policy is being made from the immediate past history of feudal land distribution or lack of distribution. Paine, and I think his contemporaries, saw that the biggest problem in the creation of a class of completely wretched poor was the rigid ownership of land through aristocracy and inheritance, and that the way to break that was to begin to establish the principle that profits from those lands had to be redistributed. The idea of taxing wealth with the purpose of maximizing revenues would take a more modern set of circumstances. For example, Henry George was looking at the situation after the Industrial Revolution and its effect in transforming the United States—at essentially urban civilizations. Only then is the principle logically extended.

Question: On birthday celebrations—in 1791, at the London Revolution Society Dinner—they toasted Thomas Paine on the great success of *Rights of Man*. He responded with what I think was one of the prettiest witticisms. His own toast: "To the Revolution of the World," which I think he said with a smile on his face.

Seth Cotlar: That quote, by the way, received lots of play in American newspapers; the toast was often re-circulated in America. The Federalist newspapers certainly didn't like that one. That's when they start thinking, "Wait a minute; do we really want to trust this fellow, Paine?"

Notes

[1]Thomas Paine, *Agrarian Justice Opposed to Agrarian Law, and to Agrarian Monopoly, Being a Plan for Meliorating the Condition of Man, &c* (1797), in *Thomas Paine: Collected Writings*, ed. Eric Foner (New York: Library of America, 1995). Quotations from *Agrarian Justice* will be abbreviated parenthetically as AJ. *Agrarian Justice* has had its critical admirers, and has divided commentators as to whether it should be seen as a major step in Paine's thinking, and the extent to which it should be considered radical in its political implications. David Freeman

Hawke wrote that "*Agrarian Justice* ranks among Paine's greatest essays" in *Paine* (New York: Harper and Row, 1974), p. 326. Eric Foner observed that *Agrarian Justice* did not indicate a departure from Paine's continuing belief in the rightness of private property, but also noted that it "established Paine as one of the pioneers of the nineteenth-century land reform movement in Europe and America." (p. 251). See *Tom Paine and Revolutionary America* (New York: Oxford University Press, 1976). Gregory Claeys offered an extended reading of the essay's significance, terming it "the most neglected of Paine's chief works" in *Thomas Paine: Social and Political Thought* (Boston: Unwin Hyman, 1989), p. 196. Most recently, Adrian Little has argued that *Agrarian Justice* was, for its time, "a radical attempt to incorporate a prototype basic citizen's income into his defence of natural rights," but concluded that, in the context of contemporary discussions of income redistribution, "Paine's ideas do not provide a substantive challenge to market-based economic systems" and thus do not adequately address the inequalities that such systems generate. See Adrian Little, "The Politics of Compensation: Tom Paine's *Agrarian Justice* and Liberal Egalitarianism," *Contemporary Politics* 5 (1999): 63-73, quotation from p. 63.

[2]On Quesnay, see Elizabeth Fox-Genovese, *The Origins of Physiocracy: Economic Revolution and Social Order in Eighteenth-Century France* (Ithaca: Cornell University Press, 1976); and Gianni Vaggi, *The Economics of François Quesnay* (Durham: Duke University Press, 1987).

[3]Thomas Jefferson, *Notes on the State of Virginia* (1789) reprinted by the e-text Center at the University of Virginia Library:
http://etext.lib.virginia.edu/toc/modeng/public/JefVirg.html. All quotations from *Notes on the State of Virginia* will be taken from this source.

[4]Ibid.

[5]Ibid.

[6]Ibid.

[7]Ibid.

[8] Timothy Sweet offers an important perspective on the work of both Jefferson and Crèvecoeur by reminding us that "farming in eighteenth-century America was not a single, uniform activity, but a group of diverse and conflicting practices." (p. 59) Of particular significance is Sweet's observation that wage labor, tenant farming, and migratory backwoods subsistence farming were more characteristic forms of agricultural labor than the work of the independent, freehold farmer that Jefferson and Crèvecoeur idealize. See Timothy Sweet, "American Pastoralism and the Marketplace: Eighteenth-Century Ideologies of Farming," *Early American Literature* 29 (1994): 59-80. For a discussion of Paine's connections with the American working classes during the period of the Revolution, see Harvey J. Kaye, *Thomas Paine and the Promise of America* (New York: Hill and Wang, 2005). Kaye per-suasively describes Paine's deep commitment to egali-tarianism.

[9] The change of tone and outlook from the optimistic early portions to the darker conclusion has occasioned considerable critical commentary on Crèvecoeur's work. For further details, see Thomas Philbrick, *St. John de Crèvecoeur* (New York: Twayne, 1970); and David M. Robinson, "Crèvecoeur's James: The Education of an American Farmer," *Journal of English and Germanic Philology* 80 (October 1981): 564-66.

[10] J. Hector St. John de Crèvecoeur, "Letters from an American Farmer" [1782], and "Sketches" from *Eighteenth-Century America* [1925], ed. Albert E. Stone (New York: Penguin, 1981), p. 52. Further citations in parentheses.

[11] As Eric Foner noted, many progressive French thinkers took an admiring and uncritical view of Americans as "a simple uncorrupted people living in an agrarian arcadia" (*Tom Paine and Revolutionary America*, p. 235), and received Americans such as Franklin, Jefferson and Paine quite warmly.

[12] See Claeys (*Thomas Paine: Social and Political Thought*, pp. 198-200), who argues that *Agrarian Justice* represents an important step forward from Paine's thinking in *Rights of Man*.

[13] Foner, *Tom Paine and Revolutionary America*, pp. 249-51.

[14]Kaye (*Thomas Paine and the Promise of America*, pp. 86-88) emphasizes the egalitarian principles upon which Paine based his plan. Because payments were to be made to all persons including women, Paine was proposing "an important democratic principle and practice" (p. 87). Both Foner (*Tom Paine and Revolutionary America*, p. 251) and Claeys (*Thomas Paine: Social and Political Thought*, p. 207) note Thomas Spence's more radical challenge to Paine's plan for redistribution through small payments, and his call for almost complete land redistribution to fulfill the principle of universal ownership.

PANEL 3:
PAINE, RELIGION, AND POLITICS

Moderator: Vikki Vickers

I am Vikki Vickers, your moderator, and I hail from Weber State University in Utah. I am excited about this panel, in part because I personally have studied Paine's religion and deism extensively. There have been lots of new scholarship in this area. I'm also excited because we'll be discussing not just Paine's beliefs and their importance in his time, but also as meaningful today.

Our first speaker will be Eric Schlereth from Brandeis University. He will be discussing the importance of Paine's religious beliefs in antebellum American politics. The second presenter comes from Paris, Nathalie Caron, who will be talking about Paine's deism and contemporary deism. Finally, Kirsten Fischer from the University of Minnesota will speak about the relevance of Paine's deism for the political discourse about religion today. Please hold all your questions until the end of the presentations, when there will be time for a good discussion.

REMEMBERING THOMAS PAINE AND RECKONING WITH RELIGION IN ANTEBELLUM AMERICAN POLITICS

Eric R. Schlereth

The Debtors' Prison in New York City was an unlikely location for festivities in 1835. Yet on the evening of January 29th inmates celebrated Thomas Paine's birthday with dinner, wine, and a series of regular and voluntary toasts. Though he had died in 1809, Paine's memory was very much alive for those whose economic woes landed them in municipal custody. Of the regular toasts, the first was a straightforward nod to the memory of Thomas Paine. Toasts that followed included one to the memory of Thomas Jefferson: "He was for a Union, but not of Church and State." Another toast was made to "Civil and Religious Liberty — Unshackled in either mind or body by designing Priests or heartless Creditors." The debtors of New York City concluded their celebration with a volunteer toast asserting that incarceration for debt would cease only after the "Age of Reason" arrives and the "Rights of Man" are respected.[1]

Debtors' prison was not the typical venue for celebrating Paine's birthday. Nevertheless, such commemorations—consisting of both orations and toasts, both regular and voluntary—became more common in American cities and towns after 1825. Kenneth Burchell's talk earlier in this conference did an excellent job describing the texture of these events, and explaining their popular resonance throughout the nineteenth and into the twentieth centuries. In this paper I focus on the religious aspects of Paine commemorations. Although this paper addresses Paine birthday celebrations through the 1850s, much of the argument draws from orations and toasts given during the first decade that Paine was celebrated—from 1825 to 1835—in nearly a dozen cities from Philadelphia to Boston. I chose to emphasize the decade after 1825, not only because it was the first decade of celebration, but also because it overlaps with a period of American religious history in which the alignments between religion and politics were changing. My argument is that the main purpose of these celebrations was not only to remember Paine's political writings, but also his critique of revealed religion. The Paine birthday celebrants did this in order to address a question of pressing urgency during this period: what forms of religious belief are most compatible with a democratizing political culture?

To the celebrants of Paine—consisting mainly of self-proclaimed deists, free enquirers, and "moral philanthropists"—the answer was not revealed religion, but rather religious ideas verifiable only by nature and reason, or deism. Paine's admirers thus argued that the only way to rectify the most problematic aspects of religion was to continue Paine's legacy of politically dismantling all forms of arbitrary power, be they ecclesiastical or civil. These admirers sought to articulate a political sensibility out of a theological and epistemological claim: that revelation offered no useful religious or moral knowledge. This position was granted meaning and resonance in terms suitable to antebellum American life through the informal politics of association and festivity. During the course of these events, Paine's admirers articulated two central themes. First, they claimed the memory of the American Revolution as an event that clearly restrained the political power of revealed religion. Second, they articulated a conception of citizenship that translated their understanding of the American Revolution into political practice. I will address each in turn. My main point is that the growth of evangelical religion in the United States was considered a controversial development that caused some Americans to seek political solutions founded upon the rejection of religious revelation.

Accounts of Paine birthday commemorations offer direct entry into the lives and ideas of the participants, both men and women, primarily of middling or mechanic status, and almost certainly white. When celebrants were distinguished by gender, it was clear that men and women had different reasons for celebrating Paine. Furthermore, between 1825 and 1835, these events became closely identified with the individuals who participated in them. One example of this is the volunteer toasts that were given at the New York City celebrations. In 1827 there were 12 volunteer toasts, and when they appeared in print all of them were anonymous. By 1835, however, there were 33 volunteer toasts, and only two remained anonymous. People over this decade were becoming increasingly willing to have their names associated with these events. The printing of the toasts also became more elaborate, expanding from usually small sections in various freethought newspapers, to actually publishing them as individual pamphlets for distribution throughout the city in which they were given. These accounts are detailed enough to allow an understanding of their place in an organized campaign to engage contentious debates over the religious and moral underpinnings of antebellum American life.

The events drew inspiration and often participants from celebrations in England, where the first organized birthday celebration was held in London in 1818. Benjamin Offen reminded the Paine birthday celebrants in New York in 1828 that, just three years before, only one location had a proprietor willing to host an event honoring Paine, whereas in 1828 celebrants "have their choice of situations; and the day will be celebrated in different parts of the city, both in public and private." The advance of "liberal opinions" was even greater in Britain, he declared. Celebrations in 1828 were held throughout Scotland and England. Offen thus opened his address to the men and women attending the New York celebration with the optimistic appraisal that, "This day, which has been considered by fanatics the birthday of a *monster* rather than a man, is now remembered and observed by thousands both in England and America."[2]

Paine birthday celebrations in the United States reveal a strong awareness of European, and particularly British, religious and political culture in the 1820s and 1830s. However, these celebrations were bolstered by events in America during the same period that imbued the festivities with a seriousness of purpose. Just as Paine's admirers in the United States began commemorating his birthday, the stirrings of Sabbatarianism were rippling throughout American culture. The main goal of the Sabbatarian movement was to uphold the sanctity of the Christian Sabbath through legal and political measures limiting economic and governmental business on Sunday. The institutional organ of this movement was the General Union for Promoting the Observance of the Christian Sabbath, an organization consisting largely of individual Presbyterian and some Congregational churches. Formed in 1828, the General Union bound its members to observe the Sabbath through pledges while utilizing petitions to Congress and moral suasion to encourage observation of the Sabbath throughout American society. Only three years after the first Paine birthday celebration in the United States, the most institutionally and financially endowed of the nation's Protestant churches embarked upon an effort to shape the public sphere through a reinvigorated Christian cultural campaign. This campaign also had a political facet exemplified in leading Presbyterian divine Ezra Stiles Ely's call for a "Christian party in politics." As one strand of an increasingly diverse evangelical discourse in antebellum America, Ely's controversial call for a Christian party combined theological postmillennialism and a progressive emphasis on Christians' social responsibilities. This combination comprised the religious disposition that drove moral reform efforts and characterized the Second Great Awakening. However, Ely gave this disposition a weighty political burden by wedding Christian obligations to electoral outcomes.[3]

Celebrants of Paine's birthday were deeply concerned with such immediate evidence of Christianity's political presence in the public sphere, so they sought to give their own perspective an equally weighty political imperative. In a representative set of toasts, participants in an 1833 New York celebration warned that the success of "The Church and State Party in the United States" would dash "the hopes and liberties of half the world."[4] Though the views of Ely and other New School Presbyterians were controversial, public celebrations of Paine and strident denials of Christianity were still more provocative, so Paine's devotees sought to ground their cause on an unimpeachable foundation: the legacy of the American Revolution.

No greater source of legitimacy was at hand in the United States during the 1820s and 1830s than the memory of the American Revolution, which was deployed as an ideological tool in contemporary political and social debates. Paine birthday celebrations also claimed the Revolution, but they subscribed to a very specific interpretation of American history. Paine's admirers characterized the Revolution as a political and social watershed that proved untenable all claims for the public authority of revealed religion, especially Christianity. From this perspective, the rise of a politically infused evangelical Protestantism was contrary to the nation's revolutionary history and, therefore, to the political values shaping American life between 1825 and 1835.[5]

An important part of claiming the memory of the Revolution was recognizing Paine's place, albeit posthumously, in the pantheon of America's founders. This effort to rehabilitate Paine's role in the Revolution defied decades of hostility to him and his ideas. Even before Paine's death in 1809, his descent into derision was well underway throughout the Anglo-American world, and opinion of him continued to decline through the 1810s. The main reason for Paine's fall from popular admiration was the publication of *The Age of Reason*, a book widely denounced in England and the United States as a blasphemous threat to established political and social order. However, celebrants of Paine's birthday viewed *The Age of Reason* as a fitting extension of his ideas in *Common Sense* and *Rights of Man*. To an audience of more than one-hundred, filling the largest room in New York City's Tammany Hall in 1832, John Morrison celebrated Paine's tenacious pursuit of liberty, even after his writings had contributed to political revolution in the United States and the overthrow of monarchy France. Paine turned his attention toward contesting "a power continually opposed to the civil power—consisting of a body of priests, who, in virtue of their pretended *divine* mission and *sacred* office, arrogated the right of giving laws to the universe." Volunteer toasts following Morrison's also celebrated Paine's work challenging the political pretenses of revealed religion. J. Wells toasted *The Age of Reason* exhorting, "Christians read it; it will convince you of the impositions of priestcraft." Soon after Wells, "A Guest," raised a drink to the demise of religion, the "Belief in unintelligible dogmas . . . May the word be erased from all languages, and morals substituted in its place." Paine's birthday was worthy of celebration precisely because his admirers believed he was the most effective prophet of revealed religion's pernicious influence on society and politics.[6]

Indeed, Paine's place among America's founders was beyond reproach because his writings stripped bare the religious and political machinations that had oppressed the world for centuries, or so Morrison argued in his oration. Although Washington, Jefferson, and Franklin were worthy of America's collective admiration, Paine surpassed all in "*moral courage*." Morrison asked who among them "would have had the daring, like him, to unveil the frauds and deceptions practised by the ministers of a mysterious theology?" Washington concealed his opinions, Franklin remained apprehensive, and Jefferson did not write publicly about his religious views out of concern for his political career. Thus, Paine, according to Morrison, was not only a patriot, but was perhaps the most patriotic and important of the nation's early political leaders.

He alone wrote clearly and acted publicly in pursuit of the Revolution's primary goal, to set the United States on a republican political foundation free from the corruptions of revealed religion.[7]

Two years later, in 1834, Paine's credentials as hero of the Revolution were reiterated at a celebration in Boston. The dinner for this event served two-hundred participants, and the following address was delivered before an audience of approximately five-hundred, a large number of whom were women. Abner Kneeland was the evening's speaker, and he extolled Paine for doing more "to break the yoke of both Political and Religious intolerance, than any other heroes of the American revolution." Later in the event Kneeland challenged alternative historical interpretations with a volunteer toast in honor of Benjamin Franklin, Paine, and Thomas Jefferson. Though all three had similar religious views when alive, Kneeland argued, "Christians are trying to claim the first and the last [Franklin and Jefferson], when dead."[8]

It was a small interpretive step to move from understanding Paine as one of the central figures shaping the republic's early history to viewing the Revolution as an event that established Paine's ideas as the foundation of the nation's new political order. In orations and toasts honoring Paine, the contentious religious and cultural history of the early republic's first decades was conflated into a progressive narrative of declining superstition in the wake of advancing free enquiry. This was a politically potent remembrance of the American Revolution, one succinctly expressed in an 1833 Providence, Rhode Island, celebration attended by a few hundred participants. The city's First Society of Moral Philanthropists organized the public celebration, inaugurated with cannon fire from atop the hills surrounding Providence, and reprinted the proceedings for distribution. Included in the voluntary toasts was a nod by Providence painter, Samuel E. Brown, to Paine as "the great apostle of religious and republican liberty in every hemisphere." One Mr. Peck toasted "The worthies of the revolution by whose indefatigable exertions, Church and State were separated; the reunion of which may we nor our sons never live to see." Moreover, an anonymous "Lady" offered cheers to Free Enquiry: "may it flourish in this land of Liberty, until bigotry and priestcraft are buried in oblivion." A similar historical understanding was reiterated two years later at an 1835 Rochester, New York, celebration. That year,

110 of Rochester's "Free Inquirers" met in the City Hotel to honor Paine's birthday. They commemorated Paine, "who devoted a long and laborious life to the emancipation of man from political and spiritual tyrants." In an event complemented with music and attended by men and women, toasts were made to "The sages and heroes of our glorious revolution—Almost to a man untrammeled by the dogmas of the church," and to the downfall of "Temporal and Spiritual Tyrants—We have free'd ourselves as a nation from one, and will ere long from the other."[9]

The interpretation of the Revolution and the republic's early history put forth at Paine celebrations characterized Sabbatarianism as a novel development, one highly disruptive to an American civil society premised on institutional circumspection toward sectarian religious beliefs. The rise of an institutionally advanced, financially equipped, and politically mobilized variant of Protestantism seemed nothing less than a complete rejection of a political settlement on religious matters in place since the Revolution, which accounts for the alarm expressed at Paine birthday celebrations over any hint of a "church and state party." This also accounts for why celebrants developed an interpretation of the Revolution defined in Paineite political, and more importantly, religious categories. Nevertheless, rehabilitating Paine's place in the pantheon of American founders, and claiming the memory of the Revolution for the history of free enquiry, was merely one strategy for reckoning with politically tangled religious questions after 1825.

In addition, the Paine celebrants developed a conception of citizenship necessary to translate their understanding of America's revolutionary past into effective political practices for the present. In January, 1833, the *Rhode Island American and Gazette* carried an announcement for a Providence event that contained a far from subtle political judgment regarding who should attend. According to the Committee of Arrangements for Providence's First Society of Moral Philanthropists, "All patriots and lovers of a democratic form of government" were invited to attend an event honoring Paine. This festivity would commemorate his services to the republic with the likes of illustrious patriots from the past including Washington and Jefferson. Patriotism and love for democracy were attributes easily accepted or shed depending on the political or ideological needs of the user, thus fairly meaningless in and of themselves. Paine's admirers, however, attached a clearly normative significance to his writings and the celebration of his memory[10]

For them, the meaning of patriotism and respect for democracy were evident: to commemorate Paine, including his critique of Christianity, was to declare oneself on the proper side of political and cultural debates that had shaped so much of Atlantic history from the late eighteenth century onward. For the celebrants, to be patriotic and inclined toward democracy was to be against revealed religion. Furthermore, the message of many Paine birthday celebrations between 1825 and 1835 explicitly pronounced what was implied in the announcement for the Providence event. If the United States was to maintain its Revolutionary settlement concerning religious belief and political liberty, then ideas about citizenship must incorporate denials of revealed religion as detrimental to the body politic.

The advent of Paine birthday celebrations in the United States occurred at the very intersection of ideas about religious belief and citizenship. Recent scholarship on the history of citizenship in early nineteenth-century America has highlighted the degree to which citizenship in the modern sense—as a formal, constitutional category linking the individual to the federal state—was, in the words of historian William J. Novak, "but the last form of membership in a continuum of public functions and civil associations." Instead, Novak argues, what often mattered most in people's lives were forms of "non-constitutional citizenship." Non-constitutional citizenship refers to the ways that status and political power were determined by access to local, voluntary associations. These associations were typically formed to pursue a philanthropic or religious purpose; thus, membership was often based upon acceptance of religious confession or a moral outlook.[11]

Paine celebrants also understood citizenship in non-constitutional terms, albeit as a combination of political identity with critiques of revealed religion. According to this conception, a society organized to celebrate Paine provided an institutional field for fulfilling citizenship, and free enquiry provided the intellectual and moral means. Celebrants concluded by arguing that full citizenship was tantamount to mental emancipation, and both were connected by free enquiry. Machinist Amory Amsden of Rochester elucidated the epistemological and political components of Paineite notions of citizenship in his toast to "Free Inquiry—The chief cornerstone of republicanism."[12] Paine birthday celebrants opposed what historian Richard Carwardine has described as the "duties of the Christian citizen" (cf. note 13 below), a linking of Christianity to the power and privileges of citizenship. These duties required frequent political participation informed by religious belief and also sectarian involvement in benevolent societies and voluntary associations—the very organizations that transformed individuals into citizens. For Paine birthday celebrants, defining citizenship through Christianity was sure to weaken citizenship. Isaac Fitz, a Rochester laborer, expressed this sentiment in his toast to "Christian believers—As citizens we respect them, but as slaves we pity them," a less-than ringing endorsement of a Christian's ability to be a fully effective citizen in a republic.[13]

Paine's admirers continued to link republican citizenship and mental emancipation throughout the early 1830s. John Morrison's 1832 oration at Tammany Hall credited Paine for asking the question, "For what avail is it to be *politically* free while *mentally* enslaved?" Celebrants at New Hartford, New York, in 1830 were aroused by accounts of various evangelical efforts toward the mass distribution of religious tracts and Bibles along with western missionaries, declaring them institutions "with which this country is literally deluged—formed for the purpose of supporting revealed religion." New Hartford's orator warned that evangelical associations were attempting to use their institutional networks to influence the national government, and only mentally emancipated citizens could successfully challenge the nation's clergy, reminding his audience that "you will be as truly mentally free, as you already are politically so."[14]

Mental emancipation was not only the basis of citizenship, but it could also determine electoral preferences. Occasionally, Paine celebrations offered opportunities to support political candidates who would best represent the mentally emancipated citizen. This was particularly true of celebrations in New York, where the state assembly had a member from the ranks of the free enquirers: Thomas Herttell, who entered public life by writing criticisms of an 1820 New York Supreme Court decision on religious oaths in courtrooms. Herttell argued that this decision supported an unconstitutional religious test. In doing so, the court was complicit in reifying the

"the combined power and influence of political and ecclesiastical government directed to the common object of rendering the people, both in body and mind, the very dupes and slaves of spiritual and political tyrants" (cf. note 15 below). Once in the Assembly, Herttell championed causes such as the unconstitutionality of state-sanctioned clerical chaplains and the necessity of married women's property rights. At the 1835 celebration in Rochester, an S. Campbell acknowledged Herttell's public service by toasting him with a hope that Herttell's "voice never cease to be heard in our Legislative halls until orthodoxy in all its designs is vetoed." Support for Hertell, whose politics were tied to the Workingman's movement, suggests the broader connections between free enquiry and what would become the free-thinking wing of the Democratic Party, the wing that caused the greatest consternation for the Whig reformers during the ensuing decades. In the course of Paine celebrations are thus hints of the intellectual and political divides that came to shape, in part, the formal partisan alignments of the second-party system.[15]

Both in claiming the Revolution and in asserting a related understanding of citizenship, we see a real effort on the part of the Paine birthday celebrants to reckon with what they thought was a significant change in American religious culture. But mental emancipation, the primary concept that connected efforts to claim the Revolution and define citizenship, was not without ambiguities and limitations. By analyzing Paine celebrations through the lens of gender, mental emancipation emerges as a concept that contained a conservative understanding of actual individual freedom relative to competing understandings of gender and women's rights that gained currency in antebellum American.

It seems fairly certain that the concept of mental emancipation offered the men who celebrated Paine a way to link their suspicion of evangelical Christianity to a political identity and a broader historical narrative: republican citizens upholding the principles of 1776. Paine's admirers, primarily urban mechanics, thus turned to free enquiry as an alternative to the emerging cultural dominance of Christian reform in America's northern towns and cities. Yet women also appeared in the celebration accounts, both as participants and in the gendered language of their male counterparts. The men who lauded Paine used gendered references to promote an ideal of the free enquiring woman, usually in reference to women who expressed their criticisms of Christianity in the most public of ways—as writers and lecturers. Mary Wollstonecraft, author of the controversial *A Vindication of the Rights of Women* published in 1792, was frequently toasted, for example. Salutations were also made of a more general tenor directed at diminishing the authority of the clergy. These remarks were often imbued with negative gendered assumptions about female susceptibility to sly clerics, in order to demonstrate that the nation's religious authorities were losing their foothold even among those perceived most vulnerable. Thus, during Rochester's 1835 celebration a toast was made in honor of "The American Fair," though long "pray to a designing priesthood" may they soon "spurn with contempt the infamous designs of a hireling clergy to enslave their minds."[16]

A gendered discourse concerning female capacity for mental emancipation versus their tendency toward mental acquiescence was evident in other celebrations. Russel Canfield engaged this discourse in order to critique what he believed was the inherently unjust nature of the Bible teachings, and by extension challenging claims to its divine authorship and the utility of religion in general. Canfield expressed this view during an 1835 oration before Philadelphia's Society of Free Enquirers and it anticipated his later writings on the physiology and sociology of sexuality. Canfield addressed a large portion of his 1835 oration to the women in the audience and declared that, historically, Biblical justifications of social relations and conceptions of gender had done nothing but render women "slaves, liable to be sold to the first purchaser, either as wives or prostitutes" (cf. note 17 below). Only the progress of free enquiry and mental emancipation could dismantle the social and political restraints imposed upon women, Canfield argued. Such restraints were often justified by religious principles that prevented women from achieving their full value and dignity. Ultimately, the central theme of Canfield's Biblical critique was his declaration to the women in his audience that, "Every where, and at all times, has religion been adverse to your rights, your reputation, your enjoyments."[17] Canfield thus concluded with optimism about women's potential for free enquiry.

Opponents of Paine commemorations shared the gendered assumptions of Paine's male admirers, but they used them to highlight the pernicious implications of female participation. That some women admired Paine and, in particular, *The Age of Reason,* struck observers as contrary to the interests of women, even if their admiration was cloaked in actions and ideas thought becoming of an early nineteenth-century lady. In March, 1837, an Amherst, New Hampshire, paper, *The Farmer's Cabinet,* carried a description of a recent Paine birthday celebration in New York City. The author of this piece could not understand why women attended the event. First and foremost, "The purity imputed to the female mind is so entire, that a single stain mars the whole" (cf. note 18 below). Celebrating a writer who taught the world to doubt revealed religious truths was certain to irreparably harm the female mind, or so this writer believed. Mental damage aside, this writer also argued that women had religion to credit for their recent elevation from material and mental drudgery to the role of man's "companion, friend, and almost superior." For the author writing in *The Farmer's Cabinet,* the road to antebellum ideals of middle-class womanhood was apparently paved with good religion, not the infidelity of Thomas Paine.[18]

For all the writing about whether women should celebrate Paine, in the end it suggests a fairly seamless extension of what the male writers understood about the broader social and political implications of efforts to diminish Christianity's authority. Less easy to explain is why women chose to celebrate Paine. Women, by most accounts, frequently attended Paine commemorations, listened to the orations, and even offered toasts that were then printed for popular consumption. The festivities offered female celebrants a role in civil society and a voice, albeit limited, in public discourse. However, these moments of female political participation were ultimately a response to evangelical religion, an ostensibly curious target of female opposition. Of all the opportunities for women to enter the antebellum public sphere, it was through evangelical reform movements that women had the greatest influence and appeared in the greatest numbers. The motivations of the anonymous female Paine celebrants referred to in the newspaper reports and published toasts must be inferred from the few remarks by named women that did make it into print. These remarks were informed by an ideal of female participation in the public sphere that reaffirmed the authority of women in the private sphere. In other words, female celebrants viewed free enquiry and critiques of revealed religion as the source of an alternative understanding of feminine authority and femininity lodged primarily in the home and not premised on evangelical religion. Celebrating Paine was a way for women to define themselves against emerging ideals of nineteenth-century femininity premised on the extensive pursuit of benevolent causes. Assuming the women who celebrated Paine shared the status of their male counterparts, they probably lacked the social resources and perhaps even the interest in attaining a place in the evangelical movements that typified northern religious culture.

Thus, between the few women exceptional for their public diatribes against revealed religion and lofty toasts to the "American Fair," were women such as Mrs. Matthies, who hosted and helped organize the 1835 event in Rochester, New York, at the hotel that her husband operated. Similarly, at the 1842 Paine commemoration in Salubria, Iowa, a communal experiment that was organized by Abner Kneeland after he left Massachusetts, one "Miss Adams" toasted: "The daughters of Iowa—may they learn less of priestcraft, and lay aside their Bibles for the distaff and loom" (cf. note 19 below). Miss D. J. Rice also toasted Iowa's young women with the hope that "their buoyant minds and guileless hearts never be ensnared by the artifices of the priest."[19] Ultimately, then, the women who participated in Paine celebrations adhered to a conception of mental emancipation and free enquiry that enforced dominant cultural constructions of gender-appropriate labor and female psychology. Enforcing these notions was the best means for female celebrants to critique the demands of evangelical femininity that were difficult to attain if indeed they even desired them.

In the end, celebrants of Paine were a self-selecting group who brought to the birthday events radical views on religion and its place in society, but they voiced intellectual and political concerns about the problematic nature of religion that ran deep in nineteenth-century American life. For many Americans in the early nineteenth century, it was by no means commonplace that the authority of divine revelation and the assumptions of republican politics were reconcilable. Many Americans in the late 1820s and 1830s welcomed the advent of a more robust and politically engaged evangelical Christianity, but other Americans were not as sanguine. Paine's admirers fit the latter position. I close with a story from Ithaca, New York, in 1830. In that year the city's residents resolved that calls to suspend Sunday mail delivery through political action were part of an intentional, organized plan by a "religious sect in the United States to coerce the government into measures tending to establish their peculiar construction of the law of God, and ultimately to establish a particular religion as the religion of the State" (cf. note 20 below). In a series of resolutions submitted to their congressman, they concluded that legal restriction of Sunday mail delivery violated civil and religious liberty and subverted "the first principles of self-government."[20]

Suspicion about aligning political power and religious belief cut across religious persuasions in the early national United States. Evangelical Protestantism's emergence as a cultural force created a contentious strain in the political and religious life of the early republic. At issue were disparate views about whether an accommodation between religious belief and a democratizing political culture was possible or even desirable. Between 1825 and 1835, admirers of Paine addressed the problem of religion from the perspective of free enquiry, and in explicitly political terms. First, they adhered to an interpretation of the American Revolution as an event that circumscribed the political, public authority of revealed religion. Second, they developed an idea of citizenship that relied on their interpretation of the American Revolution as justification for political activity. Additionally, celebrants of Paine drew inspiration from their place in an Anglo-American culture of Paine commemorations that developed in the early nineteenth century. Beyond understanding the events themselves, the history of Paine commemorations also demonstrates that changing relationships between religion and the public sphere in the early republic were not primarily carried out through legislative enactments or legal decisions. Rather, these changes occurred in the less rarefied realms of popular sociability and voluntary organizations, or in some instances even a debtors' prison.

Notes

[1]*The Free Enquirer* (New York, NY), February 8, 1835. Also in the concluding toast were references to Paine's *Common Sense* and *Crisis,* although clearly the most political weight was given to *The Age of Reason* and *Rights of Man.* New York's Society of Moral Philanthropists, organizers of that city's annual Paine birthday celebration, provided the debtors' food and

wine using surplus revenue raised from ticket sales for the event's ball.

²*The Correspondent* (New York, NY), February 2, 1828.

³Richard R. John, *Spreading the News: The American Postal System from Franklin to Morse* (Cambridge: Harvard University Press, 1995), who devotes a chapter to the Sabbatarian controversy. Also, James R. Rohrer, "Sunday Mails and the Church-State Theme in Jacksonian America," *Journal of the Early Republic* 7 (1987): 53-74. Ezra Stiles Ely, *The Duty of Christian Freemen to Elect Christian Rulers: A Discourse delivered on the fourth of July, 1827, in the Seventh Presbyterian Church, in Philadelphia* (Philadelphia: W. F. Geddes, 1828).

⁴*The Free Enquirer*, February 9, 1833.

⁵On the workings of historical memory in relationship to the American Revolution see, Michael Kammen, *Mystic Chords of Memory: The Transformation of Tradition in American Culture* (New York: Knopf, 1991), pp. 9-10. The political and cultural implications of remembering the Revolution during the 1830s are nicely discussed in Alfred F. Young, *The Shoemaker and the Tea Party: Memory and the American Revolution* (Boston: Beacon Press, 1999), pp. 143-54.

⁶John Morrison, *An Oration Delivered In Tammany Hall, In Commemoration Of The Birthday Of Thomas Paine* (New York: Evans & Brooks, 1832), pp. 24 and 29. The events of the celebration were printed for distribution at the request of the birthday celebration's Committee of Arrangements. The account of the celebration was also carried in the *New York Daily Sentinel,* February 2, 1832. This celebration's vice-president was the ubiquitous Offen. For further indication of the size of Tammany Hall's 1832 Paine birthday celebration see a tangential reference to the "big room" of Tammany Hall as the location where the event was held, thus forcing a smaller political meeting to be held elsewhere. See, *New Hampshire Sentinel* (Keene, NH), February 10, 1832. This seems likely since nearly four-hundred men and women attended the social ball that followed the Tammany Hall oration.

7*An Oration Delivered In Tammany Hall, In Commemoration Of The Birthday Of Thomas Paine*, pp. 12 and 14.

8*Boston Investigator*, February 7 and 14, 1834. For other celebrations where Paine's status as a founder was declared and the American Revolution claimed as an event in the struggle to separate religion from politics see, *The Correspondent*, February 2, 1828, for a New York City celebration; *The Free Enquirer*, February 22, 1835, for a Buffalo, New York, celebration. Equally telling are the members of the Revolutionary generation who were "forgotten," including Samuel Adams and Benjamin Rush, who both linked the Revolution to Christianity.

9*An Oration, Delivered Before The Society Of Moral Philanthropists, At The Celebration Of The Ninety-Sixth Anniversary Of The Birth Day Of The Hon. Thomas Paine* (Providence: [no publisher listed], 1833), pp. 12-13; *Boston Investigator*, February 8, 1833; and *The Free Enquirer*, March 8, 1835.

10*Rhode Island American and Gazette* (Providence, RI), January 29, 1833. The paper's editor, C. B. Peckham, was no neutral party, but an active participant in the Moral Philanthropists.

11William J. Novak, "The Legal Transformation of Citizenship in Nineteenth-Century America," in *The Democratic Experiment: New Directions in American Political History*, eds. Meg Jacobs, et. al. (Princeton: Princeton University Press, 2003), p. 94.

12*The Free Enquirer*, March 8, 1835.

13*The Free Enquirer*, March 8, 1835. On Amsden and Fitz see, *Charter and Directory of the City of Rochester* (Rochester: Marshall and Dean Printers, 1834). Fitz is listed as "Fitts" in the directory, but they are very likely the same person. Morrison, *An Oration Delivered In Tammany Hall, In Commemoration Of The Birthday Of Thomas Paine*, p. 6. John Carwardine, *Evangelicals and Politics in Antebellum America* (New Haven: Yale University Press, 1993), pp. 22-30.

14*The Free Enquirer*, February 20, 1830. The theme of mental emancipation was also central to Paine birthday orations in

New York City and Providence, Rhode Island. Before Providence's Society of Moral Philanthropists, N.C. Rhodes, the day's orator in 1833, celebrated *The Age of Reason* that upon reading "the superstitious curtain drops at once, and the mind, freed from the power of Demons, emerges into the open air of liberty and happiness." See *An Oration, Delivered Before The Society Of Moral Philanthropists, At The Celebration Of The Ninety-Sixth Anniversary Of The Birth Day Of The Hon. Thomas Paine*, p. 9.

[15]Thomas Herttell, *The Demurrer* (New York: E. Conrad, 1828), p. 18; *The Free Enquirer* (New York, NY), March 8, 1835. Herttell, *Remarks Comprising in Substance Judge Herttell's Argument in the House of Assembly of this State of New York, in Support of the Bill to Restore to Married Women "The Right of Property"* (Boston: J. P. Mendum, 1867).

[16]*The Free Enquirer*, March 8, 1835. The historiography on women's access to the public sphere in antebellum America, even though they were denied direct access to formal, electoral politics, is voluminous and growing. For two examples, see Mary P. Ryan, *Women in the Public between Banners and Ballots, 1825-1880* (Baltimore: Johns Hopkins University Press, 1990) and Elizabeth R. Varon, *We Mean To Be Counted: White Women and Politics in Antebellum Virginia* (Chapel Hill: University of North Carolina Press, 1998).

[17]*The Free Enquirer*, March 1 through March 15, 1835. Russel Canfield, *The Besom of Truth; or A brief reply to the question "Is the resurrection of Christ from the dead so taught in the Bible as to be a subject of rational belief?"* (Boston: Geo. A. Chapman, 1837) and *Practical Physiology: being a synopsis of lectures on sexual physiology, including intermarriage, organization, intercourse, and their general and particular phenomena* (Philadelphia: J. Wixson & Co., 1850).

[18]*The Farmer's Cabinet* (Amherst, NH), March 3, 1837.

[19]*The Free Enquirer*, March 8, 1835; on the Salubria celebration see, *Berkshire County Whig* (Pittsfield, MA), April 14, 1842. Salubria's connections to Massachusetts perhaps explain the interest of the *Berkshire County Whig* in the town's happenings.

On Salubria see, Margaret Atherton Bonney, "The Salubria Story," *Palimpsest* 56:2 (1975), 34-45.

[20]*Ithaca Journal and General Advertiser,* February 10, 1830.

THE RELEVANCE OF THOMAS PAINE'S RELIGIOUS THOUGHT TODAY

Nathalie Caron

As has been emphasized by other participants in this symposium, the radical republican deist Thomas Paine resonates in the public consciousness in ways he had not before, but he does so somewhat unexpectedly and ironically. "Paine has achieved near-celebrity status" (p. 9), contends Harvey Kaye in his book *Thomas Paine and the Promise of Democracy*, and indeed not less than eight books on Paine have been published in the United States in the last two years.[1] One is even tempted to say, Paine has never been so close to being included in the pantheon of the Founding Fathers. Part of the irony is that today the most progressive of the American revolutionaries appeals to liberals and conservatives alike. But the greatest irony might be that the new interest in the infamous author of *The Age of Reason*—who called the Scripture "a book of lies" and Christianity a "system of falsehood, idolatry, and pretended revelation"[2]—is occurring in a country where reliance on the Bible is high for modern societies and where roughly 80% of the population are Christians.

Paine serves the interests of politicians and public figures who otherwise would have nothing to do with his religious outlook. President Bush, a born-again evangelical, to name but one, has quoted the author of *Common Sense* repeatedly.[3] By the same token, many others have appropriated or discussed Paine's political ideas despite his deism and the memorable attack that he launched in the 1790s on all revealed and organized religions, Christianity in the first place, an act which, in Susan Jacoby's words, "proved the primary cause of his fall from American grace."[4] Paine, however, is back on the scene also *because of* his deistic views, and the new attention that is paid to him extends to people who share his religious posture. Paine's political and social thought makes him relevant and appealing as a powerful reminder of past ideals. Likewise, his eighteenth-century rationalist rhetoric and constructive deism, reflected as they are in contemporary attitudes toward religion and religiosity, continue to inspire not only staunch secularists, but also neo-deists, religious liberals, spiritual seekers, and other types of freethinkers.

Thomas Paine claimed that his religion was to do good, and he devoted most of his late career to deistic activism. He was a man of the Enlightenment, who, as intellectual historian Henry F. May put it, "believed passionately in God and hoped for a future life."[5] What is popularly known of his religious views, however, is confined to his strident attack on Biblical Christianity, described as superstition in *The Age of Reason*. Because he was a deist and because American historians of religion have tended to overlook the late Enlightenment critique of Christianity, little has been published on his underlying approach to religion.[6] Because Paine was too radical, he has been dismissed as a shallow theologian. As a consequence, the multifaceted nature of his all-encompassing deism, the articulation of his religious views and his republicanism, his reflections on diversity and on Church-and-State relations do not always get the attention they deserve.

In this paper I explore Paine's religious legacy. My aim is to connect his revolutionary Enlightenment deism to current religious attitudes, so as to provide some keys to understanding Paine's resurgence today and to contribute to a better understanding of the evaluation of his impact on American culture.[7] Like his political and social vision to which they are closely tied, Paine's religious views are being rediscovered, even rehabilitated. At a time when conservative Christians are more vocal than ever, Paine's ideas on the relationship between religion, politics, and society are being summoned up to sustain discussions over Church and State and religious-freedom issues, as Susan Jacoby's book on secularism illustrates.[8] Besides, Paine's individualistic and secular approach to religion, based on human responsibility and the rejection of mystery—as articulated in *The Age of Reason* but also in *Rights of Man* and other writings—echoes current religious and spiritual expressions that reveal a sense of estrangement from institutions as well as a lack of preoccupation with doctrine, while stressing private forms of belief, spiritual exploration, and personal fulfillment. The interest in Paine's deism is further materialized by the growing neo-deist movement that is developing on the Internet.

In *The Age of Reason*, Paine's radical criticism of the Bible and Christianity was preceded by a "profession of faith," in which he articulated a definition of what I call elsewhere his political deism, namely a form of deism that engages the believer in worldly action.[9]

> I believe in one God and no more; and I hope for happiness beyond this life. I believe in the equality of man, and I believe that religious duties consist in doing justice, loving mercy, and endeavoring to make our fellow-creature happy.[10]

Paine believed in a unitarian God ("one God, and no more"), a God who was not revealed in the Bible, but in nature, God's creation. Paine, like other representatives of the Enlightenment, was fascinated by Newtonian science. Science was "the true theology" that alone could lead to the knowledge of God.[11] His deism, however, went beyond the debunking of Christianity and the belief in a distant Maker whose existence was evidenced by sensuous perception and the use of reason. Paine's constructive deism was also a statement of liberty and went hand in hand with a forceful defense of freedom of conscience.

In a book on the First Amendment religious clauses, the authors argue that James Madison and Thomas Jefferson, two influential advocates of religious liberty in the early Republic, conceived of freedom of conscience in a broad sense. To those founders, "the freedom of conscience [was] the source from which the freedoms of religion, speech, the press, and association [were] derived."[12] Paine's reasoning was founded on the same broad understanding. It backed Jefferson's *Bill for Establishing Religious Freedom* (1779) and Madison's *Memorial and Remonstrance* (1785) drafted to expand religious liberty in Virginia, and which, together with the *Virginia Declaration of Rights*, form the philosophical basis of the First Amendment to the federal constitution, designed by the founders to "set in motion a process of expanding liberty."[13] Expanding the process of liberty was also Paine's purpose after the revolutionary process had got under way in the British colonies in North America: "From a small spark, kindled in America, a flame has arisen not to be extinguished."[14] In 1791, the year when the U.S. Bill of Rights was added to the Constitution, Paine based his *Rights of Man* upon an appraisal of the French Constitution, which he wrote "had abolished or renounced *Toleration* and *Intolerance* also, and hath established UNIVERSAL RIGHT OF CONSCIENCE."[15]

As his Virginian friends had some years before, Paine demonstrated that the freedom of conscience was one of the unalienable human rights that could not possibly be relinquished to civil government. Freedom of conscience, which Paine called an intellectual right or right of the mind, consequently and inevitably incurred religious liberty, that is, the free exercise of religion.[16] Because free speech was derived from it, freedom of conscience created the condition for "free discussion" and the free expression of opinions. All individuals have "the same right to their opinions as others," he wrote about religion in the young Republic.[17] As one commentator has it, the founders' purpose was "the common debate of a free people where all are permitted to persuade others of their views."[18] The plea for the free conscience of a free-thinking individual created the philosophical basis for Paine's otherwise paradoxical critique of revealed religion and insistence on the superiority of deism. Indeed, how could Paine reconcile his defense of religious liberty with his assault on Christianity irrespective of other people's beliefs? *The Age of Reason*, as it were, was a demonstration aimed at stimulating public debate and making the case that the individual should not be afraid to think. As Paine points out in *Rights of Man*, "it is only those who have not thought that appear to agree."[19]

Paine defended the freedom of conscience to the point that—although he regarded atheists as "half-rationals"—he did not exclude the right not to believe.[20] Besides, concurrently with his scathing assessment of Christianity in *The Age of Reason* and his late papers, he entertained respect for all religions. Paine ranked Quakerism high, and in *Rights of Man* asserted that "Every religion is good that teaches man to be good; and I know of none that instructs him to be bad."[21] Christianity had been corrupted by political use and the religious establishment and had been made "a political machine." "Take away the law-establishment," Paine wrote for his Anglican audience, "and every religion reassumes its original benignity."[22] He added: "In America, a Catholic priest is a good citizen, a good character, and a good neighbor; and an Episcopalian minister is of the same description: and this proceeds independently of the men from there being no law-establishment in America."[23] On his return to the United States in 1802, however, Paine was to somewhat revise this view as he personally experienced the effect of the alliance of the Federalist Party and the conservative clergy.

Paine was a forceful exponent of the separation of Church and State. He condemned "national gods" and, as such, appeals to secularists today.[24] But, to use present-day terminology, he fell short of expressing strict separationist views. Paine took religion seriously and looked forward to a religious revolution that would enable people to think freely in religious matters. He favored a limited use of external forms of religious devotion, but assumed that religion had a public role to play as the moral guide of all citizens and expected the State to encourage the expression of "a variety of devotion" by guaranteeing freedom of conscience.[25] Religious pluralism is an argument Paine used to contend for religious freedom: "For myself, I fully and conscientiously believe, that it is the will of the Almighty that there should be a diversity of religious opinions among us," he argued in *Common Sense*.[26] In the 1776 pamphlet, Paine recommended the drafting of a Charter that would "secure [...] above all things the free exercise of religion."[27] In 1794, after proclaiming the advent of deism as a universal religion, he concluded the first part of his *The Age of Reason*—not without a touch of pragmatism—with these words: "in the mean time, let every man follow, as he has a right to do, the religion and worship he prefers."[28]

Paine's consistent separatism regarding Church and State relations, like Jefferson's or Madison's, allowed for a great diversity in terms of beliefs and practices. This diversity meshes easily with the prophetic vision he outlined in *Common Sense* regarding the religious pluralist ideal of the American nation.[29] Paine, however, went a step further than Madison and Jefferson. By publicizing his intolerable views, he challenged the claims to full religious pluralism as presented in the founding documents. The limits of tolerance for an open exchange of views were demonstrated by his "fall from grace." In 1809 the celebrated author of *Common Sense* and *Rights of Man* died in poverty, abandoned by his friends, disenfranchised, and having lost his American citizenship.[30]

A perfect embodiment of the ethnocentrism of the Enlightenment, Paine was confident that the deism he promoted was a system of simple belief to which all would eventually turn in the future, now that the political revolutionary process had opened the way for further development in the field of "civilization" and religion."[31] Deism was to outlive all other systems of faith once all free-thinking individuals had shed superfluous beliefs. As the pure belief in God, which did away with mysterious dogmas, deism was the core of religious belief, the common denominator of all religions. A freethinking man, who believed that only free debate could advance the cause of progress, Paine insisted that deism was the only true religion, and yet his emphasis, always, was on human dignity, human freedom, human capacity for exploration, in other words, intellectual independence. In *Rights of Man*, he claimed in Enlightenment rhetoric, "independence is my happiness."[7]

To Paine, independence of the mind came first and was manifested not only in religious pluralism and the individual's capacity and willingness to choose one form of worship from among many others, but also in one's ability to forge one's own ways of devotion. In his criticism of toleration—which he says "places itself [...] between God and man"—Paine refers to an original compact between man and God:

> The first act of man, when he looked around and saw himself a creature he did not make, and a world furnished for his reception, must have been devotion; and devotion must ever continue sacred to every individual man, *as it appears right to him* [italics are Paine's] and government do mischief by interfering.[33]

Paine was a champion of democratic politics and, aware that notions of the self were changing, he appealed to individual responsibility and creativity. He articulated deistic apologetics, not always devoid of Christian overtones, and on his return to the United States in 1802 he supported the institutionalization of deism on American soil initiated by Elihu Palmer, and yet, at the same time, influenced as he was not only by Enlightenment philosophy, but also his Quaker upbringing, he conceived of an intimate religiosity that limited intermediaries between the believer and his Maker while creating the possibilities of personalized worship outside any organized institution. "Religion is a private affair between every man and his Maker," he claimed in 1797.[34]

As sociologist Robert N. Bellah and his co-authors have noted in their critical analysis of the culture of individualism in the United States, "already in the eighteenth century, it was possible for individuals to find the form of religion that best suited their inclinations," suggesting that it is then that the source of contemporary individualistic responses to religion can be found.[35] "My own mind is my own church," Paine wrote in *The Age of Reason*, a statement echoed by Jefferson's private declaration of faith: "I am of a sect by myself."[36] Both Paine and Jefferson attested to "the presence of individuals who found their own way in religion even in the eighteenth century."[37] Both were wary of religious institutions—because of the fanaticism they could generate and because of the possible alliance of Church and State—and implied that it was up to individuals endowed as they were with the use of reason to make up their minds as to what and how to believe.

Undoubtedly, the new interest in Paine in the United States today is related to the relevance of his reflection on religious belief to our modern societies, and to American society in particular, where the democratic ethos and the culture of choice—which Paine helped to promote—have shaped contemporary responses to religion and styles of religiosity. Paine condemned the hereditary principle that founded monarchical government. Likewise, he encouraged his contemporaries and future readers to decide for themselves and stand up to anything inherited. Like his co-religionist Elihu Palmer and others, he was "an earnest and religious seeker."[38] Today, as sociologists of religion have shown, in the United States (and this is in large part true of Europe as well) inherited religion has become less important than one's own choice and personal fulfillment. These scholars have brought to the fore the "quest culture" that has replaced the reliance on tradition in the second half of the twentieth century. Sociologist Wade Clark Roof in particular has argued that "the current situation in the United States is characterized not so much by a loss of faith as a qualitative shift from unquestioned belief to a more open, questing mood."[39] Conversely, "a culture of non-affiliation" has emerged.[40] The non-affiliated sector, a diverse constituency that comprises unbelievers and believers who are dissociated from organized religion, is growing and has recently increased to 14%.[41]

More broadly, the case Paine made for the privatization of religion in the eighteenth century contributed to the expressions of current forms of religiosity that are turned inward and are based on a growing attention to personal well-being as well as on a sense of the self in its connection with nature. Those forms of religiosity are likely to appeal to the increasing number of "spiritual but not religious" people as much as religious people. As was typical of Enlightenment thinking, Paine laid strong emphasis on happiness. "There is a happiness in Deism," he wrote in one of the *Prospect* papers.[42] To Paine, deism was liberating because it reconciled reason and belief ("It is necessary to the happiness of man that he be faithful to himself") and also because the deist "looks through nature up to nature's God."[43] In sum, Paine is one of those who fostered the expansion and stretching of the notion of religion, by dissociating spiritual feeling from religious doctrine and institution, by stressing individual agency ("Reader, put thy confidence in thy God, and put no trust in the Bible"), and by putting forward the possibility of personal well-being through intellectual and sensuous harmony with nature.[44]

The persistence of deism in American society has been noted by a number of commentators, including, interestingly and most recently, an evangelical sociologist. In a book published in 2006 on the spiritual and religious life of American teenagers, in collaboration with Melinda Lundquist Denton, Christian Smith articulates the connection between the eighteenth century and contemporary religiosity:

> The de facto dominant religion among contemporary U.S. teenagers is what we call Moralistic, Therapeutic Deism [...] Like the deistic God of the eighteenth-century philosophers, the God of contemporary teenage Moralistic Therapeutic Deism is primarily a divine Creator and Lawgiver.[45]

Smith argues that a shared American religion, analogous to what Bellah called "civil religion" but operating at a different level, is now visible in the United States. He expresses his concern that this type of deism—which is primarily about feeling good and being happy—is, without anyone noticing, colonizing many established traditions and congregations in the United States.[46] He consequently provides a negative definition of a diffuse trend in a way reminiscent of the paranoid fear of deism in the eighteenth century. Deism, however, is also an assertive way of defining oneself religiously, and it has become one of the many options available to Americans on the religious market. A survey published in 2001, American Religious Identity Survey (ARIS), shows that from 1990 to 2000, the number of deists increased from 6,000 to 49,000.[47] The estimation for 2004 is 69,000.[48]

Today, Paine's most articulate heirs are what I call the "neo-deists," or "new deists," who over the past decade have used the Internet to share their views with others and as a base for the steady development of their beliefs. The presence of organized deism in cyberspace is currently evolving as new sites pop up every few months, older sites vanish, and names are changed or swapped. These websites present the many and frequently changing faces of deism to Internet users.

The first attempt at creating a virtual community of deists on the Net was the World Union of Deists, online since 1996.[49] Explicitly political, somewhat intolerant, it was within a few years outpaced by a more moderate and sophisticated website, PONDER (Presence on the Net of Deists for Enlightenment and Reason), launched in 2002. Soon these two sites had to face the stimulating competition of new sites from a number of splinter groups. Today PONDER is called Deistnet. Its goal "is to present Deism in a positive light for all visitors and to serve as a comprehensive reference for Deists to find information."[50] A Deist Alliance was recently set up to coordinate five active websites—Deistnet, Positive Deism, Modern Deism, Dynamic Deism, and Deism Information. Other websites are currently regularly updated, to which a number of forums must be added.[51] The neo-deist movement is feeling its way, exploring possibilities, striving to find the best communication strategy to reach out to people on the competitive American spiritual marketplace. All relate back, at some point or another, to Thomas Paine and direct the religious surfer's attention to *The Age of Reason*, now available online. Most neo-deist groups embrace a definition of deism which, in keeping with Paine's views, emphasizes reason, nature, and human experience, while wishing "to go beyond historical deism" by adapting Paine's advocacy of spiritual exploration to present time and putting forward the capacity of the believer to mix codes and "appropriate symbols, teachings, and practices from many times and places."[52]

Although not all cyber-deists retain Paine's strong emphasis on progressive political commitment, it seems that the renaissance of deism should be seen as a liberal response to a troubled political context and the worrisome alliance between government and evangelical Christianity in the United States. Among the reasons why Paine's thought appeals to many Americans today, there is the nature of his deism, which was not so much a system of beliefs as an encouragement to "think for oneself" and to question the prevailing authority. Paine's attitude toward religion is today more compelling than Jefferson's because he spoke out and Jefferson did not. Moreover, Paine was not a statesman, but an ordinary citizen, caught between fear and hope for a better world, who reminds us of our dreams as we come "face to face with the modern mind."[53] Paine participated in the secularization of public space, but did not promote the decline of religion. Rather his deism, like that of some of his eighteenth-century contemporaries, advanced the cause of liberal religion and pluralism, and contributed to the expression of the protean nature of religion.

Notes

[1] Harvey J. Kaye, *Thomas Paine and the Promise of Democracy* (New York: Hill and Wang, 2005), p. 9. See also Edward Larkin, *Thomas Paine and the Literature of Revolution* (New York: Cambridge University Press, 2005); Paul Collins, *The Trouble with Tom Paine: The Strange Afterlife and Times of Thomas Paine* (New York: Bloomsbury, 2005); Vikki Vickers, *"My Pen and My Soul Have Ever Gone Together": Thomas Paine and the American Revolution* (New York: Routledge, 2006); Christopher Hitchens, *Thomas Paine's Rights of Man: A Biography* (London: Atlantic Book, 2006); Craig Nelson, *Thomas Paine: Enlightenment, Revolution, and the Birth of Modern Nations* (New York: Viking Adult, 2006); Michael Burgan, *Thomas Paine: Great Writer of the Revolution* (Minneapolis: Compass Point Books, 2005).

[2] *The Age of Reason*, in *The Writings of Thomas Paine*, Moncure Daniel Conway, ed., 4 vols. (New York: AMS Press, 1967), vol. 4, pp. 104, 112.

[3] Like Ronald Reagan, George W. Bush seems to enjoy quoting Paine's *Common Sense* (Kaye, *op. cit.*, pp. 9, 223): "[the] ideal of America is the hope of all mankind" (Sep. 11, 2001); "We are serving in freedom's cause—and that is the cause of all mankind" (Sep., 2003); "The cause we serve is right, because it is the cause of all mankind" (Jan., 2004).

[4] *The Age of Reason*, in Conway, *op. cit.*, vol. 4, p. 21. Susan Jacoby, *Freethinkers: A History of American Secularism* (New

York: Metropolitan Books, 2004), p. 36. Among scholars who have recently downplayed Paine's radicality by integrating his thought into conservative narrative, see Gertrude Himmelfarb, *The Roads to Modernity: The British, French, and American Enlightenments* (New York: Vintage Books, 2004).

[5] Paine, *Rights of Man*, in Conway, *op. cit.*, vol. 2, p. 472. Henry F. May, *The Enlightenment in America* (1976; Oxford: Oxford University Press, 1978), p. 174.

[6] Some articles but few books are devoted to Paine's religious views. See, however, Jack Frutchman, Jr., *Thomas Paine and the Religion of Nature* (Baltimore: John Hopkins University Press, 1993) or Edward H. Davidson and William J. Scheick, *Paine, Scripture, and Authority* (Bethlehem, PA: Lehigh University Press, 1994). See also Nathalie Caron, *Thomas Paine contre l'imposture des prêtres* (Paris: L'Harmattan, 1999). Only three monographs have been published on American deism—including two in the 1930s. Gustav A. Koch, *Religion of the American Enlightenment* (N.p.: No publisher, 1933; New York, Crowell, 1968); Herbert M. Morais, *Deism in Eighteenth-Century America* (New York: Columbia University Press, 1934); Kerry Walters, *Rational Infidels: The American Deists* (Wolfeboro, NH: Longwood, 1992). Several historians have noted in passing that the history of deism is poorly understood. See James Turner, *Without God, Without Creed* (Baltimore: John Hopkins University Press, 1985), p. 78; Jon Butler, "Coercion, Miracle, Reason: Rethinking American Religious Experience in the Revolutionary Age," in Ronald Hoffman and Peter Albert, eds., *Religion in a Revolutionary Age* (Charlottesville: University Press of Virginia, 1994), p. 2. Susan Jacoby's bibliography brings to the fore the scarcity of secondary sources. It is to be noted that a new interest in American deism is currently emerging among early American historians.

[7] I use Henry May's terminology, *op. cit.*, p. xvi. May distinguishes between four categories: the Moderate Enlightenment, the Skeptical Enlightenment, the Revolutionary Enlightenment, the Didactic Enlightenment. The Revolutionary Enlightenment is defined by May as "the possibility of constructing a new heaven and earth out of the destruction of the old" (p. xvi).

⁸Jacoby, *op. cit.*, pp. 3-8, 58. The author emphasizes that, although Paine's propagandist literature was crucial to the revolutionary cause, he has not received his due in American history because of the "heretical views" (p. 5) put forth in his *The Age of Reason*. Her reference to Paine, whom she inaccurately calls "the first American freethinker stigmatized to be labeled an atheist" (p. 5), is intended to fuel her criticism of the influence of religion on "the communal psyche and public life" (p. 3) in a nation founded on the separation of Church and State. She denounces the customary denigration of secularists and exposes the current "institutionalization of religion" (p. 8). Her analysis of Paine, however, tends to overemphasize his anti-ecclesiastical views and fails to acknowledge Paine's acceptance of a variety of religious beliefs and practices and defense of religious pluralism.

⁹Caron, *op. cit.*, p. 359.

¹⁰Paine, *Rights of Man*, in Conway, *op. cit.*, vol. 4, pp. 21-22.

¹¹*The Age of Reason*, in Conway, *op. cit.*, vol. 4, p. 191.

¹²Phillip E. Hammond, et al., *Religion on Trial: How Supreme Court Trends Threaten Freedom of Conscience in America* (Walnut Creek: Altamira Press, 2004), p. 39.

¹³*Ibid.*, p. 36.

¹⁴*Rights of Man*, in Conway, *op. cit.*, vol. 3, p. 454.

¹⁵*Ibid.*

¹⁶*Ibid.*, p. 307.

¹⁷*Prospect Papers* (1804), in Conway, *op. cit.*, vol. 4, p. 342. In his essay "On Dreams," Paine refers to the "American Revolution, which, by establishing the universal right of conscience, first opened the way to free discussion" (in Conway, *op. cit.*, vol. 4. p. 364).

[18] Barbara McGraw, *Rediscovering America's Sacred Ground: Public Religion and Pursuit of the Good in a Pluralistic America* (Albany: State University of New York Press, 2003), p. 37.

[19] *Rights of Man*, in Conway, *op. cit.*, vol. 3, p. 516.

[20] See "The Existence of God," in Conway, *op. cit.*, vol. 4, p. 243: "The atheist who affects to reason [. . .] is a half rational for whom there is some hope."

[21] *Rights of Man*, in Conway, *op. cit.*, vol. 3, pp. 504, 515.

[22] *Ibid.*, pp. 327, 515. In a letter, Paine assured Samuel Adams, who had written to express his disappointment that Paine had turned [his] mind to infidelity, that he did not believe that all "priests" were "perverse." He concludes his letter by saying "the Man who is a friend to man and to his rights, *let his religious opinions be what they may*, is a good citizen" (letter to Samuel Adams, Jan. 1, 1803, in Conway, *op. cit.*, vol. 4, pp. 205, 208, my emphasis).

[23] *Rights of Man*, in Conway, *op. cit.*, vol. 3, p. 327.

[24] *Ibid.*, p. 516.

[25] *Ibid.*

[26] *Common Sense*, in Conway, *op. cit.*, vol. 1, p. 108. It was in his letter to Camille Jordan, written in 1797 in post-revolutionary France, that Paine developed his views on public worship (like the use of bells or public processions) and argued for "quiet and private domestic worship" (in Conway, *op. cit.*, vol. 4, p. 253).

[27] *Common Sense*, in Conway, *op. cit.*, vol. 1, p. 98.

[28] *The Age of Reason*, in Conway, *op. cit.*, vol. 4, p. 84.

[29] William R. Hutchison, *Religious Pluralism in America: The History of a Contentious Ideal* (New Haven: Yale University Press, 2003), p. 58.

³⁰Bernard Vincent, "A National of Nowhere: The Problem of Thomas Paine's American Citizenship," *The Transatlantic Republican: Thomas Paine and the Age of Revolution* (Amsterdam and New York: Rodopi, 2005), pp. 109-14.

³¹"A revolution in the state of civilization is the necessary companion of revolutions in the system of government," *Agrarian Justice*, in Conway, *op. cit.*, vol. 3, p. 342.

³²*Rights of Man*, in Conway, *op. cit.*, vol. 2, p. 472.

³³*Ibid.*, p. 354.

³⁴"A Letter to Mr. Erskine," in Conway, *op. cit.*, vol. 4, p. 229.

³⁵Robert N. Bellah, et al. *Habits of the Heart: Individualism and Commitment in American Life* (Berkeley, CA: University of California Press, 1996), p. 233.

³⁶*The Age of Reason*, in Conway, *op. cit.*, vol. 4, p. 22; letter to Ezra Stiles Ely, June 25, 1819, The Thomas Jefferson Papers Series 1. General Correspondence. 1651-1827 http://memory.loc.gov/ammem/collections/jefferson_papers/index.html, page viewed Sep. 18, 2006.

³⁷Bellah, *op. cit.*, p. 233.

³⁸May, *op. cit.*, p. 231.

³⁹Wade Clark Roof, *Spiritual Marketplace: Baby Boomers and the Remaking of American Religion* (Princeton: Princeton University Press, 1999), pp. 9-10.

⁴⁰*Ibid.* p. 125.

⁴¹Barry A. Kosmin and Ariela Keysar, *Religion in a Free Market: Religious and Non-Religious Americans* (Ithaca, NY: PMP, 2006), p. xvi.

⁴²*Prospect Papers* (1804), in Conway, *op. cit.*, vol. 4., p. 316.

⁴³*Ibid.*, p. 311. *The Age of Reason*, in Conway, *op. cit.*, vol. 4, p. 22.

[44]*Examination of the Prophecies* (1807), in Conway, *op. cit.*, vol. 4, p. 412.

[45]Christian Smith and Melinda Lundquist Denton, *Soul Searching: The Religious and Spiritual Lives of American Teenagers* (New York: Oxford University Press, 2005), pp. 162-72.

[46]Robert Bellah, "Civil Religion in America," *Daedalus* (Winter, 1967): 1-21.

[47]Kosmin and Keysar, *op. cit.*, p. 27. The authors define the word "deists" as believers in a "deity."

[48]See also http://www.adherents.com/rel_USA.html (page viewed Sep. 18, 2006).

[49]http://www.deism.com/ (page viewed Sep. 18, 2006).

[50]http://www.deistnet.com/ (page viewed Sep. 18, 2006).

[51]See the "Other Deism websites" page on deistnet.com (pages viewed Sep. 18, 2006).

[52]Email from David Pyle, administrator of www.dynamicdeism.org, Sep. 30, 2005.

[53]Will Eno, *ThomPain (based on nothing)* (London: Oberon Books, 2004), p. 16.

"AS NEAR TO ATHEISM AS TWILIGHT IS TO DARKNESS": THOMAS PAINE'S DEISM IN A RELIGIOUS REPUBLIC

Kirsten Fischer

After the 2004 presidential election in which, as victorious Republicans claimed, "values won," many liberals wonder whether and how to use a language of religion in the public sphere. "Values talk" has been monopolized by conservatives, making the "me-too religion" of Democratic contenders seem by comparison an after-thought, a political strategy rather than the source of deeply-held convictions about a political platform.

Many liberal commentators have touted a reclaiming of religious language to clarify (presumably to swing voters) that progressives *do* have values and that these include social justice, equal opportunity, fiscal responsibility, ecological sanity, the right to privacy, and civil rights. Some of these pundits understand Christianity as a leftist movement begun by Jesus, a charismatic radical who has since been hijacked by the religious right and made to serve their greedy, dogmatic ends. I am thinking especially of Jim Wallis, the evangelical author of the best-selling book *God's Politics: Why the Right Gets It Wrong and the Left Doesn't Get It*.[1] Wallis says the prophetic tradition is infused with a radical agenda of social justice and that the left needs to reclaim the language of Christianity to talk back to conservatives and reach American voters where they are—and where 90-plus percent of Americans are, apparently, is in conversation with God. Many liberals and leftists agree with Wallis. It appears that liberals are losing political clout they won't regain in this lifetime if they continue to avoid discussing religion in public. If not sincerity of belief, then *Realpolitik* and the importance of framing issues advantageously would have Democrats challenging Republicans in 2008 on religious ground.[2]

I find this proposition enormously troubling. For one thing, talk is cheap, and presidential hopefuls will subject us to endless and always unverifiable claims of their religious devotion. Most of all, I dread theocratically imposed doctrines on an array of life-and-death issues. Any talk of religion in the political realm seems to me a hazardous concession to the framing of social issues by the religious right. But while I would rather not hear about religion in politics, I find myself pressed to rethink my opinion about the role of religion in the public sphere because the secular sphere I prefer doesn't hold up very well against its critics. In a moment I'll explain why a secular public sphere may be neither possible nor even desirable. These are questions of political ethics: which beliefs may people bring to the public conversation, and how should religion inform political decisions? The strategic problem also remains: how to campaign successfully for public office when so many voters claim that religious opinion on a single issue outweighs all other concerns?

Fortunately, Thomas Paine offers a productive way to think about both the ethical dilemma (the role of religion in the public sphere) and the strategic concern (how to win the next election). Paine demonstrates how to engage in religious talk in the public sphere without supporting fundamentalist claims to knowledge of a divine will. Before liberal politicians rush to take up the cross, they would do well to look at the way Paine promoted ethical political action without referring to any creed at all. Paine was motivated by his understanding of God and God's relationship to the human race, but Paine rejected as irrelevant (and usually hypocritical) any effort to authorize a social and political platform with references to God's will. With contemporary political disagreements shaped by clashing religious views, and with contests raging over the meaning of the separation of church and state, Paine's writings may help liberals to renegotiate a language of faith in the political realm.

What is the problem, exactly, with a secular public sphere, one without reference to religious mandates and religiously-inspired agenda? The problem is that those who insist on an entirely secular public sphere—their critics call them "secular fundamentalists"—force people either to compartmentalize their inner lives and leave vital aspects of their world views at the door or to remain on the fringes of public, political debate. Religious conservatives have long deplored what one called the "naked public square," a secular public sphere presumably stripped of all moral sensibility.[3] Conservatives have argued that this is a terrible misunderstanding of the founders' original intent. The Constitution's establishment clause, they say, did not mean to imply or impose a separation of church and state.[4]

More recently (and for me, more interestingly), leftist and liberal intellectuals have also challenged the separation of church and state, not on the basis of original intent, but on the grounds that such a separation is impossible and undesirable. The "impossible" argument is that one cannot separate one's political values from moral, ethical, religious ones. Every political decision and social policy is shaped by the values and beliefs of its promoters. How could it be otherwise? Honesty requires that we admit the many sources of our political views. The related argument, namely, that a strictly secular state is undesirable, claims that the exclusion of religious language from the public sphere does violence to those (the many) whose political agenda is fueled by religious values. A truly secular public sphere constrains people to speak of their religious beliefs in a secular code, without explicit reference to the moral mandates that give their politics coherence and meaning. This truncation of religious thought is especially unfair when we consider that certain normative religious values (such as Christianity in the United States) pervade the public sphere more than "separation advocates" would like to admit. In reality, therefore, the allegedly secular nature of the public sphere has a recognizable but unspoken and unacknowledged Christian norm or standard, which is in turn protected from competing religious views by the pretense to a secular public space.

William Connolly is a political theorist who makes the case for a "post-secular" society. According to Connolly, a public sphere that is both non-theistic *and* a-secular (pause a minute to think about this: neither theistic nor secular) would look like this: "partisans of several types might negotiate a public ethos of engagement drawn from several moral sources. Here no constituency would be allowed to represent authoritatively the single source from which all others must draw in public life, even as each continued to articulate the strengths of the source it honors" (Connolly, p. 6). For Connolly, "the objective [of a post-secular society] is not to eliminate secularism, but to convert it into one perspective among several in a pluralistic culture" (Connolly, p. 11). A "democratic ethos of generosity and forbearance" (Connolly, p. 16) is both the means and the goal for this vision of a non-theistic a-secular space, one in which partisans engage with each other with a kind of respect that is currently hard to imagine. Connolly envisions "a general ethos of engagement among adherents of divergent moral sources. None commandeers a universal moral source complete, auThomasatic, or authoritative enough to generate a masterful response to every difficult issue ... [E]ach contributes something to an appreciation of the indispensability and constitutive fragility of ethics in political life" (Connolly, p. 17).[5]

Arguments such as these help me to reconsider my separatist stance regarding politics and religion. In an age where the president of the world's greatest military power claims to make war because God told him to, this reconsideration is quite a challenge.[6] It seems as though any concession in politics to a language of religious inspiration (even worse: religious mandate) is the same as a hefty push down the slippery slope to theocracy. One of the reasons I'm willing to reconsider the role of religion in public political debate is that Thomas Paine managed to do it in a way I can appreciate. He, too, faced a moment of intensified evangelical activism. Paine responded to that challenge by speaking out in ways that honored his own deist belief system, acknowledged the right of others to their source of spiritual guidance, and yet denounced absolutism from any corner. In the 1790s, when the contest between the churched and the un-churched was at a fevered pitch, Paine used a language of ethics in politics that might prove useful to us now.

To clarify, I am not talking here about the constitutionality of religious talk in the public sphere, which I take to be a given whether one is a private citizen or an elected or appointed public official. At issue is not constitutionality, but applied political philosophy: what self-restraints, if any, are appropriate and useful in a pluralistic democracy? To what extent should politicians, judges, and citizens draw on their religious (or nonreligious) beliefs to explain their political decisions? I do not explore that problem fully here, nor the vexed question of whether a distinction can and should be made between religious *arguments* in the public political sphere and religiously motivated political *decisions* by government officials (which I view as improper). I sidestep that difficulty, and focus here on the limited question of how liberals can join in the fray of religiously-inflected public debate without it becoming a major concession to the religious right. I explore what liberals might learn from Paine about how to talk about religious beliefs in a way that does not support fundamentalism or doctrinally based political decisions.

Paine's use of religious language reflected his beliefs about God, organized religion, and Christianity in particular. As a deist, Paine believed in a benevolent but non-interventionist Creator whose works anyone could observe in the natural world. In contrast to the Bible, which raised more questions than it answered, Paine said, "the creation we behold is the real and ever existing word of God, in which we cannot be deceived. It proclaimeth his power, it demonstrates his wisdom, it manifests his goodness and beneficence."[7] That God was good Paine never doubted. "Do we not see a fair creation prepared to receive us the instant we were born—a world furnished to our hands that cost us nothing? Is it we that light up the sun; that pour down the rain; and fill the earth with abundance? Whether we sleep or wake, the vast machinery of the universe still goes on" (AR, p. 674). Paine viewed natural philosophy as the only true theology: "natural philosophy is properly a divine study. It is the study of God through His works. It is the best study, by which we can arrive at a knowledge of His existence, and the only one by which we can gain a glimpse of His perfection."[8] What falsely passes as theology, Paine said, "is not the study of God himself in the works that he has made, but in the works or writings that *man* has made" (AR, p. 691, emphasis added). "The only true religion," Paine claimed, "is deism, by which . . . mean the belief of one God, and an imitation of his moral character, or the practice of what are called moral virtues" (AR, p. 806).

Belief in one God made sense to Paine, but the idiosyncrasies of any given dogma—what Paine nicely called "the redundancies annexed to that belief" (AR, p. 719)—were bogus invention with sinister intent. "All national institutions of churches, whether Jewish, Christian or Turkish, appear to me no other than human inventions, set up to terrify and enslave mankind, and monopolize power and profit" (AR, p. 666). But Paine did not seek to suppress the religions he opposed. He was willing to "let every man follow, as he has a right to do, the religion and worship he prefers" (AR, p. 719). Paine also conceded, as did Benjamin Franklin, that religions could be useful and could have an appropriate place in society, depending entirely on their results. In *Rights of Man*, Paine asserted that "every religion is good that teaches man to be good; and I know of none that instructs him to be bad" (RM, p. 644). Nevertheless, while Paine was sure that "it is the will of the Almighty that there should be a diversity of religious opinions among us," he could not see any value in Christianity (CS, p. 43). He scorned the notion that the Bible was divine revelation, and he mocked the miracles described in the New Testament as implausible and merely hearsay. Christian adoration of the man Jesus was crude and misguided idolatry that Paine called "manism." To Paine, the Christian faith seemed "a species of atheism; a sort of religious denial of God. It professes to believe in a man rather than in God. It is a compound made up chiefly of manism but with little deism, and is as near to atheism as twilight is to darkness. It introduces between man and his maker an opaque body which it calls a redeemer . . . It has put the whole orb of reason into shade" (AR, pp. 690-91).

Paine viewed as both ludicrous and harmful Christianity's central tenet that innate human sin required redemption through the sacrifice of Jesus, whose resurrection promised eternal life. "Moral justice cannot take the innocent for the guilty, even if the innocent would offer itself. To suppose justice to do this, is to destroy the principle of its existence, which is the thing itself. It is then no longer justice. It is indiscriminate revenge . . . [T]he probability is . . . that, in truth, there is no such thing as redemption; that it is fabulous; and that man stands in the same relative condition with his Maker he ever did stand since man existed; and that it is the greatest consolation to think so" (AR, p. 685). Paine hoped his Biblical exegesis would liberate Christians from their belief in original sin. "It is by [man's] being taught to contemplate himself as an out-law, as an out-cast, as a beggar, as a mumper, as one thrown, as it were, on a dunghill, at an immense distance from his Creator, and who must make his approaches by creeping and cringing to intermediate beings, that he conceives either a contemptuous disregard for every thing [. . .], or becomes indifferent, or turns, what he calls, devout" (AR, p. 685). The devout man, Paine said, was filled with grief— real or affected. Ungrateful and reproachful, "He calls himself a worm, and the fertile earth a dunghill; and all the blessings of life by the thankless name of vanities. He despises the choicest gift of God to man, the GIFT OF REASON" (AR, p. 685).

Like the Enlightenment *philosophes* who lambasted Christianity for rejecting reason and glorifying superstition, Paine's passion was to debunk the Biblical myths that shackled believers and disgraced God. "It is the fable of Jesus Christ," Paine said, "and the wild and visionary doctrine raised thereon, against which I contend." He found the story "blasphemously obscene" (AR, p. 792). With scathing sarcasm, well-placed questions, and sometimes pedantic logic, Paine did his best to unseat Biblical authority and to redefine Christianity as a form of disbelief, as "near to atheism as twilight is to darkness." Paine advocated, instead, "the plain, pure, and unmixed belief of one God, which is Deism" (AR, p. 796) and saw it as "a duty incumbent on every true deist, that he vindicates the moral justice of God against the calumnies of the bible" (AR, p. 740). The Bible is entirely unnecessary, Paine asserted, because "THE WORD OF GOD IS THE CREATION WE BEHOLD; And it is in this word, which no human invention can counterfeit or alter, that God speaketh universally to man" (AR, p. 686).

Yet Paine was not simply a naysayer. He debunked the Bible so thoroughly because he believed that if people could be persuaded to ditch the notion of human depravity and a vengeful God, they could instantly go out and remake the world. That's precisely what his opponents feared, be they Edmund Burke in the eighteenth century or certain Paine scholars in the twentieth. Paine cheerfully leads the way to disorder, a complete remaking of the social world, which begins with individuals thinking for themselves. Paine was fundamentally an optimist, and even in his last and least popular days he adhered to his long-standing conviction that a liberation movement would build and spread. Paine predicted and promoted the freeing of the individual mind from undue authority, and he fully believed it would happen in his lifetime. In the future he envisioned, people would overthrow the state and church powers that oppressed them psychologically as well as economically, and they would take on the responsibilities and pleasures of free thinking and true self-government, in both an individual and a societal sense. Paine had faith in this transformation, and he believed he was doing the important work of promoting self-liberation among ordinary people.

The link between belief and social practice is crucial in Paine's thinking. Prayer alone is a meager way of enacting one's devotion in the world, because prayer is at botThomas a self-serving practice: "A man does not serve God when he prays, for it is himself he is trying to serve."[9] Instead of prayer, Paine advocated universal philanthropy, with which he meant not merely "the sentimental benevolence of wishing well, but the practical benevolence of doing good" (Ibid., p. 420). The Deity, as Paine put it, "needs no service from us. We can add nothing to eternity. But it is in our power to render a service *acceptable* to him, and that is not by praying, but by endeavoring to make his creatures happy" (Ibid., p. 420). Here we have the classic statement of a deist, namely, that the pursuit of happiness in this world, and the efforts of individuals to help others achieve happiness, constitutes a worthy moral striving, one that would please the same God who had given humans the ability to raise their condition through their own means. As Paine saw it, ". . . the *practice* of moral truth, or in other words, a *practical imitation* of the moral goodness of God, is no other than our acting towards each other, as he acts benignly towards all . . . [T]he only idea we can have of serving God, is that of contributing to the happiness of the living creation that God has made" (AR, p. 712, emphasis added). Consequently, he said, "every thing of persecution and revenge between man and man, and every thing of cruelty to animals, is a violation of moral duty" (AR, p. 719).

Paine's politics were steeped in notions of morality, and he used a strong idiom of ethics to propose radical social reforms. Paine's agenda included abolishing the death penalty, a progressive estate tax to limit the accumulation of property, tax relief for the poor, special relief for families with children, a system of social security for the elderly, public funding of education through a voucher system, financial support for newly married couples and new mothers, and employment centers for the jobless.[10] His vision of social justice was bound up with his hopes for the free and democratic society he believed the new United States to be.

But Paine's *Age of Reason* did not frame his critique of power or his proposals for social reform in a language of religious faith, as Jim Wallis would have liberals do. On the contrary, Paine used a language of moral duty that was removed from any particular theological belief system. He offered morality without a creed, but one with a mandate for action. Paine separated ethics from religion, expressing values without endorsing a religious doctrine. Today, the religious right has reframed matters so that religion seems to occupy the entire field of ethics, making "secular ethics" seem an oxymoron to many. But Paine's deist faith inspired him to separate ethics from any religious creed. Paine was neither a secularist, nor a fundamentalist. I believe he exemplifies the non-theistic, a-secular thinking that Connolly describes.

Except that Connolly would not agree. Paine does not offer the respect for others' beliefs that Connolly envisions. Paine is disgusted and sarcastic when he describes how religious talk is used to justify unethical conduct. He scorns all things supernatural and cannot imagine that anyone would really believe that stuff of their own volition. His invective is very much akin to the right-wing hyperbole that currently has so many liberals flailing. Paine's venomous pen will not help usher in a post-secular space of generosity and forbearance. This part of Paine's persona—the underdog fighting against entrenched beliefs—has my full sympathy, but his vitriolic language does not help us to re-conceptualize the kinds of conversations about religion and politics we need to have in this religious republic of ours.

More useful, however, is Paine's language of values without a corollary creed on which those values rely. I especially appreciate his insistence that one person's God is just that: one person's God. Liberals and leftists can and must talk about their values when they talk politics, and if some wish to speak of their political inspiration from Jesus and the moral code they see in the Bible, they can have at it. But as Paine points out, their spiritual inspiration has no more persuasive power than that of a person who does not subscribe to a religion of the book. The religious faith of another is ultimately unknowable—and liberals should admit that as they appeal to voters by referencing personal religious beliefs. Furthermore, all talk of revelation, of knowing the will of God, *must* expect explicit skepticism. Paine was right about this: revelation stops with the recipient. To all others, it is merely hearsay. All we learn, when someone speaks of the will of God, is that they claim to know what it is and are willing to say so in public. One can acknowledge, without *accepting*, believers' claims to their knowledge of God and his preferences.

Then again, "values talk" need not be couched in the language of religion at all; certainly religious language is not needed to make the case for social change. One can even wrap oneself in the flag, claiming that privacy of religion is American and patriotic. Paine was an ardent patriot and champion of the American Revolution precisely because the Constitution abolished religious tests for office, established freedom of religion, placed religion beyond the purview of the legislative process, and made claims only to popular rather than divine authority. Insisting on the privacy of one's religious beliefs has a venerable tradition in American history that's worth upholding, even as some choose to take on a religious tone.

But since we cannot expect to keep religious talk out of the public sphere, and since it may even be beneficial to include an open discussion of faiths, we might do well to remember Thomas Paine. The respectful engagement William Connolly calls for is not the same as reverence, and Paine was good at being irreverent. He had the courage to say when another person's religion appeared to him "As near to atheism as twilight is to darkness" (AR, p. 690). Respect for other people means holding them accountable for unethical actions they justify with their religious beliefs. Respect means engaging in conversations and confrontations about moral practice, and public debate involving religion must support the right of everyone to disbelieve the religious tenets of another. Liberals will have lost too much if they claim to know God's will better than the religious right. No matter how powerful religious beliefs are for those who hold them, they are binding only for the believer. As for everyone else, as Paine said, "We should never force belief upon ourselves in anything" (AR, p. 819). Thank you.

❧ ☙

Question: I'm confused. You said that Thomas Paine was opposed to Christianity and Jesus Christ. Are you saying that Thomas Paine was opposed to Christianity?

Kirsten Fischer: I'm saying that he had no time or respect for it.

Question: I have two questions. Regarding Paine's idea of economic justice, were other prominent founders allied with that kind of idea? Secondly, I'm interested in the process by which he came from his Quaker background into his deism.

Vikki Vickers: I can address the Quaker background issue, as I discussed this in my own book. His father was a Quaker, and Paine did believe that, of all the Christians sects, the Quakers came closest to being true Christians. Nevertheless, as Kirsten has said, there was still no reverence for Christianity, itself. But of all the Christians, he did respect the Quakers most of all. His father's influence, I think, had more to do with his general moral sense than Quakerism, per se.

Eric Schlereth: I am by no means an authority on the economics of Paine, but I'm thinking of his references in *Common Sense* to the idea that political liberty for the American colonies would be justified and protected by free trade. That was, I think, an economic idea shared by many of the other prominent Americans who were thinking at that time, and it tapped into that idea in the late eighteenth century that free trade was in some sense liberating, and thus it was a fairly radical idea.

Question: I'm a member of the American and British Humanists Associations, and of course Thomas Paine is a hero for them. I have learned at this symposium that there were many associations that tried to promote the values of the humanists, of Thomas Paine, and those values have been enunciated. I've learned that there's a rationalist religion, the religion of deism; I've heard about the Center For Inquiry; I've heard about revolution, peaceful revolution, to try and promote all these values; and I've heard about numerous Websites through which one can get information on deism. What I'd like to know is, what can we do to unite to promote all these ideals and these values, and if there's any other way than to join a political party? While I'm not a Democrat, I do see that the only way these values can be promoted is through political activism and, hence, through the Democratic Party.

Kirsten Fischer: My own personal opinion about that is yes, I think the political public sphere is the place in which to have these kinds of conversations—and that may mean running for office, or it may mean having conversations with those who do run for office, or it may mean, among ourselves and in the groups of people with whom we communicate, that we learn to speak about religion possibly in new ways, in the ways that I'm trying to suggest Tom Paine did himself. For me, the struggle is to avoid being a Rush Limbaugh of the left, and to actually engage in more respectful ways than in the past with those who hold different beliefs than mine, and to remind them continually that their beliefs may not be imposed upon me. In other words, I see this segregation, the so-called red state/blue state divide, as being a device, a trope, maybe even a fiction that continues to separate people and continues to hinder these kinds of conversations from happening. To come out in the public sphere in this way, I think, is the right way to go.

Question: I'd like to ask Eric Schlereth . You were talking about the Paineite movement in the 1820s and 1830s; I was just wondering what kind of interaction, if any, there was with the Jacksonian movement of the common (white) man. I wonder if they overlapped. I also wonder about the contradiction of Jacksonianism, speaking of freedom while oppressing Native Americans.

Eric Schlereth: There was overlap of movements. In many ways, the people who were participating in the Paine birthday celebrations in the 1820s and 1830s were the same people who were involved in various workingman's parties and such, in New York City, for example. Even in some toasts, right after the 1830s, you have references to Jackson. There was a clear political thinking that aligned with the Jacksonians. It doesn't seem to be as strong later with the Whigs. I think there was probably a different form, almost a Whig-ish type of free inquiry. But for the material I focused on, the people were mainly aligned with the Jacksonians.

The issue of Native Americans is worth probing. One of the fascinating things about this idea of mental emancipation is, I think, there was such a confidence among these people that if you emancipate the inner thinking of a person, then everything else outside of that will take care of itself. But that makes it very limiting in many ways.

Question: Regarding Paine's experiences in France, I'm wondering if he's had any lasting effect there, and how would he assess the form of government in France and also their religious views there, today?

Nathalie Caron: About the influence of Paine in France, I can say that *The Age of Reason*, which was translated into French, had no impact at all. I thought that was pretty amazing, that there was absolutely no reference to the book in the 1790s in France. I can say that Paine is known in France among historians of the French Revolution. He stayed in France ten years and was a deputy, a representative, to the National Assembly. He played not a major, but he played a role there, and he voted against the execution of the King. Also, after he was released from prison, he went back to the Assembly once to criticize the fact that the new constitution would do away with universal suffrage. Suffrage based on profits was reintroduced, and Paine was one of the few who criticized that change. As to what Paine would think today, I can't answer that question. I don't think we can give relevant answers to those questions.

Question: Walter Cronkite was once thought to be the most respected or trusted person in the United States, and he said that the American public is not sufficiently educated to pick its public representatives. I'd like to hear the comments of any of you in the context of your knowledge of Paine's writings on that.

Eric R. Schlereth: I think that Paine would put a greater burden on the individual to be educated, obviously. I would take issue with Cronkite's statement. I think if people are making political decisions regarding who they think best represents them, even if we fundamentally disagree, I wouldn't necessarily call that uneducated. But Paine certainly did believe in the obligations of the citizen to be educated. Of course, we're not sure how to apply Paine directly toward those kinds of contemporary questions.

Vikki Vickers: He was very democratic, Paine. Hamilton was not. Hamilton was among those who thought the people were not at all fully qualified to govern themselves. But I think Paine was one of the more democratic of the thinkers in American history.

Notes

[1] Jim Wallis, *God's Politics: Why the Right Gets it Wrong and the Left Doesn't Get It* (San Francisco: Harper San Francisco, 2005).

[2] See, for example, the op-ed by Boston University professor, Stephen Prothero, "Democrats: Get Religion!" in *The Boston Globe*, Nov. 10, 2004.

³Richard John Neuhaus, *The Naked Public Square: Religion and Democracy in America* (Grand Rapids, MI: W.B. Eerdmans, 1984).

⁴The conservative claim that the founders' original intent was *not* a separation of church and state came only after decades of berating the same founders for creating a secular Constitution and after numerous failed attempts to amend the Constitution to recognize a divine authority. This history is charted in Isaac Kramnick and R. Laurence Moore, *The Godless Constitution: The Case Against Religious Correctness* (NY: W.W. Norton and Co., 1997), chapter 7.

⁵See William E. Connolly, *Why I am Not a Secularist* (Minneapolis: University of Minnesota Press, 1999), pp. 6, 11, 16-17.

⁶According to the Israeli newspaper *Ha'aretz* for June 26, 2003, Bush told the Palestinian prime minister, "God told me to strike at al-Qaida and I struck them, and then he instructed me to strike at Saddam, which I did, and now I am determined to solve the problem in the Middle East." Quoted in Thomas Frank, *What's the Matter with Kansas? How Conservatives Won the Heart of America* (NY: Henry Holt and Company, 2005), p. 305, note 5.

⁷Thomas Paine, *The Age of Reason* in Eric Foner, ed., *Thomas Paine: Collected Writings* (NY: The Library of America, 1995), p. 718. Hereafter cited in the text as AR. Paine's *Rights of Man* is cited in the text as RM and *Common Sense* as CS. Both are also from Foner's edited volume.

⁸From Thomas Paine, "The Existence of God" (1797), quoted in Jack Fruchtman, Jr., *Thomas Paine and the Religion of Nature* (Baltimore: Johns Hopkins University Press, 1993), p. 159.

⁹Letter to Sam Adams, Jan. 1, 1803, in Foner ed., *Thomas Paine: Collected Writings*, p. 420.

¹⁰This list of proposed reforms comes directly from Harvey J. Kaye, *Thomas Paine and the Promise of America* (New York: Hill and Wang, 2005), p. 75.

PANEL 4:
THE RIGHT OF REVOLUTION AND THE LEGITIMACY OF GOVERNMENTS

Moderator: Ronald King

The last panel of a conference often contains some of the most wonderful and interesting and important things to talk about. Yet sometimes people also have to rush out, on their way to the airport so we do apologize, especially for enforcing time limits. This panel is the last one for our conference; to my mind it engages the most important topic of all, the right of revolution and the legitimacy of governments. We have three papers: from Jason Molloy of Oklahoma State, from Drew Maciag of Rochester, and from Aaron Keck of Rutgers. The first addresses the controversy between Paine and Adams. The second addresses the controversy between Paine and Burke, and the third addresses a controversy internal to Paine, himself.

THE PAINE-ADAMS DEBATE AND ITS SEVENTEENTH-CENTURY ANTECEDENTS

Jason S. Maloy

The intense personal rivalry between Thomas Paine and John Adams in the late eighteenth century was not only remarkable in its own right but also, arguably, formative in the development of American political thought and culture. The literary legacy of that rivalry is well known, as are its broad ideological oppositions: between optimistic and pessimistic views of human nature and perfectibility, between progressive and conservative attitudes toward social and political change, between populist and elitist accounts of the proper distribution of political power in republican regimes. Less well known, perhaps, is the fact that the Paine-Adams debate has a seventeenth-century genealogy stretching back to the beginnings of the tradition of Anglo-American constitutionalism. Their political argument was another episode in a long-running debate, with both English and American antecedents.

Instead of offering a comprehensive review of what was a wide-ranging and spirited dispute, this genealogical exercise will focus on a rather narrow and apparently technical aspect of it: the disagreement over different types of political regime, and more precisely over the merits and demerits of unicameral vs. multicameral constitutions. It is an important subject because it concerns the translation of democratic values into constitutional design, that is, the institutionalized distribution of political power. With respect to the theme of this symposium, examining the genealogy of the Paine-Adams debate offers definite theoretical pay-offs today. For, notwithstanding the relative francophilia of Paine and his American supporters vis-à-vis Federalist anglophiles like Hamilton, the Paine-Adams debate was really an episode of intramural struggle within Anglo-American constitutionalism itself. Understanding this debate and its antecedents, then, may prove useful for assessing, in these times of global "democratization," the complexities and potentialities of one of the most historically successful and currently influential approaches to constitutional design.

My genealogy will proceed in three steps, moving backward chronologically. First, I will outline the disagreement between Paine and Adams over regime types, as it appeared in print in the 1770s, 1780s, and 1790s. Then I will consider two seventeenth-century debates that anticipate many of the same arguments, one nearly as famous as the Paine-Adams debate, the other rather more obscure. The second step in my backwards chronology is the debate between Levellers and Cromwellians during the English Revolution of the middle seventeenth century. The third step is the foundational dispute about regime types and constitutional structure in the Massachusetts Bay Colony during its first two decades of existence, ca. 1630-1650.

Neither Paine nor Adams was shy about publication, and to a degree unmatched in early-republican America this political rivalry left a literary record. It began with the publication of Paine's *Common Sense* early in 1776. Adams, in a private letter, called its author "very ignorant of the Science of Government" and complained particularly of Paine's "crude, ignorant notion of a government by one assembly," which lacked the requisite "equilibrium or counter-poise."[1] Adams' own *Thoughts on Government*, published later in 1776, was meant to guide the making of the post-Independence state constitutions, and particularly to counter the influence of Paine's pamphlet. Adams had no quarrel, of course, regarding the superiority of republican over monarchial government, the right of revolution, or the desirability of American independence. On all these points the two men agreed. In fact, Adams rather enviously disparaged *Common Sense* as "a tolerable summary of the arguments which I had been repeating again and again in Congress for nine months."[2] In France it was long believed that Adams, not Paine, was the work's true author. It was squarely on the question of regime type that Adams' *Thoughts* sought to refute Paine.

Paine's views on this subject were borne by his sharp criticism of the British constitution, not only for being hereditary (the point of greatest force and elaboration in *Common Sense*) but also for being a species of "mixed government." Paine argued that Britain's mutual checks among separate branches—Crown, Lords, and Commons—rendered it in some sense self-contradictory or self-defeating: "a house divided against itself" and "a *felo de se*."[3] In response, Adams' *Thoughts* attacked unicameralism with elements of the doctrine of checks and balances. Mixed government was necessary in order to prevent tyrannical designs from being conceived and carried out. Because human nature is naturally vicious, Adams argued, a single assembly cannot be trusted any more than a single monarch. A second chamber is required to act as a "controlling power" to veto the tyrannical measures of the first.[4] The basic argument has become, by now, a familiar defense of the current American political system against the so-called Westminster or parliamentary alternative.

There was a practical as well as theoretical dimension to these first salvoes. The newly-independent states had set about making new constitutions for themselves, and Pennsylvania, home to Paine and his patron Franklin, famously adopted a unicameral constitution in 1776. It featured a single legislative assembly and a plural executive lacking veto power. It also granted a relatively wide franchise (including all taxpayers, even those without property of their own), required representatives to be elected annually with no consecutive terms, and provided for regular constitutional revision via a Council of Censors elected every seven years.[5] The Pennsylvania Constitution and its boosters in the Paine-Franklin circle came under fierce attack by conservative critics inspired in part by Adams' multicameralism. Among these critics was Paine's former ally, Benjamin Rush, who defended his ideological switch by citing *Thoughts on Government*.[6]

The next series of publications associated with the Paine-Adams debate over unicameralism began with the translation from French into English of Jacques Turgot's "Letter" in 1785, which attacked the multicameral constitutions of the various American states. Turgot, Louis XVI's Minister of Finance, originally sent this letter in 1778 to Richard Price, the prominent English radical and friend of Paine. Adams responded in 1787 with *A Defense of the Constitutions of the United States*, an effort to vindicate the American states against the likes of Price, Turgot, Franklin, and Paine (all of whom were named by Adams in his "Preface").

Turgot's letter briefly but provocatively criticized the tri-partite structure of all the American state constitutions (save Pennsylvania's, which Turgot attacked solely for its religious qualifications for office-holders):

> The customs of England are imitated without any particular motive. Instead of collecting all authority in one center, that of the nation, they have established different bodies . . . They endeavor to balance these

different powers, as if this equilibrium, which in England may be a necessary check to the enormous influence of royalty, could be of any use in republics founded upon the equality of all the citizens, and as if establishing different orders of men were not a source of divisions and disputes.[7]

These remarks were clearly identifiable with Paine's approach to constitutional design, for they adumbrated the three major points of Paine's critique of mixed regimes: first, inapposite imitation of Britain; second, self-defeating complexity (that is, failing to "collect all authority in one center"); third, violation of the ideal of equality (via the class composition of different agencies of government).

Adams' *Defense* was a lengthy reply to these strictures of Turgot's in the form of a constitutional survey of republics, ancient and modern. His conclusion was that all the most stable republics had in fact exhibited "a multitude of curious and ingenious inventions to balance, in their turn, all those powers."[8] "Those powers" referred to Adams' belief that human societies naturally produce what Turgot had called "different orders of men." For Adams, constitutional structures do not create and cannot destroy social hierarchies, but they might be designed to limit the violence that classes can do to one another. The purpose of a second, elitist legislative chamber was to empower but at the same time to isolate and to contain the natural aristocracy of a society. Otherwise, in Adams' view, civil war was the probable result. The only two ways to regulate partisan conflict were "by a monarchy and standing army, or by a balance in the constitution."[9]

The final and most famous stage of the Paine-Adams debate began with the French Revolution and its appropriation into American party politics. Adams reportedly believed that Jacobinism was the result of the "blind love" of French republicans for the unicameral Pennsylvania constitution of 1776; he also called this baneful ideological disposition "Paine's yellow fever."[10] Adams' attribution to Paine of influence over the Jacobins is problematic in several respects, but the key point for now is that the Paine-Adams contest became central to the American reception of the French Revolution. Jefferson, Madison, and the Democratic-Republicans welcomed that revolution and many still embraced Paine himself when he finally returned from Europe; Adams and the Federalists excoriated both the man and the event.

Adams' own response to Jacobinism was the *Discourses on Davila*. This, of course, was not the most telling such response; it was explicitly Burke's *Reflections* that Paine targeted when he wrote *Rights of Man*. The issue of unicameralism made a brief but important appearance in this debate. Paine celebrated the French National Assembly because it originated in the declaration of the Estates General against the privileged orders of nobility and clergy with their distinct prerogatives; that is, it appeared to be a genuine unicameral organ of popular government. In Part I of *Rights of Man*, Paine restated his 15-year-old criticism of mixed government from *Common Sense*: "in Mixed Governments there is no responsibility; the parts cover each other until responsibility is lost."[11] Constitutional complexity was thus seen to protect powerful elites from inspection and indictment by the citizenry at large. Paine went on to reject the notion found in Adams' *Defense* that a multicameral regime is needed to reflect natural social stratification: "as there is but one species of man, there can be but one element of human power, and that element is man himself. Monarchy, Aristocracy, and Democracy are but creatures of imagination; and a thousand such may be contrived as well as three."[12]

Republicans in America embraced Paine's latest defense of what they recognized as their own cause. Part I of *Rights of Man* was published by a friend of Jefferson's in an edition that included fulsome prefatory praise by Jefferson himself (then Secretary of State). Everyone at the time understood this American edition to be a personal attack on Vice-President Adams. As Madison had said of Adams' *Defense*, "under a mock defense of the Republican constitutions of his country he attacked them with all the force he possessed."[13] Jefferson was more ironic but no less clear in a letter to Washington: "I have a cordial esteem [for Adams], increased by long habits of concurrence in opinion in the days of his republicanism; and even since his apostasy to hereditary monarchy and nobility, though we differ, we differ as friends should do."[14] Paine himself confirmed, "I had John Adams in my mind when I wrote the pamphlet, and it has hit as I expected."[15]

Broadly speaking, therefore, there were two points on which Paine and Adams differed regarding regime types in general and the question of unicameralism in particular: constitutional complexity and class division. First, while Adams touted checks and balances among distinct agencies of government as a necessary mechanism for preserving public liberty, Paine decried what he saw as their mystifying and self-defeating character. Second, while Adams touted the class composition of various departments of political authority as a way to guard against civil war, Paine decried what he saw as its artificial and destructive rending of national unity. Interestingly, Part II of Paine's *Rights of Man* (the last major contribution to the debate) put a wrinkle into this pattern of disagreement. However, before considering that late turn and the lesson behind it, I will look at the two seventeenth-century debates that established the essential structure of Anglo-American debate over unicameralism — one in England and the other in colonial America.

The argument between Levellers and Cromwellians over the direction of the English Revolution and the shape of a new constitution is best known for the so-called Putney Debates of 1647 on the proper extent of the franchise. But equally subject to contest was the related question of unicameralism. The Levellers, with the support of a significant portion of the rank-and-file of the New Model Army, not only sought a broader franchise but also, in line with their generally populist vision of post-monarchial politics, recommended a unitary legislative body as the central organ of public authority. On the other side, Cromwell and his officer corps tended not only to defend existing property qualifications but also to advocate hedging the power of a representative assembly with other, elitist agencies.

Like Paine over a century later, the Levellers alarmed most of their contemporaries by the extent of their democratic demands, including the abolition of all forms of hereditary rule. For them, a reformed House of Commons was the only possible legitimate organ of government since hereditary bodies such as the House of Lords were patently unrepresentative of the sovereign people. As early as 1646, they were complaining that the Lords "are become arrogators to themselves of the natural sovereignty the represented have conveyed and issued to their *proper* representers [i.e. to the Commons]," and in the seminal *Petition of 11 September 1648* they explicitly joined King and Lords as chief authors of the nation's troubles while demanding that both agencies be stripped of veto power over the Commons.[16]

This initial defense of unicameralism, somewhat by implication, appeared to have been realized after the regicide in 1649 with the abolition of the House of Lords and of the monarchial office. But when Cromwell ignored many elements of the Levellers' proposals for constitutional reform (the so-called "Agreements of the People") and set up the Council of State and the office of Lord Protector, many Englishmen perceived that the old tripartite mixed regime had been re-established under new names. The Levellers' second version of the Agreement of the People, in response, included emphatic calls for the dissolution of the Council of State.[17] Their unicameralism was now fully self-conscious.

In general, the so-called "Instrument of Government" under which Cromwell governed was an institutional mishmash precisely of the sort Paine would have detested. It was much closer to John Adams' favored "multitude of curious and ingenious inventions" than to the unicameralism for which Adams (incredibly) blamed both Cromwell and Milton.[18] The "Instrument of Government" advertised itself as rule by "one person *and* the people assembled in Parliament.[19] Moreover, the "one person" (the Lord Protector) had a veto over the "people assembled." Adams' real complaint about the Cromwellian regime was not that it was truly unicameral, on any common-sense counting of chambers, but rather that Cromwell's mixed regime was tipped more in the direction of autocracy than of aristocracy. For Adams, the main point of multicameralism, for the achievement of liberty and stability, was the legislative veto given to the elitist, senatorial second chamber; in the Instrument of Government, by contrast, the Lord Protector — but not the Council of State — had the legislative veto.

It would not be fair, then, to say that in the late eighteenth century Adams was merely repeating Cromwell's argument or squarely taking his side against the Levellers. The likeness of Paine's arguments for unicameralism to the constitutional radicalism of the Levellers is rather more profound. In particular, the basic structure which defenses of unicameralism (or of "parliamentary systems," in modern parlance) have always taken, and which find articulation in Paine's writings, was a restatement of the Levellers' mind rather than a unique invention of his own: nothing else but a single sovereign assembly can be truly representative of the nation, and nothing else can be accountable to the people of the nation; therefore, nothing else can be either legitimate or safe.

Whenever the question of anticipation arises in the history of political thought, the question of influence is sure to follow. Was Paine aware that he was in effect taking a side in a seventeenth-century debate, that is, that of the Levellers against the Cromwellians? John Adams was a keen student of history and thus would have understood the un-innovative character of the debate he was having with Paine, and he was generally rather approving of Cromwell, despite his conviction that the Instrument of Government represented multicameralism of the wrong sort. Adams put forward the standard Whiggish interpretation of the Puritan Revolution, as a blow for liberty in a historic struggle against tyranny. Adams, then, was likely well aware of his and Paine's seventeenth-century antecedents; as for Paine, for reasons of temperament and the documentary record, the case is less clear.

What is clear, as I hope now to show, is that the debate over unicameralism was even older (slightly) than the English Revolution. The Leveller-Cromwellian controversy had its own antecedent, and, perhaps surprisingly, an American one. Conventional wisdom imagines that the Puritan commonwealths were simply illiberal theocracies with little to offer in terms of interesting political debate. In fact, there was a long-running political struggle in Massachusetts Bay, from the earliest years of settlement, between the governing establishment (which later, in the 1640s and 1650s, would be friendly to Cromwell in ways both practical and philosophical) and a kind of "country opposition" movement.

The government of the Bay Colony was tri-partite. There was a Governor, a Board of Assistants, and a General Court that all citizens were entitled to attend but which was usually composed of town deputies functioning in a representative capacity. To the country opposition that arose in the 1630s, led by deputies from the various towns around Boston, this system in practice showed visible oligarchic tendencies. According to Israel Stoughton, one of the leaders of this early opposition movement, "the government was solely in the hands of the Assistants. The people chose them Magistrates, and then they made laws, disposed lands, raised moneys, punished offenders, etc., at their discretion."[20] Responding to this perception, a remarkable movement for constitutional reform arose in the General Court of 1634. It won a few immediate victories and re-emerged in fits and starts over the next ten or fifteen years.

The 1634 reforms won by Stoughton and other opposition deputies represented a shift in ruling structure. They gave a variety of powers to "none but the General Court": "to make and establish laws . . . to elect and appoint officers . . . to set out the duties and powers of the said officers . . . to raise moneys and taxes, and to dispose of lands."[21] In short, precisely the same powers that allegedly had been monopolized by the natural aristocracy of the Bay Colony—Governor John Winthrop together with the prominent merchants and ministers sitting on the Board of Assistants—were ostensibly shifted wholesale to the General Court. The Massachusetts opposition, by absorbing Governor and Assistants into a single voting assembly, was attempting to move the colony toward a unicameral representative democracy.

But one obstacle remained: the Governor and Assistants had a legislative veto, and they employed it with regularity. This was the type of aristocratic veto that Adams would later favor, unlike the Cromwellian executive veto. Because the colony charter recognized no distinction between ordinary (statutory) and fundamental (constitutional) acts of the General Court, the magisterial veto was used to preserve itself. Paine would later attack the British constitution for precisely the same problem, that ordinary legislation and basic constitutional reform were entrusted to the same body.[22] Facing this checkmate, the opposition deputies offered a new proposal: "that there shall be power of suspension on either party in cases where they agree not, until the mind of the whole body of the Country may conveniently be known: and then the issue to be on the Major part's side."[23] In short, they were proposing a mutual veto, a kind of symmetric bicameralism, coupled with a version of referendum. Winthrop and the magistrates, however, initially held firm.

The issue of the magisterial veto and the broader question of regime type came up again and again in Massachusetts throughout the 1630s and early 1640s. Opposition deputies always criticized the veto as inconsistent with the popular nature of their government, and magistrates always defended it as necessary for wisdom and stability. Yet neither side was entirely immune to the spirit of compromise. The deputies periodically re-tabled their bicameral proposal, and the magistrates began to give ground, conceding the essentially "democratic" nature of the Bay Colony's constitution but insisting on the need for their veto as a useful "aristocratic" admixture.[24] Finally, in 1644 (after a foreign-policy blunder had embarrassed Winthrop), an agreement was reached on constitutional reform: bicameralism and the mutual veto, but (crucially) without any referendum-like appeal directly to the people of the colony.

It is interesting to notice that the lines of ideological influence in the seventeenth-century Anglo-American world traveled eastward as well as westward. The opposition deputies in Massachusetts not only anticipated some of the themes developed by the Levellers ten years later, and by Paine over a hundred years later; they also had personal ties among the Puritans back in England who shortly would be participating in civil war and constitutional reconstruction, and out of whose ranks the Levellers emerged as a radical splinter. Then again, the Bay Colony itself had splintered, and the leader of the breakaway colony, Roger Williams of Rhode Island, kept close ties with like-minded Londoners dabbling in a new ideological coupling of religious toleration with democratic constitutionalism, including future Levellers like Richard Overton. In a sense, then, the seventeenth-century debates over unicameralism resembled intramural quarrelling more than inter-tribal warfare. The Leveller-Cromwell contest, for instance, took place in a relatively remote corner of the English ideological landscape of the time, among people who had consciously distanced themselves considerably from hardcore royalists, moderate Anglicans, and Presybterian parliamentarians alike. For their part, the Massachusetts elites agreed with the opposition deputies that the *raison d'etre* of their colony was partly to do with opposition to the absolutist rule of Charles I.

Now we can return to the debate between Paine and Adams. One lesson taught by these seventeenth-century antecedents is that the Paine-Adams debate was not especially unique. The two protagonists shared beliefs common to the Anglo-American tradition of liberty-loving, broadly republican constitutionalism; they differed over a specific and, in their eyes, momentous issue of institutional design. Yet there was a final twist in the Paine-Adams debate, in which the Adams side gained a partial victory in the final round. In Part

II of *Rights of Man*, Paine offers a partial concession to multicameralism.

To understand the nature of the concession, we must notice that there were two grounds to Paine's opposition to the notion of mixed governments, related but distinguishable. One was the very idea that having different bodies check one another is absurd; it leads to gridlock and self-contradiction. The second reason was the class character of the different bodies. As has been pointed out previously in this symposium, Paine did not believe in class or interest group politics. He was very keen on the unity of nation. His objection to mixed government was that the little councils, the senatorial bodies, tended to take on a class character, representing aristocratic forces and giving them a veto to obstruct the will of the nation as a whole. The concession Paine makes concerns the first point, as he softens his opposition to constitutional checks and balances. Of course, he never yielded on the second point, as he did not want mixed government ever to become the basis for class politics.

In Chapter 4 of Part II in *Rights of Man*, he proposed dividing the national representative assembly into two or three parts (significantly, by the ancient Athenian device of lot) for purposes of deliberating on proposed legislation; the final vote, however, was always to remain in the unicameral body, with no veto power allowed to separate branches thereof:

> In order to remove the objection against a single house, that of acting with too quick an impulse, and at the same time to avoid the inconsistencies, in some cases absurdities, arising from two houses, the following method has been proposed as an improvement upon both. First, to have but one representation. Secondly, to divide that representation, by lot, into two or three parts. Thirdly, that every proposed Bill shall be first debated in those parts by succession, that they may become the hearers of each other, but without taking any vote. After which the whole representation to assemble for a general debate and determination by vote.[25]

Paine's proposal is vague and might be considered just another somewhat half-baked constitutional idea. Yet it was a clear step in the direction of constitutional complexity, responding to the idea that a unicameral legislature might act without adequate deliberation. Every bill would be debated by the parts, separately; however, the parts were still aspects of a single assembly for representation and voting. To Paine, this would reduce the possibility of tyrannical measures getting through.

It is a partial concession to the now famous Madisonian structure of 1787 that Paine and Jefferson had supported on broad grounds of national unity, but not on narrower grounds of constitutional design. It also reflected the same spirit of compromise that led the Massachusetts opposition to accept the idea of symmetrical bicameralism in the 1630s and 1640s. Similarly, the Levellers' later proposals for constitutional reform preserved unicameralism at the national level but introduced checks and balances between local authorities and the national Parliament, precisely in order to safeguard public liberty against the potential inroads of national authority.

Paine at first offered very strong arguments against the system in the U.S. that we have been living under for more than two-hundred years, the multicameral system. Yet he did suggest, in his final comment on the issue, that even radical democrats should take seriously the notion of constitutional complexity and internal checks. To put it another way, there are genuine theoretical, and not just practical, grounds for thinking that a Paineite program of radical democratic reform would not necessarily resort in a reflexive way to simplistic unicameralism, centralism, or nationalism, for example, by abolishing the Senate, the Electoral College, or the states. In a world where most nations have adopted parliamentary systems of government, and where democratization is increasingly on the agenda, it is a point worth considering. Thank you.

Notes

[1] J. Fruchtman Jr., "Foreword," in T. Paine, *Common Sense, Rights of Man, and Other Essential Writings*, ed. S. Hook (New York: Signet, 2003), p. x; D.F. Hawke, *Paine* (New York: Harper and Row, 1974), pp. 48-50.

[2]E. Foner, *Tom Paine and Revolutionary America* (Oxford: Oxford University Press, 1976), p. 79.

[3]Paine, *Common Sense and Other Essential Writings*, pp. 9, 10.

[4]J. Adams, "Thoughts on Government," in *The Revolutionary Writings*, ed. C.B. Thompson (Indianapolis: Liberty Fund, 2000), p. 289.

[5]Foner, *Tom Paine*, pp. 132-33.

[6]Ibid., pp. 135-36.

[7]"Letter from M. Turgot," in R. Price, *Richard Price and the Ethical Foundations of the American Revolution: Selections from His Pamphlets*, ed. B. Peach (Durham, N.C.: Duke University Press, 1979), pp. 218-19.

[8]J. Adams, *Works*, 10 vols. (Boston: Little, Brown, 1856), vol. 4, p. 380.

[9]J. Adams, *Works*, vol. 4, p. 588.

[10]M.D. Conway, *The Life of Thomas Paine* (New York: G. P. Putnam's Sons, 1909), p. 118; Foner, *Tom Paine*, p. xviii.

[11]Paine, *Common Sense and Other Essential Writings*, p. 249.

[12]Ibid., p. 251.

[13]Conway, *Life of Paine*, p. 120.

[14]Ibid.

[15]Ibid., p. 132.

[16]A. Sharp, ed., *The English Levellers* (Cambridge, U.K.: Cambridge University Press, 1998), pp. 61, 133, 135.

[17]Ibid., p. 172.

[18]Adams, Works, vol. 4, p. 466.

[19] S.R. Gardiner, ed. *The Constitutional Documents of the Puritan Revolution, 1625-60* (Oxford: Oxford University Press, 1906), p. 405; emphasis added.

[20] I. Stoughton, "Letter to John Stoughton," *Proceedings of the Massachusetts Historical Society*, vol. 58 (1925), p. 452.

[21] N.B. Shurtleff, ed. *Records of the Governor and Company of the Massachusetts Bay* (Boston: W. White, 1853-4), vol. 1, pp. 117-18.

[22] Paine, *Common Sense and Other Essential Writings*, p. 301.

[23] Stoughton, "Letter," p. 452.

[24] See J. Norton, "Concerning the Negative Vote" (1643), *Proceedings of the Massachusetts Historical Society*, vol. 46 (1912).

[25] Paine, *Common Sense and Other Essential Writings*, p. 311.

Ronald King

The debate over unicameralism versus multicameralism remains, as there are very few truly multicameral legislatures in the world today. Empirically, these few tend to be in nations composed from initially separate parts or that wish to give special representation to regionally-concentrated religious or ethnic minorities. This implies that the U.S. governmental system is quite atypical. By the way, for anyone who wants to think about it, a majority in the Senate (52 votes) can be constituted from states representing as little as 18 percent of the population, according to Robert Dahl of Yale, who has asked directly, how truly democratic is the American constitution?

The next speaker is Drew Maciag, who will discuss the modern implications of the Paine versus Burke debate.

REVENGE OF THE ANTI-PAINE: THE UNCOMMON WISDOM OF EDMUND BURKE (AND WHY IT STILL TRIES OUR SOULS)

Drew Maciag

It's late, and this is the last panel. It has been an outstanding symposium, and as a result, I am sure, all of our heads are almost filled to capacity with ideas and information. In the interest of time and mercy, I will be as brief as possible.

Americans have long accepted (even internalized) the proposition that Paine and Jefferson won the seminal debate against Burke and Adams, and in the process established the dominant vision of the United States as a product of Enlightenment thought. Consequently, the vanquishing of Old World hierarchies and superstitions by democracy and reason freed humankind (for America was a harbinger of global transformation) from ages of oppression and ignorance. To the extent that varieties of liberalism supplanted traditional orthodoxies, a triumphant "happy ending" to Western history might seem warranted. But just as revolutions often spawn counter-revolutions, the evolution of "progress" has triggered counter-forces that now call for a fresh evaluation of the finality of Paine's apparent victory.

While a critical examination of Paine's own writings is

essential, so too is a reappraisal of the chief writings of the archetypal anti-Paine, Edmund Burke, as well as those who claim to speak in Burke's name. This effort is especially relevant today, at a time when the Age of Reason seems to have run its course, and the assumptions behind liberalism and modernization are openly challenged from both the left and right. The Burkean persuasion was often dormant but never extinct in America, and it has returned with a vengeance since World War II. Of late, it contributes to a broader irrationalist sensibility that denies the primacy of reason and the benefits of the Enlightenment legacy. Such phenomena as anti-modernism, religious fundamentalism, the counterculture, and New Age obscurantism indicate that an eclectic mix of Americans believe that intuition, mystery, faith, transcendence, and reversion to age-old practices can provide personal "meaning" and public guidance. Put another way: Burke's view that we must "venerate" that which "we cannot presently comprehend," now threatens Paine's assertion that Burke was "labouring in vain to stop the progress of knowledge."[1]

In today's America, the Irish-born British politician Edmund Burke, who lived form 1729 to 1797 (which makes him about seven years older than Paine), is known mostly as the "father of conservatism," thanks to the enduring reputation of his anti-revolutionary tract: *Reflections on the Revolution in France* (1790). The revival of Burkean thought by "new conservative" intellectuals during the Cold War transformed Burke's eighteen-century anti-Jacobinism into twentieth-century anti-communism. This convenient interpretation proved so powerful that the balanced, progressive-traditionalism of Burke's "Whig vision" has been forgotten, and many conservatives have installed Burke as their guru. This ideological stereotype ignores the considerable body of reformist, progressive, proto-liberal thought that Burke articulated (for the most part) early in his political career. On such matters as slavery, capital punishment, freedom of the press, *habeas corpus*, religious toleration, government corruption, colonial rule, royal prerogative, and imprisonment for debt, Burke stood against the entrenched establishment, and on occasion even allied himself with radicals. That said, Burke was never temperamentally a creature of the left, and his later conservative writings divorced him from the liberal tradition. Moreover, post-war American conservatives in search of a modern father figure had surprisingly few choices available. Post-war liberals had fathers in abundance. Thomas Paine and Thomas Jefferson were the most self-evident, but the family tree could be traced back to John Locke or forward to John Dewey without much effort. Certainly Burke was the most eloquent and quotable on the short-list of conservative candidates. In consequence, it is the anti-radical, anti-Enlightenment Burke—the defender of monarchy, chivalry, aristocracy, religion, mystery, and tradition—whose likeness we now recognize.

It may surprise many to learn that the purple prose for which Burke has become famous, and which separated him so vividly from Paine, represented a small, even tiny, portion of his output, and most of his inflated rhetoric was merely grandiose; only a minute fraction was what we might call (for lack of a better term) mystical. Yet without the mystical touch, Burke would not have been Burke, nor would his late-modern reputation be so unique. Above all else, Burke's approach to politics was based on moral intuition. His inner certainty about good and evil was not amenable to rational inquiry or logical proof, what we might here call common sense. It was not so much irrational, as it was (like instinct or religious faith) a-rational or extra-rational.[2]

Paine too may have been guided by his own internal sense of right and wrong. But, unlike Burke, he specialized in the art of plain speaking. Thus, he sought to dispel mystery, majesty, and hoary tradition, what Burke called "all the pleasing illusions," and replace them with unadorned realities. Not that Paine was lacking in eloquence. Despite writing for the common man in what has been called the vulgar style, his statements routinely transmitted a simple dignity and a quiet profundity.[3] But there is little grandiosity in Paine, and nothing mystical whatsoever. Most important, Burke's polemical poetics sought to awe his readers into submission; Paine's forensic advocacy invited his audience to exercise its own reason. Hence, not only was Paine more democratic than Burke, but his style was more participatory. While Paine may be justifiably faulted for assuming that human nature was simpler and more benign than it actually was, and therefore that social, political, and economic problems were ripe for relatively easy solutions, Burke may be faulted for asserting that "man's nature" and the "state of civil society" were so complex and mysterious, that it was fruitless or counter-productive to attempt all but the most marginal adjustments to existing, inherited practices.

While Burke granted hypothetically the idea of "natural rights" akin to the "rights of man," he denied that such rights could be understood well enough to serve as political principles. Besides, he preferred wisdom over reason, because wisdom combined the sum total of ancestral reason with a moral intuition that was not beholden to intellectual machinations. Locke, Rousseau, and Paine extolled the realization that men could think for themselves; Burke believed that in most cases, especially on the big issues, they should not even try. Burke's reliance on prejudice and prescription represented the polar opposite of Paine's reliance on common sense. In America—where according to Jefferson: "Paine's principles . . . were the principles of the citizens of the U.S., where even John Adams (allegedly the American Burke) spoke of superstition abating in a land where "the people were universally too enlightened to be impressed by artifice" and government ruled "without a pretense of miracle or mystery"—the Old World sensibility of Edmund Burke was already an alien anachronism by the 1790s.[4] No wonder that Paine's *Rights of Man* outsold Burke's *Reflections* by a huge margin.

As we know, their rivalry did not end with the Age of Revolution.[5] Paine's immortality is unsurprising, given America's glorification of its rebellious origins. Yet it is baffling that Burke has not just avoided extinction, but experienced a revitalization in the past fifty years. Prior to World War II, Burke appeared to be slowly fading from the scene. Even before the Civil War, important voices had praised Burke's ability and character while distancing themselves from his reactionary philosophy. Similarly, the (culturally conservative) genteel writers of the Victorian era praised Burke's artistry in prose and his respect for Western civilization, but they shied away from endorsing his militant anti-radicalism. By the twentieth century, Burke was recognized more as an exemplary rhetorician than a relevant political philosopher. When the United States government honored him with a statue in Washington, D.C. in 1922, it cited only his support of the colonists during the Revolution, with no mention of his reaction to the events in France. All this changed dramatically after World War II, when a small yet determined group of conservative intellectuals rediscovered Burke's ideological usefulness.

In what might be called a "Burkean moment," writers

Moorhouse Millar, Ross Hoffman, Russell Kirk, Peter Viereck, Peter Stanlis, and others consciously reshaped the manner of Burke's appearance in light of problems identified as crucial to the survival of civilization as they chose to see it. Their entrepreneurial efforts yielded a revised and proprietary image of Burke that supplanted all prior interpretations, and this resulted in a paradigm shift in the application of Burkean thought that has set the pattern to this day. The Cold War and communism supplied the golden opportunity for a renewed interest in Burke's anti-Jacobinism. But the Cold War merely popularized a Burkean revival that had already been initiated by a concurrent rediscovery of Natural Law, specifically with a conservative spin to it.[6] After the Cold War's demise, the Natural Law interpretation of Burke remained active, not because it withstood scholarly scrutiny, but because it sought to combat the perceived maladies of the Enlightenment legacy: positivism, relativism, skepticism, pragmatism, utilitarianism, and secularization. Alternatively, it sought the re-imposition of a pre-rational world view.

Post-war "new conservatives," especially the Catholic scholars among them, lamented the moral decline supposedly encouraged by modern thought, and by liberal intellectuals.[7] The connective tissue binding their sentiments was an abhorrence of moral relativism, which traditionalists perceived to be the logical outcome of post-Enlightenment thinking. In their view, once reason had been unleashed upon the world, heterodoxy quickly followed. This was not a new theme for American conservatives, who had struggled to cap the well of social and intellectual experimentation since at least the 1780s. Unfortunately for them, the intellectual dynamism of the nineteenth century hinged on replacing long-held traditional and religious beliefs with scientific and rational analysis; the modern mind had swapped a belief in old certainties with the promise of new universal laws. Intellectual dynamism by the twentieth century instead hinged on replacing the ideal of certainty with the pragmatic inevitability of uncertainty and the new realities of relativism. In other words, certainty was converted from an absolute, permanent, universal concept into a probabilistic, temporary, or case-specific one, which also depended on the perspective and even on the values of the observer. To liberal intellectuals at the vanguard of Western thought, this represented a maturation of modern society. But to conservatives, the belief in certainty, especially moral certainty, was timeless. Not only were they unwilling to abandon this comfortable notion, but they were determined to stop others from abandoning it.

While Thomas Paine's version of optimistic reason served as a precursor to the less idealistic quest for scientific certainties in the nineteenth century, Edmund Burke's pessimistic view of human nature, combined with the mystical sensibility of his later work, provided a dramatic precedent for the twentieth-century reaction against the triumph of liberal thought. Unlike Paine, for whom reason was almost a law of gravity, Burke subordinated reason to virtue, wisdom, prudence, custom, and related agents of stability. Such concepts were intrinsically murky, which only enhanced their contra-rational handiness. Technically, Burke was not an adherent of Natural Law theory, at least not in the way his postwar champions claimed. But he did believe in a natural moral order that was more mysterious than it was comprehensible. Again in contrast to Paine, Burke was not shy about cutting reason down to size. Even in writings that had nothing to do with politics or current affairs, he spoke of the "natural weakness of understanding" and the inadequacy of "naked reason." As for skepticism (religious or political), Burke believed that "in general, it is not right to turn our duties into doubts. They are imposed to govern our conduct, not to exercise our ingenuity."[8] What better maxim was there for late-modern conservatives who asked, as one of our contemporary Burkeans has put it: ""[W]hy can't we turn back the clock? . . . [H]ow may we heal a society that has overdosed on liberalism?"[9]

Surely one way is to repudiate the entire Enlightenment legacy. That is, to question or to pervert virtually all post-traditionalist thought that has unfolded since the Age of Reason, or even before. Today's conservatives have learned not only how to adopt the language of liberalism for their own purposes, but also how to twist it against itself (such oxymorons as Creation Science and compassionate conservatism form the linguistic tip of an ideological iceberg). Moreover, conservatives have proven adept at changing people's minds about the benefits of liberal thought and modern values. Figuratively speaking, Paineites have recently been forced to give some of their winnings back to the Burkeans. Meanwhile, the prospect of reason ultimately defeating non-rational alternatives no longer seems assured.

American culture has always contained strains of anti-modernism.[10] Still, during most of the nineteenth and twentieth centuries the momentum of modernization and the advance of liberalism were too strong to counter, let alone to reverse. Since roughly the 1970s, however, the house of liberal reason began to weaken from within. The political aspect of this phenomenon has received much attention. Researchers have documented the decline of the New Deal order, the rise of the religious right, the white-ethnic and blue-collar backlash, and so on. Yet, as important as these political, social, and economic trends have been, they were subservient to even more fundamental shifts in the intellectual and cultural arenas. Around the turn of the twentieth century, modernization began eating away at itself, though it took several generations before the damage became obvious. The observable climax of Enlightenment modernism occurred in the early to mid-1960s.[11] This was followed by a fairly precipitous decline, as the post-modern consciousness spread beyond the avant-garde and other small circles of the initiated, to the broader educated public, and as the symptoms of this transition became apparent to the less educated as well. At the same time, the American belief-in-progress lost ground to various permutations of the perennial conservative jeremiad on the decay of civilization.

"Common sense," both in the way Thomas Paine used the term and as it applied to the Scottish branch of Enlightenment thought, might be restated as: "simple reason." Another option is to think of it as the workable combination of personal reason, experience, and intuition. During Paine's lifetime, and for a generation or so thereafter, science, politics, economics, medicine, and technology fit (or came close to fitting) a "seeing is understanding" template. But as the nineteenth century progressed, and more dramatically once the twentieth century began, the growing culture of professionalism and the new complexities of science resulted in a climate in which knowledge was no longer so sensibly comprehensible. A parallel trend of sophisticated exclusivity also developed in the arts and classical music. Aside from creating a world of unfathomable complexity, such developments guaranteed a personal experience of incomprehensibility in all but a few fields of selected expertise. Much new knowledge had to be accepted on faith, and this made it as mysterious to the uninitiated as religion, sorcery, or divination had been to our pre-modern ancestors. As a practical matter, so long as modernization continued to deliver the goods economically, technologically, medically, even socially, doubts concerning the comprehensibility of its latest discoveries could be shrugged off by the masses. Once the perception of success faded, or once it was recognized that technocratic society was incomplete at best and perhaps psychically damaging or (with the prospect of nuclear war or environmental disaster), even fatal, for the species, millions of persons on the cultural left became unintentional allies with others on the cultural right in their challenge to modern thought.

As for Paine's rational critique of religious orthodoxy in *The Age of Reason*, not only was it ineffective during his own lifetime, but, if he were writing it today, he would have to contend with a range of religious and quasi-religious beliefs that start with the premise that reason is not the primary key to personal deliverance or social harmony. Concurrent with the recent resurgence of religious orthodoxy has been the revival of astrology and witchcraft, a Western vogue for Eastern religions, the rise of numerous New Age belief systems, a turn toward alternative medicine, a widespread interest in the paranormal (ghosts, E.S.P., telekinesis), along with UFO-logy and countless variations on such non-rational themes.[12] It is doubtful that Edmund Burke would have been susceptible to any of these movements. Contrary to the claims of post-war and contemporary Burkean conservatives, he was not even sympathetic to theological orthodoxy within traditional Christianity.[13] Yet, as we have already observed, Burke reverted to the mysterious and ancient whenever reasoned argument proved to be inadequate, or worse, when it better suited the position of his adversaries. Similarly, Burke's late-modern conservative admirers have adopted the same technique.

It is this element of mysterious authority (in contrast to the clarifying light of human reason) that survives as the most serious challenge to the Painean legacy in America. The other major points in the Burke-Paine controversy have been settled in Paine's favor: democracy overtook monarchy, egalitarianism (at least in principle) replaced inherited social class, a written constitution with a bill of rights prevailed, a culture of progress supplanted one of custom, and progressive reform has (recent elections notwithstanding) been the long term pattern of American political activity. Hence, by process of historical elimination, the reason-wisdom tug-of-war survives torical elimination, the reason-wisdom tug-of-war survives as the last serious point of contention between Paineites and Burkeans, and there has always been something mysterious about the acquisition of wisdom.

Traditionalist-conservatism gave ground very grudgingly throughout the modern era, and it was never comfortable with the liberal frame of mind and its reliance on human reason. Yet as long as American life remained predominantly concerned with the ideals of liberty and the attainment of material progress, the spiritual, transcendent, religious, ancestral, and mythical aspects of culture remained subservient to rational, scientific, economic, or technological imperatives. While a broad national consensus developed around the benefits of modernization, the various contra-modern constituencies were relegated to isolated pockets. For much of the nineteenth century, most contra-modern impulses were culturally and socially conservative, although, as with Thoreau's transcendental and anti-industrial anarchism, they were not exclusively so. But as the twentieth century approached, there were already signs that even among free-thinking cultural liberals, reason did not supply a comprehensive enough, or a satisfying enough, world view. Granted, turn-of-the-century flirtations with what we now call New Age spirituality were confined to small bohemian circles. Yet they anticipated the sort of non-rational belief systems that would later become common.

In conclusion, it is tempting to dismiss the lure of the mysterious, regardless of whether it manifests itself in old-time religion or New Age obscurantism, or whether it leads to liberal or conservative behavior. Perhaps a generation ago such a dismissal would have been justified. Today, however, there is no mistaking the loss of passion, even loss of respect, for rational, scientific, secular, and Paineite common sense approaches to public policy and personal philosophy.[14] This is not only understandable, but, in hindsight it should have been predictable. At the dawn of the modern age, enlightened thinkers saw limitless possibilities for improvement of the human condition. The realization that these early hopes were unsupportable was delayed by early victories over the residual ignorance and injustice of earlier eras. But, just as in war, initial euphoria fades once the prospect of easy, painless victory is thwarted. By the final third of the twentieth century, the United States and much of the developed world lived in the midst of (what Jurgen Habermas has called) a "disenchanted modernity." The disenchantment had multiple roots, but the taproot may have been its own common-sense belief that reason was virtually the sole method for obtaining knowledge and for solving problems. In other words, the faculty of reason became transformed into the *Weltanschauung* of rationalism.

By the later twentieth century, American culture was ripe for a resurgence of transcendental experience, and the mysterious nature of the Burkean revival played to this theme. One may interpret this to be either an atavistic regression or a necessary corrective to Enlightenment over-reach. Perhaps the sense of comparative balance between reason and transcendence was captured by the British historian, Alfred Cobban, when he wrote about Burke in 1929. While Cobban contrasted Burke with Locke, the same point could have been made by inserting the name of Thomas Paine: "The great achievement of [John Locke] had been to free political thought from theological authority and bring it into the more reasonable realm of secularity and individual responsibility. The greatness of [Edmund Burke] lay in re-inspiring politics with a cosmic spirit and in teaching men again the deeper realities of social life."[15] Now, three-quarters of a century after Cobban's remarks, we might ask in the American context: is it still possible to infuse a reasonable society with a sense of awe and a spirit of imagination, and in the process to infuse secular life with a deeper (that is, beyond material) purpose, or must reason be sacrificed to the transcendent and obscure, simply because it cannot by itself deliver human contentment?

Notes

[1] Edmund Burke, "Appeal from the New to the Old Whigs," in Daniel E. Ritchie, ed., *Further Reflections on the Revolution in France* (Indianapolis: Liberty Fund, 1992), p. 199; the "Appeall" was published in August, 1791, nearly a year after Reflections appeared on November 1, 1790. Thomas Paine, *Rights of Man, Part One*, in Michael Foot and Isaac Kramnick, eds., *The Thomas Paine Reader* (London and New York: Penguin Books, 1987), p. 244.

[2] Burke called such moral intuition "untaught feelings," or a

"natural sense of right and wrong," Edmund Burke, *Reflections on the Revolution in France* (New Haven: Yale University Press, 2003), pp. 70, 74.

³An excellent examination of Paine's rhetoric is "Thomas Paine's Rights of Man: The Vulgar Style," in James T. Boulton, *The Language of Politics in the Age of Wilkes and Burke* (London: Routledge & Kegan Paul, 1963), pp. 134-50.

⁴Lester J. Cappon, ed., *The Adams-Jefferson Letters* (Chapel Hill: University of North Carolina Press, 1959), 250; Charles Francis Adams, ed., *The Works of John Adams, Second President of the United States: With A Life of the Author*. 10 vols. (Boston: Charles C. Little and James Brown, 1851), vol. 4, pp. 292-93.

⁵See Francis Canavan, "The Burke-Paine Controversy," *Political Science Review* 6 (Fall, 1976).

⁶See for example, Benjamin Fletcher Wright, Jr., *American Interpretations of Natural Law* (Cambridge, Mass.: Harvard University Press, 1931), p. 327. A more recent work that pushes the envelope on the subject is David Braybroke, *Natural Law Modernized* (Toronto: University of Toronto Press, 2001). Especially relevant to the post-war revival is Roscoe Pound, "The Revival of Natural Law," *Notre Dame Lawyer*, 17:4 (June, 1942), 287-372.

⁷Patrick Allitt, *Catholic Intellectuals and Conservative Politics in America, 1950-1985* (Ithaca: Cornell University Press, 1993).

⁸Burke, "Appeal from the New to the Old Whigs," *Further Reflections*, p. 163.

⁹Mark C. Henrie, "Edmund Burke and Contemporary American Conservatism," in Ian Crowe, ed., *The Enduring Edmund Burke: Bicentennial Essays* (Wilmington, Delaware: Intercollegiate Studies Institute, 1997), p. 203.

¹⁰See T.J. Jackson Lears, *No Place of Grace: Antimodernism and the Transformation of American Culture, 1880-1920* (New York: Pantheon Books, 1981).

¹¹See Michael E. Latham, *Modernization as Ideology: American*

Social Science and "Nation Building" in the Kennedy Era (Chapel Hill: University of North Carolina Press, 2000).

[12]See Paul Kurtz, *The Transcendental Temptation: A Critique of Religion and the Paranormal* (Buffalo, N.Y.: Prometheus 1986).

[13]Burke was concerned with the stabilizing effect (political and social) of religion, which is why he was conservative on matters such as maintaining an established church with firm rules, but as his "Speech on Clerical Subscription" (1772) revealed, he was well aware of the widely different interpretations of Scripture that were reasonably possible; furthermore, his writings display no interest in discovering ultimate religious truths. Paul Langford, gen. ed., *The Writings and Speeches of Edmund Burke*. 8 vols. to date (Oxford: Clarendon, 1981-2000), vol. 2, pp. 361-62.

[14]Examples are numerous: the *New York Times* (August 31, 2005) cited a poll by the Pew Forum on Religion and Public Life that finds that 42% of Americans hold "strict creationist views," and that 64% "are open to the idea of teaching creationism in addition to evolution" in the classroom.

[15]Alfred Cobban, *Edmund Burke and the Revolt Against the Eighteenth Century* (London: Allen and Unwin, 1929), p. 96.

Ronald King

I am reminded of a comment by Lewis Hartz, who says in America that Locke has become Burke—or for today's conference, it would be Paine has become Burke. To Hartz, the philosophy of rationalism is accepted in the U.S. as a traditional way of life and therefore is asserted non-rationally, without being subject to rational discourse. One of the things this paper has asked us to do is examine the powers and the limits of reason. Are we still in the Age of Reason? Must we now live in an Age of Unreason? It is a challenging issue, and certainly relevant to our proceedings this weekend.

The next paper, equally provocative, is from Aaron Keck of Rutgers University.

THOMAS PAINE AND THE RIGHT OF REVOLUTION

Aaron Keck

Earlier today, Kirsten Fischer mentioned that political theorists are not easy to please. As a political theorist myself, I can confirm that wholeheartedly. With respect to Thomas Paine, I am displeased by the extent to which we tend to characterize him as a revolutionary democratic republican, without engaging the problems and contradictions that inevitably result. Of course he is all of these things. But to characterize him in this way is sometimes to forget that the three concepts—revolution, democracy, and republicanism—don't necessarily go hand in hand. In fact, in many cases they are very much at odds with each other, a reality that Paine himself had to confront, in his own writings, before the end of his life. Understanding Paine as a political thinker, then, involves identifying which of these three concepts he privileges when it becomes necessary for him to do so. That is the topic I will address today.

I will argue that Paine is best understood not as a revolutionary, nor as a democrat, but as a republican. To put it another way: Paine was certainly revolutionary, but he was not *a* revolutionary. Rather, he *used* revolution, and democracy as well, as the means to a higher republican end, and was perfectly willing, if only implicitly, to throw the idea of revolution out the window when that became necessary to serve republican ends. To put it even more strongly: Paine did not merely *oppose* anti-republican revolutions; he also denied the *right*, or even the *possibility*, of a people to revolt against republican institutions, in any direction. Conservative counter-revolutions against republicanism and progressive revolutions *beyond* republicanism were all the same: Paine was willing to allow generations to bind their posterity—indeed he demanded it—as long as they prescribed the proper form for the institutions of government, namely, republican, representative democracy.

Paine dedicated his career, first and foremost, not to promoting the right of self-governance but rather to the advancement of a specific political program, republicanism and popular representation in democratic institutions, as the inevitable byproduct of a constitution grounded in reason. It is noteworthy that Paine uses these two phrases, *republicanism* and *representative democracy*, almost interchangeably in his writings. In Paine's hands, the idea of popular sovereignty, so crucial for contemporary republicans like Rousseau, is secondary to the existence of representative democratic institutions, removed as they may be from the direct voice of the people. (James Madison, though perhaps a little disingenuously, makes the same move in *Federalist 10* and *39*, as do many eighteenth-century republicans.)

Near the end of his life, Paine wrote: "It was to bring forward and establish the representative system of Government that was the leading principle with me in writing that work [*Common Sense*], and all my other works during the progress of the revolution. And I followed the same principle in writing the *Rights of Man*, in England."[1] The near-total lack of republican institutions in Europe (Italy excepted), coupled with the long-standing tradition of monarchy in England and France, led Paine inexorably to attack the established order as neither a necessary or sufficient justification of government's legitimacy. "That which a whole nation chooses to do," he asserts, "it has a right to do," whether or not there is any sort of historical precedent.[2] As we have already seen in this conference, this becomes the theoretical basis for the revolutions in America as well as France, republican revolutions which bring about the new system of representative government. But this attack on the established order exists in Paine's writings not for its own sake, but in service of a higher purpose: only by discrediting tradition as a source of legitimacy in itself would it become possible to overthrow the *ancien regime* and erect a republic in its place.

To be sure, Paine's assertion of the right to self-government is forceful and visible in his writings, but it is not always consistent. Paine never argued that tradition alone *could* serve as the sole justification of power in any case, but the attack on tradition in his thought is nevertheless always secondary to, and largely a consequence of, his advocacy of the republic. The creation of a republic brings these two principles, revolution and republicanism, into inevitable conflict. Once republican institutions become the established authority, it becomes impossible to defend revolution without rejecting republicanism, and equally impossible to defend the republic without opposing, to some degree, the right of a people to rebel against it. Permitted a choice *within* representative institutions, people are not permitted the choice *against* them.

Faced, if only subconsciously, with this issue, Paine sides with the republic, quickly dropping the natural right of self-determination and the natural equality of generations. When describing post-revolutionary republican societies, Paine shifts suddenly, though very subtly, from angry revolutionary to traditionalist conservative, praising the glory and the *permanence* of the new republics in language almost identical to Edmund Burke's. "Every age and generation," Paine declared in *Rights of Man*, "must be as free to act for itself *in all cases*, as the ages in generations which preceded it . . . Man has no property in man; neither has any generation a property in the generations which are to follow."[3] But Enlightenment, once established, cannot be rescinded: attempting to counter it would be, in Paine's words, like "darkness attempting to illuminate light."[4] Enlightenment, for Paine, is irreversible. The revolution of reason effectively precludes any possibility of returning to pre-modern, pre-Enlightenment forms of society, and while the exclusion of traditionalism, provincialism, fundamentalism, and pre-modernity in general is certainly not undesirable, it nevertheless poses a problem, theoretically speaking, for Paine's oft-repeated assertion that no generation may bind its posterity in any way or for any time.

This raises a further point, far more troubling and even more important: if the republic is to be permanent, as Paine asserts, then the republican revolution, by his own reasoning, closes off not only the possibility of reactionary, pre-modern counter-revolutions, but also progressive, postmodern revolutions *beyond* the narrow republicanism of the European Enlightenment. Representative, republican political institutions hold their ground, not only against attempts to bring back the *ancien regime,* but also against attempts to progress beyond them. The triumph of Enlightenment in human psychology not only closes off the possibility of returning to the age of "darkness," but also closes off the possibility of *critique,* of challenging the scientific method and objective reason that Paine takes for granted. Paine himself implies that such critique is literally impossible—clearly an overstatement, in the wake of Derrida and Foucault—but even if we allow for the possibility, any such critique would be highly objectionable, even illegitimate. For Paine, after all, the purpose of the revolution was not to criticize but "to instruct," to "make men as wise as possible,"[5] not to challenge existing institutions for their own sake, but to reveal an objective truth and to found new institutions—objective, and therefore *permanent*—upon it. To use Peter Gay's terms, Paine was less concerned with *criticism* and more concerned with redistributing *power* in positive and progressive—and republican—ways.[6]

If Paine does recognize this implication, he's remarkably unconcerned by it. Through all his declarations that generations have no right to bind their posterity, Paine is surprisingly tolerant, even full of praise, for generations that bind their posterity to a republic. "Can we but leave posterity with a settled form of government," he laments in *Common Sense,* "an independent constitution of its own, the purchase at any price will be cheap."[7] In the *Letter to the Abbé Raynal,* he characterizes the creation of the American republic as "not a temporary good for the present race only, but a continued good to all posterity."[8] But it is in *Rights of Man* that Paine drops all pretense and speaks of the republic's future in almost Burkean overtones, even appealing to tradition as a source (though not *the* source) of political legitimacy: "A thousand years hence, those who shall live in America or in France, will look back with contemplative pride on the origin of their governments, and say, *This was the work of our glorious ancestors!"*[9]

This is not, of course, to say that Paine was a conservative in the popular sense of the word. Certainly not. Within the broad framework of representative democracy, he allowed for, and in fact even encouraged and worked for, massive social reforms. Earlier we talked a great deal about agrarian or land reform, only one of the significant political projects Paine supported in his active life. The one thing he would not allow, however, is a revolution against the basic institutions of the republic, its representative democratic institutions. In that sense, Paine continued as a reformer, but, to the extent that the republic triumphed and was firmly established, he was no longer a revolutionary, in spite of his own declarations to the contrary.

Is this mincing words? Maybe. But I think the distinction is significant. Despite his rabble-rousing reputation, Thomas Paine was no revolutionary, only a die-hard republican who used revolution as a means to a just end. But in spite of this—I would argue *because* of this—Paine's thought, particularly his theoretical turn in the wake of the French Revolution, offers a good deal of insight into the problems and pitfalls facing progressives today. What happens to Thomas Paine at this point in history, this particular moment when revolutionary doctrine and republican institutions cease to be compatible and go their separate ways, should be of great interest to us, not only to historians of the Enlightenment, but also to the theorists and activists of the modern-day Left, who still hold Paine up, rightly, as a model and an inspiration.

The French Revolution is the climax of the "century of lights," as well as one of the greatest and most transformative democratic upheavals in human history, and Paine was both its and the Enlightenment's most popular spokesperson. That such a symbol of progressivism and social justice as Paine should choose, at this precise moment, to effectively abandon his revolutionary impulse (in practice, if not on paper) should give pause to those elements of today's fractured Left that choose instead to privilege critique and resistance while largely abandoning the Enlightenment principles of objective reason and universal human rights. For many on the Left, to be sure, this emphasis on critique is precisely the point: after all, the Left is generally opposed to the concentration of power; and as Foucault (among many others) has so pointedly observed, *any* social institution represents the concentration of power in the hands of one group or another. But to resist power for its own sake is effectively to withdraw from politics altogether, a declaration of impotence that cedes the playing field entirely to the Right. Paine's "conservative" move, by contrast, allows him to remain politically relevant, even two-hundred years after his death.

By choosing system over method, wedding himself to republican principles at the expense of the rights of revolution and self-determination, Paine places himself squarely (though only implicitly) on the right side of the divide between the radical democrats and the more temperate republicans of the Left (which may help explain his imprisonment by the Jacobins). Opposing him on the critical side are a variety of intellectual traditions, many of which have significant influence over current progressive movements: postmodernism, critical theory, anarchism, radical democracy, existentialism, and ethnic nationalism (all of which compete with one another as well). These are the forces that drive much of the Left today, and while these movements hold Paine up as a revolutionary forebear, they have little use for his emphasis on objective truth, instrumental reason, and universal rights. Such approaches often share a fundamental impotence in offering concrete institutional responses to actual political problems. But Thomas Paine's legacy, in contrast, continues to inspire real progressive movements—again, not *in spite* of his "conservative" approach, but in many ways *because* of it.

Faced with the implicit choice between the self-determination on which he so firmly insisted and the republic in which he so firmly believed, Thomas Paine chose the latter. This did not, of course, preclude him from supporting progressive reforms after the revolution; as we have seen, the republican principle often requires a society to pursue major reform projects, to manifest the republican ideal *socially* as well as *institutionally*. Paine leaves plenty of room for progress after the revolution, in order to advance that ideal: the social reforms he proposes at the end of *Rights of Man* are an example, as is his famed argument for periodic constitutional conventions. Such progress is necessarily incremental and reformist in nature, however, rather than fundamental and revolutionary; that is, it works within existing institutions rather than challenging them from the outside. (This is the case even with constitutional reform: Paine supported a people's right to periodically re-constitute itself but insisted—as he made clear in his 1804 letter *To the French Inhabitants of Louisiana*—that the new constitution be republican and representative as well. Paine urged republican societies to rewrite their constitutions, that is, but only if the new institutions effectively resembled the old.) But Paine's reformism, incremental as it may be, is also inherently *concrete*, a quality that contemporary critical movements often lack.

Paine's reformism is also inherently *progressive*, a quality often lacking from radical democratic philosophy, which emphasizes democratic *procedure* and the importance of discourse but rarely concerns itself as much with the political *outcome*. Many of us, in the last two days, have characterized Thomas Paine as a radical democrat or a forerunner of modern radical democracy, but Paine himself would have been decidedly uncomfortable with the nature of our most radically democratic institutions. The initiative-and-referendum process, most notably, is one of the most democratic institutions, strictly speaking, currently in existence; historically, though, it has actually tended to produce *reactionary* and decidedly *anti*-progressive policies, as we saw, vividly, in the last national election (and as those of you from California have experienced repeatedly), nor would Paine have been entirely at ease among those radical democrats who, in true post-modern fashion, embrace *discourse* as the highest ideal because they deny the possibility of *progress* in any objective sense.

Paine, by contrast, never lost sight of the end. He supported democratic institutions not so much for their own sake, but rather because he believed that they would result in good laws and positive social effects. The social program he spells out at the end of *Rights of Man* largely is unconcerned with discourse, nor does it insist upon a space for public resistance. Rather, Paine's central aim, here as everywhere, is the enactment of good policies, effective institutions, and responsible government, a goal that continues to challenge and inspire, even to this day. Even more than this, activists continue to draw inspiration from the principles—cosmopolitanism, human rights, social justice, the quest for *truth*—that Paine's "conservative" move allows him to embrace. That modern-day activists still draw inspiration from this long-dead pamphleteer is an indication not of his status as a revolutionary, but rather of the continuing power of those principles—principles that remain the property of progressive movements everywhere, if only they will claim them for their own.

Question: I have a question for Professor Keck, about what Tom Paine would do regarding the U.S. government now. We have a rigged system in this country. We have a gerrymandered House of Representatives, so all the seats are safe practically. We have single-member districts, so minor-party people can't get elected. In the Senate, we have two votes for Alaska and two votes for California, which is obviously not a republican thing. We have money, and the Supreme Court says that money is free speech, so you have money ruling everywhere. Then we have the Electoral College, which is a constitutional fossil that gives more power to the smaller states and divides us up into red states and blue states. Then we have the executive who goes ahead and sends troops all over of the world, even though Congress is supposed to make war, and we have secrecy and we have them ignoring the separation of church and state. Would Tom Paine support revolution against this government?

Aaron Keck: You've listed a number of institutions that are obviously seriously, seriously flawed. I'm not going to speculate which reforms Paine would advocate, which institutions he would throw out and which of them he would advocate that we keep. But obviously he would be opposed to a great deal of the events and trends that have been happening in American society today. My argument is that he would want to resolve those problems, not through revolution *per se*, but through the institutions of representative government. Whether that means we would have to somehow transform those institutions, that's up for debate. But in the end I think Paine would continue to advocate representative democratic structures, maybe slightly altered but essentially the same basic framework that we have now.

Jason Maloy: I'd like to comment. First of all, I think many of the gentleman's points are well taken. That's why we're here, because Paine would say something about them. The most obvious, I think, from the Paineite perspective is the point about defective representation, not only in Congress but in countless state legislatures as well. Like the Levellers before him, Paine *sine qua non* is known for legitimate government, and the only thing that could make the single voting assembly legitimate was if it were truly representative. In order to be a truly representative, it had to reflect the various interests and points of view and characteristics of the people. This redistricting process—where the legislatures themselves get to draw the boundaries (giving the key to the hen house to the fox)—I don't think he would find that kosher at all. I'll leave the many other things you listed to one side but will say that Paine, I think I agree, would advocate a peaceful procedure.

Question (Seth Cotlar): These are great papers. This is a question for Aaron Keck in particular. First, the distinction between revolutionary and republican is very intriguing, but I wonder if there's anyone in the world who counts as a revolutionary the way you've defined it. In other words, are there revolutionaries who can imagine creating a revolution but they don't really care what comes from it? In other words, they're okay with the idea of past things reemerging, or that something in the future might come about that will be different than what they believe in—in other words, a revolutionary without a content. Paine certainly wasn't that, but I can't think of anyone who is, so I'm wondering if you're holding him to a standard that is maybe not right.

My second question is, what do you think about Paine's comments about constitutional revision? Throughout *Rights Of Man* (and this is something that quickly gets excised from American political discourse), Paine and also Jefferson say regularly you're going to have a constitutional convention every twenty years; for Paine it was a set of revisions every seven years, I believe. Paine talks, regarding the Pennsylvania Constitution, about continually taking the mold that is your political system and giving it back to the people, saying let's revise this, let's rethink this, let's talk about this again; it's something that Paine imagines going on in perpetuity. This is a measure, he says, of the health of the body politic, that has to be reinvigorated every so often by the constitutional process. Now, over the course of American history, constitutional conventions even at the state level have happened only occasionally.

Maybe this is where we start getting to Drew Maciag's point about the unreason. Paine had this incredible faith that the American people, when given the opportunity to revise their Constitution, would do it in a reasonable way. In America today, they might write a constitution that outlaws the teaching of evolution.

Aaron Keck: There were two questions. First of all, it is a very good point and fair about the question if anyone is really a revolutionary by my standard. The first people who come to mind are the critical theorists, the Frankfurt School, although they ended up abandoning politics. I would say that it is possible to identify people, particularly in the twentieth century, and I spelled out the list at the end of the speech, and you can name others—Bolshevism comes immediately to mind—that advocated further revolutions beyond the basic principles of Enlightenment, or that repudiated those principles and advocated different institutions from those of representative democracy and republican principles. Paine definitely would be opposed to that.

In response to your second question, yes, I think Jefferson said a constitutional convention every 25 years and Paine said every seven years. Exactly right, although I think, again, even in those constitutional conventions, Paine would not have supported or even defended people who favored a new Constitution that was opposed to representative institutions. Those were first and foremost.

Brian McCartin (from the audience): Just two things. First, you mentioned before about Paine not being a revolutionary, but advocating a republic was itself revolutionary at the time. Therefore, he is a revolutionary if he's advocating revolutionary principles, and his revolutionary idea of a republic radically changes the meaning of these terms. Paine takes those republican virtues of previous thought and gives them a whole new twist, adding equality and justice and dignity to the very essence of the virtues. In addition, there is no revolution in America until *Common Sense*. There's a resistance movement, there's an insurgency, there's a rebellion, but there's no independence movement and there's no true revolution until *Common Sense*, and so I really disagree with you when you say he's not revolutionary, because the principles he advocates are revolutionary, and they haven't been instilled today, and that's the reason that the previous gentleman is complaining so vigorously.

The other thing I wanted to mention is that Paine was not a Leveller. Wealth, he says, is not usually built on oppression but sometimes causes it later. But he advocates capitalism—at that time it's still the very early stages of capitalism, and so he does not see monopolization and corporate structures—but he believes that wealth is fine as long as you've earned it legitimately and that you don't exceed so much wealth while there are so many others still suffering. He stayed with the wealthiest people around. He hobnobbed with the wealthiest people. He did not have a problem with wealth as long as the wealth was not used for self-aggrandizement and is distributed to some degree to those who had nothing at all.

Aaron Keck: I totally agree with you. Obviously Paine was revolutionary for his time. But I would question whether Paine would be as revolutionary today as he was in 1776, again, for all of the reasons that you list. Paine remains salient today, as many in this conference have argued. In spite of that, he wouldn't come across today as quite so revolutionary. He still remains progressive, and he still remains an inspiration for progressive movements that are grounded on these basic principles of social justice and reason and rationality.

Jason Maloy: Two points on the Levellers and Paine. First, I was addressing the Levellers' constitutional ideas and constitutional design, and in that respect Paine is, whether self-consciously or not, restating the Levellers' constitutional ideas. The very notion of a written constitution that is supposed to structure how the government operates and also to limit what the government can do, and also the idea of unicameralism—these are all in the Levellers and later they're in Paine. Regarding economic ideas, I'm just not qualified to comment.

The second point is that, in a sense, the Levellers were not even Levellers. They didn't name themselves. It was a pejorative name that was given to them by their opponents, who wanted people to think that they were crazy utopian communists. The Levellers themselves, just as Paine did, came out and said we're not for economic leveling, so maybe there is another similarity between them.

Ronald King: I want directly to raise a topic that we have been skirting around: to what extent can we trust the common sense of people today? Is the pressing issue, as that gentleman asked in the first question, the distorted institutions of government and the faulty representation system? To what extent might the problem lie elsewhere, that common sense might be absent from the American people? When we think about issues of race, for example, to what extent might rationalist common sense always have been somewhat absent in America?

Drew Maciag: This issue has come up a number of times in this conference, when we were talking about a reversion to fundamentalism versus independent thought. If you want to use that as the test, we're in pretty bad shape. Modern liberalism in general has suffered, although it is necessary to note real improvements in certain areas.

Jason Maloy: Regarding Professor King's question about common sense among the citizen body, my own view — and I think it turns out to be a fairly Paineite view — is that there exists a great reserve of common sense among ordinary citizens. But the processes of political choice, the processes by which citizens can translate their common sense into political choices are skewed in so many ways. I think Paine's point would be, going back to the point about the unrepresentative character of our representative system, that you've got to fix the processes so that the common sense of ordinary people can be translated into public policy, so, again, I would encourage us to cast our eyes back to the issue of institutional-structural reform. I do worry sometimes — everyone worries — about what the democratic majority is going decide. It might offend us or injure our interests in some way. But I think Paine would say, and I would agree, that you won't know for sure until you actually fix the political structure so that it does reflect ordinary people's choices.

Drew Maciag: You basically made the point I was going to make, in essence that common sense has to be organized in order to be channeled into effective action. We think about the most recent reform era — things like the Civil Rights Movement, anti-Vietnam War Movement and all that — it went through a period of institution building, organizational building before it became effective. That's one thing missing now. There may be this well of common sense, joined to this well of frustration now, but it has to be properly organized and channeled. I would hope, possibly, we are on the eve of that.

Aaron Keck: Just echoing those points, Thomas Paine believed that once the institutional structures were properly in place, human beings would then become better people and the common sense of human beings would transform as well, becoming necessarily progressive and good. Echoing the earlier point, we're not going know what the common sense of the people says until we complete that revolution. You are exactly right; it hasn't been completed. Once that's done—and we can do that through reform within the system, as Paine would agree—then I think we'll see.

Drew Maciag: I would add that bottom-up reform, or common-sense reform with the masses of the people, is not bottom-up in any simple way. It requires proper leadership, too. For whatever reason, over the past generation or so, the proper leaders have not emerged. It's a mystery (which might make it Burkean). I don't know why, but the leaders have been emerging on the other side. I would hope that that would correct itself over time, just for statistical purposes alone. But I think it's a very important element, that there is a leadership in the wellspring of public sentiment that needs to form itself.

Ronald King: Since I get the last word, I am going to dissent. I am not optimistic about progressive reform in America today, with or without institutional change. Historically, the beneficiaries of world empire very rarely turn their backs on its advantages.

I thank you all for coming to this wonderful and most educational conference.

Notes

[1] Paine, "To the Honorable Senate of the United States," in *The Complete Writings of Thomas Paine*, ed. Philip S. Foner (New York: Citadel Press, 1945), vol. 2, p. 1491.

[2] Paine, *Rights of Man* (New York: Penguin, 1984), p. 42.

[3] Ibid., pp. 41-42.

⁴Ibid., p. 45.

⁵Paine, "Dissertation on First Principles," in Foner, vol. 2, p. 587.

⁶Peter Gay, *The Enlightenment: An Interpretation, Volume 1: The Rise of Modern Paganism* (New York: W.W. Norton, 1995) p. xi.

⁷Paine, *Common Sense* (Mineola, New York: Dover, 1997), p. 34.

⁸Paine, "Letter to the Abbé Raynal," in Foner, vol. 2, p. 238.

⁹Paine, *Rights of Man*, p. 118. Compare Burke: "I would not exclude alteration, neither, but even when I changed, it should be to preserve. I should be led to my remedy by a great grievance. In what I did, I should follow the example of our ancestors." *Reflections on the Revolution in France*, ed. J.G.A. Pocock (Indianapolis: Hackett, 1987).

Contributors

Joyce Oldham Appleby is Professor Emerita of History at UCLA. She is a former President of the Organization of American Historians and the American Historical Association. Among her many published books and articles, *Ideology and Economic Thought in Seventeenth-Century England* won the 1978 Berkshire Prize. She recently finished a biography of Thomas Jefferson and has edited a volume of the writings of Thomas Paine. She continues to co-direct the History News Service, an informal association that distributes op-ed essays written by historians to over 300 newspapers weekly.

Elsie Begler holds a Ph.D. in cultural anthropology from Columbia University and serves currently as founder and Director of the International Studies Education Project (ISTEP) at San Diego State University.

Kenneth W. Burchell is a Lecturer in the History Department at the University of Idaho. His work focuses on the life, influences, and followers of Thomas Paine, including Gilbert Vale and other great democratic reformers of the nineteenth century.

Hazel Burgess is an independent scholar living in Australia. She is working on a new biography of Paine and compiling an edition of works not previously attributed to him.

Nathalie Caron is *maitre de conference* (associate professor) in the department of Anglo-American Studies at the University of Paris 10 (Nanterre). She is the author of *Thomas Paine contre l'imposture des pretres,* as well as several articles on Paine, American Deism, and new forms of religiosity in the United States.

Bryson Clevenger, Jr. is a full-time research advisor for the University of Virginia Library and a part-time reference librarian for Shanghai Library in China. He also teaches courses at Northern Virginia and Piedmont Community Colleges.

Elizabeth Cobbs-Hoffman is the Dwight Stanford Professor of American Foreign Relations in the History Department of

San Diego State University. Her first book, *The Rich Neighbor Policy*, earned awards from the Society of American Historians and the Society for Historians of American Foreign Relations. She serves as a member of the nine-person Historical Advisory Committee to the U.S. Department of State.

Seth Cotlar is Associate Professor of History at Willamette University in Salem, Oregon. His book on trans-Atlantic radicalism in the 1790s is forthcoming from the University of Virginia Press.

Kirsten Fischer is Associate Professor of History at the University of Minnesota. She is the author of *Suspect Relations: Sex, Race, and Resistance in Colonial North Carolina*, published by Cornell University Press, and currently is researching the contest between reason and faith in the early American republic.

Eric Foner is DeWitt Clinton Professor of History at Columbia University. He is the former president of the Organization of American Historians, the American Historical Association, and the Society of American Historians. He is an elected fellow of the American Academy of Arts and Sciences and the British Academy. Included among his many published works are *Tom Paine and Revolutionary America*, and the Library of America collection of Paine's writings. His book, *Reconstruction: America's Unfinished Revolution, 1863-1877* won, among other awards, the Bancroft Prize, Parkman Prize, and Los Angeles Times Book Award. His most recent book is *Forever Free: The Story of Emancipation and Reconstruction*.

Tony Freyer is University Research Professor of History and Law at the University of Alabama. His books include *Producers versus Capitalists* and *Antitrust and Global Capitalism, 1930-2004*.

Susan Jacoby is program director for the Center for Inquiry in New York City. Her book, *Freethinkers: A History of American Secularism*, was named a notable nonfiction book of 2004 by *The Washington Post* and *The Los Angeles Times* and as one of the outstanding international books of 2004 by the *Times Literary Supplement* and *The Guardian*. As an essayist, she has contributed to leading journals of commentary on topics including law, religion, medicine, women's rights, and Russian literature. She has been the recipient of grants from the Guggenheim, Rockefeller, and Ford Foundations, and from the National Endowment for the Humanities.

Harvey Kaye is the Ben and Joyce Rosenberg Professor of Social Change and Development at the University of Wisconsin-Green Bay. His publications include the award-winning books, *Thomas Paine: Firebrand of the Revolution*, a young adult biography published by Oxford University Press, and *Thomas Paine and the Promise of America*, published by Hill and Wang.

Andrew Keck is currently a Ph.D. candidate in Political Science at Rutgers University. His dissertation traces the history of cosmopolitanism in American political thought from 1776 to 1876.

Timothy Killikelly is an Instructor of Political Science at the City College of San Francisco. He is the editor of a volume on American political thought, *Readings in American Politics and Liberalism*.

Ronald King is Professor and Chair of the Political Science Department at San Diego State University, specializing in American politics and American political development. His most recent work examines the expansion and contraction of franchise rights in the United States.

Eve Kornfeld is Professor of History at San Diego State University. A specialist in early American history, American cultural history, and the history of childhood and gender, her published books include *Creating an American Culture, 1775-1800*, and *Margaret Fuller*.

Michael Kreizenbeck is a graduate student in the Political Science Department at San Diego State University, writing his thesis on the public funding of electoral campaigns. He served as staff coordinator for the Paine conference.

J.S. Maloy is Assistant Professor of Political Science at Oklahoma State University. His work focuses on Anglo-American political thought, emphasizing the relationship between democratic theory and constitutional design.

Drew Macaig is visiting Assistant Professor in the History Department at Nazareth College of Rochester. His work focuses on Edmund Burke and his connections to both Whig reform and American civilization.

Brian McCartin is President of the Thomas Paine National Historical Association. He and his family reside at the Thomas Paine Museum in New Rochelle, New York. A teacher at an alternative public high school in the South Bronx, he is the author of the book, *Thomas Paine: Common Sense and Revolutionary Pamphleteering*.

Dawn Marsh Riggs is Assistant Professor of History at Purdue University. Her current work focuses on issues of Native American sovereignty and social thought.

David M. Robinson is Oregon Professor of English and Director of the Center for the Humanities at Oregon State University. His books include *Natural Life: Thoreau's Worldly Transcendentalism*, published by Cornell University Press, and *Emerson and the Conduct of Life*, published by Cambridge University Press.

Sophia A. Rosenfeld is Associate Professor of History at the University of Virginia. Her current work focuses on the production and uses of "common sense" in early eighteenth-century England.

Eric Schlereth is a Ph.D. student in history at Brandeis University. His work explores how debates over the sources of religious knowledge influenced political thought and motivated political action following the American and French Revolutions.

Vikki Vickers is Assistant Professor of History at Weber State University. Her book, *My Pen and My Soul Have Ever Gone Together: Thomas Paine and the American Revolution*, was published by Routledge.

William Weeks is a Lecturer in the History Department at San Diego State University, specializing in nineteenth-century U.S. history. His written work examines the cultural, ideological, and political links between the American nation and American empire.